Kathleen Muldoon - The fiery Irish beauty who gave up her only son for the glitter and privilege of fabulous wealth.

Stonewall Barton - The smooth-talking lover who would never forget the innocent girl he had abandoned.

Schuyler Martin - The possessive husband whose lust for power compromised his own daughter.

Elizabeth Martin - The young wife whose driving ambition blinded her to the lies at the very heart of her marriage.

Mother Jean Marie - The Catholic nun who took a dark secret to her grave.

Their lives were inextricably bound to the destiny of one man -

JERICHO SMITH

Also by Maggi Brocher:

THE CHEERLEADERS
AMERICAN BEAUTY
PARTINGS

MAGGI BROCHER

Jericho

LEISURE BOOKS ❧ NEW YORK CITY

ACKNOWLEDGEMENTS

My deep appreciation and thanks to Anita Carey of Golden, Colorado, who provided me with authentic history, and who lived through and survived the devastating years of the dust bowl.
And to Thomas J. Brocher, who assisted me in putting it all together.

A LEISURE BOOK

Published by

Dorchester Publishing Co., Inc.
6 East 39th Street
New York, NY 10016

Printed in the United States of America

'They shall mount up with wings like eagles,
They shall run and not be weary.'

Isaiah: 40:31'

1

By the clock it was high noon, but the sky above showed the eerie light of early dusk as Kathleen Muldoon, sixteen and heavy with child, struggled on against the cutting wind in her search for shelter from the approaching storm. The sun had become a rapidly dimming, angry, red ball with little warmth, and the mare's tail dust plumes, which always preceded the main wall of the storm, already reached far to the east behind her. She knew without any doubt that the coming night of dust would envelope the stricken land for days, as it had before, and she glanced apprehensively at the darkening sky.

Almost instinctively she moved to the fence and grasped the wire to aid her progress westward into the driving wind. Slowly, she made her way past what had once been a plum orchard. Now, the dead tree tops reached gnarled fingers to the bloody sky; the trunks had long since suffocated in five-feet or more of mounded wind-blown dust. The orchard was followed by what had once been a lush prairie pasture, but was now sere and almost bare. It had been the peaceful grazing ground for a large herd of cattle, but the remnants had been sequestered in barns and makeshift shelters in the hope that at least some would survive the approaching devastation that would soon strike the suffering land again. The

Depression. The Early Thirties—the Dust Bowl years.

Kathleen struggled on against the wind. There was no one to whom she could turn, and no one who really cared. She'd been hired out at the tender age of twelve and because of this lacked any real education. As a result, Kathleen had a burning desire to learn, which was only partially satisfied through her church and through others more fortunate than she.

To say the least, life had not been easy.

The one person to whom she had turned with no misgivings had been a handsome young man who worked on the adjoining farm. He'd introduced himself to her on one of her rare excursions into town. His name was Stoney, and he'd been forced to make his own way in much the same manner as Kathleen. As time went on, he showered this woman-child with words of flattery and beguiling tales of "the wonders of the world." He also spoke to her of love.

Kathleen Muldoon was an Irish beauty with hair as dark and shining as ebony, set off by a creamy complexion and eyes of deepest violet framed with luxurious lashes that swept her cheeks. Her full bosomed figure belied her age. She was the seventh child born into the Muldoon clan, a large Catholic family, and she'd been taught little but obedience and the sanctity of their religion.

Stoney and Kathleen had shared many happy times together, and had ultimately fallen in love. But to Stoney love was all consuming, and although Kathleen's church teachings advocated the sacredness of one's body and taught virginity as the highest virtue, those words of wisdom were soon forgotten in their passion for one another.

On the day Kathleen realized that she was pregnant with Stoney's child she'd experienced a thrill of delight, for she was certain that he would share in her joy. Also, true to her religious convictions, she believed that propagation was the primary reason a woman lived, so her pregnancy was doubly pleasing to her.

When she joined Stoney at their secret meeting place it was impossible for him not to see her exhilaration.

"Kate," he said in a demanding tone as he pulled her down close beside him, "what's happened? You've never looked this way."

She laughed deeply and her smile was secretive as she kissed him full on the mouth. Deftly she began to explore his body, something that she'd not attempted before as Stoney had always been the aggressor. He stopped her ministrations with a frown wrinkling his brow.

"What gives?" he demanded.

Softly Kate whispered, "Stoney, we're going to have a child."

"A child?" he snarled, his face taking on a look of rage. "Did you say a child? My God, Kate!"

At his words a cold chill swept through her and she pulled away quickly. This was a side of Stoney that she'd never encountered. When he looked at her it was with loathing, as though he were seeing a stranger.

He jumped to his feet, his lust for Kathleen now forgotten, while she cowered like a frightened doe beneath the tree with a look of fear etched on her face.

"Stoney," she ventured, and when he failed to respond she crawled to her knees, hands outstretched pleadingly. "Stoney, what's the matter?"

It was then that he turned on her. "Matter, you ask? You say this kid is mine, you whore! You'll not use me," and he kicked angrily at the dry ground causing a spray of dirt to fall on Kathleen's outstretched hands.

For a moment she stared at the dirt, then calmly brushed it away and got to her feet. With head held high she looked the father of her unborn child in the eye and said proudly, "I'll not claim you as my child's father. Goodbye, Stoney," she whispered.

Never once did she look back as she walked away swiftly.

The years leading to the great Depression of the 1930's were ones of an almost euphoric pattern. Speakeasies were pervasive in the large metropolises, and the mobs which ruled them also ruled the politicians. The United States existed in an era of near hysteria, and there was no one who could possibly foresee the depths of the economic devastation that would soon engulf the country.

The Middle West also took its lumps; homes and farms were lost by foreclosure, and the people who lived through this horrendous experience found themselves existing in a strange and alien world.

In the early 1920's, the Muldoon family, which consisted of Casey, the father, Colleen, the mother, and their brood of seven children, had left the old city of Boston to embark on a new venture—farming. They settled in Western Kansas near the small town of Staley. This particular area had been carefully selected because many of its inhabitants were members of the same faith, Catholisicm. However, after their departure from the familiar shores of the eastern seaboard, they soon discovered that the riches which they'd dreamed of accumulating did not exist, and that hard work was the only answer to their continued survival.

Casey Muldoon, who'd once been in the Merchant Marine, had been the instigator of the move. Colleen, after suffering months of the searing Kansas heat along with the electrical storms and tornados which frightened her half to death, began to threaten Casey with returning to Boston and the life they'd had before. It was true that they'd been poor Irish in Boston, but to her even that was far better than the prospect of being rich Irish in Kansas.

To keep themselves afloat financially, the Muldoons had finally placed their children up for hire to the prosperous wheat and cattle ranchers. Each young Muldoon had secured a job as a hired hand, and Kathleen, the youngest at age twelve, became a hired girl. The pittances which they received for their services, outside of room and board, found its way back to Casey who, because of his lack of success, soon became one of the town's known gamblers and drunks, using their hard earned money for bottleg whiskey and gambling debts. Even Colleen was forced into becoming a wash woman for the local rich, and she never forgot—or forgave—Casey. She knew that the move to Kansas had been a mistake, and one for which she paid bitterly.

Before Kathleen Muldoon had become infatuated with Stoney, she'd spent the few hours that she was allowed away from her job at the Catholic Convent which was located near Staley. She'd become friends with the Sisters, and they'd taken the time to instruct this eager child in the tools of reading and writing. She had served them with a happy heart, until Stoney had taken her away.

On this awesome day, with the dust storm rolling in from the west, Kathleen, with each step, was drawing closer to the convent where she hoped that she would be welcome. As she continued to move along the fence, each step she took through the mounds of dirt became more difficult. It was while she was struggling against the biting wind that she experienced the first sharp pain of labor.

Kathleen gasped for air, only to inhale the dust which permeated the air like a black plague, and she coughed in agony.

When she'd recovered sufficiently she looked once again to the west, shielding her eyes from the dust with her hands. What she saw caused her to heave a sigh of relief, for only a short half-mile in the distance were the dim lights of the convent.

Once again Kathleen moved toward the welcome symbol, each step seeming like a mountain to climb. A sudden swirl in the wind pushed her cumbersome body forward and she stumbled, a cry of outrage screaming from her parched throat. She lay quite still on the dirt laden land while pain after pain racked her body. Finally she pulled herself up and, on hands and knees, began to crawl forward, stopping only when the pains of labor struck yet again.

When she reached the bottom step which lead to the door of the convent Kathleen rested, almost peacefully. It was at that moment that the door to the brick building opened slightly and the Sister who looked out saw what seemed to be a human body huddled on the steps below. She turned and ran to the Mother Superior's quarters, fright in her eyes.

Sister Jean Marie looked up, a frown creasing her brow at the unexpected interruption, and snapped, "What is it, Sister?"

Then she saw the look of terror written on the young nun's face and she moved to her quickly.

"Sister Ann," the Mother Superior asked more kindly, "are you not well?"

The young nun shook her head and then made an effort to speak, but the words which she needed to say wouldn't come. Instead, she took the Mother Superior by the hand and led her down the hallway to the entrance. There she pushed open the door so she could see the body which was now stretched full length at the base of the steps.

Angrily, the Mother Superior pushed the door wide, and with her habit blowing wildly about her from the driving force of the wind, she took a strong hold of the hand railing and cautiously made her way to the bottom of the steps where she knelt beside the body of the woman who was obviously in the final stages of pregnancy. The wind had blown a scarf across the woman's face, and when she lifted it gently she found herself looking into the pain-filled eyes of Kathleen Muldoon.

First shock and then anger swept through her, but it was at that moment that Kathleen screamed out in agony. Through clenched teeth she managed, "Help me, Mother. Please help me!"

Mother Superior all but forgot the possible consequences and waved to the nuns who were now crowded together in the entryway. Two of the braver ones ventured down, each holding tightly to the iron railing to keep from being blown off the steps. When they reached the bottom and recognized Kathleen Muldoon their eyes clouded and they drew away, both wondering why the Mother Superior would become involved.

In the effort to be heard over the howling wind, the Mother Superior was forced to shout as she gave instructions to her obviously reluctant helpers.

"Sisters," she said, "we're going to get Kathleen inside and out of the storm. You'll both have to help. She's in labor."

The two women exchanged long glances and for a moment hesitated.

When she saw their hesitation her wrath descended upon them. "As God is in his heaven, ye do not judge," she shouted into the wind. "Now help!"

Obeying her command, they struggled together to get Kathleen to her feet and then very slowly, taking each step one at a time between pauses to rest, they moved up and up until they entered the convent's hallway where they found the other inhabitants huddled together in small groups, eyes wide with wonder.

"Prepare a clean bed," Mother Superior ordered to no one in particular, and with that the majority rushed from sight, almost like mice scurrying to safety. They all knew that the Mother Superior could easily make their lives unbearable, and her words were their command.

As though from nowhere a rickety wooden wheelchair appeared and Kathleen was helped into it. Then she was pushed over the bare wooden floors while the chair's turning wheels crunched loudly through the dust which had accomulated. In a short time they entered a small, candle lit room, furnished only with a twin sized iron bed, a chair and a small chest—the usual sparse necessities provided for a nun's privacy. The Sister who'd formerly been the occupant had succumbed a few days previously to what Staley's one doctor had diagnosed as dust pneumonia, an ailment he'd attributed to the devastating storms. Fortunately, the room was located in the center of the two story brick structure and lacked any outside openings, thus lending itself well to serving as a makeshift delivery room.

When Kathleen first saw the bed, tears streamed down her cheeks, but then a sharp, knife-like pain engulfed her and she doubled over, almost falling from the chair.

Two Sisters had gone ahead and had removed the hand woven rustic bed covering in preparation, but when Mother Superior saw the homespun muslin sheets were covered with a layering of dust she shook her head in despair, wondering if the child who was about to enter the world could possibly have a chance at survival.

"Take those sheets off and shake them out," she demanded, and the two nuns quickly removed them and left the room. Old newspapers, now yellow from age, covered the two inch tick mattress, but to Kathleen it didn't matter as it looked like heaven to her.

When the sheets were back on the bed Kathleen, with the help of the women, was assisted from the chair and onto it. Wearily she lay down while her benefactors began to remove her clothing. Mother Superior stood to one side, a false sense of security going through her. She'd once been assigned to a Catholic hospital and she knew that it would be up to her to deliver Kathleen Muldoon's child. However, even the thought of it caused a shudder to pass through her.

After Kathleen was undressed she was covered with a single sheet. Then the two Sisters retreated into the shadows of the small room as Mother Superior moved to Kathleen's side.

"Kathleen," she said kindly, her anger gone, "I've been chosen to be the one to help you bring your child into the world." She sighed deeply. "I once served in a hospital, but not in surgery or the delivery room, so this will be a first for me, too." Her mouth crinkled slightly in a smile.

"Let's pray together that God will help we two novices," and she crossed herself reverently and mumbled a prayer.

Then she turned to the two women who waited. "Boil plenty of water and sterilize my cutting scissors." She frowned for she really knew little about what she would need. Still, she went on. "Get lots of clean cloths. You might look in the sealed barrels. Surely the dirt hasn't gotten to them.''

But she was wrong. Nothing was sacred to the dust storms, not even the Convent.

The Convent had proven to be, in many ways, a self-sustaining order of the Catholic Church. The previous year, when moisture had been plentiful, they'd produced a bountiful harvest from the large garden they'd planted. The Sisters had canned every possible fruit and vegetable and, in the deep cellar which ran beneath the structure, had stored potatoes, onions, carrots and other vegetables and fruits.

One parishoner had built, as his contribution (or retribution) a sturdy chicken house with an adjoining wire pen, and had stocked it with some of his finest poultry. A milking cow had somehow found its way to them, so their real needs were few, with the possible exception of staples, such as flour, sugar, coffee and tea, which they secured from the general store in Staley. The Convent had weathered previous dust storms which had swept unmercifully across the countryside and would continue to do so, and Kathleen Muldoon knew that she was indeed fortunate to have their help.

While Kathleen and Mother Superior waited patiently for the baby to make its appearance, one of the Sisters served them cups of hot broth and tea. Kathleen sipped hers eagerly, for it had been hours since she'd had even a trace of food and she realized that the battle which loomed before her would take all of her youthful strength and energy.

Mother Superior had removed her dark habit and had slipped into a gown which had once been white, but which was now a dingy grey. She'd scrubbed her hands and arms with homemade lye soap while she'd prayed desperately that all would go well.

In the quiet of the late afternoon, Kathleen's labor became more pronounced and before long her water broke. This sign of approaching birth caused Mother Superior to fly into action. She hurried into the hallway where the Sisters waited and instructed them to bring the boiling water as her patient's time was drawing nearer. Dutifully they hurried away.

While the Sisters were away, Mother made Kathleen as comfortable as possible by placing pillows under her knees and moving her legs into position in anticipation of the impending birth. Her contractions were now only minutes apart, and with each one Kathleen clung to the head of the iron bed, biting her lips to keep from screaming.

During a brief respite from the now almost constant pain, Mother Superior had asked her only one question. "Kathleen," she said softly, "who is the father?"

The young woman's eyes had taken on a frightened look and she shook her head vehemently as though denying the knowledge. However, her benefactor thought differently, and knew that the day would come when Kathleen Muldoon would reveal the name of her child's father.

Finally, the crown of the baby's head begin to appear. With brief, curt instructions provided by the Mother Superior, the Sisters who'd responded to her call took their places around the iron bed; two positioned at the head and two at the foot. They grasped Kathleen's arms and ankles. It was to prove to be a difficult situation, for not one had witnessed, let alone participated in, the birth of a child.

Because of the mounting pain, Kathleen fought them like a tiger and several times broke lose from their hold, only to be recaptured once again. Mother Superior, even without proper medical knowledge but with the same instincts as all women, encouraged Kathleen to push when she felt the first indication of pain. The actual birthing process would take only minutes, but to those present it would seem like forever.

Finally, with one last frantic push, and a scream wrenched from Kathleen which echoed throughout the Convent, a strapping boy child came hurtling into the world screaming with rage, as though he knew even then that it was not of his own choosing.

After cutting and tying the umbilical cord which had joined the child to its mother, Mother Superior handed the baby to the Sister whom she trusted most not to panic, and then went to work on her patient. Fortunately, the bleeding had not been profuse, and although Kathleen was physically and emotionally exhausted from her experience, she managed to ask, "May I see my child?"

The Sister who held the infant glanced at the Mother Superior and, when she nodded her approval, she took the tiny baby, now wrapped in a soft muslin blanket, and gently placed him in his mother's arms.

Through tear-filled eyes Kathleen looked down in awe at the son of Stoney. The baby's dark, thick head of hair she knew was an inheritance from the Muldoons, but the strong facial features, at even such an early age, with the square, dominating jaw and the straight aquiline nose, was a definite product of his father.

The baby nuzzled against Kathleen's breast and its rose bud mouth instinctively began to search for her nipple. As though she'd been through the same experience many times, Kathleen lifted her breast to help her son with his need, and the feeling as he tugged at her bosom was one of completeness.

Mother Superior and the Sisters watched, enchanted by the peaceful and beautiful scene. A trace of a tear trickled down the Mother Superior's cheek which she brushed aside, but not quickly enough, for her fellow Sisters had caught a brief glimpse of the true nature which lay beneath her habit.

When the baby's need had been satisfied, he drifted into his own small world. Then it was Kathleen's turn, and she gave an audible sigh of contentment and slowly closed her eyes, her dark hair streaming like a banner across the pillow, with a slight smile on her lips, as she too drifted into sleep.

Mother Superior signalled the others to leave, and once her assistants had gone and the three were quite alone, she dropped to her knees, crossed herself, and then bowed her head in prayer. The candle flickered and went out, leaving the young mother, her new born son, and a Mother Superior who had been shaken deeply by her experience, in the stillness of the night.

2

When the occupants of the convent came to life the following morning they discovered that a break had appeared in the dust storm, and because of this Mother Superior discharged two of her most trusted Sisters to travel into Staley. One of the neighboring ranchers had stopped by to check on their safety and she duly imposed upon him the task of driving her aides to town.

"But Mother Jean Marie," he protested, "the storm will surely begin again when the wind rises. Are you certain?"

She looked him straight in the eye, surprised at the thought that he would even question her authority. "Of course I'm sure," she snapped. "We need some things," and with that she hustled the two Sisters out the front door with the reluctant rancher, having seen to it that they were all well clothed against the possibility of the wind rising once again before they could return.

When they were out of sight, she hastened to Kathleen's room where she found the new mother holding her son.

"Good morning, Kathleen. How are you today?" she asked, almost shyly.

The radiant smile which the young woman gave her was all the answer she needed.

"Has the baby nursed?"

17

At her question Kathleen laughed, and it was then that she discovered that all her muscles were sore. She gasped slightly at the twinge of pain which would not let her forget the previous day.

"Many times, Mother Jean Marie. Many times. He's a very hungry and demanding child," and she touched him lovingly.

"Have you given any thought to a name?" Mother Superior pursued.

For a moment Kathleen's eyes narrowed as she thought of Stoney's rejection, and knew that their son would never bear his name. Then she looked up, a slight smile playing about her lips.

"Yes, I've chosen his name."

Curious at her sudden sureness, Mother Superior asked, "Would you care to tell me?"

Kathleen reached out for her hand, held it to her cheek, and then kissed it. In obvious embarrassment Mother Superior pulled her hand away as she felt her emotions begin to rise.

"His name will be Jericho," Kathleen said softly.

"Jericho?" Mother Jean Marie queried, a slight frown creasing her brow. "Jericho?"

Kathleen nodded. "Someday he'll make the walls come tumbling down," she said firmly, pride showing in her voice. "You see, my son will be somebody when he's grown. A man, a true man in every sense of the word," and there was a touch of irony in her voice that was mixed with pride.

Mother Superior nodded. "I'll make a record."

At that Kathleen frowned, and a touch of concern came into her eyes.

"A record?"

"Yes, my dear. We have to record both Jericho's birth and his mother's name. It's merely for our own use, and no one else's. Why? Are you worried?"

Kathleen's eyes brimmed with tears. "I don't possibly know how I'll take care of him."

"Don't you worry," the Sister said kindly, "Jericho will have only the best. We'll care for him here."

"But I'll have to work," Kathleen protested.

"I know. But someday you'll be able to provide him with a home, and until then he'll be safe here with us."

"You know that I'll want to have him with me when I'm able,"

Kathleen replied, "and I don't want to have to worry that when I do come for him that he'll be gone."

"Nonsense," Mother Superior replied, almost angrily. "You should know that after what we've shared here together you can trust us." And with that their conversation came to an end.

By afternoon the wind had again started the first moaning sounds which served as a warning to everyone that yet another dust storm was on its way.

Mother Superior waited nervously in her quarters for her two charges to return from Staley, and as the sky began to darken and look ominous she began to reconsider her decision. Then, chugging and coughing because of the dirt which had settled in the gas tank, the rancher's old truck came into view and sputtered to a halt in front of the convent. The two Sisters emerged, their arms filled with packages, and they hurried up the steps to be greeted by the Mother Superior herself. The relief in her voice was evident.

"My, but I'm glad that you've come back safely. I'm not sure that you should have been sent."

The two nuns looked at each other, eyebrows raised, for Mother Superior was at last beginning to demonstrate that she could be human after all.

"We're glad that we could go, and knew that God would bring us safely home," one Sister responded reverently, and then both crossed themselves while Mother Superior followed their example.

"Bring the packages to my quarters," she ordered, once again reverting to her usual manner. Dutifully and at a respectful distance, the two Sisters followed her. When they'd deposited the bulky shopping bags on the table in her small apartment, she turned to them. "Were any questions asked?"

Both nodded.

"Well, tell me," she barked, looking first to one and then the other, impatient with their obvious reticence.

"Mr. Dowell wanted to know why we needed all the baby things," the braver one replied and then paused. "In fact, he so much as inferred that it could be for one of us," and with that revelation she turned scarlet.

"Nonsense! He's just an old busybody," Mother Superior replied sharply. "I do hope that you put him straight."

Then the other Sisters spoke up. "Of course we did, Mother Superior. We told him," and she once again crossed herself and looked toward heaven, "that a family had taken refuge with us because of the storm and that they'd lost all of their belongings." As she finished, she smiled, almost happy that she'd had the courage to lie.

"Good," Mother Superior replied with open approval. "Although you both know that we don't tell stories that aren't rightly true." Then she looked out the window at the storm which was now approaching full crescendo. "However," she continued thoughtfully, "what you told him is true, for when Kathleen arrived she had nothing but the clothes on her back," and her eyes became bright with a mischevious look that neither Sister had had the pleasure of seeing before.

"Now, off to your duties," she ordered. As the Sisters started to leave she stopped them.

"I do want to thank you for your good judgment and for going out in this dreadful weather. You will be blessed."

Both sisters genuflected and then hurried on their way, eager to tell the others that the Mother Superior had actually seemed grateful.

It had been many years since Mother Jean Marie had even thought about her long ago childhood, but as she removed the tiny baby shirts, diapers, soft kimonos and blankets from one of the packages, she remembered vividly how she'd helped her own mother when a new brother or sister had arrived almost every year. She'd been the oldest daughter of twelve children, and she'd actually looked forward to leaving her home and entering the convent. She'd been a child herself when she'd had to share the responsibilities and burdens of a brood of sisters and brothers. Now, in her later years, she was rediscovering once more the magic of a new born child.

Selecting a shirt, kimono and several diapers from the different piles of clothing, in her eagerness she almost ran to Kathleen's room. Upon her arrival she found the door was standing slightly ajar, and Kathleen's bed was surrounded by a group of her charges, all oohing and aahing while they passed Jericho from one pair of arms to another. She couldn't help but smile to herself as she watched them from a distance. Then, clearing her throat loudly, she entered the room. She almost laughed at the shocked looks on the Sister's faces at being discovered.

"Ladies," she said rather brusquely, in the hope of hiding her own amusement, "You may now return to your jobs." With this announcement they scurried away, leaving Kathleen, the baby and herself alone.

"See what I've brought Jericho," Mother Superior said proudly as she held up a small shirt and kimono so Kathleen could see them. Tears formed in the eyes of the young woman as she handed them to her.

"Would you like me to dress him?" Mother Jean Marie asked.

Kathleen shook her head, finding herself at a complete loss for words. Then, she finally managed, "I will, Mother Jean Marie. How will I ever be able to thank you?"

"The day will come, my child, and perhaps sooner than you think, when you'll remember us with a kindness," and she paused and turned away to keep the rush of emotion which had suddenly engulfed her from showing. Then she continued. "I'm certain that in the years ahead you'll find some way, either through your own work or through your son, to help our Order. That's really all the thanks we need. We serve God, dear one, and want you to leave here and go on to a better life, where you also will serve." Then she smiled for Kathleen had dressed Jericho and was openly admiring his new attire.

"Let me hold your precious lamb," Mother Jean Marie said gently as she held out her arms. Kathleen gave him to her and then watched, a soft smile on her lips as the older woman moved slowly around the room, humming softly to the sleeping infant. After a time she placed Jericho in the dresser drawer which served as his bed, covered him, and then gazed at him for a long time, almost visualizing what a man he would be.

When she looked up and saw Kathleen watching, she moved to the side of the bed and sat down beside her.

"You'll be up and about soon. You're young and strong." Then she hesitated, almost afraid to go on. "How long will you be with us?"

Kathleen's look was pained, yet she knew that the time would soon be there when such a decision needed to be reached.

"I haven't given it much thought, but you're right, of course. I should start planning for our future," and she paused momentarily. "I'll have to leave Staley for my family would certainly run me out of town if I didn't," and he sighed. "Perhaps I'll go to Kansas City. It's a big town and surely there will be work for me there."

Mother Superior nodded. "If that should be your decision, I'll provide you with the name of the Mother Superior at St. Mary's. I'm certain that she'd be glad to take you in until you're able to support yourself."

When Kathleen started to thank her, Mother Jean Marie held up her hand.

"Please," she said softly. "We'll have Jericho, at least for a little while, and he'll be all the blessing we'll need."

As the two women, one so very young, and one who'd seen many years pass by, sat together in the quiet of the evening, neither could possibly envision the train of events that would enter the life of Kathleen and of Jericho, and which would ultimately change dramatically both of their existences.

And, perhaps, it was best that they couldn't.

3

The dust storms continued unabated and proceeded to destroy the wheat and oat fields that the farmers had planted that early Spring. The grasslands had become parched from the stifling heat and wind, leaving little to eat for the small herds of cattle which thus far had survived the devastation.

Because of the continued inclement weather, Kathleen Muldoon stayed on at the convent. In that interim, Mother Jean Marie had dispatched a letter to the Mother Superior who presided over St. Mary's in Kansas City, and had received a prompt and affirmative reply to her request that Kathleen be allowed to stay there until she could find suitable employment.

Jericho continued to thrive and became the most important person in the Convent.

When late Fall arrived, the dust storms quieted somewhat, and on occasion there appeared a few pleasant days. However, those few days of apparent reprieve were a deception, for still the winds howled and the dust blew over the farmlands.

People crowded into Staley's churches every Sunday, and it mattered not what their denomination for they all prayed the same prayer—that God would deliver them from this terrible holocaust.

As if in answer to their fervent supplications, one day the clouds

burst open and rain fell. People rushed into the streets of Staley
and into their burned-out yards crying with joy, then sank to their
knees to offer their grateful thanks.

As the day loomed closer for Kathleen's departure, two of the
Sisters once again traveled to Staley where they purchased, under
the interested and watchful eyes of Mr. Dowell, suitable clothing
for her journey. Once again he questioned them, but they both
turned stoic faces to him and did not respond.

Jericho was now approaching his third month's birthday and
because of her impending departure, Kathleen had seen fit to wean
him from her breast. Even so, he continued to thrive on the whole
milk provided by the convent's lone cow. Secretly, she harbored
misgivings about leaving her son, but following several conversations with Mother Jean Marie she knew it was her only
alternative—and far better for Jericho.

Mother Superior had enlisted the services of the nearby rancher
once again and swore him to secrecy about the journey he was
about to make. Readily—and in part because he was afraid of this
demanding woman—he agreed, and Kathleen's transportation to a
nearby town where the Santa Fe stopped to take on passengers was
consummated.

On the day of Kathleen's departure, Mother Jean Marie
presented her with one of her own simple treasures—a golden
cross. The young mother gave the Sisters an affectionate goodbye,
and then retired with Mother Jean Marie to her quarters for a
private farewell.

For a time there was only a peaceful silence as each woman was
fighting desperately to keep from showing emotion. As Kathleen
rose to leave, Mother Jean Marie pulled her into her arms and it
was at that time they both shed silent tears. Still, they remained
silent, and when they went to the entry of the convent they were
quite alone.

As Kathleen opened the door of the convent that she and Jericho
called home, she looked down at the base of the steps where her
transportation awaited her. Then she pulled her heavy new winter
coat closely around her, picked up the small bag in which her
meager belongings were packed, and slowly started down the steps.
She stopped once and turned back with tears streaming down her
cheeks to look one last time at Mother Jean Marie.

Finally, she murmured softly, "I'll never forget you, Mother Jean Marie . . . never."

Then she almost ran down the balance of the steps. Before she entered the battered old truck, she turned again and waved. Silently, Mother Jean Marie returned her salute and then watched as the decrepit vehicle moved noisily out of sight.

Mother Jean Marie closed the convent door and returned to her quarters. Once alone, she started to cry as though her heart would break.

That evening, Mother Jean Marie moved Jericho into her private apartment and then proceeded to take full charge. The other Sisters had hoped, in vain, that they would all share in his everyday care, but this was not to be. Mother Superior's rationale was that she was far more experienced in the care of infants than all of the others combined, and in addition, she was not above using the fact that she had the authority. So, in all reality, Jericho became her grandson, or Godchild, or whichever title suited her best at the moment. She doted on him thoroughly.

The days, weeks and months moved swiftly by, and on occasion a postcard would arrive from Kathleen informing Mother Jean Marie of the progress she was making. After spending several months at St. Mary's while she searched for a housekeeping position, she suddenly found herself being considered as a housekeeper for a rich, young widower who'd recently lost his wife, and who had two children of his own. Being a mother herself, the position appealed to Kathleen, and when it was finally offered to her, she accepted without hesitation. The salary was quite adequate and she knew that at last she'd be able to send funds to Mother Jean Marie for her son's care until she could come for him.

In short order, Kathleen found herself becoming so totally involved in the family life of Schuyler Martin and his children that she had little time left to consider, or be concerned, about Jericho. She knew that he was being well cared for from the monthly progress reports that Mother Jean Marie sent, and it was only at those times that she longed to hold her son in her arms. Then she'd forget about him as she busied herself with the running of the palatial mansion she now called home.

It wasn't long before Schuyler Martin, because of his intense liking for this beautiful Irish colleen, added a maid and cook to his staff to assist her. This released Kathleen from many of her former duties so she could spend time with Schuyler on some of the family outings, although she felt rather awkward and out of place occasionally.

At numerous times, Schuyler had questioned Kathleen concerning her background and family, but she'd made a concerted though unobtrusive effort to avoid providing him with any particulars. She was not proud of her past, or her family.

The months passed quickly and although on numerous occasions Kathleen had requested a few days off so she could return to Staley to visit Jericho and Mother Jean Marie, there was always a pressing need for her to remain with the Martins.

Jericho's first birthday came and went, then his second, and finally his third, and the guilt which Kathleen had first harbored at not seeing her son soon dissipated, for she was being well groomed to become the wife of Schuyler Martin. It mattered not to him that she had little education, for his greatest desire was to possess—and bed—this dazzling raven haired beauty who had thus far eluded him.

During those years, Jericho had become the center of Mother Jean Marie's life. With each passing month, as Kathleen's communications diminished and her apparent indifference to the welfare of her child became obvious, there were many anxious moments and some deep regrets on the part of the Mother Superior, as well as the Sisters.

The one male member of the convent had grown into a handsome child, and one blessed with an inquisitive and curious mind. Under Mother Jean Marie's tutelage he had learned quickly, and by the age of four had mastered reading exceedingly well. The long letters that Mother Jean Marie wrote to Kathleen were filled with glowing praise and pride in Jericho's accomplishments. But although the letters were never returned, they did not provoke any replies.

Kathleen, of course, had provided the convent with the Martin's address when she became employed there. Her lack of response to Mother Jean Marie's letters, decided the Mother Superior to make a trip to Kansas City. When she informed her assistant that she would be away for several days, the question, "Where are you going?" had naturally arisen.

"I'm going to see Kathleen Muldoon," Mother Jean had replied, her words almost caustic.

"But why, Mother Jean Marie?"

"Because it's high time she became a mother to her child," she'd responded. "And besides, I need to see her."

That had proved to be their entire conversation and, without a companion accompanying her, she'd left Staley and headed for Kansas City.

When she arrived, Mother Jean Marie went directly to St. Mary's Convent where the Mother Superior greeted her warmly and with obvious affection as they'd served as novices together and had shared many moving moments during their indoctrination into their chosen Order.

Following a pleasant evening supper when Mother Jean Marie had been proudly introduced to the other Sisters, she and her friend retired to the Mother Superior's quarters.

"Jean Marie, my dear," Mother Frances questioned, "why are you here? And by yourself?" There was a trace of admonition in her voice as Sisters normally traveled in pairs.

Mother Jean Marie paused for a moment before answering in the hope that Frances would prove to be the one who would understand. She got up from the comfortable chair and moved slowly around the room, casting admiring glances at the artifacts which had been gifts to St. Mary's from grateful parishoners, and then she turned to face her old friend.

"It's a long story, Frances," she began, "a very long story."

The Mother Superior of St. Mary's remained silent, but her eyes never once left the troubled face of Jean Marie, for it was apparent to her that the mission that had brought her old friend to the city was painful indeed.

Finally, Jean Marie seated herself across from her friend and gazed into her eyes.

"Promise me that you'll remain silent about what I'm going to tell you," she said firmly, knowing full well that she could be reported to the Diocese for harboring a young woman and her child.

Frances reached over and took Jean Marie's wrinkled hand in her own. "Jean Marie, you know full well you can trust me," then a thought came to her. "Does this by chance have anything to do with the young woman you sent to us, Kathleen Muldoon?"

"Yes, it does. Why do you ask?"

Her friend laughed slightly and Jean Marie found this to be rather disturbing, for Kathleen's behavior where her son was concerned was certainly not a laughing matter.

"You don't receive the Kansas City papers, do you?" her friend asked.

Jean Marie shook her head. "No. Has something happened to Kathleen?" She felt a sudden alarm.

"Oh, my, yes. Something really rather wonderful."

"Wonderful?" Jean Marie replied, puzzled.

"I'm surprised that she didn't inform you about her marriage."

Before she could continue, Jean Marie interrupted, "Marriage? To whom? Where?"

"You mean you didn't know? I'm really surprised, for she spoke so fondly of you. Perhaps she'll be writing to you."

"But I made this trip especially to see her. I *have* to see her," and her voice began to rise in anger.

Frances glanced at her sharply.

"My dear, there's nothing to be so upset about. Kathleen and Schuyler Martin were married in a High Mass just this past Sunday at St. Joseph's, and are now on their honeymoon." She paused. "I doubt if they'll be home soon. I believe the newspaper story said they were going to Nassau," and she got up and went to her desk where she rifled through a neatly stacked pile of newspapers.

The information which her friend had just revealed had put Jean Marie into almost a state of shock.

Frances handed a newspaper to her. "Here's the story about Kathleen, and the wedding photograph. Didn't she make the loveliest bride?"

Jean Marie took the paper from her and stared for a long time at the picture of Kathleen and her husband, then put it aside. Her face was pale and her heart pounded, and she suddenly realized that there was little reason for her to remain in Kansas City.

"Now then," Frances said as she seated herself again. "Do tell me what's troubling you."

"There's nothing to tell now."

"Nothing?"

"No, it's all been decided, so I'll be leaving tomorrow to return to Staley." She sighed. "Do you suppose that I could retire now? I'm suddenly very tired."

"Why, of course. How thoughtless of me to keep you up so long after such a hard trip." She looked at her friend with concern in her eyes. "Are you certain that you're only tired?"

"Yes, just tired. Now may I go to my room?"

Frances guided her through the silent hallway to a pleasant bedroom where a lamp had been left burning. As she turned to leave, Jean Marie put out her hand. "Thank you, dear friend, for not prying. God and I have a lot of decisions ahead of us, and there's no one else who can do it."

They embraced, and then Frances returned to her own quarters, still wondering why Jean Marie had been so upset at the news of Kathleen's marriage.

On the return trip home, Mother Jean Marie considered just how she'd handle the problem which now faced her. It was obvious that Kathleen wanted nothing more to do with her son, and she had to assume that Schuyler Martin was totally unaware of his existence. However, she also realized that Jericho would be ready to begin school in the Fall, but certainly not in Staley where the Muldoon family still resided.

Late that afternoon she was met at the door by her assistant, who'd been fortunate enough to see the bus drop her off at the steps. She took one look at Mother Jean Marie and the exhaustion on her face, took her bag, and silently followed her down the hallway. On the way, several of the Sisters made an effort to speak to the Mother Superior, but she merely waved them aside and retreated into the peace of her own quarters.

Once alone, she slipped off her heavy habit and pulled on a patched worn robe. When she returned to her desk she saw a beige envelope of obviously rich quality lying there and recognized immediately the handwriting of Kathleen. It was apparent that the letter had arrived while she was on the way to Kansas City, and that their paths had crossed.

Mother Jean Marie picked up the envelope and settled into a

comfortable chair. She opened it. Inside was another envelope with her name boldly written on it. A sheet of paper fell to her lap, but she let it lie and instead opened the heavy linen-like card on which was engraved in formal gold script the announcement of Kathleen's marriage to Schuyler Martin.

She placed the announcement to one side and picked up the note. Very carefully she opened it and then read:

> "My dear Mother Jean Marie,
>
> "I'm sure you've often wondered why I haven't kept in touch with you because of Jericho, but during the time that I've been away my life has changed completely, and I've had to make a decision you may find hard to understand.
>
> "First, I want you to know that I did intend to come back for my son. However, after being away from him, and although I lived a part of his childhood through your wonderful letters, it wasn't enough. Then I met and fell in love with the man who is now my husband, and he and his children have become my life. It may not sound fair to you, but I feel now that it is in Jericho's best interest that you find a good Catholic family who need a small boy to enrich their lives.
>
> "You and the other Sisters at the convent have displayed a wonderful responsibility in caring for Jericho, and he has indeed been fortunate to be loved by so many. I was fortunate too, when I came to your door and you so generously took me in. I shall never forget the love that you gave me, but you must realize that I have found a man who respects and loves me, and to bring a bastard child into this relationship would ruin everyone's lives, including Jericho's.
>
> "When you find a family that wants Jericho and will love him, I will gladly sign the adoption papers. Should he ever ask about me, please tell him that I no longer live. I realize that this will not be an easy task for you, Mother Jean Marie, but I believe it to be a necessary one.

"God Bless you, dear one, and I pray that you will
not think too harshly of me.

                                    With love,
        Kathleen

Thoughtfully, Jean Marie put Kathleen's note aside and then
noticed that a folded slip of paper had dropped onto the floor.
After she'd retrieved it she'd glanced at it rather casually, then she
was startled, for what she'd thought at first was an insignificant slip
of paper was a check in the sum of ten-thousand dollars, made
payable to the Convent, and signed by Kathleen Martin.

Mother Jean Marie sank into her chair, now completely
confused. *She's paying us off*, was her first thought, then she
shook her head. No, that wasn't it. Kathleen wanted to do the
kindness they'd talked about a long time ago. She sighed and a lone
tear trickled down her cheek. Slowly Mother Jean Marie got up,
went to her small altar, knelt and bowed her head in homage.

The road ahead, she knew, would be one of sorrow. Losing
Jericho would be the most difficult act that she'd ever been faced
with.

After her prayers were over, she snuffed out the candle, took off
her robe and crawled into the safety of her bed. She turned her face
to the wall and cried, wrenching sobs racking her body. Finally,
exhausted, she slept.

4

The search for a home for Jericho now began in earnest, but not before Mother Jean Marie informed the sisters of Kathleen's decision, her marriage and her gift. Several had expressed their feelings quite openly, insisting that Jericho should stay, while others looked somber and disbelieving.

Through Mother Superior's vast acquaintanceship she'd made several discreet inquiries and had been fortunate to learn of a Jacob and Martha Smith who had requested to adopt a Catholic child. The age of the child made no difference to them and thus she felt that Jericho might be the answer should they, themselves, prove to be suitable.

Then came the day when Mother Jean Marie had to inform Jericho that he be prepared to leave the Convent. It was a heart-breaking experience for both of them. During the years that Jericho had been close to her, she'd instilled in him a part of her own stocism. When she revealed that his stay at the Convent would soon come to an end his eyes filled with tears, yet he stood before her like a man and let not one tear fall.

His first question, of course, had been "Why?" as he perched on the edge of the straight backed chair which faced Mother Jean Marie.

"Jericho, it's time for you to begin school. You're nearly five."

"But I can learn here, Mother Jean Marie," he'd replied, his words almost pleading.

"I know, my boy, but you need a family. Living at the Convent will simply not do. We know that you love us just as we love you, but it's necessary for your own sake that you go. You see Jericho, we all have to come to terms at some time in our lives with decisions that we don't fully understand," and she reached over and patted him on the cheek.

"But what about my mother?" Jericho pursued. "Why isn't she coming for me?"

That was the one question that Mother Jean Marie had hoped wouldn't arise.

"We've just recently learned that your mother succumbed to an illness a few months back. I'm sorry, Jericho."

For a moment a forlorn look crossed his face, and it was then that he first came to the realization that he was indeed very much alone.

"Mother Superior," he replied almost formally, "who will be my family if not you and the Sisters?"

Jean Marie was taken aback by his sudden show of maturity and knew that she'd had a brief glimpse of the man he'd eventually become.

"A man and his wife will be coming to visit on Saturday, Jericho. They've not been blessed with children of their own, and have wanted a child for many years. I've had correspondence with the Monsignor of their parish and after receiving his recommendations, I'm certain that they are kind and loving people."

For a moment a flicker of interest sparkled in Jericho's eyes. "What's their name?"

Mother Jean Marie smiled, pleased by his positive response. "Smith. It's a very common name, but one that's easily remembered."

"Smith," Jericho murmured, then, "Jericho Smith. Would that be my name?"

"Yes, should you both decide that you'd like to be together."

"Where do they live?"

"In Wichita. That's about 150 miles east of Staley. Mr. Smith is a businessman and farmer and he and Mrs. Smith have helped many of the less fortunate in their lifetime.''

"How old are they?" Jericho continued with his interrogation.

"In their forties. They are mature and know what is needed to enrich their lives, and as I said before, they've wanted a child for a long time." She paused. "However, should you feel uncomfortable with them, we'll continue to search for another family until we find one that proves to be suitable."

"May I be excused, Mother Jean Marie?" Jericho suddenly asked.

Although a bit surprised at the abruptness of his request, Mother Superior nodded and Jericho almost ran from the room, pausing only long enough to give her a fleeting smile and a wave of his hand before he was out the door.

Resolutely, Jericho marched down the long hall looking straight ahead, his eyes focused on the front door of the Convent. With some difficulty he pulled the door slightly ajar and slipped through it; then he proceeded to bound down the long flight of steps. With the energy of extreme youth he catapulted across the newly born grass which was just beginning to emerge from the parched ground to try its luck once more in the Spring weather of Kansas.

At breakneck speed he rounded the corner of the building and literally flew into a small grove of trees which were just starting to bud, then shinnied up one of the large cottonwoods much like a monkey and settled himself on one of the limbs with his legs dangling earthward. This was Jericho's favorite place, and although the Sisters and Mother Jean Marie were quite aware of it, they always respected his need for privacy.

As he swung his legs to and fro his face took on a dreamy quality and he murmured softly to himself, "Jericho Smith, Jericho Smith." The sound of the name had a magical ring and a shiver of childish delight went through him. He'd known for the past year that his life at the Convent was far different than that of the children whom he'd watched almost jealously from the windows as they'd gotten on the school bus, and he'd also wondered why the Mother Superior was so protective of him. Now he felt that he knew.

For a moment he thought about the death of his mother, and although he was a sensitive child, the fact that she was no longer a hope in his life—as she'd been in the past—really didn't matter, for now there was new hope.

"Jericho, time for prayers before supper," came a voice from out of nowhere. He sighed, then scrambled backward down the cottonwood and brushed his soiled hands on the back of his pants as he ran toward the back door of the convent.

"Coming," he called out, and pounded noisily up the wooden steps which creaked and groaned from even his light weight, then burst into the large kitchen where the evening meal was being prepared. He sniffed hungrily at the pungent odor of the food and smiled. It was obvious to him, even at such a young age, that the Sisters were outdoing themselves on his behalf. He skipped over the wooden plank floor until he reached the small chapel. At the door, waiting for him, was Mother Jean Marie.

"Have you been up in the tree?" she asked softly.

"Yes, Mother Superior."

"We'll excuse your appearance just this once, Jericho," she admonished and gave him a slight pat on the rear, just to remind him that she was still in charge. He gazed up into the wrinkled face that he'd grown to love, and smiled slightly, then pressed her hand as they moved together to the front of the holy room.

From her habit pocket Jean Marie produced Jericho's rosary and handed it to him as they knelt together to begin their evening prayers. As Jericho recited the words, Jean Marie stopped her own recitation and looked at the small boy kneeling beside her. A sigh escaped her, and when Jericho looked up he saw the pain in her eyes. He reached over and patted her gnarled fingers as if to say, "I understand," then turned his attention to the worship service.

Jacob and Martha Smith had weathered the Depression with little obvious discomfort and had proved to be staunch pillars of St. Peter's Church. They had willingly given of their own wealth to the less fortunate, and were highly respected citizens.

When Monsignor O'Connell had requested that they meet with him at the rectory office, they'd both wondered why, but he'd failed to divulge the reason.

Rather apprehensively they'd entered the rectory office, to be greeted almost effusively by the Priest. Jacob had glanced at his wife, who appeared to be relieved, and he also relaxed.

After they were seated comfortably, the Monsignor began.

"Jacob, Martha, I have some news that I hope you'll find of interest."

Once again Jacob looked at his wife, then reached over to take her hand. "Yes, Father, we hope so, too," Jacob replied, though obviously puzzled.

"You have both exhibited great compassion for the less fortunate during this devastating time in our country's history, and have willingly shared your own good fortune not only with others, but also with the church." Then he leaned back in his chair and his look became even more serious.

"Thank you, Father," Martha Smith replied, gratified that their help had not gone unnoticed.

"We've known here at St. Peter's that you've always wanted to have a family," and a trace of compassion appeared in the old Priest's eyes, "but you haven't been blessed in that way, so far."

Jacob and Martha sat up in their chairs even straighter for they'd both caught the words *so far*. Their excitement mounted.

"Please go on, Father O'Connell," Martha burst out, then blushed at her boldness as she was not usually that forthright.

The Priest smiled at her display of eagerness, then leaned forward and placed his arms on the top of his desk so he could see their reaction clearly.

"We've just been informed that a young boy, who's almost five, is available for adoption, and naturally our thoughts turned to you first."

Jacob's eyes lit up and he turned to look at Martha, whose eyes were also shining, and he smiled.

"When can we meet him, Father?" Jacob asked.

"I'm afraid not today. You see, the young lad is at the Convent in Staley at the present."

"Staley? That's way out West!" Jacob exploded.

"We're quite aware of where it is," the Priest replied coldly and paused. "If you're not interested, then there's no need to continue our discussion."

Martha Smith's expression was filled with disgust as she turned to look at her husband.

"Father O'Connell, it makes no difference where he is; we can go there. I'll not miss out on a chance to have a child in our home." She bridled a bit at her boldness.

Mollified by Martha's response and embarrassed by his first reaction, Jacob bowed his head. When he looked up it was directly into the eyes of the Priest who was staring at him intently.

"Jacob," he said gently, "is Staley too far for you?"

"Of course not, Father. I was simply surprised, that's all. Of course I want to see the child. Can you tell us more about him?"

The old Priest shook his head. "I'm sorry, but we know very little about him, other than that his parents were never married, and that the Mother Superior at the Convent has the authority to place him for adoption with a good Catholic family."

"You mean he's a bastard child?"

"Yes, Jacob. He's illegitimate, but he's one of God's children, just as we are, and you must always remember that he himself had nothing to do with the way he entered our world."

Martha and Jacob exchanged long glances.

"When do we have to give you a decision?" Jacob asked.

"I'd like to know if you're seriously interested as soon as possible," and he paused. "Why don't I give you some time by yourselves. Perhaps that would help." He got up from his chair and moved to the door. "Ask the Sister to come for me when you're ready." He opened the door and went out, closing it softly behind him.

Jacob turned to his wife. "Martha, a bastard!" he snarled, "My God, we have no idea what kind of parents he had. He could be not right."

Martha Smith looked at her husband with growing distaste.

"Jacob, I can't believe that you'd take such an attitude. We've wanted a child for so long," and her lips quivered. "I don't care about his parents . . . I want to meet this boy."

Jacob Smith knew when he was beaten and he put his arms around his wife and held her.

"All right, Martha. We'll go to Staley, but if he's not what we want, then we'll not attempt to adopt him. Will you agree?"

"Yes, Jacob. But I pray that you'll be pleasantly surprised. Now, go find Father O'Connell," and she almost pushed him out the door.

When the two men returned they seemed to be in accord and Jacob was smiling.

"Martha," Father O'Connel said pleasantly, as he seated himself, indicating that they should do the same, "Jacob and I have agreed that I'll make arrangements with the Mother Superior for Saturday next. I do hope that you find these plans to your satisfaction."

"Oh, yes, Father," she replied, "I just wish it could be sooner."

Then she turned to her husband. "Jacob, you'll have to get the car ready for the trip and I'll bake cookies and we'll buy some toys."

Before she could elaborate further he touched her arm. "Martha dear, we're merely going to meet the child. These things take time."

"He's right, Martha. There's no reason for you to go completely overboard," the Priest interjected, although there was a definite sparkle in his eyes.

Jacob got up from his chair and nudged Martha, who followed suit. The Priest went with them to the door and told them goodbye, but not before he spoke directly to Jacob.

"Jacob," he said, "all I ask is that you not judge this child by the behavior of his parents. Hopefully, the Mother Superior will give you more information on his background, but don't be surprised if she is unwilling," and he laughed softly. "I've known Mother Jean Marie for many years. She's one of the finest in her Order, and is most discreet."

"I understand Father, and we thank you for giving us this opportunity," Jacob replied. "Both Martha and I will be open minded; who knows, we may come back prospective parents," and with that they all laughed happily.

On the morning that Jacob and Martha Smith were expected at the convent, Mother Jean Marie rose before dawn and went to the chapel. As she knelt at the altar to pray, tears of sorrow flowed silently down her cheeks, and she begged forgiveness for her sinful and selfish hope that the Smith family would prove to be unsuitable. She'd never realized until now how much she loved the boy and even though there had been times when she'd lectured herself harshly, it made no difference to her heart. Now she was consumed by grief at the thought of his leaving, and as she cried out in anguish she failed to hear the opening of the chapel door.

Jericho had bounded from his bed that day when the first crease of dawn echoed across the sky, and as he'd looked out the window of his tiny bedroom he saw that it would be a spectacular day. Still, he felt an inner restlessness and because of his deep religious beliefs he dressed hurriedly and went to the chapel. When he entered he saw that someone was already there, and knew that it could only be Mother Jean Marie.

Slipping quietly into one of the pews he listened to her sorrowful lament and tears of sadness for her drifted down his cheeks. Finally, as she lay prostrate before the Virgin Mary with sobs racking her bulky frame, he quietly went down the aisle and knelt beside her. For a time he remained silent, then as her crying began to subside, he touched her arm gently.

Startled, Mother Jean Marie raised her head, her lined face red and moist with tears. Still, she made no effort to smile.

"Jericho," she whispered, her voice sounding much like the croaking of a bull frog, "why are you here?" Then Mother Jean Marie forced herself to an upright position as the serious eyed child, now sitting crossed legged on the floor beside her, gazed at her almost sternly.

"Mother Jean Marie," he stated firmly, "You mustn't do this. Did you think you'd lose me? I'll not let that happen, ever."

"Oh, Jericho," the elderly woman said, and pulled him onto her ample lap where they clung together as the first rays of the sun which pierced the stained glass window burst around them.

While they nursed their sadness, the Mother Superior's assistant had crept silently to the door and looked in. A lump had formed in her throat at the sight of the Mother Superior and Jericho and she quickly made the decision that no one would enter the chapel for morning prayers until the two had come to terms with their parting.

Finally, gathering a semblance of courage, Mother Jean Marie released her hold on Jericho, and then looked him in the eye.

"You're right, Jericho," she said, and sighed deeply. "You've shown more backbone then I have; I'm ashamed," and she bowed her head in obvious embarrassment.

At that Jericho's childish laughter pealed throughout the chapel and he jumped to his feet, tugging at the old woman's hand.

"Come, Mother," he said, the sound of joy in his words, "let's go to the woods. It's a beautiful morning and the birds will be up," and he laughed happily.

At first Mother Jean Marie made an effort to protest, but she quickly acquiesced to his invitation and with Jericho's help struggled to her feet. His enthusiasm for life was what she needed, and hand in hand they hurried from the chapel, neither noticing the Sister standing in the shadows with tears of sadness coursing down her cheeks as they passed.

5

The long trek to Staley took Martha and Jacob Smith nearly eight hours. They'd left their comfortable home in Wichita at four o'clock that morning and had arrived at the convent hot, dirty, virtually exhausted, and with a trace of their first enthusiasm at the prospect of finding a child gone.

Mother Jean Marie heard their arrival and moved to the window to watch. As they alighted from the dusty automobile she was pleased to see that Mr. Smith showed good manners and helped his wife from the car, then placed his hand under her arm as they moved slowly up the flight of steps which led to the convent door.

After their walk in the woods that morning, Mother Jean Marie and Jericho had shared breakfast in her quarters, and she'd informed him that he must bathe, wash his hair and wear his Sunday best.

"But why?" he'd protested, his dark eyes flashing their anger.

"Because I want the Smiths to see what a handsome young man you are," she had replied matter of factly.

Obviously chagrined by her instructions, Jericho morosely nodded his head in agreement and left to do her bidding. He'd been dressed and waiting for close to four hours, and now his patience

41

was beginning to ebb. Then the Mother Superior came rushing into his room.

"They're here, Jericho," she announced, and as he jumped to his feet to accompany her, she stopped him.

"I must talk with them first. Then we'll have refreshments and I'll come for you."

Disappointed, he flung himself down on the bed. Another wait. Jericho's courage faltered as tears welled in his eyes. He didn't like what was happening and yet he knew that Mother Jean Marie wanted only the best for him.

Sister Ann met the Smiths at the convent door and greeted them, then guided the couple down the hallway until they came to the Mother Superior's office. She knocked but once, and Mother Jean Marie's strong voice called out, "Please enter." The Sister opened the door, then stepped to one side as the guests entered to find Mother Jean Marie sitting behind her desk looking much like a queen on a throne. Her eagle-bright eyes raked over the man and woman standing before her, obviously ill at ease, and then she smiled warmly and held out her hand; first to Jacob, who gripped the frail fingers ever so gently; and then to Martha, who kissed her hand out of respect.

"Please sit down," she said and waved toward the two straight backed chairs which had been placed next to her desk. Dutifully, her visitors took their seats and then looked once again into the stern face of the Mother Superior.

"I do hope that your trip was enjoyable," Mother Jean Marie remarked, and Jacob and Martha glanced at each other apprehensively, then nodded. Then she continued on, all socializing now over. "The first order of business we must discuss is *why* you wish to adopt a child," and she raised her brows slightly to gaze at them shrewdly.

Jacob Smith looked confused. "Didn't Monsignor O'Connell tell you?"

"Of course he did," Mother Jean Marie snapped, "but I want to hear it first hand . . . from you." Looking much like a judge as she settled back comfortably in her chair, she waited for their answer.

Jacob nudged his wife, but the gesture did not escape Mother Jean Marie. It was obvious that Martha felt ill at ease in the audience before the Mother Superior, and she was almost afraid to speak, but bravely she cleared her throat and then looked up shyly into the eyes of the elderly woman.

"Don't be frightened," Mother Jean Marie said softly.

The wariness in the woman's look had been apparent, but those few words of kindness helped Martha Smith, and then the story of their childless years poured out, revealing the lack of fulfillment they'd both experienced.

Jean Marie listened with rapt attention, her eyes never once leaving Martha's face. Jacob shifted uneasily in his chair as his wife told of the efforts they'd made and explored in order to have a child of their own. Nothing was left to the Mother Superior's imagination. At the conclusion, Martha wept unashamedly. Mother Jean Marie stood up, moved around the desk to her side, and placed her arms around her.

"My child," she consoled, "I believe everything that you've told me, and you deserve to be a mother."

Martha dabbed at her eyes, and suddenly a smile raced across her heretofore somber face.

"You mean it?"

Mother Jean Marie nodded. "I'm going to have Sister Ann take you to a quiet place where you can freshen up and rest," and she took the younger woman by the arm and helped her from the chair. Jacob started to rise, but Mother Jean Marie motioned for him to stay, and obediently he sat back in his chair.

"I need to talk with Mr. Smith alone, my dear," Mother Jean Marie explained to Martha who had hesitated at leaving her husband behind. When Jacob nodded his approval, she went to the door, opened it and found Sister Ann waiting.

Then the Mother Superior shut the door and leaned against it for a moment to gather her courage. Almost like a soldier, she marched back to her desk and seated herself, then picked up the sheaf of papers.

During all the years she'd written her monthly letter to Kathleen concerning Jericho's progress, she'd laboriously made copies of each one, not only for her own self protection, but also to have a record of his obvious intelligence and ability. He'd learned to read by the age of three, and although the reading materials for a child at a Catholic Convent were sparse at best, Mother Jean Marie had unearthed some of her own ancient primers that she'd used when a child and which were an important part of her personal belongings. The vow of poverty that she'd taken years before did not allow for any luxuries; however, her own Mother Superior had relinquished that hard and fast rule in order to let her keep the books that were her only prize possessions. And, as if foresight had been possible, they'd obviously been put to good use, for Jericho had devoured each and every one of them and she knew that when he entered either a regular school, or a parochial school, he'd prove to be superior to the other children.

Jacob Smith watched Mother Jean Marie intently, realizing that she'd artfully removed his wife from the scene as Martha had proved to be highly emotional. Now it was just the two of them, the Mother Superior and himself, who would come to terms—one way or the other.

"Mr. Smith," the Mother Superior addressed Jacob, her voice expressing little emotion. "I wanted to talk with you in private about this child," and she paused to look at him sharply, then continued. "After being with your wife for only this short a period of time, I'm certain she will make an excellent parent," and once again she paused, a slight frown creasing her brow. "But I do have reservations about you."

Jacob's look was one of bewilderment.

"Mother Superior," he protested, "I want a child, too. Why would you feel this way?"

Mother Jean Marie smiled slightly.

"My dear man, Father O'Connell and I go way back, and he conveyed your hesitancy about the distance to Staley."

Jacob paled and he felt that their trip would prove to be in vain.

"However," she went on, "in our long and informative correspondence," and she waved some of the papers at him, "we've both come to the conclusion that given enough time you just might turn out to be a good father and parent."

At her statement, Jacob released a deep sigh, which caused Mother Jean Marie to chuckle slightly. Then she became serious.

"You're aware that this child was born out of wedlock, I know. Does this bother you?"

The man's face reddened for he remembered vividly his first reaction at St. Peters.

"It does present some doubts, Mother Superior. I'll admit to that."

"I'm sure that it would and I can understand why. However, if this young lad were not perfect in every way he'd stay here where he'd be loved and cared for, but that's certainly not the case. He's an extremely bright, sensitive and loving child," and she laughed slightly and added, "even after being raised by a stoic group of Sisters." Then her eyes clouded. "You see, Jacob, we *all* love Jericho very much," and tears suddenly misted her eyes.

Her visitor couldn't help but see the deep agony she was going through, and as he looked at the elderly woman his heart was filled with compassion.

"I'm certain that you do, Mother Superior," and he hesitated, then continued bravely, "but weren't you the one who made the decision to place him for adoption?"

The Mother Superior nodded her assent.

"Yes, that's true. You must understand that when Jericho's mother first left him with us she had planned on coming for him, but unfortunately she developed an illness and ultimately succumbed to it. Then, after consultation with my superiors, it was decided that he should be placed with a good Catholic family."

"How truly sad," Jacob responded. "Does the boy know?"

"Yes, we've told him. However, it is fortunate in one respect."

"Really? How?"

"Jericho has no memory of his mother whatsoever, and even though we talked with him about her frequently, her death was merely the ending of a fantasy for him," and she sighed.

"But what about his father?"

The look Mother Jean Marie gave Jacob was icy. "We know nothing about him. Nothing at all," she snapped.

"He deserted his own flesh and blood?" Jacob stammered.

"That's correct. But enough of this. Are you prepared to make your acquaintance with Jericho?"

Jacob Smith beamed, for he now felt that all was not lost. "Of course. Shall I go find Martha?"

"That won't be necessary. Sister Ann is with her in the sitting room reserved for the few guests we receive here at the Convent. I'll show you the way," and she paused momentarily. "Then, I'll go fetch Jericho.''

After seeing Jacob on the way to join his wife, Mother Jean Marie moved slowly down the hall toward Jericho's room, realizing deep within herself that this could be one of the last times she'd make the familiar journey, and she suddenly felt very tired.

When she reached Jericho's door she found it closed, and knocked softly. Receiving no response, she pushed open the door and entered the small room to find her young charge sprawled out on the bed, sound asleep in his now rumpled Sunday-best. One arm lay across his eyes as though to shut out the world, and Mother Jean Marie sensed immediately that he was dreading the thought of leaving the familiarity of his surroundings.

She bent over to kiss him lightly on the cheek and then Jericho stirred. He withdrew his arm from across his face and slowly opened his eyes to see the beloved face of his Mother Superior peering down at him. He smiled, then pushed himself up, rubbing at his eyes with the back of his hands.

''Sorry, Mother Jean Marie, I didn't mean to go to sleep,'' he apologized, and glanced at his pants and shirt which didn't resemble in the least their appearance when he'd first put them on. Still, Mother Jean Marie did not reprimand him for his wait had been long.

''It's time for us to join Mr. and Mrs. Smith, Jericho,'' she said, making an attempt to smooth his wrinkled clothing. ''Comb your hair and then we'll be on our way.''

''Should I change?''

Mother Jean shook her head. ''No, it really isn't that important.''

At his question she paused, for she'd been considering her own feelings, and she did like the Smiths. They were good people and would make excellent parents, yet it was her own need that seemed to come first, and that was wrong.

''Don't you like them?'' he asked, looking intently at her.

''Oh my, yes, I do like them,'' she replied, putting enthusiasm in her voice. But Jericho knew Mother Jean Marie extremely well, and was aware that she wasn't telling him the whole truth.

''Will they like me?''

Mother Jean Marie laughed. ''Of course, silly boy, and in time they'll grow to *love* you, just as we do.''

''It won't be the same,'' Jericho said emphatically.

"You've got to give it time, dear one," and Mother Superior patted Jericho on the head with affection.

"But it will never be the same," he repeated.

"Jericho," she replied, a firmness in her voice, "nothing is ever the same, but we all have to learn. Now is the time for you to enter a new life. Shall we go?"

The small dark-haired child, gazed up at the old woman, then slipped his hand in hers.

"I'm ready, Mother Jean Marie, but I'll always love you best."

Suddenly the Mother Superior pulled out her kerchief and blew her nose loudly. Then, without another word between them, they began the walk that would take the child that she loved out of her life.

6

Stonewall Barton was his name, but to conceal the fact that his father was a known murderer, and his mother a 'madam,' he'd refrained from using it when he'd run away from the only home he'd ever known, which happened to be a small apartment located at the rear of the Ladies Palace. This impressive edifice was his mother's grand attempt at being an entrepreneur, and she had undertaken this mode of survival only after his father had been incarcerated. To hide any connection to either his father or his mother, he'd adopted the only name he could possibly handle . . . and that was Stoney.

In the 1930's the State of Kansas was almost devoid of these houses of ill repute; however, Madam Bess, as they referred to Stoney's mother, ran hers like a business and in due time turned a tidy profit. As a young child Stoney had basked in the almost motherly attention bestowed on him by the ladies in his mother's employ. But as he grew older and more knowledgeable of the travesties of life, he found the cruel, snide remarks offered by his schoolmates far too much to cope with, and he'd escaped from what he now knew was a questionable occupation by disappearing in the night without so much as leaving a word as to his whereabouts.

Besides the good looks he'd been borne with, the one and only talent that Stoney possessed was working with his hands. Ultimately, this led him to a somewhat menial job as an apprentice mechanic on a ranch near Staley.

Stoney had kept to himself in the bunk house which he shared with the other hands, and had cultivated only a few that he could call friends, for in the main they were much older than he. At times he was forced to hide in his bunk feigning sleep when the older men would return from a 'hot' Saturday night on the town. Their ribald and deprecating remarks about Madam Bess and her ladies embarrassed him. From such experiences he'd placed a wall around his heart, and when he was asked to accompany the others to 'learn the ropes,' as they so laughingly put it, he'd refused. Because of his youth, they'd accepted his decision and learned that it was best to leave him to his own devices.

On one of the few trips that Stoney had made to Staley, he'd encountered Kathleen Muldoon quite by accident, and her dark haired, velvety eyed Irish beauty had taken his breath away at the sight of her. Almost boldly, and completely out of character, he'd introduced himself. Kathleen proved to be his first love and his growing desire for her mounted as they spent more and more time together. With the inexperience of extreme youth, they had both tossed all concern to the wind about what the future might hold in their mutual search for just one person to really love.

The day that Kathleen had told him of their expected child, Stoney had cruelly cast her aside, much as he would have done to one of his mother's ladies. He was not yet mature enough to realize that she was the one person in the world who could possibly have made a difference in his life. At times, late at night as he lay in his bunk unable to sleep, he'd think of her, and a rather strange feeling, but not one of desire or lust, would almost overwhelm him. Stoney did not recognize that this was a mark of an all consuming love for Kathleen, and a path that he'd never, ever cross again.

On occasion he'd hear idle gossip concerning Kathleen supplied by the neighboring ranch hands, and that was his main source of information. He'd hoped, and unashamedly, that she'd lose the child that she carried, but that was not to be the case. As the months passed quickly and the dust storms rolled across the arid plains of Kansas, Stoney decided that it was now the time for him to leave. Not only was the country itself becoming devastated, but it was approaching the time for the birth of the child Kathleen carried, and he could not face either.

When Stoney left Kansas, he'd headed for the Northwest and had finally settled in a small town in Montana. The town he chose was called Salmon, nestled against the base of the Rockies near the Canadian border, with the black gold called oil its primary product. Because of the mechanical ability that he possessed, he'd applied for a job as a member of a rigging crew with Pride Oil, and had been rewarded immediately by being hired on. His youth and strength proved to be an excellent resource to the burgeoning oil company, and after he'd easily accomplished the tasks assigned to him, within a few short months Stoney had been promoted to foreman.

It was only natural that when Joseph Walowski, the President of Pride Oil, became aware of Stoney's intelligence and his ability to get along with the other employees, Stoney shed the heavy work clothes of the rigging crew and became a member of management. Soon he found himself sitting at the right hand of the Polish immigrant who'd founded Pride, and who also had dreams of greatness, much like Stoney himself. When newly discovered wells came in they were placed under Stoney's supervision, for he was now second in command, answering only to Joe Walowski himself.

Stoney had kept himself aloof from the melting pot which inhabited Salmon and led a very private and almost reclusive existance. The one exception he'd made was his relationship with the Walowski family. With them he felt accepted and at ease.

The town of Salmon itself had proved to be a far cry from the staid village of Staley. With the discovery of oil, the bars and saloons seemed to have cropped up almost overnight. It also brought an influx of foreigners. These transients frequented the bars along with a majority of Pride's employees. However, because of Stoney's experience with the Ladies Palace, he'd never considered entering them.

Joseph Walowski, himself a respectable married man and blessed with a large family, saw in Stoney the attributes that he so prized, and welcomed the young man into the privacy of his home.

In time, Joe's oldest daughter, Julia, made a marked impression on Stoney. Julia had not only graduated from high school, but college as well, and though she lacked real beauty and was some years older, he sought her out because of her intelligence and knowledge of the outside world. He knew that if he were to get ahead, he needed a woman such as this in his life.

It was hardly a surprise that when Stoney Barton asked Joe Walowski for Julia's hand in marriage, he was given his whole-hearted blessing without hesitation. Julia was also elated by this fortuitous turn of events.

After Stoney became caught up in the hectic lifestyle of the Walowskis, he thought it would be easy to forget Kathleen Muldoon. But still, there were frequent times when he'd awaken long before dawn to find himself murmuring her name, and his body would ache from his desire. On those days he would withdraw into his shell, and nothing, not even business, could interest him.

Joe Walowski was quick to sense Stoney's varying moods, but excused them as pre-marital symptoms. He'd even gone so far as to confide in Julia about Stoney's seeming unhappiness, and had intimated that perhaps it would be wise to show him more affection.

This suggestion, especially coming from her father, was shocking to Julia. Didn't their religious upbringing preach chastity? However, not wanting to lose Stoney, she began to pursue him aggressively.

Due to his sheer frustration and need for release, he soon bedded her. To Julia their first sexual union was a frightening and unsatisfactory experience, for after Stoney had drained himself, he'd pushed her away savagely. She then burst into tears. This had brought her soon-to-be husband back to her side, and he'd comforted her, convincing her that he was as nervous as she.

Satisfied with his explanation, and having known nothing about the art of love making, Julia, as most women of those years, believed that she'd performed her part successfully. But Stoney, who'd experienced the epitome of sexual gratification, knew that he could never give of himself fully to Julia, and that she would merely be the pillar he needed for his future.

Out of that rather dismal experience Stoney decided to stay his distance from his bride-to-be, and at first this had puzzled Julia. When they were alone he'd stroke her hand tenderly, and on occasion would bestow a chaste kiss on her brow, but he never once indicated that he wanted her physically again. In a way this pleased her, as she believed with all her heart that she had given Stoney proof of her love, and that out of respect for her convictions, he wanted to abstain.

The wedding day of Julia Walowski and Stonewall Barton was approaching rapidly and would take place almost two years to the day since Stoney had first arrived in Salmon. Before their marriage, Joe Walowski insisted that he wanted to build the bride and groom a house on land that he owned, situated not far from the granite manion he'd erected for himself. That was the first time that Stoney had words with his intended father-in-law.

The conversation had taken place following a sumptuous meal prepared by Mrs. Walowski and Julia's sisters. Stoney and Julia, at her father's invitation, had joined him on the veranda when he'd indicated that he wished to talk with them privately.

Stoney's look remained passive as he listened to Joe's carefully woven plan, and he'd glanced once at Julia who appeared bright eyed and eager. Finally he could no longer contain himself.

"Joe," he said, almost angrily, "I don't want to be obliged to you. You pay me well. For God's sake, let me be the one to provide a home for Julia," and he pushed himself up from his chair and began to pace back and forth, his hands thrust deep into his pockets to conceal his clenched fists.

"My boy," Joe began, an almost condescending air to his voice, "why can't you let me give you a home as a wedding gift? I see no harm in it."

Then Julia chimed in. "Oh, Stoney, it would be wonderful to be near my family," and her eyes almost begged him to say yes. But still he remained adamant.

"I know that you mean well, Joe, but I'd like to make it on my own," and Stoney looked once more at Julia, her look one of disappointment.

"Julia," he said, stopping before her, "if you are to be my wife, I'll be the one who takes care of you. We will have a home of our own, but in good time. Until then, we'll find a small place and build from there."

"But Stoney," Julia protested feebly, "it's all in the family. Don't you understand?"

"Yes, I do, but from the stories that your father's told me, he had no one to help him, and he made it on his own. I intend to do the same."

Joe Walowski could find no fit argument to counter his protege's reasoning and threw his hands up as though in dismissal. He'd also been given the opportunity to see the prideful and stubborn nature of Stoney Barton, and in a way he had to admire those qualities.

Rising to his feet he slapped Stoney on the back paternally, then took Julia's hand and looked into her eyes.

"My dear, you are a very fortunate young woman to have a man with such self-pride for a husband." At his compliment Stoney turned away, but still Joe continued. "I hope that you'll bless him with many children, as your dear mother has me."

Julia blushed at his words. "I'll try, father," she murmured, and then accepted his kiss as he left to enter the house.

Then she turned to Stoney. "We'll do whatever you think's best," she said and moved close to him. She placed her arms around his neck and pulled his head down so she could kiss him. But Stoney was not in the mood, and gently he removed her arms to free himself. At this apparent rejection, Julia stomped into the house, leaving him alone.

For a time Stoney, deep in thought, stared out across the vast countryside. Then, without so much as a goodbye, he left the Walowski house and headed back to his rooming house. On the way he was approached by several young, flashily dressed girls plying their trade, and he found himself searching their faces, almost afraid that Kathleen might have fallen prey to this kind of life.

The preparations for Julia's and Stoney's wedding became the main focus of attention in the Walowski household. A seamstress had been hired to make Julia's wedding dress, the bridesmaids' gowns and her mother's dress as well. As a result, Stoney was left pretty much to his own devices and spent many evenings at Pride's offices catching up on his always heavy workload.

One evening, after he'd locked up the office, he'd wandered through the bar and saloon district of Salmon and saw many of Pride's employees having a helluva time, as they so aptly put it. As he strolled along, minding his own business, he noticed an older woman lounging in front of one of the bars, obviously waiting for some man to show an interest. He glanced at her again for she seemed vaguely familiar, and as he drew closer he saw that it was Butterfly Belle from the Ladies Palace. For a moment Stoney panicked, but before he could turn away she'd spotted him and came running.

"My God," she whispered, "My God, it's little Stoney," and she stepped back to appraise him, then added, "all grown up," and a glitter came into her eyes. "So this is where you've been these past years," she said accusingly. "Your mother almost went crazy when you dropped from sight. God, but Bess will be glad to know where you are."

Stoney knew that she had him dead to rights and that there wasn't anything that he could do but listen to her babble.

"Where you living?" she said point blank.

"I have a room, if it's any of your concern."

"You got a woman?" she pressed on.

"Not the kind you mean," he replied.

"Oh, so you're a straight one," and when Stoney nodded she laughed uproariously, causing passers by, some of whom were employees of Pride, to pause and look.

Stoney knew that this meeting with Belle would cause gossip to run rampant, and he knew that that was the last thing he needed. Taking Belle by the arm he pulled her down the street while she protested loudly. When they'd forsaken the main thoroughfare, and were out of the eyes of the curious, he'd turned into a lightly traveled side street and then released her.

Belle stared at him indignantly and rubbed her bare arm where red marks from the pressure of his fingers were noticeable.

"Just who the hell do you think you're pushing around?" she rasped.

"Belle, I have to talk to you."

"What about? I'm not doing anything wrong."

"I want you to get out of Salmon."

"Get out? Why the hell should I? This town is a gold mine for dames like me," and she flashed a suggestive smile.

"For old times sake."

"Old times? Just because I wet-nursed you when you were a kid?

There has to be a better reason than that," she said mockingly.

"There is."

"Care to tell me?" she asked archly.

"I guess I'll have to."

"Well, spill it, kid."

"Okay, Belle, let's find a place where we can talk," Stoney said reluctantly, and glanced up and down the unfamiliar street. Then his eyes came to rest on a small run down cafe whose lights still burned.

Taking Belle by the arm, now more gently, Stoney guided her down the street where they entered the cafe. They moved to a small table located at the rear and far from the windows. Stoney pulled out a chair for Belle, then took the one opposite her.

In a short time, a woman appeared and slapped two dirty, fly specked menus on the table, then waited.

"What would you like, Belle?" Stoney asked, as his companion read the sparse menu eagerly.

"Everything looks good to me," and then added, "haven't eaten today."

"You haven't eaten?"

Belle shook her head.

"Well, for God's sake order something that'll stick to your ribs."

At this comment the woman standing beside them laughed wryly. She knew well that when you were in the *business*, there could be many days without even so much as a cup of coffee, and especially when your looks had begun to fade.

"Gimme your special steak," Belle ordered almost haughtily, as she'd been quick to notice the woman's manner. "And good hot coffee, right now," she added and then glanced with loathing at the woman.

The woman ignored her look and turned to Stoney.

"How about you, mister?"

"Coffee will be fine, and could you hurry?"

At his request she looked at him rather disdainfully, then replied, "Of course, sir," with undue emphasis on the 'sir.'

While they waited for Belle's dinner they both remained silent. Neither Stoney nor Belle knew just how or where to begin, but finally Belle could stand it no longer.

"What are you doing way out here, Stoney?"

"I might ask you the same question," he replied, hedging.

"Well, God knows you know my business. I'd still be at your Mom's place if they hadn't raided it."

"Raided the Ladies Palace?" he asked in astonishment for he knew that his mother had paid the law well.

"Yeah. Some of those Christians decided that we shouldn't be around. Fortunately, one of the deputy's came ahead and told us so we were gone when they arrived."

"But whatever brought you to Montana?" he pursued.

"Oil. What else? Everybody in Kansas wants to leave that damned dried up place. Besides, money was getting scarce and it was time for me to move on."

"What about my mother?"

Belle laughed. "Hell, you needn't worry about Bess. She got herself a rich one from Wichita, so losing the Palace didn't hurt her that much."

Stoney gave an audible sigh of relief and murmured, "Thank God for that."

Then Belle leaned her elbows on the table and look Stoney square in the eye. "Now kid, tell me what the hell you're doing here? The last time we heard anything you were ranching, then we lost track."

Stoney nodded. "You're right, but when the dust storms got bad, I figured I'd look for greener pastures," and he laughed slightly at the obviously unintended humor.

"So?" Belle remarked.

Stoney sighed, then told her why he was there. "You see, Belle, one of the hands' brothers drifted out here some years back, and when he found that jobs were becoming plentiful and the money good, he let him know. I was ready to leave Kansas anyway, so we hoofed it out here together. He went on to Cut Bank and I stayed here."

"What kind of a job you got?" Belle pursued, as she'd noticed how well dressed he was.

"I work for Pride Oil. Started out there a couple of years ago on the rigging crew and then made foreman. Now I'm in the office."

"Whew!" Belle said, pursing her lips. Then her eyes brightened.

"You're a big shot? And that's the reason you want me to leave. Right?"

Stoney squirmed. He knew now that he'd have to tell her.

"Come on, kid," Belle encouraged, "Remember, I was like a second mother to you."

"I know, Belle," but still he hesitated.

At that moment he was granted a brief reprieve, for the waitress appeared with a tray filled with steaming food, and for the moment Belle's attention was drawn to it.

She literally dived into the food and ate ravenously. While Stoney watched in silence as she gorged herself, a sinking feeling came over him. He's never known hunger himself, but it was obvious to him that this woman was starved, and he wondered if her story about not eating just that one day was really true.

When the edge had been taken from Belle's hunger, she paused and looked at Stoney with open affection in her eyes.

After she'd wiped her mouth on a paper napkin, she took a sip of the hot coffee, all the while appraising her companion.

"You know, Stoney, you're a damned good kid," and she laughed huskily. "I guess I shouldn't call you a kid, 'cause it's obvious you're now quite a man and doing very well."

He nodded.

"Now then, why do you want me out of Salmon?"

Stoney knew that he had to be honest with her.

"Belle, I've done well out here, as you've already noticed," and he smiled tightly. "I was fortunate when I hired on at Pride. They needed young, good mechanics on the rigging crews, and thank God that old geezer I worked with in Kansas had been a hard task master," and his eyes reflected a trace of kindness. "I've been here well over two years now, and after I'd proved myself on the crew, I was made a foreman."

"That's great. But you said the office," Belle persisted.

"I was getting to that," he replied and shifted nervously in his chair.

"Joe Walowski, the President and owner of Pride, noticed my work and took a liking to me. Now I work with him and am in charge of all the new wells."

Belle's eyes widened. "So you *are* a big shot," she said and slapped her hand on the table with such enthusiasm that it caused the dishes to rattle.

Stoney had to smile. " 'Fraid so, Belle."

"And that's the reason you want me to leave?"

"Not only that, Belle. You see, I'm going to be married in a few weeks to Joe Walowski's daughter, Julia. They're a very respectable family and know nothing of my past," and his look shifted away from hers.

"I kinda figured that it was something like that, and I can't say that I blame you," Belle replied kindly. "But you see, Stoney, I haven't got a dime. I'm getting a little too old for this game, I guess, and frankly, I'm growing tired of the life. Three of us share a flea bag room, taking turns," and she looked at him archly. "It's not like it was at your Mom's."

"Where would you like to go?" Stoney asked.

"I've given some thought to that. Your mom is my only real friend, but Bess married well and doesn't need me hanging around to remind her of the past."

"I can help you."

Belle laughed. "How?"

"I've accumulated some money, and I'd be happy to share it with you."

A sudden hardness crossed her face. "Pay me off, you mean?" she rasped.

"Nothing of the sort. You were good to me when I was growing up and I owe it to you."

Belle's look softened somewhat. "So what's the plan?"

Stoney cleared his throat, knowing that he had a hard sell to make.

"I know a lot of people in Cut Bank, and I'm certain if you'd consider working in someone's home, they'd be glad to hire you, if I recommend you. There's one thing, though; you'd simply have to change your appearance and manners."

"In other words, be someone's servant? Is that what you're saying?"

Stoney nodded. "It could be a good, decent life for you, Belle. People out here don't have the caste system that they do in the bigger cities, or even in Kansas. We're all in this together and I'm sure that after awhile, you'd find it to your liking."

Belle shrugged almost resignedly. She knew that Stoney was talking sense, and she was also aware that she needed a good, long rest.

"I'll give you money for a decent room and some good clothes, and tomorrow I'll put out some feelers. In the meantime, you have to stay off the streets," and a grimness etched his face. "I mean it, Belle. If you want my help, I'm glad to be here for you. You see, I ran away from home because of the Ladies Palace, and I don't ever want anything like that to cause me trouble again. I'm straight, Belle. It took me awhile, but I got there."

Belle had listened to him with rapt attention and realized that Stoney now wielded a great deal of power. She was thankful that he was on her side, and it didn't take her long to make up her mind.

"Okay Stoney, you gotta deal," and she stuck out her soiled hand which he grasped without even noticing the grime.

Then Stoney took off his money belt and removed five twenty dollar bills and handed them to Belle. Her eyes widened as she gasped, "My God, I haven't had this much at one time in years," and sudden tears filled her eyes. Then her shoulders started to shake as she began to cry.

Stoney reached over to take her hand. "Belle, there's nothing to cry about. I'll always be your friend. You were mine and I've never forgotten your kindness."

The sorely bedraggled woman looked up into his handsome face and smiled through her tears. "You make me feel like a real person, Stoney," she whispered, "a real person," as she attempted to dry her eyes on the back of her sleeve.

"You're a good woman, Belle," and he patted her hand with affection. "Now tomorrow you get some new duds and clean yourself up, then come by my office."

"Your office?"

"Of course. I'll introduce you to Joe as a friend from Kansas who came out here looking for work in Cut Bank."

"He won't object?"

"Not at all. He'll probably help."

"Oh, Stoney, how will I ever repay you?" she asked.

"By becoming the good woman you are," he replied with a trace of emotion catching at his words.

Stoney paid the bill. They left the cafe and headed for a small hotel he knew that didn't cater to the 'trade.'

When they entered, the clerk looked at them sharply, taking in the cheaply dressed woman and the well dressed young man.

"Sorry, we don't rent rooms to the likes of you," he rasped.

Stoney's fist banged down on the counter, startling both Belle and the clerk.

"I'd like a room for my friend. She'll be quite alone, I assure you," and he stared at the man with obvious distaste.

The clerk was obviously taken aback and decided to accede to his demand.

"Yes, sir," he replied. "Any luggage?"

"No. Miss Belle will be moving to her new home tomorrow. Her personal belongings are being sent there," Stoney replied.

The man's look was dubious.

"That'll be three bucks," he said and waited while Stoney handed him a five.

"Keep the change and see that Miss Belle has access to the bath and plenty of clean towels, linens and hot water. She's traveled a great distance," hoping that this explanation would provide his friend with a trace of esteem.

"Of course. I'll see to it right away. Now, if you'll come with me."

Belle and Stoney followed the clerk down the dimly lit hallway, then entered a small but clean room.

"Satisfactory?" he asked.

"This will do fine, for now."

After the clerk had disappeared, Belle moved around the room reveling in its almost sterile atmosphere.

"God, Stoney, I never thought this would happen to me again," and her dark eyes danced with newfound happiness, which caused her to look far younger.

"I'm going to say good-night now, Belle. Don't let that guy bother you, and remember what you have to do."

"I will, Stoney," and she reached up to kiss him on the cheek. "Good night, friend."

Stoney closed the door behind him, then wandered down the hall and out into the night. Slowly he made his way home. He'd helped a dear one from the past and it was then that his thoughts turned to the mistake that he'd made years before when he'd left Kathleen.

7

To Kathleen, the journey to Kansas City had been almost frightening. She'd been unable to remember anything of real significance about the early days in her life when she and her family had lived in Boston, and leaving the quiet and almost docile atmosphere of Staley had inflicted an almost momumental degree of anxiety. But most of all, leaving her friends at the Convent, and her beloved child, Jericho, behind without so much as knowing when or where she might seen him again, made the first few months she'd spent at St. Mary's lonely and depressing.

Mother Jean Marie's friend, Mother Superior Frances, had been thoughtful and kind, and the sisters who served at St. Mary's had been open and friendly. Without their support, Kathleen might have given up and returned to Staley. However, such was not to be the case, for when she acquired the position of housekeeper to the rich widower, Schuyler Martin, her whole existence changed practically overnight.

Schuyler Martin's ancestors had been among the founding families of the now large midwestern metropolis. When they'd embarked on the journey from the East to Missouri years before, they'd stopped at the settlement of Westport, and it was there that their first home was established. Generations later, as the town's growth burgeoned, the Martins left their homestead to move farther South into the more fashionable district. There they constructed a magnificent mansion on Ward Parkway, called by the common folk, Millionaires' Row. The interior of the palatial three story colonial style house was constructed from the finest mahogany paneling that the Philipines offered, and the hand cut, highly polished marble which enhanced the entry hall and the mansion's ornate bathrooms was a product of Italy. Persian rugs in profusion were strewn about the hand hewn oak floors. The house's grandeur was truly overwhelming.

Kathleen had been interviewed for the position of housekeeper by Schuyler Martin's mother, the reigning matriarch. Kathleen's association with St. Mary's and her Catholic background had caused the elderly woman to lean toward her when she'd taken on the task of hiring a new housekeeper for her only son and heir apparent. The one thing that had concerned Emily Martin was Kathleen's youth (she was now approaching 18) and her striking beauty. However, the respect that Kathleen displayed for her elders had pleased her, and she'd requested that Schuyler join her so that he could meet this young woman.

Schuyler Martin was not prepared for the fresh and unmarred beauty of this Irish colleen, and for the first time in many months he'd become excited at seeing a woman. Since his wife's death several months before, he'd lived an almost reclusive existence. His only interest had been his two young sons. Now he was having doubts, for he became literally captivated by Kathleen Muldoon.

When Schuyler and Kathleen were introduced she bowed her head slightly and offered a shy smile. He ignored her obvious reticence and rushed to take her hand. This impulsive act on his part caused Kathleen to blush, and she withdrew her hand as quickly as possible. She returned to the straight backed chair she'd occupied next to his mother.

Emily Martin had watched her son with interest and was amused. She'd been concerned by the fact that he still remained in a state of deep depression, but the excitement he'd exhibited at meeting Kathleen Muldoon gave her every reason to believe that at last he was coming alive.

Schuyler took a seat on the divan next to his mother, which

provided him with a good vantage point to watch Kathleen. He stared at her unabashedly. Kathleen noticed his look but kept her eyes averted, directing her full attention to his mother.

"Miss Muldoon," Mrs. Martin said, "we understand that you are friends with Mother Superior Frances and the sisters at St. Mary's," and she looked at her appraisingly.

"Yes, ma'am, I am. When I came to Kansas City to look for work, they kindly let me stay at the convent. But I've done my share," she added quickly.

"I'm certain you have, dear," Mrs. Martin replied. "Do you by chance have experience in the care of young children?" she pursued.

For a moment Kathleen was baffled as she knew that she couldn't reveal she herself had a child. Then she replied. "Yes, I do. I come from a large family," and she laughed lightly. "There seemed to be a new baby almost every year."

The elderly woman and the younger man exchanged glances, then smiled at her show of humor.

"My son has two young children who will undoubtedly demand a great deal of attention. Do you feel that you could possibly handle the house as well as two wild ones?" She looked at her son with affection, for both she and Schuyler knew that her grandchildren were holy terrors.

Kathleen was conscious of the fact that this would indeed be a challenge, but her experience and long hours of labor on the ranch in Kansas as a hired girl would finally be of value. She answered without hesitation. "I have no doubt," she said firmly, then added, "that is, if you think I'm qualified."

At that moment Schuyler Martin started to interrupt, but his mother hushed him. He was often too impulsive, and this was a serious matter.

"We'll give you consideration, and we'd like for you to do the same. Then, if we come to a mutual understanding, we'll discuss financial arrangements."

Abruptly Kathleen was dismissed, and she left the Martins feeling depressed.

Several days passed without so much as a telephone call from Mrs. Martin and Kathleen made an attempt to adjust to the possibility that she'd been rejected. She was now almost to the point of desperation. If something didn't happen soon, she'd be required to return to Staley. On days such as these, when she experienced depression and her outlook on life appeared bleak, she'd read the letters that Mother Jean Marie had so faithfully written. The minute description of Jericho and his every changing ways would cause her heart to ache from loneliness, but she knew that without a job she couldn't possibly have him with her.

A full week went by and still Kathleen heard nothing. Then early one morning of the second week, the Mother Superior sent word for her to come to the office. Kathleen's curiosity was aroused, and she even considered the possibility that Mother Frances might simply ask her to leave. Reluctantly, she knocked at the office door.

"Come in," Mother Frances responded in a cheery voice.

Kathleen opened the door and then closed it behind her, dreading what could happen.

"Sit down, Kathleen," and the Mother Superior smiled warmly.

After she was seated, she looked up into Mother Frances' smiling face.

"I have some good news for you," she began, and saw an immediate change in her guest's expression.

"Good news?" Kathleen echoed.

"Yes, my dear. Very good news."

Kathleen waited expectantly.

"Mrs. Martin just called me and asked if you'd be interested in accepting the position as their housekeeper."

The look which came over the young woman's face was ecstatic.

"Oh, Mother Frances, am I interested? Yes, yes, yes," and her eyes danced.

"I'm pleased that you're happy. The Martins are highly respected and very generous to our church. Would you like for me to inform them that you'll accept?"

"Please. I'm so excited. When do I leave?"

The Mother Superior held up her hand to quiet her. "Enough questions, dear girl. That is to be handled between you and Mrs. Martin."

After the call was made and she'd informed Mrs. Martin that

Kathleen would be happy to accept their offer, she handed the instrument to Kathleen.

Hesitantly she spoke into the phone, "Hello. . . ."

"Kathleen, my dear, I'm delighted that you've decided to come to my son's home. We'd appreciate it if you could make arrangements to arrive here no later then tomorrow. You see, I'm leaving for our winter residence in Florida soon, and I want this business finalized to my satisfaction before I leave."

"Of course, Mrs. Martin," Kathleen replied, her voice reflecting her eagerness. "I'll be there right after breakfast," Then she added shyly, "Thank you for giving me this chance."

"You're most welcome, my dear. Both Schuyler and I feel that you'll be an asset to the household." Then abruptly, "Goodbye."

Gingerly, Kathleen put the phone back, her thoughts awhirl.

Mother Frances had to smile at Kathleen's starry-eyed look, for she knew that a miracle had indeed been performed for this beautiful young woman.

Into this atmosphere of luxury Kathleen Muldoon ventured, not realizing that someday she would be the mistress of all she surveyed. During the first few weeks in the Martin home she felt almost humble and ill at ease, but she soon discovered that her duties never ceased. Ultimately, she found herself not only in charge of the household, but also of Schuyler Martin's children, who'd taken to her like ducks to water.

Within a few weeks time Kathleen had mastered her duties and was organized to the point where she could almost always find the time to play with Schuyler, Jr., whose nickname was Sky, and Brandon, called Brandy. The young boys were five and four years of age respectively, and were indeed roustabouts. On that fact she'd agreed with their grandmother. However, they came to adore Kathleen, and when they teased her—which occurred frequently at the outset—she never responded with a cross word. Soon that game came to an end and they sought her out for her loving companionship. In time, Kathleen gradually introduced them to helping her in small ways and their eagerness to learn came as a complete surprise to their father.

Schuyler Martin had kept a close watch on his new housekeeper and his first attraction to her increased with each passing day. Still, Kathleen was as shy as a newborn colt whenever he was present, and she would leave him and his children to themselves after the evening meal was over to retire to the privacy of her room.

He'd insisted from the first that she share dinner with them, and her obvious lack of proper manners didn't go unnoticed, but he knew that that limitation could easily be corrected. Also, the complete indifference she exhibited to vanity was a positive attribute. It wasn't only her natural beauty, but her caring ways that made her even more desirable.

Sky and Brandy ultimately insisted—when their father took them on outings to the park, the zoo or the movies—that Kathleen be included. At first she'd refused, but the boys pleaded with her and then Schuyler had interceded.

"Kathleen," he said kindly, "we want you to go," his eyes expressing the same excitement as his sons.

"But I'm your servant, Mr. Martin," she protested, "and besides, I don't have the proper clothes." She paused. "I'm afraid that you'd be ashamed of me."

At her words Schuyler Martin exploded.

"Ashamed? Of You? My God, Kathleen, you'd look good in anything, but if you're really concerned, I'll find something from my wife's collection," and he strode purposely from the room, leaving a very surprised young woman staring after him.

When he returned, he carried in his arms a bevy of dresses which created a rainbow effect and laid them carefully over a chair.

"Take your pick," he said, indicating the dozen or so garments he'd hastily pulled from the closet.

"But they were your wife's, Mr. Martin," Kathleen protested feebly. "Wouldn't it bother you?"

For a moment, his first enthusiasm waned, but then rekindled. He'd briefly forgotten about his dear Alice, and found it surprising that she was gradually becoming only a pleasant memory.

"Kathleen," he said softly, looking deep into her eyes, "my wife would have loved you just as the boys and I do. She was a very generous woman," and he laughed slightly. "In fact, she bought dresses that she could never possibly wear but she didn't want to disappoint the sales clerk."

It was now obvious that she couldn't refuse him and she dutifully picked up a few of the dresses and headed for her room. At least she could try several on just to please him, if nothing else.

While he waited for Kathleen to return, Schuyler slumped on the davenport and thought back to the day she'd entered his home. For a long time he'd felt dead inside, but the first sight of this lovely country girl had for some unknown reason changed him completely. As he sat quietly pondering, he didn't hear Kathleen enter the room. Then suddenly he became aware that someone was present and he turned to see a vision of beauty.

As he struggled to find the right words, Kathleen moved toward him.

"Aren't you pleased?" she whispered softly.

"Oh, my God! Pleased?" he managed. "You are so beautiful," he said as he jumped up to pull her into his arms and then whirl her around the room. He stopped as suddenly as he'd begun and stepped back so he could gaze again at her beauty.

Embarrassed by his action, Kathleen started toward the stairs but he hurried after her. It was obvious that she had been alarmed by his behavior.

"My dear," he said gently, "you are so lovely. Please wear the dress, and don't think harshly of my actions."

When Kathleen looked into Schuyler Martin's eyes she saw his desire for her, one that she'd seen many times before . . . from Stoney.

The weeks and months seemed to race by, and Kathleen found herself so completely involved with the Martins that she barely had time to consider Jericho. Mother Jean Marie's detailed letters telling her of Jericho's progress came faithfully. At first, she'd acknowledged each one with a note or card. But as time went on her replies became more infrequent, and finally stopped completely.

Schuyler had been openly curious about the bulky letters she received every month, and on one occasion he'd questioned her. She'd explained it by telling him that they came from an old friend. This happened to be true, but she failed to reveal that it also concerned her own child, and one for whom she now had little motherly feeling.

Several months after she'd completed her first year with the

Martins, Kathleen requested a few days holiday with every intention of returning to Staley and the convent. Instead, she found that Schuyler Martin had other plans.

"Kathleen," he'd said, "we'll be going to our summer place in Colorado soon, and it wouldn't be fun without you being with us."

His reasoning pleased her. Howevere, she knew that Mother Jean Marie was anxious about her continued absence and lack of correspondence, but when Sky and Brandy approached her about Colorado, there was simply no way that she could refuse them. Jericho and Jean Marie, once again, were forgotten.

The holiday at the Martin's summer residence in Colorado proved to be a unique experience for Kathleen. When Schuyler had first mentioned the summer excursion she'd assumed that they would be going to a rustic cabin in the mountains, but upon their arrival in Colorado Springs she entered yet another world of enchantment.

After the boys alighted from the taxi which had brought them from the train station, they ran pell-mell toward the house leaving Kathleen and their father to follow. For a moment Kathleen stood silently while she gazed in awe at the large native stone home with its lush green lawn manicured to perfection. When Schuyler took her elbow, she realized that she'd been gawking like some country bumpkin.

"Come, Kathleen," he urged, and she glanced up into his smiling eyes.

"I had no idea it would be like this," she managed, "it's simply beautiful." Then she regained her composure. "Where are the boys?" she asked, for they had now disappeared.

"They've gone inside and are probably deviling Cook for something to eat."

"The cook?" she said a trace of alarm evident in her voice.

"This is a surprise for you, my dear," Schuyler replied. "I've always had summer help here when we're in residence, and besides, you're to enjoy yourself and not have to worry about the care of the house or our meals." Then his look became serious. "I want you to devote all of your time to me, Sky and Brandy."

At this comment, Kathleen edged away. She was almost sorry that she'd agreed to make the trip.

Schuyler noticed her hesitation and cocked his head to one side
to give her a rakish grin. "Cold feet?" he asked.

Kathleen's Irish temper bristled. Her reply was short. "Certainly
not. Since we're here, let's go inside. I need to find the boys."

"Not so fast, my dear," he said. He took her arm and turned her
so that she faced him. "You have nothing to fear from me,
Kathleen."

The majestic splendor of the Colorado mountains proved to be
idyllic for Kathleen. She found it sheer luxury (and something she'd
never dreamed could possibly happen) to lie in bed until at least
seven o'clock and then not be required to rush to the kitchen to
prepare breakfast for the always famished children, and Schuyler,
too.

The Cook and the other members of the household staff ran the
house much like a ship's crew, and acknowledged Kathleen as the
Governess of the Martin children. However, it was apparent to all
that their employer had more than a passing interest in this lovely,
charming young woman.

In time, Kathleen's eyes sparkled like rare jewels from the fresh,
clear mountain air and her usually pale complexion turned a
delicate pink which caused Schuyler to be even more taken with this
Irish lass.

On occasion, when she had time to spend alone, Kathleen's
thoughts would turn to Kansas. She knew that Kansas was now
beginning to return to some semblance of normalcy after the dust
bowl years, and she thanked God for it. The days that she'd lived at
the Convent, and through the devastating dust storms, now seemed
just an unpleasant memory.

During the daytime hours Schuyler, Sky and Brandy would often
go fishing, riding or on hiking trips, whichever one suited their
fancies best at the moment. Kathleen had accompanied them on
several such excursions but ultimately decided that she'd rather stay
quietly at home and read a book from Schuyler's vast collection or
simply laze on the veranda. On a few occasions when the male
entourage would return from their chosen outing, they'd discover
Kathleen asleep in the hammock with her book or magazine now
lying on the floor. The boys took delight in waking her, and would
shout with glee when she'd discover that the hours had slipped by

so quickly.

Then came the day when Schuyler and the boys arrived home from one such trip to once more find Kathleen sound asleep. Quietly, Schuyler had shipped Sky and Brandy off to their rooms to bathe and freshen up before dinner, while he stayed behind to awaken Kathleen. As she slept peacefully he gazed down at her, drinking in the exquisiteness of her beauty, much like a humming bird absorbs the honey from a flower's bloom. Then swiftly he bent to kiss her gently on her full red lips, and his excitement mounted.

At his touch, Kathleen stirred restlessly in her sleep and brushed her hand across her face, but then quieted again. In a moment of sheer impulse Schuyler dropped to his knees beside her, placed his mouth full on hers, and kissed her with all the passion he'd withheld for so many months. Kathleen's first reaction to his kiss had been responsive, for in her dream she'd been making love with Stoney. Then suddenly her eyes flew open and she discovered that it was not Stoney but Schuyler Martin whose handsome face hovered over her.

For a brief moment she'd simply stared into his eyes, quite unbelieving. Shocked by his boldness, she pulled herself to a sitting position and found herself at a complete loss for words. Still Schuyler remained on his knees beside her, as though waiting for her response, but when she remained silent he took her hand, turned it palm up and planted a kiss in its softness. Hastily Kathleen pulled free, appalled and embarrassed by his actions. Then, almost defiantly, she slipped from the hammock and without so much as a goodbye ran into the house, but not before she heard him call her name. She hurried on, stumbled, almost fell on the steps landing to the second floor, and then almost collided with Sky.

"What's wrong, Kathleen?" he asked as she pushed past him.

He could tell that something was wrong but she failed to respond to his questioning, which for her was completely out of character. She continued on to her room where she slammed the door. Then he heard the click of the lock.

For a six year old, Sky Martin was an exceedingly bright and intuitive youngster, and he sensed that some action of his father's lay at the bottom of this. At a run, he took the stairs two at a time in his haste to find him. After he'd searched the veranda and found no one, he returned to the house and hurried to the den where he discovered his father standing facing the window as though he were oblivious to the world.

"Father," he said quietly.

Schuyler Martin did not respond as he was deep in thought.

Then Sky insisted loudly, "Father, what's happened to Kathleen?"

At the mention of Kathleen's name, Schuyler turned to find his oldest son looking at him, obviously concerned.

"Sorry, Sky. I didn't hear you. Now what was it you asked me about Kathleen?"

"I want to know what's wrong. She came running up the stairs and almost knocked me down," and he paused. "She looked scared out of her wits. Did you make Kathleen unhappy?"

A sudden frown crossed Schuyler's face for he knew that he'd made a complete fool of himself. Now his family was faced once again with the results of his impulsiveness, and he remembered the many times his mother had curbed that facet of his personality, and for good cause. For a moment he wished that she'd accompanied them.

He gave Sky a half-smile, then seated himself in the well worn leather chair and beckoned for his son to join him. Sky crawled into the matching chair which faced him, a serious look on his face, and waited for his father to speak.

"Sky, my boy, you know how lonely I've been since your mother died," and he looked deeply into his son's eyes. "I also realize that you and Brandy have missed her as much as I have."

Sky nodded, although he and Brandy had been of such a young age when she'd died that he couldn't really recall her clearly.

Then he questioned again. "But why is Kathleen so upset?"

Schuyler smiled slightly, realizing that there was no possible way to keep his sons in the dark.

"I care about Kathleen very much," he said and shrugged slightly. "Probably a lot more than she does for me. I also act on impulse on occasion, and that's what happened this afternoon. I'm hoping that she'll excuse and forgive me."

Sky's sunny disposition took over and he laughed aloud. "She will, father. Kathleen loves us," and he paused. "Brandy and I have wished many times that she were our mother."

"You have?"

Sky nodded. "We both love her a lot. Oh, Dad," and his voice was almost pleading, "why don't you marry her?"

Now it was Schuyler Martin's turn to be shocked. It seemed rather strange to be having an adult conversation with one so young, but he also was aware that children normally speak the truth, and in this instance he was glad.

"I've considered that, Sky, but the time just hasn't seemed right. It's not me, for I'd have her in a minute. There seems to be something troubling her."

"Then we'll fix it," his son responded very matter-of-factly.

Schuyler threw back his head and laughed, then reached over to tousle his son's hair. "You do have a point. Perhaps after dinner this evening I can coax Kathleen into talking with me."

"She'll talk with you," Sky replied firmly, never once believing that a Martin could be refused.

After dinner that evening Kathleen took her usual place at the table, but her actions now seemed to be almost automatic. She listened intently to Sky and Brandy's account of their hike in the mountains and said all the right words, but her usual enthusiasm was noticeably lacking. Schuyler hadn't pressed her into conversation, and he kept silent.

The boys hurried through their dinner and dessert and then asked to be excused. For a moment, a flicker of annoyance crossed Kathleen's face as she had little desire to be left alone with Schuyler Martin.

"Off with you," Schuyler replied to their request, and the two youngsters placed their linen napkins in the silver holders, and ran from the room. Kathleen kept her eyes focused on the large bay window which overlooked the grounds, completely ignoring Schuyler's presence.

After coffee had been served, Schuyler got up from the table and moved toward Kathleen. When she saw him approaching, she placed her hands firmly against the table and pushed back her chair. It was then that the demitasse cup, which was filled to the brim with the steaming liquid, spilled onto her lap. She jumped to her feet and almost screamed, "Look what you've made me do." Then she burst into tears.

Without once considering the fact that Kathleen was angry with him, Schuyler pulled her into his arms and held her in a gentle embrace, while she sobbed uncontrollably against him. With a soft voice, he murmured words of endearment, and soon felt her body relax, while he savored her warmth.

Then, just as suddenly as she'd cried out, she pushed him away, and wiped at the tears which now streaked her face.

"I'm sorry, Schuyler. It wasn't your fault. Please excuse me," Kathleen said and started to leave.

"Kathleen, please don't go," he pleaded.

She turned back and saw the stark loneliness reflected in his look and the longing in his eyes.

Slowly, Kathleen moved toward him and smiled sweetly. "What is it you want, Schuyler?"

"I need to talk with you, Kathleen." His nervousness was evident. "I've needed to for a long time."

Her look was questioning. "Yes?"

"I'm dreadfully sorry about this afternoon," and he blushed much like a school boy, for he'd never felt the need to apologize to a woman before. "I do get carried away at times."

Kathleen smiled, remembering the warmth of his kiss. It was strange that she'd been dreaming of Stoney, yet it was Schuyler's kiss that had stirred her emotions and she knew that a strong current ran between them.

"Your apology is accepted," she said demurely, and then laughed. "As I hope mine has been."

"Of course," he said, then blurted out, "would you take a walk with me?"

"A walk?" Kathleen echoed. "I see no reason not to," and she extended her hand to him, which he grasped eagerly. Together they made their way through the house and out the front door, failing to notice Sky and Brandy hiding behind the flowering bushes.

On that unforgettable night, Kathleen Muldoon and Schuyler Martin discovered just how much they loved and needed each other. It was eye-opening for Kathleen. Her first love—if she could call it that—had been short lived and cruel, but one she would never forget. The love that she felt for Schuyler was not only one of passion, but also one of deep respect, and that had been sorely lacking with Stoney.

When they returned to the Martin residence in Kansas City at summers' end, Kathleen sported a two-carat diamond ring on her left hand, a symbol of her betrothal to Schuyler.

Emily Martin had been delighted with the news when they'd made a special trip to tell her, and Sky and Brandy could hardly contain themselves. Because of the Martin's prominence in the city, Schuyler's mother took the reins and planned the wedding of Kathleen and her son down to the minutest detail.

One year later, on a balmy, clear day, Kathleen Muldoon and Schuyler Martin exchanged their wedding vows at St. Joseph's Catholic Church, with all the fanfare accorded the very rich.

Ironically, only a few days prior to the Martin-Muldoon nuptials, Stonewall Barton and Julia Walowski had recited their wedding vows in St. Peters's Church in Salmon, Montana. But to Stoney, his marriage was one of convenience.

Kathleen's was one of love.

8

The rumblings of war in Europe caused grave concern to the United States and its populace in the late 1930's. Jericho had now been with Martha and Jacob Smith for well over two years, and shared in his father's obvious anxiety. Jacob, fortunately, was now approaching his fiftieth year, and was also a farmer, which were doubly sufficient reasons to prevent him from serving in the armed forces.

The realization of this had lifted a huge burden from Jericho's shoulders, for after becoming an integral part of a loving family and one that he could call his own, he couldn't help but feel relief that he'd not lose the one man that he'd grown to love and admire. Over the months they'd been together, the two had developed a special kind of relationship and Jacob had accepted Jericho on an adult level, for the young lad had demonstrated beyond any doubt that he possessed a maturity far greater than his years.

Martha Smith, his adoptive mother, showered him with affection almost to the point of embarrassment, but Jericho wisely let her exercise this latent motherhood which she so obviously enjoyed. Nothing was too good for her son, and he thrived and lived a happy and fulfilling life.

Mother Jean Marie, however, was not to be forgotten. Jericho

painstakingly wrote long and informative letters to her, describing
in vivid detail his home life, school and church activities. The
elderly Sister looked forward with anticipation to his letters, and
often considered how happy Kathleen would have been if she'd
seen fit to claim her child.

During the years of crisis after the United States had entered the
war, Jericho shared in the farm chores alongside his father. They
were often in the fields from early morning until the last light of
day, for help was not to be found. When the time came to harvest
the ripened crops, the farmers banded together as one to assist each
other, and Jericho was always there. Through the teachings of both
his mother and father, he'd become a patriotic young man, and
this, in itself, would serve him in good stead as he grew into
adulthood.

Stoney Barton worked his crews in the oil fields like a drill
sargeant during the war years. He'd taken over the reins of Pride
Oil when his father-in-law, Joe Walowski, had suffered a crippling
stroke after learning that the part of his family which still remained
in Poland had perished at the hands of the Nazis. It was out of
sheer necessity that Stoney was exempted from military service, for
Pride Oil had been the recipient of several large and profitable
government contracts.

At times, Stoney found himself working as he had in the
beginning, in the fields right alongside his employees. He knew that
it was inevitable that he would ultimately become the head and
owner of Pride, and he already dreamed of his bright future when
the chaos in Europe and the Pacific ended.

Stoney's life with Julia was bland at best, to his way of thinking,
but still he remained faithful. Julia had borne Stoney one child,
which had arrived in the first year of their marriage, and had found
the experience of childbirth one that she could barely tolerate.
Thus, any intimacy that they'd had before become virtually non-
existent.

When Joe Walowski had been stricken, Stoney, with Julia and
their child Adele, had moved into the big house where Stoney had
immediately taken charge. The two Walowski sons had long since
departed; one serving in the Air Corps and the other in the Army.
Julia's only sister, Ann, had joined the Red Cross. Subsequently

she'd been sent to a military hospital where she served as a nurse, leaving only Joe and his wife, Stoney, Julia and their daughter, in residence.

Finally, Stoney had called Belle in Cut Bank and insisted that she come to Salmon to assist with the care of the ailing man because it was too much for Julia and her mother. Belle had literally jumped at the chance, gave her employer notice, and then journeyed to Salmon where she fit into the Walowski's household like an old shoe. She also provided Stoney Barton with someone with whom to talk, and thus her presence served two purposes.

When the telephone call came from Washington, D.C., Schuyler Martin wasn't particularly surprised. Harry Hopkins, one of F.D.R.'s right hand men, had been its instigator. He'd asked his friend Martin to come to the capitol as one of the 'Party's Dollar-a-Year-Men', to lend his financial wizardry to the complex problems which faced the nation.

Schuyler hadn't even hesitated. He'd responded in the affirmative to Hopkin's invitation and Kathleen, who was now happily and very obviously pregnant after having tried for months to beget a child, enlisted the aid of the household staff in the preparations for the move. The boys were withdrawn from Pembroke Country Day School and were enthusiastic about the adventure ahead. After their father's marriage to Kathleen, they'd been taken on a trip to Washington and had been quite impressed by all the attention showered on them. In reality, they felt little reluctance at the thought of leaving their friends, and what they termed their dull school and its instructors.

Prior to the family's departure from Kansas City, Schuyler had made a hurried trip to Washington to confer with the President and his cabinet members. At the same time he had seized the opportunity to lease a palatial residence in Georgetown, one which would provide quick access to his assigned office in the capitol building. He knew that it was an absolute necessity to have a home to go to upon their arrival, primarily because of his wife's condition, for Kathleen was now approaching her ninth month of pregnancy.

Schuyler's mother, Emily Martin, who was now in her mid-seventies, was still active and in excellent health. Because of this,

Kathleen asked that she accompany them to Washington. She was
aware that her mother-in-law not only knew the proper protocol
since she'd been a resident in the capitol during World War I, but
also that she'd kept up her social contacts there. She agreed
immediately, delighted that Kathleen had included her.

After Schuyler and Kathleen had been married, Emily Martin
had taken it upon herself to move from the family home to a
somewhat smaller, but quietly elegant, residence of her own in
order that Schuyler, Kathleen and the children could start their life
together as a family group. She knew that her daughter-in-law
cared for her, as she did Kathleen, but the prospect of having two
women in the same household, who'd both been in charge but at
different times, could indeed become difficult. That she didn't
want. Now, some three years after her son and Kathleen's marriage
had proven to be as sound as a rock, she had few qualms about
joining them on their trek to Washington.

The Martins private railroad car possessed every convenience
that they might possibly need. Schuyler had even gone so far as to
cajole Kathleen's doctor and his wife, who was also a registered
nurse, to accompany them, just in case. Without too much
hesitation, they'd agreed.

On a lovely April day, the two Martin limousines, one carrying
Schuyler, his family and their guests, and the other loaded with
several of the household staff and luggage, left the house on Ward
Parkway for Kansas City's Union Station where they would board
the private car for their destination.

After Kathleen had been settled comfortably in their stateroom,
Schuyler left her by herself so he could see to the comfort of his
mother, the boys and Dr. and Mrs. Emergy.

Kathleen gazed out the window of the train at the bustling
crowd. She sighed deeply as she saw the worried faces. That could
be me out there, she thought, as she caught a glimpse of a young
woman with a small boy holding fast to a man in uniform who was
obviously leaving. For a moment, the woman's and Kathleen's eyes
met and held. Then Kathleen pulled the curtain across the window,
shutting out the vision of what might have been.

9

1951

Jericho was approaching thirteen when the fighting on both fronts reached its climax. In time, the GI's straggled home, but only to discover a vastly different environment. The jobs which they'd held before leaving to serve their country and which had been products of peacetime were either nonexistent or had changed dramatically. Many returned home to nothing except the joy of being alive, but that in itself proved to be enough for the majority.

Franklin Delano Roosevelt's sudden death in the Spring of 1945, only a few months before the final fruition of his years of strategy were attained, had rocked the world. Fortunately, it had been Harry S. Truman, his feisty Vice President, who had readily taken command. The one-time haberdasher from Kansas City proved to be a real surprise to the nation, for Harry Truman possessed a no-nonsense attitude. Truman's only deviation from this attitude was in the love and devotion that he held for his wife, Bess, and their only child, Margaret. To him these women, and rightly so, were the most important part of his life.

All this was history-in-the-making for young Jericho Smith. It had happened during hs formative years, and because of this he reached the decision that he, too, would some day serve his country. In just what specific capacity he was still not sure, but he knew that this would be his ultimate goal. Jacob and Martha were amazed at his intense interest in, and comprehension of, the political scene, for Jericho spoke fluently and very wisely on many aspects of the problems which faced a nation recovering from war.

The years swept by at a rapid pace and soon it was 1951, the year for Jericho to enter college. A few years before, Jacob had met with Monsignor O'Connell at St. Peter's, and had asked his support for Jericho's application to Notre Dame. It was only natural that the old priest, who had spent many hours with Jericho and who at one time had urged him to don the cloth only to be graciously refused, would write a glowing letter to the president of Notre Dame. The result was that Jericho's acceptance into the school was almost automatic.

Prior to Jericho's departure for school, he decided to make one last trip to Staley to visit Mother Superior Jean Marie. The last time he'd seen Mother Jean Marie her health had deteriorated and she had been quite feeble. Her eye sight had failed considerably but she had still possessed some of the same dry humor and spunkiness of old.

As Jericho prepared for the trip, Jacob and Martha had asked if he'd like them to accompany him. The request didn't come as a surprise, for his instincts were correct. It was obvious to him that they felt that once he was alone with Mother Jean Marie, he might ask too many questions. His reply was one of patience and given with a disarming smile.

"Of course I'd enjoy your company. There's little doubt of that, but this once I'd like to spend some time alone with Mother Jean Marie. It may be the last time I'll see her alive," and for a moment a shadow crossed his face. Then he smiled again. "I do hope that you don't mind."

Jacob and Martha exchanged looks, and both realized that it was best to let him go alone.

"Of course we don't, son," Jacob replied, placing his hand on Jericho's shoulder with affection. "I'm sure that Mother Jean Marie will live much longer," but he knew in his own mind that this was just wishful thinking.

Their one concern was that, by chance, Mother Jean Marie might reveal to Jericho the name of his natural mother which could provoke a desire on his part to launch a search for her. The only name that they'd been provided when the adoption papers had been finalized was Kathleen. The Mother Superior had produced a Power of Attorney and had signed the papers on behalf of the unknown Kathleen, giving them their son, but she'd refused to disclose the mother's last name and that still remained her secret.

When Jericho arrived at the Convent late that morning he was greeted at the door by Sister Ann, Mother Jean Marie's faithful assistant. She drew him aside, "Jericho," she said, as she clasped both his hands in hers, "I feel you need to know what you'll be facing when you see the Mother Superior." There was deep sadness in her eyes.

"Is she worse?" he replied, now feeling almost impatient.

"I'm afraid so. She seems irrational at times, and rambles on about happenings of the past," and she dropped her eyes. "She remembers things far differently than they actually were."

"Oh, my God," Jericho murmured, and gently placed his arm around Sister Ann's shoulders. "Does she know that I'm coming to visit?"

"Yes, and that has proved to be balm to the hurt and anger within her."

"Let me see her. Perhaps I can help." Then he paused. "You know that I'm leaving for Notre Dame shortly and won't be able to visit her as often as I have."

"We know. Just keep her in your prayers. Time means nothing to her now, but she will miss you."

Sister Ann knocked on Mother Jean Marie's door and a voice that held little strength or expression acknowledged, "Enter."

The room was almost dark as Jericho entered, even though it was bright daylight outside. He stood still while his eyes adjusted to the dimness, and then saw that the blinds and drapes had been pulled tight across the windows and that only a candle's light flickered before the Virgin Mary. From out of the depths of the large easy chair, Mother Jean Marie looked up. Her face showed little expression, but as Jericho drew near and knelt down beside her, she recognized him. The transformation which took place as she gazed at him was unbelievable. Her eyes and face suddenly came alive and she pulled him into her arms. In silence they embraced each other; then Jericho got up and moved to the ancient straight backed chair close to her, which he'd occupied on many occasions as a child.

Gently Jericho took the frail hand that she extended, noting that the gold wedding band which had been the symbol of her marriage to God had been removed.

"Jericho," she said softly, "how good it is to see you." She pressed his fingers gently. "Are Jacob and Martha with you?"

"Not this time, Mother Jean Marie. I came by myself."

A pleased smile crossed the wrinkled face, for at last she had her son to herself.

"When are you coming home?" she asked abruptly, her eyes piercing into his.

"Home?" Jericho responded, not yet comprehending her thinking.

"Of course, son. You belong here with me. You've been away much too long."

Suddenly Jericho realized that the warning Sister Ann had given him was manifesting itself right before his eyes. For a moment he felt outrage at seeing the woman that he loved more then anyone decaying into a lump of nothingness. Still, he restrained himself, and even though tears pressed hard against his eyelids he replied in as steady a voice as he could muster, "I'll be here from now on, Mother Jean Marie," and pressed the fingers which still clung to him.

"Good," she replied, and then searched his face to see if he were telling her the truth. Satisfied, she released her hold and began to rock back and forth while an almost catatonic look crept over her.

For what seemed like hours the two sat quietly. Finally, Mother Jean Marie turned to Jericho and said almost accusingly, "Why aren't you helping in the garden?"

Jericho was taken aback by the sharp change in her manner.

"I'll go now, Mother Jean Marie," he said quietly, hoping to placate her.

"Don't keep calling me Jean Marie," she snapped, "that's not my name." A strange look came over her face and the smile which suddenly appeared seemed to erase part of the many years that she'd lived. "My name is Kathleen."

At that crucial moment, Sister Ann entered the room. Motioning to Jericho to move aside, she went straight to the Mother Superior.

"Mother Superior," she said kindly, "it's time for you to rest."

Sister Ann assisted a now docile Mother Jean Marie to her feet and then slowly guided her to the bed which occupied the far side of the room. Not once did Mother Jean Marie look in Jericho's direction, and it was almost as though he'd never been there. After she was settled comfortably, the Sister kissed her hand and crossed herself, then beckoned for Jericho to follow her.

When the door to Mother Jean Marie's apartment had closed, Jericho's tears began to fall and then hard, racking sobs shook his body. Sister Ann took him gently by the arm and led him to the chapel where she left him to find peace with God and within himself.

While he sat quietly in the small chapel all the long ago memories came rushing back and he remembered vividly the day that he'd discovered Mother Jean Marie lying prostrate before the altar, devastated at the thought of losing him. Now, he had lost her, for she imagined that she was someone else. Jericho shook his head in bewilderment and thought of the name, Kathleen, which she'd called herself. It meant nothing to him, but Sister Ann had hurried him from Mother Jean Marie's presence and this bothered him.

When he had calmed himself sufficiently, Jericho went in search of Sister Ann and found her in the kitchen overseeing the preparation of lunch. After greeting the Sisters that he knew, he approached her.

"Could we have a talk?" he asked.

The woman hesitated and a slight frown furrowed her brow. "What about, Jericho?"

"There are a few things I'd like to clear up before I return home. Won't you please come to the rose garden with me?" His manner was persuasive.

Sister Ann quickly removed the white starched apron which covered her habit and then proceeded to give final instructions to the other Sisters. With a nod to Jericho, she indicated that he should follow her. They left the steamy kitchen through the back door and carefully made their way down the flight of wooden steps, now worn thin from long usage. In silence, they moved together along the dirt pathway leading to the rose gardens which at one time had been Mother Jean Marie's personal pride and joy.

When they came to a concrete bench and one which Jericho had occupied on many occasions in the past, he pulled his handkerchief from his pants pocket and swept away the thin layer of dust and leaves. Then, they seated themselves. At first they remained silent while both enjoyed the warmth emanating from the late summer sun, now high in the heavens.

Finally, it was Jericho who broke the silence. "Sister Ann, I'd appreciate it if you'd explain something to me," he said and glanced at the elderly woman sitting beside him. "You know I haven't any desire that you should reveal secrets, as I highly respect the trust you share with the Mother Superior." He paused slightly, as though waiting for his companion to respond.

With a deep sigh, Sister Ann turned to look into the handsome face of the young man she'd known and loved from the moment of his birth, and she reached over to pat his hand. "Jericho, my boy, what is it that you must know? You've seen for yourself just how confused Mother Jean Marie is these days."

Intuitively, Jericho knew that she was hedging for it had been obvious to him that when she'd heard Mother Jean Marie refer to herself as Kathleen that she'd hurried him from the room as expediently as possible.

"This Kathleen that Mother Superior speaks of. Do you know who she is?" he questioned.

For a long moment Sister Ann gazed up into the blue cloudlessness of the vast Kansas sky, knowing full well that she could not tell him the truth.

"Kathleen?" she repeated.

"Yes, Kathleen. Mother Jean Marie insisted that that was her name."

"Kathleen," Sister Ann murmured again, almost as though she were trying to piece together the significance of why it should mean something to Mother Jean Marie. Then, without so much as batting an eye, she looked at Jericho and said, "I have no idea what it could possibly have to do with her. Mother Jean Marie, God Bless her soul," and this was said almost piously, "is not herself, as I'm sure you're aware."

Jericho interrupted. "But she also said that I was her son."

At this statement all color disappeared from the Sister's face and she gasped for breath.

"Are you all right?" Jericho asked with concern, for he'd noticed the remarkable change in her color.

"It must be the sun," she whispered.

"Then we'll move to the shade," Jericho offered and helped her to her feet. Together they walked slowly down the path and settled in the shade of the old cottonwood which years before had served as his hiding place.

Sister Ann wanted desperately to end their conversation, but she knew first hand how determined Jericho could be, and she also knew that he wouldn't leave the convent without some semblance of a plausible explanation.

As the color gradually began to return to her cheeks, she smiled slightly. "Please excuse my sudden faintness, Jericho. It's obviously from the heat. First in the kitchen," she sighed audibly, "and then being out here. Now, where were we?" her manner was businesslike.

Jericho had to smile to himself. If he didn't know Sister Ann so well, he'd believe every word, and he realized that she was indeed a superb actress.

"I don't want to impose upon your good nature, Sister Ann," Jericho pursued. "However, I can't help but wonder why Mother Jean Marie seems to think that I'm her son. This has never happened until today, and it really puzzles me."

"Oh, Jericho," Sister Ann replied, a soft smile caressing her lips, "you know she cared for you from the day of your birth," and her look became thoughtful. "So now, in the autumn of her life, she believes that you belong to her. Do you remember how saddened she was when you went to live with the Smiths?"

Jericho nodded, and once again the scene of Mother Jean Marie lying before the altar in her grief passed before his eyes.

"Perhaps I should never have left her," he ventured, tears misting his eyes.

"Jericho, you had to go. The convent was not a proper place for you to grow up. The Smiths have given you a good home, and they love you very much."

He nodded. "I know, and I love them, too." His voice broke suddenly and he half-whispered, "I told Mother Jean Marie the day I left that I'd always love her the best."

As he finished speaking, sobs of anger and frustration shook him, and Sister Ann placed her arms around him to comfort him while the hot, dry breeze of Kansas wafted gently through the trees.

Jericho knew that it would be virtually impossible for him to brave seeing Mother Jean Marie again, but as he and Sister Ann wandered slowly down the long hall past her living quarters he stopped at the door, where he bowed his head and murmured a silent prayer. For a brief moment his fingers caressed the rough hewn door as though in final farewell and then, with a look of determination, he hurried to the convent door.

"Let me know when she's gone," he said softly to Sister Ann as tears filled his eyes.

With evident fondness, the elderly Sister touched his face gently and then stood on tip-toe to kiss him. Solemnly she said, "That is from Mother Jean Marie, dear one," and then she turned back into the depths of the convent, while Jericho began the descent down the long flight of steps.

At the base of the steps he stopped to look back, not realizing that some eighteen years before his mother had paused there, too. Then, with a slight wave of his hand toward the wind-worn structure, he left the past behind to enter the future.

When Jericho arrived home that evening, he found that his parents had waited up for him. This bothered him. He was now eighteen, and felt that he should be accorded more respect instead of being treated like a child.

As he entered the house, Jacob and Martha greeted him eagerly, but Jericho was not in the mood for idle chatter and the long interrogation that he knew would surely follow.

"Did you see Mother Jean Marie?" Jacob asked.

"Of course," he replied bluntly, refusing to elaborate.

"How is she? What did she have to say?" Martha interjected.

As their questions continued, Jericho bit his lips so he wouldn't respond in anger, but when he looked at them there was a glint of steel in his eyes.

"I'd prefer not to discuss it tonight, if you don't mind," he replied sharply. "It's been a long and emotional day for me and I need to be alone."

"But Jericho," his father protested, voice rising in growing concern, "what's upset you so?"

If Jacob had been a wise man he would have refrained from asking that question, for at that point all the anger, fury and outrage caged within Jericho poured out.

"Why must you press me so?" he asked. "Mother Jean Marie's dying. Does that satisfy you?" and the look he gave them was chilling. "I should never have left her, never," he almost screamed.

With that, he turned on his heel and went pounding up the stairs. Then a door slammed and all was quiet.

"Could she have told him?" Martha asked, her voice filled with alarm.

Jacob nodded and his look was somber.

"What will we do?" Martha implored.

"Let it be. It's obvious that whatever happened has caused Jericho grave concern," and Jacob's look became thoughtful. "You know, Martha," he continued, "Mother Jean Marie's the only person who knows Jericho's real mother and when she's gone, God rest her soul, this will all be over. The smartest thing we can possibly do is to let Jericho handle this himself." Then he glanced fondly at his wife. "Another thing. We have to start treating him differently. We've been coddling him ever since he was little, and he's now a grown man."

Martha looked up at her husband with surprise. "You really feel that way?"

" 'Fraid so. Remember, our son is leaving for college before long, and a whole new world stretches before him."

The day before Jericho's scheduled departure for Notre Dame, the call came from Staley.

That morning Jericho had risen before dawn to help his father with the chores for the last time, and they were in the midst of demolishing one of Martha's hearty breakfasts when the telephone rang.

"I'll answer," Martha said, indicating that her two men should continue with their meal.

Almost in unison they both nodded in agreement while Martha hurried into the hall.

Jacob and Jericho continued on with their meal; then, in a moment of sudden quiet, they looked up to see Martha in the doorway. Her eyes were brimming with unshed tears and the look that she gave her son was one of sadness.

"It's for you, Jericho," she managed, and then rushed from the room.

Startled by her reaction, Jericho pushed himself up from the table and raced to the phone. With hesitation he spoke into the instrument.

"This is Jericho," he said, and waited.

"Jericho, this is Sister Ann," her voice sounding faint and far away.

"Yes, Sister Ann?"

"I trust I haven't disturbed you," she continued.

"Of course not. How nice that you called. I leave tomorrow."

"Jericho, I know that you're leaving, but that's not the reason I phoned."

At her words, a sinking feeling rushed over him. "Is it Mother Jean Marie?" he asked.

"Yes, it's the Mother Superior."

"Is she failing?"

There was a long silence while Sister Ann gathered her courage. "Jericho, Mother Jean Marie left us this morning."

"She's dead?" he cried out, bringing Jacob running into the hall.

"Dead?" he repeated.

"Yes, Jericho, she's with our God."

"Why didn't someone call me so that I could have been with her?" he asked accusingly.

"Mother Jean Marie knew that it was her time, and she didn't wish to subject you to her passing. Her last words were for you," Sister Ann replied gently.

"But I loved her so."

"I know, my child, and she loved you."

For a time Jericho remained silent while the seconds ticked away and he desperately fought the tears which clouded his vision. Then he managed, "What did she say?"

The Sister's voice was heavy with emotion when she replied. "Her words were these, Jericho," and she paused.

"Please tell me," he implored.

Bravely, Sister Ann said, "Tell Jericho that someday all the questions will be answered."

"That's all?"

"Yes, Jericho. Those were the last words Mother Jean Marie

spoke, and then she went peacefully to sleep.''

Automatically, Jericho thanked Sister Ann and then, lost in thought, slowly replaced the telephone. The message puzzled him, and he moved like a sleep walker in the direction of the kitchen. In doing so, he bumped into the door and the sudden impact jolted him back into reality. In the brilliant sunlight now streaming through the kitchen windows, he saw his father watching him with obvious concern.

"Sorry, Dad," Jericho murmured, resuming his seat at the table as he rubbed at the bump which was now becoming visible on his forehead.

Jericho," Jacob said gently, "I assume from your conversation that Mother Jean Marie has passed on.''

Mute, Jericho merely nodded.

"I'm truly sorry, son," Jacob said and then paused. "You can be thankful for one thing, though. You saw her just recently.''

The young man turned and glared coldly at his father.

"I meant what I said the night that I came home from Staley. I should never have left her.''

"But that's all in the past now, Jericho. Mother Jean Marie knew what was best for you. Haven't you been happy with your mother and me?'' the older man replied in a pleading manner.

"Yes, I've been happy, but you can't seem to comprehend that Mother Jean Marie and I shared a very special relationship. It's one that can never be replaced.''

"We know that, boy," Jacob remarked almost defensively. "But she was an old woman when you left her.''

"Show her the respect that she's due, father," Jericho snapped.

"I didn't mean to be disrespectful," Jacob apologized.

Abruptly, Jericho got up from his chair. "Please excuse me. I have a lot of things to do before tomorrow.''

With Jericho's words ringing in his ears, Jacob Smith realized that the closeness that he and his son had once enjoyed had now somehow vanished.

Early the following morning, Martha and Jacob drove Jericho to the train station, where they huddled together in the sharp early morning air of autumn.

While they waited for the train, Jericho took a stroll down the platform by himself. That morning at breakfast he'd had a glimpse of his mother's red-rimmed eyes and had known that in all probability she'd cried herself to sleep. Thus, his one desire was that their parting be a really happy one. It wasn't that he and Martha hadn't enjoyed a warm and affectionate relationship as mother and son, but she'd never been able to replace the deep and abiding love that he'd always felt for Mother Jean Marie.

As he looked down the tracks he saw the moving headlights of the oncoming train as it thundered toward the station. Then the whistle began its ear splitting shriek and he turned and hurried back to Martha and Jacob. As he joined them, there was the sound of grinding steel and the train came to an abrupt halt. The conductor swung to the platform, obviously eager to board his passengers and be on their way.

There were only a few moments in which to say their brief goodbyes, and Jericho hastily embraced Martha and then shook his father's hand. With a slight wave he ran up the steps of the waiting train and entered the railroad car. There he threw his bag on the floor and took a window seat. When his parents saw him peering from the window they waved frantically, and he acknowledged their efforts with a warm smile. As the train moved out he turned to look back only once, and then heaved a sigh of relief.

10

It didn't take but a short time for Jericho to discover that Notre Dame and college were far different than his high school days at St. Peters, where he'd been the fair-haired boy not only of the Sisters, but of Monsignor O'Connell as well. At Notre Dame he found that he was accepted as just one of the highly qualified young men who'd been accorded the opportunity to attend this fine university.

The one shining moment after his arrival had been his meeting with the young man who was to be his roommate, and that had come about in an interesting fashion.

When he'd arrived in South Bend a heavy downpour had greeted him, and with some foreboding he'd hailed one of the taxis which lined the curb waiting for a fare. After he'd thrown his bag into the rear of the cab, he got in and then leaned forward.

"Notre Dame, please."

The cab driver had chuckled, for it was obvious that this was just one more of the privileged few who were allowed to enter the hallowed halls.

"What's so funny?" Jericho had demanded sharply; he was bone tired from the long train ride and the driver's evident amusement irritated him.

"Nothing, sonny," the man replied, then paused. "You're new, aren't you?''

"Yes, why?"

"It's obvious," he'd said, and added nothing more.

By now Jericho's dander was beginning to surface. "I really can't say that I care about your opinion, sir," he'd said contemptuously. "Just get me there."

"What dorm?"

At this, Jericho became flustered.

"Let me look."

Taking the school papers from his jacket pocket, he rifled through them. Then he found the name. "Old Dominion," he said shortly.

"Old Dom, it is," replied the taxi driver and, with wheels squealing from the wet pavement, they plunged into the darkness of the Indiana night.

When the taxi entered the campus grounds Jericho pressed his face against the moisture covered window hoping to catch a glimpse of his surroundings, but because of the heavy rain his view was limited. Then, with screeching brakes, the cab came to an abrupt stop in front of an ivy covered three story brick building whose lights were ablaze.

"Here ya' are, kid," the driver said as he shut off the meter. "That'll be two seventy-five."

Jericho rummaged in his pant pockets and came up with three crumpled dollar bills which he handed over. "Keep the change."

The man chuckled at the size of the tip and remained rooted to his seat while Jericho clumsily climbed out of the vehicle with his bag.

"Good luck," the cabbie called out, and then, without any thought, drove directly through a large puddle causing the water to splash on Jericho. With disgust he looked down at his ruined trousers, and he started to feel as though he shouldn't have come.

At that moment a young man came rushing out of the building, but stopped when he saw Jericho.

"Hi," he said, looking him over, then held out his hand. "See one of the driver's got ya'," and his laughter was pleasant music to Jericho's ears. "Don't pay any attention to those characters. Come on, I'll help you find your room."

As they walked through the brightly lighted hallway, the young man was greeted by others with obvious familiarity.

Finally he turned to Jericho. "Sorry, but I forgot to ask you your name," and he stopped for a moment as a pleasant smile touched his lips.

Jericho had watched his guide with interest because of his obvious self-confidence, and when he'd asked him his name, he'd replied almost casually, "Jerry Smith."

"One of the Smith brothers?" the red haired, freckle-faced, merry eyed Irishman had replied with obvious good humor.

" 'Fraid not. I'm an only child. By the way, you never did tell me your name."

Without a moment's hesitation the young man said proudly, "I'm Brandy Martin."

From that day on Jericho and Brandy Martin became fast friends. Not only did they share the same quarters, but both were intensely interested in and concerned with the political climate of the country. Jericho proved to be far more studious, while Brandy floated through his classes on his personality and charm. He was as undisciplined as Jericho was disciplined, and their close relationship was an interesting mix which soon proved to be an excellent balance.

The first few days were taken up in long hours of boring orientation and in the scheduling of their classes. However, when the evening meal was over, they often took long walks around the campus grounds in order to become better acquainted with the surroundings that they'd both call home for four busy years. Those were the times that they discussed their personal lives, and Jericho discovered that Brandy Martin had had a far more interesting one than he.

When Jericho first learned that Brandy's father was *the* Schuyler Martin of Washington, friend and confidant to presidents and statesmen throughout the world, he became even more interested, and asked endless questions about the roles Brandy's father had played in government. To Brandy, his father's affiliation with the hierarchy of the country was almost commonplace and a part of the normal pattern of their lifestyle, but he'd humored Jericho's 'whims'—as he called them—and enthralled him with some of the more exciting experiences that he'd been a party to. Jericho hung on his every word, and his intense interest pleased his friend.

After one such conversation, Brandy remarked, "Some day I'll take you home with me, would you like that?"

Jericho's eyes glowed. "Like it? You know that I would. I'd like to be able to sit down with your father, whenever he had the time." Then a shadow crossed his face. "But it will have to be later, I'm afraid."

"Why?" Brandy had pursued, his brow creased in concern.

"My folks expect me home whenever we have a holiday," and Jericho gave an audible sigh.

"Perhaps they'd understand how important it is to you if you spoke to them about the plans you've made for your future."

"I haven't told them, as yet, that I'm going into law. They wouldn't understand or approve."

Brandy shook his head. From what he'd learned from Jericho about his parents, they seemed to him to be unusually dull and he almost felt sorry for his friend. Fortunately for him, his father and lovely Kate, his stepmother, were the highlights of the Martin family's home life; and his sister, Elizabeth, who was some eight years his junior, was an enchantress who kept them all on their toes. It was obvious that his young Irish sister was growing into a dazzling, dark haired beauty much like her mother, and he and his brother, Sky, adored her almost to the point of absurdity.

When the first year at Notre Dame came to an end, Jericho and Brandy had bade each other a reluctant, although affectionate, goodbye. Jericho's destination was Kansas, where once again he'd help on the farm; while Brandy and his brother, who was a second year student at Harvard, were bound for a summer in Europe.

In the year that they'd been together, the two young men had each received a gift from the other; Jericho's was an introduction into life's social amenities, and Brandy's was acquiring some semblance of order and discipline. Their association had proved to be beneficial, but when each returned to his respective home, it was Brandy's family that was impressed by the noticeable change for the better.

When Brandy Martin reached Georgetown he found his parents and brother waiting expectantly. Sky had arrived from Harvard a few days before, and was champing at the bit to leave for their holiday in Europe. He was far more cosmopolitan in manner than his brother, and loved the life that living in the shadow of the nation's capitol had provided. Not only was Sky a welcome guest at the various embassies because of his father's prominence, but he also enjoyed playing the role of Don Juan to the Washington debutantes and socialites. It was a fortunate young woman indeed, who was chosen to be escorted by Sky Martin, Jr., to a social function, for thereafter her popularity burgeoned rapidly.

After the first boisterous greetings subsided, Brandy's father addressed him. "My boy," Schuyler had said, "Kate and I are very pleased with the reports we've been receiving from school."

Then Kate broke in. "We're very proud of you, Brandy," and the smile she gave him was radiant.

"Thank you both," he replied, blushing slightly, "but I did have some help."

"Help?" his father asked.

Brandy nodded. "Yes sir. My roommate, Jerry Smith, really showed me the ropes. He's a real brain." Then he laughed slightly. "Would you believe that he's from Wichita, Kansas?" and he made a slight face, failing to notice that Kate looked a bit uncomfortable.

"Kansas?" Sky interrupted, and the manner in which he said it was almost patronizing.

"Yes," Brandy replied. "I'd like for you to meet him sometime," and he sighed, "but his family are farmers and he has to help them out. Perhaps someday."

"Just how did he help you?" his father pursued.

"Well, you all know what a slob I've been, and not too disciplined," and they all joined in his laughter. "He made me keep my part of our room clean and insisted that I do my homework every night and study." He paused, his look thoughtful. "You know, it wasn't all that bad." Then he shrugged his shoulders. "He wants to go to Harvard Law when he completes his undergraduate work. Do you suppose that you could help him, Dad?" and he looked at Schuyler questioningly.

"I'll do my best. But from what you've told me there shouldn't be any real problem, if he's as smart as you say."

"Oh, he is. And you know something else? He thinks he wants to go into politics."

Schuyler Martin, Sr., pricked up his ears. The Democratic party
was always on the lookout for new blood and smart young men,
and even though the fields of Kansas were a far cry from the
lifestyle of the Nation's capitol, he was certain that if this young
man truly was intelligent they could certainly provide the necessary
polish.

"How interesting," Schuyler mused, and it was only Kate who
noticed the sudden gleam in his eyes.

"Enough of this for now," Kate said ending the conversation,
and rose from her chair. "Time to get ready for your homecoming
dinner," and she moved gracefully across the room to the two
handsome young men.

"Give me a hug," Kate said and held out her arms as her eyes
sparkled mischievously. It was Sky who first took her in his arms
and hugged her with abandon, then Brandy, always the shy one,
touched her, but only briefly.

"I'm delighted that you're home. Just wait until Elizabeth
arrives."

Kate had no more than finished speaking when they heard the
sound of the Martin limousine coming to a halt in the drive. Then
young Elizabeth Martin got out of the back and spoke to the
chauffeur.

"James, you're keeping a secret from me," she said accusingly,
and then stomped her foot dramatically. Almost majestically she
turned and without so much as a backward glance glided up the
front steps, while the elderly black man, a slight smile on his lips,
followed with her luggage at a respectful distance.

Kate had hurried to the front door in order to be the first to greet
her daughter.

"Mamma," Elizabeth squealed with childish delight when she
saw Kate and threw herself into her arms. Schuyler had followed
his wife to the entryway and stood quietly as he watched the two
women whom he adored almost beyond reason. Then his daughter
caught sight of him and she turned from her mother to jump into
his outstretched arms.

Sky and Brandy, at their father's direction, had waited in the
drawing room. As Kate, their father and Elizabeth entered the
room she saw her brothers and her violet eyes widened. With a
shriek of joy she ran to them.

"I knew it, I knew it," Elizabeth shouted happily while Brandy, who had always been her favorite, hugged her to him. Then Sky held out his arms, but she stayed with him only briefly and then began to dance merrily around the room like a small whirling dervish as her dark ringlets bounced erratically about her piquant face.

Suddenly she stopped and scrutinized her parents who were smiling with pleasure at her obvious happiness.

"Why did you keep James from telling me?" she said accusingly, her eyes quickly growing dark with anger.

"Baby," her father said as he drew her to him and then lifted her onto his knees where he cradled her tenderly, "we wanted to surprise you, that's all."

For a few tense moments Elizabeth pouted, almost putting a damper on the heretofore happy occasion. Then, like quick silver, she changed back to the beautiful vibrant child they'd first seen.

There was little doubt in anyone's mind, including her family's, that Elizabeth Martin was a spoiled and pampered child. Kate and Schuyler in the years following her birth had made every effort to have additional children but had failed, so the daughter that was born out of their deep love for one another had become a child of idolatry.

The first few weeks that Jericho was at home he'd spent working in the fields with his father. Jacob's attitude was such that he believed that working together and sharing in the abundance of the harvest should prove sufficient to keep his son happy and contented. However, at times he detected a restlessness that Jericho couldn't conceal. When this became even more evident as the weeks wore on, first to Jacob and then later to Martha, they knew that keeping their son 'down on the farm', might be detrimental to their relationship. Finally, in desperation, they turned to the one man they knew would remain unbiased, and who Jericho trusted implicity.

Father O'Connell was not the least bit surprised when his new young priest informed him that Jacob and Martha Smith had requested an appointment. He'd observed Jericho, but only briefly, each Sunday after Mass, and although the young man had said all the right words, he instinctively knew that he was desperately unhappy.

He was also quite aware that the loss of Mother Jean Marie the previous year had cheated Jericho of a loving relationship, and one that he couldn't forget. Peter O'Connell also knew that this was not uncommon, as the majority of children in their formative years love, almost without reason, the one person that has given true meaning to their life. It was not that he doubted Jacob and Martha's devotion and love for their adopted son, but it could never be the same, and this they couldn't understand, or, in fact, didn't want to. So in all reality, he'd welcomed the chance to meet with them. After that he'd seen Jericho alone.

On a hot July afternoon, Jacob and Martha entered the quiet coolness of St. Peter's rectory, where young Father Pignelli greeted them warmly and saw to their comfort while they waited for the meeting with their friend and pastor. The young priest was very much aware that the Smiths were generous contributors to the parish, having been informed of their generosity by one of the novice Sisters who taught at St. Peter's school, and he fervently hoped that the Monsignor would not keep them waiting.

As the three were passing the time in idle conversation concerning the unrelenting summer heat and the upcoming elections in the Fall, the door to the inner sanctuary opened and Father O'Connell came forward to greet them pleasantly, dismissing his assistant with a slight nod.

"Martha, my dear," he said with obvious affection, "how nice to see you." Then he turned his attention to Jacob who had risen to his feet and stood facing him. "Good to see you, too, Jacob," and he laughed slightly. "You look as though you carry the burdens of the world on your shoulders. Trying to be Atlas?" and his wise old eyes twinkled in amusement.

" 'Fraid not, Father," Jacob replied seriously, clearly concerned by the manner in which the Priest was taking their visit. "We need to talk with you about our son."

"Jericho?" he questioned. "Is something wrong?"

"Could we speak in private?" Jacob asked.

"Why, of course. Please come into my office."

After they were seated, Father O'Connell leaned forward, rested his arms on his desk and looked from one to the other.

"Now, what's bothering you?" His manner was serious.

"It's Jericho," Martha blurted out. "He's different since he went away to school." She glanced at her husband and then added, "Since Mother Jean Marie died, he's not been the same boy."

"That's it?" he asked, searching their faces.

Then Jacob spoke up. "We've always had a good relationship with Jericho and now he treats us almost like we're strangers." He looked at Martha who was making a concerted effort not to cry.

"That does come as a surprise," the Priest responded, "and I know how it must concern you. However, let's take each problem one at a time." Jericho's parents nodded their agreement.

"My dear friends," Peter O'Connell began kindly, "what I say may cause you not to like me," and he paused. "However, it's necessary that you understand once and for all about Jericho and his feelings toward Mother Jean Marie." He crossed himself reverently and murmured softly, "God rest her soul."

"But she's been gone for almost a year," Jacob protested angrily. "He was away from her for almost thirteen years after he came to live with us," and then muttered, "although he did spend a holiday with her every summer and that was a mistake," an ugly look replaced his usual placid face.

At this last remark Father O'Connell glared at Jacob coldly. "Perhaps you're not prepared for what I have to say," he barked.

Martha, always the diplomat, broke in. "Please, Father, Jacob's upset. We appreciate your wisdom," and she gave her husband a savage kick on the shins. He glanced at his wife and saw the smoldering anger in her eyes.

"I'm sorry, but Martha's right. Excuse me, please," Jacob apologized, although it seemed half-heartedly.

Then Peter O'Connell related briefly the story of Mother Jean Marie and the love and attention that she'd given so unselfishly to Jericho during the years he'd spent at the convent, and also included the fact that, if she'd had her own way and not been concerned for his future, she would never have placed him for adoption.

Martha and Jacob listened with rapt attention to the words of the priest and began to understand, at least partially, the reasons for their son's unrelenting love for her.

"Will he ever get over it?" Martha asked.

The old priest smiled. "Yes, in time. He does love you and Jacob, of that I'm quite certain," and these words brought a ray of brightness to the faces of the man and woman who sat before him. Then he added. "He will love deeply again," and he laughed slightly, "that is, when the right young woman enters his life. Then he'll feel fulfilled, and Mother Jean Marie will remain in his heart only as a beautiful memory."

"But he's too young to be serious about anyone," Jacob protested.

"You're probably right, but it will come in time. Now let's get to your second complaint," and Father O'Connell's look was shrewd.

"It's not that important, Father," Martha replied. "We'll just have to grow with Jericho," and she sighed. "I love him so, but he turns from me now."

"That's a normal reaction, Martha. He now has a man's feelings and wants no woman to touch him, let alone his mother."

Martha looked at him with surprise. "Is that really true?"

"Of course. Even I felt that way about my own mother, although I loved her dearly. Boys are very different in some respects from girls."

Jacob shook his head. He still didn't fully understand, but he had to be satisfied for he knew that Father O'Connell had undoubtedly seen or heard it all.

As they rose to leave, the Priest followed them to the door where he looked Jacob in the eye. "Ask Jericho to come see me. We need to have a talk."

It was not surprising that Jericho noticed the rather sudden and dramatic change in the attitude of his parents. Instead of insisting on being included in every moment of his spare time, he happily discovered that he was, for once in his life, free to do as he pleased.

When Jacob had casually mentioned that the Monsignor had requested that Jericho visit him, his first reaction had been on the negative side. He was rather apprehensive where the old priest was concerned and for good cause; in the main because of his hereto-fore voiced desire that Jericho enter the seminary upon his graduation from Notre Dame. He'd refused him on one previous occasion, but he also was quite aware of Peter O'Connell's well known reputation for having his own way. On the other hand, the positive side was that he was indeed understanding, and Jericho instinctively knew that if he confided his desire to enter law with the ultimate intention of becoming involved in the political arena, it just might appeal to him even more so. On previous visits he couldn't help but notice the affectionately autographed photograph of Joe Kennedy and the additional pictures of the clan, and if anyone was active in the country's political picture, most assuredly it was the Kennedys of Massachusetts.

Apprehensive or not, he phoned St. Peter's for an appointment and was surprised to find that he was invited to share supper with the Monsignor. His acceptance was automatic and a surge of confidence swept through him. When he'd completed making the arrangements with Father Pignelli, he went in search of his parents.

He found Martha and Jacob on the large screened-in porch, enjoying the cool evening breeze that had followed a much needed rain. Jericho collapsed into the string hammock and for a few moments enjoyed its relaxing movement as it swayed gently back and forth. Then he pulled himself up into a half sitting position.

"Nice evening," he remarked pleasantly.

Jacob put his newspaper aside and Martha stopped her frantic fanning as they both directed their attention to Jericho. It had been extremely difficult for them to change their mannerism toward him after so many years, and when their son searched them out—and these occasions had been meager of late—they knew that he really wanted their company.

"Matter of fact, it is," Jacob responded. "Thank God for the rain," and Martha responded, "Amen!"

Jericho smiled. "I've just had a conversation with Monsignor O'Connell's assistant," and he paused, taking note of the sudden show of interest by his parents.

"Are you going to see the Father?" Martha asked point blank.

"Better than that. I've been invited to have supper with him tomorrow evening."

"Really?" Jacob replied, a pleased smile on his lips. Then he glanced at Martha who winked at him knowingly.

"Yep, I've known that he'd wanted to see me ever since I came home from school, but we've been so busy," and his voice trailed off as he had little desire to hurt his parents.

"We're delighted for you, Jericho," his mother replied. "Please give him our best." Then she looked at her husband. "Since Jericho's going to be away, how about taking me into town for dinner?"

The look that came over Jacob's face was one of horror. "Eat in town?" he sputtered.

"Why not, Dad?" Jericho interjected. "We can drive in together, and then I'll meet you later to come home. Mother deserves a break."

Jacob was surprised by his son's ready agreement. He was becoming far too liberal in his thinking these days, and he didn't know if he really liked it.

"Come on, Jacob," Martha coaxed. "It won't hurt you just this once."

"All right, if you insist. But remember this, it won't become a habit," he replied firmly.

Both Jericho and his mother laughed at Jacob's sternness. They were both aware that Martha had spoiled her husband almost beyond reason, even before Jericho had joined them, and the mere thought of breaking a long standing habit he found difficult. Still, Jacob knew that both Martha and Jericho were right. His wife had worked hard all the years of their long and happy marriage, and when he looked at them a twinkle appeared in his eyes.

"Okay, you two con artists," he'd said, and for him those words were almost flippant. Then he added. "Suppose I can't wear my overalls?"

"Definitely not," Martha snapped, and the subject was automatically closed.

"Okay, okay. It's off to the city tomorrow." Then he pushed himself up from the old rocker. "Time to hit the hay," and he motioned to Martha, who obediently got up to join him.

" 'Night, Jericho," his father said and then Martha stopped beside him. "Good night, son," and she touched his cheek with affection.

"Good night, mother. I'll turn in soon."

Then he was left alone in the stillness of the night. As he listened to the katydids as they shrilled their piercing song while the crickets chirped along almost in unison, he realized that at last he would be free. There was just one monkey in his personal life to conquer, and that was finding his real parents. Jericho dismissed the thought, as he knew there was a long road ahead, and that that would come at the right time. His immediate future was what was most important.

Jericho entered the rectory office to be greeted warmly by Father Pignelli, and especially so as he was an alumnus of Notre Dame and thus felt that they shared a common bond. This brief meeting with the young Priest provided Jericho with an opportunity to draw him into conversation about the commitment he'd made to the church, for there had been times when he'd observed Father Pignelli's rather lackluster performance in the ritual of the Mass, and at the time he'd wondered if the shine of being ordained into the priestly life hadn't already become tarnished.

"Father Pignelli," he'd said, "do you mind if I inquire as to why you felt called to the priesthood?"

The black haired, dark eyed Italian had hesitated at first at giving a reply. He knew that the Monsignor had explored many avenues in an effort to foster an interest in the young Smith boy for the church, but so far he'd failed.

"There's always been at least one priest in the Pignelli family," he replied, and for a moment a sudden wistfulness came into his eyes. "My four older brothers chose other lifestyles and I was the last son." In resignation he threw up his hands. "I really had very little choice." But then he brightened. "It's a good life and I'm very fortunate to be assigned to St. Peters. I admire the Monsignor very much." Then his face took on an earnestness as he looked at Jericho intently and said softly, "But don't ever let anyone push you into something that you really don't want."

At that inopportune moment, Peter O'Connell entered the room.

In obvious haste, Father Pignelli excused himself and practically ran from the room. At the Monsignor's appearance Jericho had risen to his feet feeling concern that Father Pignelli might have been overheard. However, from the hearty welcome he received, it was apparent that their conversation had gone unnoticed.

In a short time the rectory's housekeeper announced that supper was now ready, and Jericho followed Father O'Connell to the small patio which adjoined his office where a table for two had been set.

The light supper they were served proved to be delicious fare and after they'd finished and were lingering over iced coffee, Father O'Connell once again broached the subject of Jericho's intentions concerning the priesthood.

"Jericho, my boy," he'd said, turning on his native Irish charm, "you're aware that your family and I have high hopes that you'll reconsider entering the seminary."

Jericho had anticipated this conversation and he remembered vividly the look in Father Pignelli's eyes as he'd said, *Don't ever let anyone push you into something that you really don't want.* That statement had been a warning, and one for which he'd be eternally grateful.

"Sorry, Father," Jericho replied, as he toyed with a spoon. "I've made other plans. It's not that I lack respect in serving; it's simply that I want to do as I choose." He paused. "Perhaps you'll think I'm being selfish," and he looked up into the eyes of the old priest who watched him with interest.

"Just what do you have in mind?" he asked.

"You may think that I'm crazy."

"Try me," the Monsignor replied.

For several minutes Jericho remained silent as he mulled over in his mind just how he should say it, and then he looked up and smiled. "Father, it's really quite simple. I want to serve my country."

"In what capacity?"

"I have a great interest in being involved in our country's political structure. At Notre Dame this past year I roomed with Brandy Martin, the son of Schuyler Martin, and someday I plan to meet his father," and he flushed with pleasure at the thought.

It was now Peter O'Connell's turn to be surprised. He'd heard good things about Schuyler Martin through his friendship with Joe Kennedy and as he remembered it, this Martin wielded an enormous amount of power and influence within the Democratic Party.

"How interesting," he murmured, his expression now thoughtful. Then finally, "You've got your head set on this, Jericho?"

His young guest nodded his head vigorously.

"Well, then I won't try to discourage you, however, I do want you to know one thing."

"What's that?"

"A man isn't forced into becoming a priest unless he wants to be one."

"But sometimes families pressure you," Jericho protested, in an effort to defend the young priest.

"That's true," the Monsignor replied. "However, if you have any strong convictions toward another course, then that's the one you should take. By the way, just how do you plan on going about your venture?"

"That's one of the reasons I wanted to discuss it with you, and I do appreciate your taking this time with me," Jericho replied seriously.

"Well, get on with it."

"You see, Father, the next three years I'll be rooming with Brandy Martin and he's indicated that he'd like me to meet his family." He took a deep breath and then plunged on. "I want to go to Harvard Law after I get my B.A."

"Be a lawyer?" the old priest asked in surprise.

"Yes, but that's only the first step. Then, when I become established here in Kansas, I'll start at the bottom of the political ladder and learn the ropes. I've been doing a bit of investigating and that seems to be the best way."

"Have you told Martha and Jacob?"

Jericho hung his head sheepishly. "No, I'm afraid I haven't. Actually, I was hoping that you'd help me tell them. I'm concerned about their reaction." He paused as though in thought and then continued. "It's rather strange, you know. Of late, mother and dad have been more relaxed and lenient with me."

Peter O'Connell's eyes twinkled and he felt like laughing outright but instead he cleared his throat loudly, pushing back his amusement.

"Do you feel that they'll object?"

"I really don't know what to expect, but I don't want them to keep thinking that I'm going to be a priest. No offense, sir."

That was when he did laugh. "I know that you mean it only kindly, my boy. Tell you what, why don't you let this ride until after you go back to school?"

"But what good will that do?"

"I'll work on them for you," and he clapped his hands almost like a child who'd been pleased.

"Oh, thank you, Father. With you on my side, I know they'll accept whatever you say."

For a moment Peter O'Connell forgot in whose presence he was and said softly to himself, "They always have . . . so far."

Jericho looked at him sharply, but the moment had passed so quickly that it was almost as though the old man had said nothing.

Jericho had taken the wheel of the car on the drive back to the farm and Jacob slumped beside him, while Martha sprawled comfortably in the back. The windows of the old Chevy had been lowered to allow the fresh clean air to flow through and the wind's noise caused the occupants to refrain from any serious attempt at conversation.

When Jericho had told the Monsignor good night he'd thanked him profusely, instilled with the knowledge that the old priest would see to making things right with his parents. He felt a thrill of excitement as he considered the years ahead, and he was glad that it was nearly time for his return to Notre Dame. During the summer he'd received several postcards from Brandy, who was still on holiday in Europe, and he'd been pleased that he'd seen fit to remember him.

It was quite late when they arrived home and Jericho was tired and more than ready for a good night's sleep, but it was obvious that his parents were curious about his meeting with Father O'Connell. However, they refrained from questioning him and he bade them an affectionate good night and went up the stairs where he entered the privacy of his room.

After Jericho was well out of hearing range, Jacob turned to Martha. "He seem okay to you?" he asked.

Martha pondered the question and finally replied. "He acted normal. I do hope that he and the Father came to terms."

"I pray so," Jacob responded, "let's you and me head for bed. Four o'clock comes mighty early," and he sighed. "Somedays I think I'd be glad if Jericho would simply come back to the farm and take over here when he's finished college."

Martha looked surprised. "Don't you want him to go to the seminary? Remember, Jacob, you're the one who's been pushing for it."

"I know, but perhaps he'd rather stay on the farm."

"Poppycock," Martha replied emphatically. "He's going to be a priest."

Jacob stared at her for a moment and then headed for the stairs. He realized that if his wife had her head set on their son becoming a priest, he'd probably be one.

11

It was with apparent eagerness and without any noticeable regret at leaving home that Jericho returned to Notre Dame. Jacob and Martha hadn't pressed him about the meeting with Monsignor O'Connell, and this in itself proved to be a relief.

When his friend, Brandy Martin, arrived on campus and they were once again settled into the continuing throes of their education, he felt more at home then he had in a long time.

One evening after they'd pushed their books aside and were relaxing over a cup of hot chocolate before turning in, Brandy approached Jericho about attending the Homecoming game with him and his father. Schuyler Martin was to be in Chicago on business that week, and he'd suggested to his son that his friend Jerry Smith be included in the weekend.

"You're kidding?" was Jericho's first reaction, his eyes lighting up. "God, Brandy, if you mean it, I'll be there with bells on," and he jumped up to move restlessly around their somewhat cramped quarters.

"How long will your father be here?" he asked.

"Probably just overnight. Then he goes back to Washington. Honestly, my friend, I didn't figure an old boy like my dad could cause such excitement."

Jericho turned to face him, his eyes bright. "You've known for a long time what I've wanted, Brandy," and he paused, his look pensive. "My folks still have hopes that I'll enter the seminary, but Monsignor O'Connell is going to break the news to them that I won't be a priest, and that I plan on becoming a lawyer and then enter politics."

"Why didn't you just tell them yourself?"

"It's a long story, Brandy. It's better if it comes from the Father," and for a moment he looked rather remorseful. Then his enthusiasm returned. "Do you think that your father could possibly find time for me?"

Brandy laughed. "Of course. I told the family about you during the summer holiday and Dad seemed just as interested in meeting you as you are in meeting him."

"Really?" Jericho asked in obvious surprise.

"Yeah. I gave him the picture of how damned bright you are," and he made a face at Jericho, "and I told them how you've helped me. That did it, kid."

"How can I ever thank you?"

"Thank me? My God, Jerry, if I hadn't had you on my case, I'd probably have flunked."

Jericho shook his head. "Hey, that's a bunch of nonsense. You're plenty smart," and he laughed. "You just didn't know how to apply yourself, that's all."

Brandy yawned and glanced at the clock. "It's long after lights out. We'd better get some shut-eye," and he began to undress and toss his clothes thoughtlessly aside. Then he glanced up to find Jericho looking at him, and immediately began to retrieve the shirt and pants he'd tossed on the floor and placed them neatly on a hanger.

"Satisfied?" he grumbled as he turned from the closet to crawl into bed.

"Need you ask?" Jericho replied.

Then they both laughed.

Homecoming weekend couldn't come soon enough to suit Jericho. Even though the course load that he carried would normally have kept him occupied, he was constantly distracted by the thought of his meeting with Schuyler Martin. However, he didn't fall short, for when the first quarter grades came out just prior to the big weekend, he still ranked first in the Sophmore class.

On the Friday night before the big game, Brandy, with Jericho in tow, took a cab to the train station to meet his father. Jericho had dressed in his best slacks and jacket while his roommate seemed to care little about what he wore or how he looked.

As they waited on the platform, Jericho's palms were moist from nervousness, even though the early November evening had a definite chill. He stood tall and straight while his companion lounged casually against the building as the train pulled to a thundering stop. After the conductor jumped down and carefully placed the step-stool on the platform for the passengers who had reached their destination to alight, it was only then that Brandy seemed to come alive.

As each man stepped from the club car Jericho scrutinized him intently, and as time passed he had a slight sinking feeling. Perhaps Mr. Martin hadn't come. Then Brandy rushed forward to greet the last passenger, and this provided Jericho with an opportunity to study the man who would ultimately become his mentor.

Schuyler Martin and his son hugged each other with affection, and then Brandy murmured something to his father, who looked up to see a tall, handsome, dark haired youth standing at a respectful distance and smiling nervously in his direction.

When Schuyler had first taken a look at his son's friend, for a moment a sense of foreboding had engulfed him, but he was unable to pinpoint any reason for his reaction. With Brandy beside him talking a mile a minute, they joined Jericho.

"Dad," Brandy said proudly, "this is my good friend, Jerry Smith." Schuyler Martin now had the opportunity to see Jericho first hand and the feeling that he'd first experienced quickly dissipated.

"Jerry Smith," he repeated as he extended his hand, "How nice to meet you. Brandy's told me some good things about you," his smile was warm and friendly.

Jericho gripped his hand briefly and replied, "Mr. Martin, you can't possibly imagine how pleased I am to be included in this weekend."

"He's afraid that he'll be intruding," Brandy interjected.

"Intruding?" and Schuyler laughed. "No such thing. I've

looked forward to meeting you ever since Brandy told me of your desire to go into law and eventually into politics," and he laughed slightly, his eyes merry. "He tells me that you're a real brain."

Jericho blushed and playfully hit Brandy's arm.

"I get by," Jericho replied modestly

"Get by!" Brandy literally exploded. "Dad, he's been the top student of our class, last year and so far this year, and he was elected President of the sophomore class." He turned to look at his friend. "And he says he gets by? Bull!"

Schuyler Martin had to laugh at his son's obvious pride in his friend's accomplishments, but he was also pleased by the modesty that Jerry exhibited.

"Okay, you guys," he said, now taking charge, "let's find a cab and get to my hotel. Then we'll have a snack together."

"Great, Dad," and much to his father's surprise Brandy picked up his suitcase and started ahead to hail a cab.

"I see that you've taught my son some courtesy," Schuyler remarked and smiled at his young companion.

"Brandy's a very fine person," Jericho replied, sounding almost protective.

"Well, you've been a good example for him, and his mother and I appreciate how you've helped him." Then his manner became serious. "I do hope that I can be of service to you." Schuyler Martin's offer was far more then Jericho had hoped for.

"I'd appreciate having a few minutes of your time to explore the possibilities available for my future. I assure you that I don't want to burden you."

"I'll be glad to spend as much time as I can, within reason of course, answering any questions that I can."

"Thank you, Mr. Martin," and Jericho paused. "I see that Brandy has a cab. They're hard to come by since it's Homecoming, so we'd better get with it."

Following a rather hair-raising ride from the station to the hotel where Schuyler Martin had booked accommodations, and after he'd settled in, he immediately called room service and ordered a variety of delicacies brought to the suite. Brandy accepted this procedure very matter of factly, but to Jericho it was a totally new experience. He'd watched, almost in awe, the attention that his host had commanded on their entrance into the hotel, for every

courtesy was extended immediately and without question. Schuyler
Martin was well known to this fine old establishment. When he'd
been a student at Notre Dame some years before, he'd hosted
several lavish and expensive parties there, and his name had been
enhanced in the ensuing years.

Brandy and Jericho had already had a complete meal at the
college dining hall, but when the food arrived with it's delectable
aromas, it took no invitation from Schuyler for the two young men
to heap their plates full and eat again with obvious relish.

Schuyler had watched with amusement and thought of the days
when he'd also been a voracious consumer of almost anything in
sight. Now, he watched his diet religiously, with the help of Kate,
and ate quite nutritiously.

When the waiter had finally removed the few remnants that were
left, Brandy sprawled on the sitting room floor and quickly fell
asleep. This turn of events afforded Jericho and his host the
opportunity to talk privately.

The two men settled comfortably into the lounge chairs and then
Schuyler Martin addressed Jericho, who from observation still
seemed rather ill at ease.

"Jerry," he said, smiling warmly, "tell me of your plans. I might
tell you first that Brandy did mention that you were interested in
Harvard Law. Am I correct?"

Jericho nodded vigorously.

"Perhaps you'd like to explain just why you want to be a lawyer,
and eventually become involved in politics. Not many young men
your age," and he laughed slightly and pointed toward his son,
"have the vaguest idea of just what they are destined to do," and
for a moment he eyed his guest appraisingly. "You strike me as
being someone who knows exactly what he wants, and where he
intends to go. Right?"

It was obvious to Jericho that Schuyler Martin had read him well
and he felt a sense of relief, for he hadn't confided his plans for his
future to anyone but a chosen few. Now he was beginning to feel
more at ease with his host and he had the feeling that when and if
he needed assistance, Mr. Martin would be both willing and
capable of doing anything within his power to help him.

"I do appreciate your interest, Mr. Martin," Jericho began.
"And you're certainly correct about my plans." His look became

earnest. Then he continued. "I come from Kansas, as you know," and he laughed. "Brandy refers to me as his cowboy friend."

Schuyler frowned and Jericho, noticing his sudden show of distaste, hurried on.

"He doesn't mean anything by that, sir. It's just his way."

When Schuyler Martin replied his tone was harsh. "I don't approve of anyone in my family speaking derogatorily."

"I'm sorry I mentioned it, sir. It's just been a joke between Brandy and me. And I have to admit in all honesty that coming from a farm in Kansas isn't all that glamourous."

"It makes no difference to me where anyone comes from, and I'll certainly speak to him about it," Schuyler replied. "Brandy is a very fortunate young man, and he'd better begin to take note of it."

Jericho felt as though he might possibily have stirred up a hornet's nest.

"Again, I'm sorry," he said quietly, eyes downcast.

"Don't be. Now enough of this. Go ahead and tell me just why you want to go into law."

"I suppose that it goes way back," Jericho began. "When I was in school I was fortunate enough to have some excellent teachers and I leaned heavily toward government and it's workings, as well as to the legal processes involved. When I had free time in the summers, I spent it at the local library," and he looked up and grinned. "We do have libraries in Kansas."

Schuyler had to chuckle at Jericho's sudden show of humor, since at first he'd seemed to be overly serious, and it was good to know that this facet wasn't lacking in his makeup.

"I'll remember that," the older man replied. "Now, just what did you find in the library?"

"I read almost everything that I could get my hands on about the manner in which the elections are held, and it was surprising to learn that President Truman didn't have a law degree. In fact, he was originally a haberdasher in Missouri, but he's proved to be an excellent political leader."

"Have to agree," Schuyler replied. "Has Brandy ever mentioned that our ancestors were one of the founding families of Kansas City, Missouri?"

It was Jericho's turn to look surprised as he'd assumed from his friend's conversation, and rightly so, that he was a native borne Washingtonian.

Schuyler caught the young man's startled expression and was forced to smile. It was just like his youngest son to add glamour to his life.

"Brandy never mentioned it. How long have you lived in Washington?" Jericho stammered.

"I was asked to join Roosevelt's administration during the early years of World War II. You see, my family has been involved in politics in one way or another over many years, so when Harry Hopkins requested that I 'volunteer' my experience in finance, it seemed only right that I accept. Brandy and Sky were both small boys at the time and Elizabeth was on her way," and his eyes brightened at the mention of his daughter.

Then he leaned forward, his voice softening.

"I do hope that you'll plan on coming to Washington to meet my wife, Sky and Elizabeth one day soon. You'll find all of them just as nice as that sleeping rascal," and he glanced at his son, who was obviously lost in another world.

"I'd really like that, Mr. Martin. However, I'm all that my folks have, and it's only to be expected that they want me home whenever I'm out of school."

Schuyler Martin looked thoughtful for several minutes. He had already thought that perhaps he could find a place for Jerry in one of his friends' law offices during the summer months, which would provide him with the necessary exposure to law he needed. Furthermore, if it were close to home, his parents surely couldn't object.

"Do you have any firm plans for next summer?" he asked.

Jericho's look was one of surprise, but then he answered. "No, sir. Just going back to Wichita and the farm," and it was obvious that he lacked enthusiasm. "Why?"

"Would you consider working as a clerk in a law office?"

Jericho's face brightened considerably, but then fell again. "I'm afraid not," and his voice trailed off, although Schuyler Martin detected a trace of anger.

"If it happened to be in Wichita, would your parents object?"

"You're not putting me on, are you, sir?" Jericho replied hesitantly.

Schuyler laughed. "Of course not. You see, Jerry, I've a very close friend in Wichita who just happens to be an excellent lawyer," and he paused. "We were classmates here at Notre Dame," and he smiled in remembrance and shook his head. "We certainly had some good times." Then his manner became serious again. "I'm almost positive that he'd be glad to have a young assistant. Tell you what," and his eyes gleamed, "I'll give Paul a call before I leave for Washington."

Jericho's mind was now in a whirl. Surely Jacob and Martha wouldn't object, and he'd still find the time to help his Dad on the farm.

"If you think that I'd be satisfactory, sir, I'll see if I can't make arrangements with my folks." Then he smiled. "It's about time that I became free."

Schuyler frowned. "What do you mean, free?"

Very solemnly, Jericho replied. "I've been beholden to someone for as long as I can remember," and he sighed, "but it has to change. "It will change," and there was the sound of a new strength in his voice that Schuyler hadn't heard before.

True to his word, the following morning Schuyler placed a call to Paul Moran, his friend in Wichita, and talked with him at great length about Jerry Smith. He even went so far as to offer to subsidize the young man's salary, and this proved to be a surprise to his longtime associate.

"You certainly seem to have taken a strong interest in this boy," Paul had replied to his offer. "Have you something up your sleeve, my friend," and he paused. "Besides your usual Ace?"

Then they both laughed, for they knew each other well.

"Frankly, Paul, Jerry happens to be one of the brightest young men that I've had the privilege of meeting in a long time. Unfortunately, he's being held back by his parents. You see, they're farmers and live just outside of Wichita, and he feels obligated to be at home every summer to help on the farm. If it wasn't for that, I'd see to it that he had a summer job in the capitol where he could get to know and rub shoulders with some of my friends."

"Now that Eisenhower's been elected, how are you going to play it?"

"Just the same. I have friends in both parties, so there's no real problem. Anyway, just give us a few years and we'll produce a candidate that no one can beat."

"Anyone in mind?" Paul Moran pursued, as he knew that Schuyler was privy to the inner workings of the hierarchy in the Democratic Party.

Schuyler laughed. "Sorry, friend, even if I did know I couldn't tell you, but I will admit that we've already started the process. We realize that it's almost a certainty that Ike will serve two full terms since he's so popular with the people, being a war hero and all, but then its our turn."

"Good enough. But do keep me posted. You know that I handle Kansas pretty well, even though it's gone Republican most of the time."

"I will, Paul, but how about the matter at hand? Will you help my young friend?"

"Be glad to. Perhaps I can lure him back here when he's finished with law school."

"You never know, you just might, and thanks. I'll have him stop by your office during the Christmas break and you two can make your own arrangements for the summer."

"Good enough, Schuyler. Give my love to Kate and the rest of your brood," and with that, the conversation ended.

After the homecoming game was over, one in which Notre Dame had taken a drubbing, much to the dismay of the students and the alumni in attendance, Schuyler returned to the hotel with Brandy and Jericho. His train for Washington was due to leave at nine that evening so there was still sufficient time for a quick supper together and some final conversation. When they entered the crowded dining room, they were guided to a table where they could enjoy some measure of privacy.

Both young men ordered steaks with all the trimmings while Schuyler selected lobster. Almost in silence, Brandy and Jericho devoured their meals and then polished off dessert.

"Someday you two will flounder yourselves," Schuyler admonished half-heartedly.

"I'll bet you ate plenty when you were my age," Brandy protested. "Too bad that you and Kate stay on that dumb diet."

Then his eyes took on a mischeivous gleam. "Of course, when you get old," and he looked at his father to see his reaction, but Schuyler merely smiled.

"By the way, Jerry, I have some good news for you."

Brandy looked from one to the other. "What kind of news? Does it include me?"

His father shook his head. "Sorry, son, it doesn't. You slept through our whole conversation last evening, and you'd probably have found it boring anyway."

Brandy scowled at being excluded. "But why?"

"Because you aren't the least bit interested in law and a political career," Schuyler rebuffed him.

"Excuse me, sir," Jericho interrupted. "Could I hear the news?"

"Sorry, Jerry," and the look that he gave his son was one filled with disgust.

Brandy sat quietly, a feeling of envy sweeping over him while his father explained to Jericho the arrangements he'd made with his attorney friend, Paul Moran, to have him as a junior law clerk for the summer. When he'd finished speaking, Jericho's face was flushed with excitement and his eyes gleamed. It was obvious to Schuyler Martin that this young man's enthusiasm could be contagious and, should it continue in the years ahead, there was an excellent chance that he could find a key position for him on the Party's staff in the capitol.

"How can I ever thank you, sir?" Jericho said.

Schuyler smiled, and saw that Brandy still pouted in silence. "You can help by keeping this son of mine on track."

Jericho glanced at his friend whose look remained passive, his eyes veiled to conceal the hurt.

"Mr. Martin, Brandy's an excellent student," Jericho protested and touched his friends' shoulder with obvious affection. "He's simply not bent the same as me." There was an almost pleading note to his words, which Schuyler quickly detected.

"Brandy's a great son," he said with pride in his voice as he placed his hand on his shoulder. "He's going to be the one to take over our family's investments after he receives his Masters Degree. I'm looking forward to handing over that job, believe me," and he smiled. "I wouldn't trust that aspect of my finances to anyone but him.''

At his father's words of praise, Brandy's face lit up and the awkward moment came to an end, but not before Schuyler had looked into Jericho's eyes as though to say 'thank you.'

As the time grew short, they left the still crowded dining room, gathered Schuyler's belongings, and then took a cab to the railroad station as the hour for his departure approached. The train bound for Washington came lumbering to a stop, and Jericho moved aside to give Brandy and his father an opportunity to be alone. They embraced warmly and conversed in quiet tones.

Then Schuyler moved to Jericho. "Jerry," he said, gripping his hand with a firm handshake, "I'm glad that we finally met, and I do hope that sometime in the not-too-distant future you'll find it possible to come visit us in Georgetown. You've got a standing invitation, and Kate and the rest of my family would be delighted to have you." His voice rang with sincerity. "Brandy," and he looked at his son with affection, "could give you the grand tour of our nation's capitol," and a sudden gleam came into his eyes. "I trust that you'll be serving there one day in some capacity."

Then, without another word and with a slight wave of his hand, he swung up the steps and disappeared into the depths of the Pullman car. The two young men stood silently and watched as the locomotive moved down the tracks, whistle blaring loudly.

When the noise from the train had somewhat abated, Brandy heaved an audible sigh and Jericho looked at him questioningly.

"Something wrong?" he asked as they proceeded down the brick paved platform to the cab stand.

"Oh, it's just that sometimes I have the feeling that Dad wishes that I were more like him," and he looked up at Jericho, "and more like you." There was a trace of hurt in his voice.

Jericho put his arm around his friend's shoulders and gave him a slight hug.

"Hey, buddy, we're not all cut from the same cloth. You are you . . . and I'm me. No two people in this whole world," and he swung his arms in a wide circle, "are the same. Wouldn't it be awful if we were?" It was then that he saw the first sign of humor begin to brighten his friend's face.

"How right you are," Brandy replied now more cheerfully, and proceeded to slap Jericho on the back.

At that point a cab came wheeling down the deserted street and Brandy held up his hand almost nonchalantly while the taxi screeched to a halt.

The driver looked at the two youths and gave them a smile of recognition. "Old Dom?" he inquired, just to be sure.

"Absolutely, James," Brandy said grandly while they both clambered into the back seat of the cab. Then they proceeded to roll down the windows and began to lustily sing Notre Dame's fight songs all the way home.

12

When the Christmas holiday arrived, Jericho headed west while Brandy took off for Georgetown. They'd exchanged gifts the day before their departures and Brandy had presented his friend with a book on the judicial system, which Jericho had admitted on more than one occasion that he wanted but couldn't afford. On the train ride to Wichita he'd kept his nose buried in it, and the long trip seemed to pass quickly.

When Jericho stepped off the train, his parents rushed to greet him. Martha threw her arms around him and held on to him like a magnet does a nail, while Jacob stood and beamed. After a few moments, Jericho extricated himself from his mother's embrace, and then shook the hand that his father extended.

"Mighty glad that you're home son," Jacob said.

Martha chimed in, "You can say that again."

After collecting Jericho's bag, they found their way to the car and once they were on the road into the country Jacob turned to Jericho. "Understand from Monsignor O'Connell that you're dead set on becoming a lawyer." The manner in which he said it was toneless and lacked any inflection.

At first Jericho did not respond but kept his eyes averted and stared at the snow covered road ahead. Then finally he said very crisply, "That's right."

"How come you didn't discuss this change of plans with us?" Martha asked from out of the depths of the back seat.

"I hadn't made a commitment to anything, Mother. And even though Father O'Connell urged me to enter the priesthood, he understood why I didn't want that."

"Well, it came as a complete surprise to your mother and me," Jacob responded sharply.

"I'm sorry, but I didn't want to hurt you, and I knew that you've always had great faith in the Father. Isn't it right for me to be what I want?"

Neither Jacob nor Martha responded to his question, and nothing further was mentioned on the balance of the ride to the farm.

When they entered the house, Jericho went straight up the stairs and to his room. There he threw his bag down and shut the door. Shrugging out of his heavy winter coat, he mulled over the brief conversation in the car. It was obvious that his parents were displeased with his decision, but they'd have to understand the same thing he'd told Brandy, that each person is different and has their own destiny, and that no one should have to be or do what someone else wants.

After a short time, Jericho wandered back down the stairs to find his parents sitting quietly before the brightly burning fire in the hand-cut stone fireplace. Jericho moved toward it and held out his hands to warm them. "Feels good," he said in an effort to open the conversation. "I sure miss having a fireplace in the winter."

Jacob merely nodded, while Martha kept staring straight ahead into the flames, completely ignoring him.

Jericho pulled a pillow from the davenport and then stretched full length on the rug in front of the fireplace, his arm braced against it for support and stared into the flickering flames. The silence between his parents and himself continued and soon Jericho's head began to nod. Scrambling to his feet, he tossed the pillow back on the divan and without a word went quickly up the stairs.

As soon as Jacob heard the door to Jericho's room close, he turned to Martha.

"Damn it, wife," he barked, "you could at least have been civil to him," he almost yelled, his face red with anger and frustration.

"You didn't act so nice yourself," Martha replied sharply. Then she added bitterly, "All men are alike. They do as they damned well please," and she got up and moved toward the stairs, but changed her mind and stopped. "I'll accept whatever he's planned," and she shrugged her shoulders in resignation. "You see, there's really no choice. However, I remember only too well how you talked of having him come back and run the farm." Her voice was accusing, "And you were the one who began the priest dialogue while Mother Jean Marie was still living."

"That's enough out of you," Jacob stormed. "Button your lip."

At Jacob's harsh words, tears welled in Martha's eyes and she began to cry softly. They'd never had a cross word, so this was indeed a first.

Jacob remained silent as Martha continued to sob. He'd never been inclined to display emotion, and although he knew that his wife was truly suffering, there was simply no way that he could bring himself to console her. Quarreling hadn't been his forte either, and he found himself completely devoid of words.

In a short time Martha dried her eyes and returned to her chair. "I'm sorry, Jacob," she murmured softly. "This whole thing has been very disappointing to me, and who knows where Jericho's chosen field will lead him. I worry about that."

Jacob nodded, accepting her obvious humility. "We'll just have to take it for whatever it's worth." And then his voice became more gentle, "Would you care to go up to bed?"

Martha nodded, and together they headed up the stairs to their room where they would both spend a long and sleepless night.

The next morning following breakfast, Jericho asked if he could use the car to drive into Wichita. Without making any comment or questioning him, Jacob handed over the keys.

Martha had rattled on almost non-stop throughout the meal, and on one occasion a remark that she'd made had brought a smile to their son's lips. Although he was pleasant, it was obvious that he would keep his own counsel.

Just before ten o'clock Jericho, dressed neatly in slacks and white shirt with tie and sports jacket and with a noticeable new shine to his brogues, left the house, stating that he'd return after lunch.

Martha and Jacob had watched him leave.

"Where do you think that he's going?" Martha asked.

Jacob shook his head. "I haven't the faintest idea." Then his face brightened. "Perhaps he's going to visit Monsignor O'Connell."

"Of course," Martha replied and her look became more optimistic. "That must be it."

Martha and Jacob had made the wrong assumption, for Jericho was on his way to an appointment with Paul Moran.

Because of Schuyler Martin's influence, the old lawyer had written to Jericho at Notre Dame and had extended an invitation for him to visit his office. Jericho had replied promptly, and this day, December 17, 1952, at eleven o'clock, would be his first brush with destiny. He'd successfully concealed the anticipation and excitement from his parents, and as he cruised along the snow covered highway he dreamed of what the future might hold.

After Jericho had pulled into a parking slot near the First National Bank Building where Moran had his law offices, he looked at himself in the rear view mirror and his reflection pleased him. The thick dark hair he'd been blessed with had been trimmed only a few days before he'd left school, and the jacket and slacks he'd put on that morning had been worn very little. He looked every inch the successful young businessman, and the darkness of his heavy beard added a few years to his appearance. Satisfied, Jericho got out of the old Chevy, carefully locked it, and then walked purposefully through the revolving door of the building and entered the first elevator.

"Fifth floor, please," he said to the young and attractive operator who glanced at him with obvious admiration.

As he got off on the fifth floor, the door to the elevator closed with a bang and Jericho stopped for a moment, then straightened his shoulders and walked swiftly on down the hall. As he glanced at the various doors that he passed he saw that on each one was the name MORAN lettered in deep black and outlined with gold. Suddenly he realized that Schuyler Martin's friend was indeed important, and for a second his confidence was shaken.

Almost with trepidation he entered the door marked
"Reception." Seated behind a desk in the center of the tastefully
decorated lobby was an attractive grey haired woman. She glanced
at Jericho as he entered and then got up and moved around the
desk, extending her hand to him. "I'm Dolly Preston."

Jericho took her hand and was surprised by the firmness of her
grasp. It was almost like that of a man's.

"And I'm Jerry Smith," he said, a noticeable trace of
nervousness in his voice.

"Awfully glad to meet you, Jerry. Schuyler has certainly sung
your praises," and she smiled warmly. "Do have a seat. Mr. Moran
is busy, but it will only be for a few minutes." Then she returned to
her desk where she busied herself.

Jericho scrutinized Dolly Preston carefully. Both her manner of
dress and her hair style were impeccable and on both beautifully
manicured hands huge diamonds sparkled. At the moment, Jericho
did not realize that he'd just had the pleasure of meeting Paul
Moran's mistress of some twenty-five years, and one who wielded
more power than most men.

Suddenly one of the dark mahogany doors which lined the outer
office came flying open, and the tallest man that Jericho had ever
seen dipped his head slightly as he moved through the doorway and
into the reception room. He gave Jericho a brief glance and then
directed his attention to Dolly Preston, who looked up at him with
honest affection.

"Paul," she said as she rose gracefully from her chair and
touched his arm, "may I introduce you to Jerry Smith, Schuyler
Martin's friend."

Jericho was not prepared for the almost ear shattering voice that
filled the room, and for a moment was startled.

"Jerry Smith," the man almost roared. "Boy, am I glad to see
you," and he smothered Jericho's hand with his own and pumped
it vigorously. "Come on in." Then he turned back to Dolly,
"Make luncheon reservations at the club for noon," and he smiled.
"You're more than welcome to join us." Jericho saw the pleasure
in her answering smile.

"Certainly, Mr. Moran," and her dark eyes sparkled.

Paul Moran ushered Jericho into his spacious office, but one
that was so cluttered with papers and law books that it was difficult

to see a free chair.

Almost apologetically, he motioned Jericho toward a chair stacked high.

"Toss that stuff on the floor," he ordered, but with obvious good humor. "You can sure tell that I need someone to pick up after me," and his laughter was hearty. Then he sat down and leaned back comfortably in the over-sized leather chair, his eagle bright eyes scrutinizing the young man who sat opposite him.

"So you want to be a lawyer?" The look he gave Jericho seemed almost ferocious.

"Yes, sir," Jericho responded emphatically. "That's been the one area that I've always been interested in," and he paused. "That, and our government."

"You're at Notre Dame now," Paul Moran stated. "Schuyler mentioned Harvard Law. Right?"

"That's correct. I've two more years at Notre Dame and then hopefully I'll be accepted at Harvard."

At his statement Paul Moran broke into laughter.

"You won't have to worry about that, my boy, if Schuyler Martin is your friend."

"But my grades are excellent," Jericho protested, and it was then that Paul Moran realized that there was a defensive side to his nature.

"I'm certain that they are," he acceded. Then he leaned across the desk and looked Jericho directly in the eyes. "Let me tell you something, young man. It take power and money to become anything in this day and age, and don't ever forget it."

At that moment Jericho's spirit took a plunge. He wanted desperately to make it on his own ability, but he had to admit that Moran was right, for he wouldn't be sitting opposite this obviously powerful and influential man if it hadn't been for Schuyler Martin.

The ringing of the intercom shattered the tenseness of the moment.

"Yes, Dolly," Paul Moran said.

"Who? Hell yes, I'll talk to him. Put him on." Then he turned to his guest. "One of my clients from Montana. It'll only take a minute."

Then he shouted into the instrument, "Stonewall, you old son of a gun, how the hell are you?" While he listened to the reply, a frown creased his brow and he ran his free hand nervously through his unruly mop of white hair.

"Who the hell told you that?" he bellowed. Again he listened.

"Well, I'll be God damned!", and for a moment his face fell and he looked as though he'd lost an important case.

"Tell you what, my friend, why don't you get your ass back here. In the meantime I'll call Washington and see if any of those frigging idiots are still there. Okay. See you Thursday," and he slammed down the phone muttering angrily at himself, "Damned incompetents." Then he picked up the phone again and said, "Get me Washington, and you know who."

He turend to Jericho. "Jerry, would you mind waiting in the lobby with Miss Preston? This is rather personal," and he laughed sardonically. "Then we'll head for the country club and have that lunch."

Dutifully, Jericho left Paul Moran's office and returned to the outer office where he took the same chair he'd vacated only a short time before. They hadn't even had the opportunity to discuss his summer job and he was sorely disappointed.

The minutes dragged by and occasionally he could hear Paul shouting at whomever was on the line. Jericho began to have second thoughts about if this was really the place for him.

Dolly saw his disheartened look and moved to the chair beside him. "He's not always this way," she said softly. "Sometimes when things don't fall into place, he erupts," and she laughed. "I've been with Paul for twenty-five years now," and a trace of wistfulness was discernible in her voice, "and he's really a very kind and gentle man. You'll see."

At that moment the door to Paul Moran's office opened and once again he stooped to avoid hitting his head on the door frame as he joined Dolly and Jericho.

"Sorry about all that commotion, Jerry," he apologized, but rather half-heartedly it seemed to Jericho. "You'll find out soon enough that being a lawyer has its bad times, too."

Then he looked at Dolly. "I'm ready. How about you two?"

Dolly glanced at her wristwatch. "We'll just be on time," and she returned to her desk and picked up her bag as Paul Moran retrieved her coat from the brass hall tree and then helped her into it.

"Thanks, Paul," she said, and the look she gave him was one filled with love and devotion.

During the Christmas holidays the Wichita Country Clubs' dining room was decorated festively and to Jericho it looked like a winter wonderland. At the far end of the dining room was a table complete with silver bowl filled with egg nog liberally spiked with rum and surrounded by sufficient delicacies to whet anyone's appetite.

After they were seated and their luncheon orders had been taken, Dolly excused herself and moved to the table at the far end of the room. There she skillfully filled three crystal cups with egg nog and then proceeded to select numerous tidbits. She placed all of these on a tray and returned to their table. Jericho had watched with interest her gracious manners as she greeted other guests, and he saw several of the men greet her with obvious affection. It was apparent she was well liked.

Paul Moran had observed Jericho as he watched Dolly. "She's a wondeful woman," he volunteered, almost as though the young man had asked about her.

Jericho nodded in agreement, but remained silent.

"When do you finish up this spring?"

"The early part of June. I should be home no later than the 15th," and he looked at his host questioningly.

"That'll suit me just fine. Take a few days to get yourself used to Kansas again," and he laughed. "Then report to Dolly. She'll have your assignment."

"But I'd hoped to work with you, sir."

The older man laughed. "I'll try to find something interesting. You might find working on Pride Oil's project of interest," and he glanced at Jericho shrewdly.

"You mean *the* Pride Oil Company?"

"You bet. I'm Stonewall Barton's trusted lieutenant. He's a native of Kansas boy, you know, and has little use for anyone born somewhere else. You could sure help me out on that one."

"I'll look forward to it," Jericho replied, now feeling elated.

The balance of the luncheon was dominated by Paul Moran and the many acquaintances who stopped by their table to wish both he and Dolly a happy holiday season.

The conversation in the large dining room seemed to reach an almost frantic pitch at times, but suddenly, and without warning, it became still, and Jericho stopped eating and looked around, curious about what had happened.

He saw that Dolly had turned pale and that his host's face was twisted and angry.

Then he saw the scene which had attracted everyone's attention. He, too, was appalled by the performance of an older woman who'd taken the center of the stage and was obviously very drunk. Two men were pleading with her to leave, but to no avail, and she laughed at them.

"Shall we leave?" Paul asked Dolly.

"Please."

"We're sorry about this, Jerry, but it's time that we got out of here."

As they walked through the dining room, the woman spotted them and began to yell even more wildly. "There he is," she screamed, pointing at Paul Moran. "There he is, with that whore of his."

Without looking back, Paul took Dolly and Jericho firmly by the arms and they moved quickly through the door of the country club.

By the time they'd reached Paul Moran's Cadillac in the parking lot, Dolly Preston was in tears. Jericho got into the back seat and Paul helped his companion into the front. Then he hurried around the car to enter the driver's seat. He turned on the ignition and careened out of the parking lot like a shot from a cannon, with the rear end of the vehicle sliding from one side of the road to the other.

After slipping and sliding down the ice covered road for what seemed an eternity to Jericho, Paul Moran slowed the car. When he found a suitable turnoff, he pulled the car into it and let it idle. Without showing any noticeable concern for his guest's presence, he pulled Dolly into his arms.

"Darling," he said, "I'm so sorry," and held her gently as she sobbed almost uncontrollably against his chest. Then a stern look came over his face. "I promise you one thing, that's never going to happen again," and his eyes held a wicked gleam.

"Paul," Dolly whispered, "when is this ever going to end?" and she looked up into his face which was now filled with tenderness.

"After today, my love, and damn the Catholic Church. I'm filing for a divorce."

Jericho was shocked by his words.

"But she's fought you every time ? Dolly mourned sadly.

"She won't stand a chance this performance today was the last straw.''

It was then that he came to the reali. present and had heard every word.

"Oh, my God," Paul stammered, ... obviously embarrassed when he turned to face the young man.

"I'm sorry as hell that you had to see all this, Jerry. Please accept my apology.''

Jericho merely nodded, his face without expression.

Then Dolly turned and put her hand out to him. He took it, but rather hesitantly.

"Please don't judge us," she whispered softly, her tear-filled eyes pleading with him.

Jericho smiled at the distraught woman and pressed her hand gently, remembering Mother Jean Marie saying, *Judge not, lest ye be judged*.

"That I do not do," he replied, and once again pressed her hand.

"Thank you, Jerry. We'll never forget your understanding," the older man said, and then turned to begin the last leg of the drive back to Wichita.

Their goodbyes were brief and rather formal, and then Jericho got into the Chevy and headed back for the farm. He'd seen yet another side of how rotten life could treat people, and he found himself feeling truly sorry for the big man who'd so far been unable to claim the woman that he loved.

When Jericho arrived back at the farm late that afternoon, the excitement that he felt was difficult to conceal. Both his parents were pleased that his attitude had obviously taken a turn for the better. The Monsignor, they thought, certainly had a way with people.

Following dinner that evening, Jericho joined in the ceremony of decorating the Christmas tree, and then Martha produced a plate of her delicious fruit cake and served it with rich, hot chocolate. As they gathered around the fireplace an aura of peace surrounded them but unfortunately for Martha and Jacob it was to end rather abruptly.

d finished with their refreshments and the remnants
cleared away, Jericho took a seat which faced them,
vousness apparent.

Mother, Dad," he began, smiling gently. "I know that you're
both curious about where I went today," and he looked at them
with expectancy.

"Sure are," Jacob responded eagerly, and Martha smiled in
agreement.

Now that he had their attention, Jericho cleared his throat and
began. "I had an appointment with Paul Moran."

The moment he uttered the name Paul Moran, a look of horror
crossed both their faces.

"Paul Moran?" Jacob sputtered. "Why would you see that
scoundrel?"

"I've accepted a job as a law clerk in his office for the summer,"
Jericho stated emphatically.

"You've what?" Martha exclaimed. "He's got that woman of
his in his office. My goodness, Jericho, whatever has come over
you?"

His heart sank and although he knew that he should have
expected this reaction, he continued doggedly on. "Schuyler
Martin, my roommate's father, made the arrangements for me to
see him, and I've accepted Mr. Moran's offer. Putting all
personalities aside," and his gaze swept from one to the other,
"Mr. Moran is a good lawyer and highly respected in political
circles. His personal life happens to be his own business," and he
turned to Martha, his look cold. "If I learned one thing from
Mother Jean Marie, it was *judge not*."

"But we'd hope that you'd changed your mind," Jacob began,
but Jericho interrupted him almost rudely.

"No, I haven't changed my mind. I want to be a lawyer. There's
a lot of work ahead for me," and his eyes held a gleam of
excitement. "I'll be part of our government someday and hopefully
you'll be proud of me. I'm sorry that you feel as you do, but you're
both dead wrong about Mr. Moran and Ms. Preston. I had lunch
with them today and she's a very charming lady."

Martha turned pale for her son was siding with, in her
estimation, a fallen woman.

Jacob stared at his son long and hard and realized that deeply seated within him was a determination that he'd undoubtedly inherited from his real parents and which was now just becoming evident.

Again Martha started to protest but Jacob silenced her with a single glance and got up to poke aimlessly at the logs which caused the low burning fire to burst into flames. Then he turned to face Jericho and his wife. "You're a grown man, Jericho," he said and his smile was now kind. "What you do with your life is up to you," and he paused as Martha looked at him in astonishment for Jericho, she thought, was falling into a life fraught with degredation. "We'll be proud of you, no matter what," Jacob continued, and tears misted his eyes. "You possess good sound judgment, and I'm certain that whatever you tackle, you'll prove to be a success."

It was Jericho's turn to register surprise and he jumped to his feet and hurried to Jacob.

"Thanks, Dad," he said softly. "Your confidence in me is the best Christmas present I could possibly have," and the two men embraced. Martha had watched the emotion-packed moment feeling quite left out, but Jericho moved quickly to where she sat and knelt down beside her.

"Mother," he said quietly, "will you give me your blessings?" The look in his dark, expressive eyes was almost pleading.

For a moment Martha hesitated and then in a sudden burst of emotion she pulled him to her and held him while tears coursed down her cheeks. When she released him, a tender smile touched her lips and Jericho felt elated.

"My son, your father and I have always thought that we knew what was best for you," and she shrugged slightly as though to dismiss the thought, "but only you know what will bring you happiness and fulfillment. If it's the law and politics, then we'll support you every step of the way."

Jericho gave an audible sigh of relief and then they all burst into laughter for the problem which had loomed before them had now been solved. Once more harmony existed within the Smith family.

Later that evening when Jericho went to his room, he knelt before the small altar, crossed himself, and began his prayer of thanksgiving while the candle's glow glimmered softly in the darkness of the night.

13

Jericho promptly wrote a note to Schuyler Martin and thanked him for his assistance in securing his job with Paul Moran. When Brandy's father received the letter, he knew in his heart that this young man was destined to become his protege.

The balance of the school term seemed to almost fly, and soon Jericho and Brandy returned to their respective homes for the summer months. Jericho couldn't wait to begin his work in Paul Moran's office. Even though his parents had now accepted his decision, on occasion he discerned a certain wistfulness in their attitude, and more especially so when young Father Pignelli officiated at the Mass. At times he felt almost guilty, as though he'd wronged them, but he was determined to continue with the course he'd chosen.

That summer, Paul Moran introduced Jericho to Pride Oil. For the first few weeks Paul inundated him with stacks of manila legal folders, all of which dealt with the company's oil and mining operations. Although Jericho couldn't, as yet, comprehend much of the legal maneuvers involved, he dutifully made a list of questions in the hope that he would be supplied with understandable answers at some time in the future.

That was also the summer that Paul Moran's suit for divorce was heard. As he'd stated on that cold December day in Jericho's presence, he'd filed for divorce at once. He had moved out of the big house where he'd spent so many miserable years and into an apartment, but not with Dolly Preston as most had anticipated.

Unfortunately for Jericho, he was subpoenaed to testify as a corroborating witness to the dreadful scene that Paul's wife had created at the country club during the Christmas holidays. It was after he'd appeared in the divorce court that Jericho quickly came to the decision that the divorce mill was not his game. However, Paul Moran was extremely grateful for his testimony, which proved to be a factor in helping him secure the divorce that he'd long wanted.

A short time after his divorce became final, Paul and Dolly Preston were quietly married and Jericho stood beside him as his best man in the judge's chambers while they repeated their vows. In a way, he felt a sense of gratification at having been of help to his mentor, but his own religious conviction about the sanctity of marriage kept creeping into his mind, and this fact bothered him.

At the reception following the private wedding, a goodly number of the prominent citizens of Wichita came to pay their respects, and also one Stonewall Barton. Jericho, at the insistence of Paul and Dolly, had accompanied them to the club, and that was where he'd first met the man who now owned Pride Oil. He'd arrived unaccompanied in a Cadillac limousine, and when he stepped from the interior of the luxurious automobile he resembled a cowboy from out of the Golden West.

Although Stonewall Barton's mode of dress was definitely a surprise, he was even less prepared for the man's soft voice and gentle mannerisms. Paul had introduced Jericho to him as his 'right hand man,' and although he knew that he had a long way to go, he was complimented. When he and Barton had shaken hands, Stonewall had looked at the handsome youth who stood before him long and hard, and a flicker of interest appeared in his eyes.

"Jerry Smith," he'd repeated, his laughter subdued. "Quite a common name, Smith."

Jericho smiled, aware that he meant no offense. "Yes sir," he replied, "but it will be easy to remember," and his dark eyes brightened as he returned the older man's smile.

"Paul tells me that you're the one whose been helping him with my company's legal matters, right?"

Jericho nodded, but now felt ill at ease, as he had little idea of what his employer might have told this very important client.

"I guess you could say that, sir," he'd replied modestly.

"Well, just what have you learned about Pride?"

Jericho had spent endless hours delving into Pride Oil's history from the time of its inception by Joe Walowski up to and including Stonewall Barton's takeover. He was also aware from a few sketchy comments that Paul had made that Barton had married Julia Walowski, Joe's daughter, and that it had been a marriage of convenience, on his part at least. When Joe Walowski had passed on, his son-in-law had inherited a controlling interest in Pride, and from that day forward he'd built the company into one of the nation's largest oil conglomerates.

"I know the history, Mr. Barton," Jericho replied.

"So you know all about Joe Walowski and me?" Barton countered.

"Yes sir, I do." Then he paused, and when he continued he looked straight into the older man's eyes. "I think that you've brought Pride Oil to the forefront, and I admire you for that."

Stonewall Barton had listened intently to his youthful companion and was struck by the poise that the young man obviously possessed.

"Well, thanks, Mr. Smith," he replied rather formally, a slight smile touching his lips, and then placed a friendly hand on Jericho's shoulder.

"You're quite welcome, sir. I believe in giving credit where it's due. Being honest, I find, causes very few problems."

Stonewall Barton laughed. "You sound like an idealist," and he glanced at Jericho appraisingly to note his reaction.

"I am," Jericho replied with obvious pride, and then his words spilled out. "I believe in the law, in justice, and in my country, and I intend to do everything legally within my power," and he glanced for a moment at the man whose interest he'd aroused, "to help the poor, the downtrodden and the illiterate."

"Whew! That's quite a tall order," Stonewall remarked.

"I feel that I came into the world with this to do," Jericho replied.

"What does your family think of your goals?"

"At first they insisted that I become a priest," Jericho said, "but that wasn't for me." His look became thoughtful. "You see, my beginning have left some questions in my mind."

"Questions?" Stonewall Barton asked, his interest now becoming apparent.

Suddenly Jericho stopped speaking and his smile was apologetic. "Oh, it's nothing," and he gave a wave of his hand as though in dismissal.

"But I'm really interested."

However, Jericho withdrew, for he found this stranger's curiosity much too personal, even though he'd inadvertently invited it.

"I've already taken up too much of your time, Mr. Barton," he said politely, "and I see that Mr. Moran's signalling. Please excuse me."

They shook hands warmly and then Jericho hurried away while Stonewall Barton stared after him, wondering why he'd refused to reveal the problem that seemed to bother him.

Jericho's acceptance to Harvard Law School came late in his Junior year at Notre Dame, and he was overjoyed when the registered letter arrived.

"Brandy, I've been accepted," he shouted, which was totally out of character for him.

Brandy smiled at his friend with affection. It couldn't have happened to anyone more deserving than Jerry. He was already aware that he was headed for Yale to work toward his Masters as his entry into the prestigous Ivy League School had been bought and paid for by his father, a fact which he slightly resented, for he knew that Jerry had made it to Harvard by his own accomplishments.

"Bully for you," and he gave Jerry a bear hug. "We'll both be close to my home stomping grounds, and I'll take no excuses from you about spending an occasional weekend with the family and me."

"I'll see what I can work out but there's still plenty of time. I wish that it were this coming fall instead of a year off."

"So you want to wish your life away," Brandy replied and cocked his head to one side to look at his friend quizzically.

"Not really, but I feel as though I've learned all that I can here."

"Don't let our dear faculty hear you say that!" Brandy admonished almost sternly, although there was a hint of a smile on his lips.

"I know," Jericho conceded, knowing that his senior year should be the highlight of his college life.

Much to his surprise, his last year at Notre Dame was one that he'd long remember with fond memories. At Brandy's insistence he'd campaigned for the office of Student Body President and was ultimately elected, even though it was a hard fought battle and his opponents were not easy marks. The first thrill of a real honest-to-goodness campaign had caused him to come alive, and he found himself almost infected with the idea.

"I may run for public office someday," he'd announced to Brandy one evening as they were rehashing the election.

"Really?" his friend had replied. "You've always seemed so hesitant, and I sure had to push you into this one."

"It's conceivable that I didn't fully realize how exciting it can be," Jericho replied. "You know, Brandy, I really feel in my element now," and his eyes sparkled with excitement.

"Well, how about that for the small town kid?" Brandy said laughingly. "Just wait 'til I tell my father. He loves a good campaign himself."

It wasn't long before Schuyler Martin heard the news about the campaign and Jericho's election. He immediately sent off a hand written congratulatory note requesting that he let him know his reaction to his first 'political' venture.

The invitation to confide in Schuyler Martin was one that Jericho cherished. Shortly after he received it, he drafted a letter to him relating in minute detail the campaign strategy that they'd used, and also giving due credit to Brandy's part. When he'd finished the letter he read it to his friend, who voiced surprise.

"Boy, you remember every little detail. It's obvious that you'd be good at this, old buddy," and then he said quietly, "you know, my Dad will probably work on you some day to go into politics."

"Think so?" Jericho had questioned. "But that's way off. He'll undoubtedly have forgotten about me by that time."

"Wanna bet?"

Jericho looked at Brandy sharply and saw the seriousness of his expression. "You really mean it, don't you?"

"I know my father. He's had his eye on you from the very beginning," and his look became a trifle somber. "Neither Sky nor I seem to have a flair for the political scene," he added, sounding almost apologetic.

"Not everyone has the same interests, and Sky's happy with his teaching. At least your father and mother recognized where your abilities were and let you follow them. You have that to be thankful for."

"I suppose you're right," Brandy conceded, and the discussion was over.

The Smith and Martin families came together for the first time the following year at Jericho's and Brandy's graduation from Notre Dame. Although the two couples were vastly different in intellectual pursuits, Schuyler Martin, always the diplomat, made the Smiths feel right at home.

Kate Martin, at the urging of her husband, had accompanied Martha Smith on a tour of the campus and as time passed Kate found herself liking this plain, solid citizen of the middlewest, although her own memories of the days that she'd spent in Kansas were largely hidden away in her subconscious. As the two women made their way through the spacious grounds, out of curiosity, Kate brought up the subject of Jericho.

"My husband certainly thinks highly of your son," she said, and this remark brought a pleased smile to Martha's face.

"Why, thank you. He's been a real joy to Jacob and me. We had waited such a long time for a child."

"Waited?" Kate asked.

Martha looked at her in surprise. "Didn't you know that Jerry is adopted?"

"No. I hadn't any idea."

Martha smiled. "We haven't told many people other than our close friends. He couldn't mean more to us if he had been our own."

Kate nodded in understanding. "Was he a baby when you adopted him?"

Martha shook her head. "No. He was almost five."

"That surprises me," Kate said and frowned. "Why wasn't he adopted when he was younger?"

"It's a long story."

"I'd like to know."

Martha glanced at her watch. "I'll have to make it short, we don't have much time." She began the story of how they had found their son.

As Martha's story slowly unfolded, Kate was suddenly filled with alarm and it seemed almost as though she were living the final letter that she had written to Mother Jean Marie. How can this be happening? she thought. *My son* Jerry Smith? Yet she realized that when she had first set eyes on him, she had had some degree of apprehension.

Then Martha spoke the confirming words. "Jerry's mother had died and the Mother Superior at the convent in Staley placed him for adoption."

Kate turned pale and she wiped her brow although the afternoon was cool.

Martha glanced at her. "Are you feeling alright?" she asked with concern.

"I suddenly felt faint. Too much excitement for one day," and she smiled. Then added. "Thanks for telling me about Jerry." She paused, knowing that she could never reveal what she had just learned. "Tell you what Martha," she said softly, "I'll tell no one, not even Schuyler. This will be our secret."

Martha Smith looked at Kate and smiled. "Thanks," then she looked directly into her companion's eyes. "You know, his name isn't really Jerry."

"Oh," Kate said.

"His given name is Jericho."

A chill of apprehension swept over Kate Martin and she quickly rose from the bench were they had rested and brushed at her skirt as Martha laboriously got to her feet. Then the two women returned to join the others in the final festivities of that very important and revealing graduation day.

While Kate and Martha were gone, Schuyler directed his attention to Jacob Smith. He was a true artist at drawing people out of their shells and he soon had Jacob talking about the farm and its operation, but more importantly they talked about his son.

"I want you to know, Jacob, that I'm as proud of Jerry as you are,'' Schuyler had said, and his compliment brought a pleased smile to his companion's lips.

"We appreciate that, Mr. Martin. He's a good boy, but rather strong-willed at times."

"Really? How's that?"

"Oh, he insists on becoming a lawyer and we'd hoped that he'd enter the priesthood. But his mother and I have accepted his decision." Then his eyes sparkled. "Whatever he does, we'll stand behind him and be proud of him."

"Spoken like a true father," Schuyler replied and they had both laughed.

After the final festivities, the Smiths and Martins, along with their families, returned to their respective homes.

Jericho was due to report to Paul Moran's office and Brandy was set to have one last summer fling with Sky on a trip into the wilds of Mexico. They had invited Jericho to accompany them but he had declined as he knew that it was far more important to continue with his legal apprenticeship.

As soon as they had returned to Wichita, Jericho headed straight for Paul Moran's office. When he entered the office, Dolly Moran greeted him with a hug and a kiss, which he found a bit embarrassing, and Paul shook his hand so hard that his arm started to ache. It was obvious that they were both glad to have him back.

"So you're now a college graduate?" Paul Moran boomed in his deep bass voice. "Congratulations, Jerry."

"Thanks, Paul. You too, Dolly. Now, what have you lined up for me to do? Anything more on Pride?"

Paul laughed. "You seem to be as hung up on Pride Oil as Stonewall Barton is hung up on you."

Jericho's look was puzzled. "What do you mean?"

"Oh, every time Stonewall calls from Montana he asks about you. I guess you really impressed him."

"That's nice to hear," Jericho replied modestly and moved to the cubicle where his desk was located. When he entered he found the desk top empty with the exception of a single white envelope.

"Where's my work?" he asked. "Don't you need me?"

"Of course we do. Now why don't you check out the envelope?" Paul urged.

Dutifully, Jericho retrieved the envelope from the desk and proceeded to break open the seal. It was a graduation card and he smiled, but when he opened it to read the message he found a key taped to the inside.

He turned toward the Morans whose faces were now wreathed in smiles.

"What gives?" he asked.

"A little graduation present, that's all," Dolly volunteered.

"Could this be the key to the executive washroom?" Jericho asked.

Both Paul and Dolly broke into laughter.

" 'Fraid not, son. Come on over by the window," and they moved together to stand before it.

"See that white convertible parked in the loading zone?" Paul asked and pointed to the street below.

Jericho nodded. "Sure, I see it, but what's that got to do with me?"

Paul Moran turned and placed his hands on Jericho's shoulders. "That, my friend, belongs to you."

For a moment Jericho was speechless as he looked from one to the other. "You're not kidding me, are you?" he finally managed.

Dolly touched his arm gently. "We don't kid about things like that. The car belongs to you, with our love," her voice was choked with emotion.

Jericho stared in astonishment at his two friends and then laughed aloud. "My own car!" he shouted, but then he became serious. "You're not trying to lure me back here to practice law, are you?"

Paul Moran smiled, for Jericho was already beginning to realize that at times people used you if they were smart enough to discover any of your weak spots.

"You're under no obligation to return here, my boy. Both Dolly and I owe you for helping us through a very trying time, and we wanted to express our appreciation." Then he added softly, "We care about you, you know."

"I don't know what to say," Jericho finally managed.

"Well, how about taking us for a spin before the Chief of Police relinquishes my hold on the loading zone?"

"Let's go," Jericho replied, and together they swept out of the office.

Jericho took the wheel and Paul and Dolly crowded into the front seat beside him.

"Would you mind terribly if we went out to the farm?"

He saw Dolly wince slightly, but she quickly recovered her poise.

"To the farm it is," she said, and then she took Paul's hand to provide her with the strength that she knew she'd need when she came face to face with Martha and Jacob Smith.

When the sleek white convertible turned into the drive at the farm, Martha was standing at the kitchen window. She glanced at it only briefly, assuming that in all probability it was a traveler who'd lost his way. She wiped her hands on her apron, smoothed her hair and then opened the back door. The sight which met her eyes was one that she'd not anticipated.

Jericho waved jauntily and gave her a smile, then got out of the car and came bounding up the steps.

"Whatever do you think you're doing, bringing those people to our home?" Martha whispered before he had a chance to explain.

"Mother, please be nice," Jericho said pleadingly. "Mr. and Mrs. Moran gave me the car as a graduation present, and I asked them to come with me so you and Dad could share it with us."

"I don't care to meet them. It's bad enough having you work in that office," Martha hissed, and then she saw Jacob coming out of the barn and toward the house. "Just you wait 'til your father gets here."

Dolly and Paul had been unable to hear the conversation which had transpired between Jericho and his mother, but from the look that Martha Smith had given them it was obvious that she was greatly displeased with their presence. They both sat silently and watched as Jacob joined his wife and son on the porch.

Before Jericho could start to explain, his mother began. "Jacob, those Morans gave Jericho that car and he's had the nerve to bring them out here," she sputtered.

Jacob turned and looked at the sparkling white automobile in the driveway and its occupants. Then he turned back to his wife and son.

"Now, let's get this straight," and he directed his attention to Jericho. "They gave you the car?"

"If you'd just let me explain," Jericho began, but Martha

interrupted.

"They're trying to get a hold on him, that's what."

"Just wait a minute," Jacob replied and he looked at her sharply. "They haven't any hold on Jericho."

Martha stared at her husband in disbelief. She almost went into shock when Jacob proceeded down the steps to the car and stopped beside Paul Moran.

Jacob was quite aware that Paul and Dolly Preston had married, and that Jericho had been some small part of it. However, he'd also taken the time to talk with Monsignor O'Connell, who'd told him briefly about the miserable life that Paul Moran had endured for so many years, and he now understood, at least to a small degree, the reason behind his seeking another woman to complete his life.

Jericho hurried after his father, leaving his mother standing alone with a definite frown of displeasure on her face.

"Mr. Moran, Mrs. Moran," Jacob said politely when he reached the car, "let me introduce myself," and he extended his hand to Paul. "I'm Jacob Smith."

Paul Moran gripped the work-worn hand firmly and gazed into the eagle bright eyes that bored into his. He'd known from the onset that the Smiths were staunch members of the Catholic church, just as he had been, and that they didn't believe in divorce. It was obvious to him that Jacob was making an effort to show them some semblance of courtesy.

"We're happy that we've finally gotten to meet Jerry's family," and he glanced up at the porch where Martha sat huddled in a chair, her face averted as though she were ignoring them. "We think a great deal of your son. He's been a real help to me these past summers."

Then Dolly spoke up. "You should be proud of Jerry. He'll go far," and she gave Jacob a dazzling smile.

At their words of praise, a smile creased Jacob's face and the stiffness he'd first exhibited now vanished.

"Thanks. We're mighty glad to hear that."

Then he stepped back to inspect the shining motor car. "Mighty nice automobile," he said admiringly, and proceeded to walk around it, even going so far as to kick one of the tires.

"Dad," Jericho approached him hesitantly. "Would you ride back to town with us and bring the Chevy home?"

"Be glad to. Where do you want me to sit?"

Paul and Dolly got out of the front seat and entered the back, while Jacob and Jericho settled in the front.

Martha Smith watched with eyes of bitterness and envy as Jericho backed out of the drive and headed down the dirt lane toward the main highway. No one had bothered to look in her direction, and she got up from her chair and entered the house, slamming the door behind her to vent her anger. In due time, Jacob Smith would surely pay!

14

The summers that Jericho had spent in Paul Moran's law offices proved to be a great benefit when he entered Harvard. On many occasions in the past, he and Paul Moran had held long discussions which had covered many aspects of the law, and Jericho, being a voracious reader, devoured just about every law book that Paul owned.

The last summer that Jericho served as a law clerk he'd informed Paul and Dolly of his intention to attend summer sessions in order to complete his law studies early. This announcement didn't come as much of a surprise, and in fact, they'd urged him to do so. However, his parents hadn't proved to be all that enthusiastic.

While he was attending Harvard, he and Brandy Martin kept in touch with each other. On occasion, they would meet in New York for the weekend. These little jaunts usually consisted of blind dates with uninteresting girls and partying until all hours. He'd simply endured this type of life to please his friend.

On one such weekend, Brandy had told him somewhat casually that Elizabeth had asked about him on numerous occasions, and had even suggested that he be invited to Georgetown. Jericho was pleased. He knew that she was a precocious young woman and although very beautiful and charming, he felt quite unprepared to take on the innuendoes she invariably inflicted on him.

Schuyler Martin had paid him a visit while he was at Harvard, and they'd enjoyed dinner and a pleasant evening. Schuyler had expressed an interest in Jericho's future plans. Jericho had very carefully weighed the question as he knew that he owed Martin a debt, but he owed an even larger one to Paul and Dolly.

"Why do you ask?" he countered.

"Just curious. Paul sings your praises constantly, and I've often wondered if you intend to join his law firm."

"I'm not quite ready to take that step, Mr. Martin. I do appreciate the help that you've given me," and he looked Schuyler squarely in the eye, "but I owe Paul and Dolly a lot." He sighed, "They've become a second family to me."

"I can appreciate your feelings, Jerry, but I could see to it that you come to Washington," he replied, hoping against hope that by dangling before him the fascination of politics and government it would change his mind.

"I'm not quite ready for the Washington scene, either," Jericho replied and laughed slightly. "You know, I'm the 'cowboy from Wichita,' and besides, I owe my allegiance to the Morans." Then he paused. "For the present, at least."

"Just thought I'd ask," Schuyler responded and sighed deeply. "I'm certain that Paul will be delighted to hear you'll be back."

"I hope so. I'm planning on telling them when he and Dolly come for graduation."

"Will your family be present?"

Jericho shook his head. "No, I'm sorry to say that's not possible. You see, Dad had a slight stroke a few months back and we've hired someone to take over the farming."

"I'm sorry about your father. I enjoyed meeting him."

"Thanks. They both appreciate the courtesy that you showed them."

"That was nothing, Jerry. I'm just glad that we got the chance to become acquainted," and then he continued, "would you mind if I joined the Morans?"

"Mind? Of course not. But what about Brandy?"

"Oh, we'll be at Yale, too."

"Good, then I'll look forward to seeing you and the family again."

"Is there any chance that you might consider paying us a visit in Georgetown before going home?"

Jericho laughed. "I've already received my orders from that son of yours. I'll be there."

As the two men left the dining room they shook hands warmly and Schuyler Martin watched with continuing interest as Jerry Smith left the hotel lobby. He'd learned from their conversation exactly what he'd wanted to know. It was obvious that his young friend possessed a streak of loyalty that he'd found wanting in so many others, and one that the Party badly needed.

Following the commencement exercises at Harvard, the Morans hosted a lavish party in Jericho's honor. The Martins had arrived en masse, having come directly from New Haven where Brandy received his Masters Degree. Young Elizabeth Martin had seen fit to take leave of the exclusive girls school that she attended in Washington and was also present. The only people lacking were Jericho's parents and Sky Martin, Jr.

Elizabeth's budding maturity was now becoming even more evident. She found every opportunity available to be near Jericho, and at times he felt as though a small puppy was trailing him. Finally, in sheer desperation, he'd asked Brandy to join him in the men's lounge.

"Something up, Jerry?" his friend had asked.

"You don't mean that you haven't noticed your sister? God, Brandy, she hangs on me like I'm some kind of celebrity, or one of her movie idols. It's getting to be damned embarrassing."

Brandy was amused by the obvious discomfort of his friend.

"Just wait until you come visit us."

"For the life of me I don't know if I can stand it." Then his look became serious. "Please don't misunderstand me. Elizabeth's a lovely young girl and I do like her, but my God, she falls all over me," and he blushed. "I feel sorry for Kate and Schuyler in the next few years," and he shook his head.

"Don't be. Elizabeth is already a very capable young woman, and is very sure of whom and what she wants. You oughta' see some of the young guys that have already fallen by the wayside."

"You've gotta be kidding."

"No. It's true."

"She's also spoiled as hell," Jerry replied heatedly, hoping that his remark wouldn't hurt Brandy's feelings.

"We know it. Dad, Sky and I have all had a big hand in that, but we excuse ourselves because she's the only young female in the family. Still, she's got a good level head on her shoulders."

"I hope so. I already feel a bit sorry for whomever she marries. She'll surely be a hand-full."

"That's where you're wrong, my friend. Elizabeth will make a wonderful wife. Under the facade that she exhibits to the world she's kind, loving and loyal, and the man who is fortunate enough to claim her for his wife will never be sorry."

"Quite a speech," Jerry replied, "but then you know her far better than I do. Now, we'd better get back or they'll send out a search party."

As they started to leave the lounge, Brandy placed a hand on Jericho's arm.

"Jerry, please be nice to Elizabeth and show her a little attention. I know that she's young, but she idolizes you."

Jericho stared at his friend. "I can't for the life of me see why," and he shrugged his shoulders.

"Well, for one thing, old buddy, you've never talked down to her. For another, she knows that you respect women. And besides all that," he laughed, "you're handsome as hell."

"Oh, go to hell," Jericho retorted.

"Believe me, it's true," and then the look in Brandy's eyes became serious. "Just don't hurt her; that's all I ask."

"Have you ever known me to hurt any of the girls that I've ever dated?" Jericho replied coldly.

"No."

"Then why the hell would you think for a minute that I might begin with Elizabeth?"

"Because you're the one who could," and he paused. "I'm sorry, Jerry, I guess I've overstepped my bounds," and he opened the door.

"Wait a minute," Jericho protested. "I've no intention of leading your sister on. I'm not a cradle robber, for God's sake. Brandy, whatever's come over you?"

"Maybe it's because I'm a little jealous of the way she feels about you."

"Jealous? Of me? Oh, my God, that's really dumb." Jericho exclaimed.

"Perhaps it is. But you see, being the youngest son and next to Elizabeth, we've grown to be very close and I feel almost as though I'm her guardian."

"I can sure see 'big brother' coming out," Jericho said softly. "Tell you what. I respect how you feel, and you don't need to be concerned. Now then, let's get back to the party."

As soon as they reached the table, Elizabeth jumped up from her chair and moved toward them.

"Jerry," she said sweetly, "the orchestra's playing my favorite song. Won't you dance with me?"

Jericho knew that it would be rude to refuse her, and with a glance at Brandy as though to say "I told you so," he took Elizabeth by the hand and led her out onto the dance floor. When he placed his arm around her waist she nestled her head against his shoulder and then pressed her body close to him. For a moment he almost stopped, but then a feeling of desire crept over him, and as they moved in unison around the dance floor, neither speaking, he knew that someday, if he were fortunate, there could perhaps be something in the future for the two of them.

When the music stopped, he reluctantly let her go and then smiled down into her eager upturned face, now flushed with pleasure. Then, completely out of character, he bent and kissed her gently on the lips.

With interest, Brandy, Schuyler and Kate Martin had watched the romantic interlude taking place. Kate felt alarm; Schuyler was overjoyed; and Brandy smiled smugly, knowing that Elizabeth was in good hands.

After the party was over, Jericho returned to his small walk-up apartment. He'd already packed and shipped his books and extra clothing back to Wichita, and all that was left for him to do was to pack the remainder of his belongings and head for Georgetown and the week of vacation that he'd promised to spend with Brandy.

He threw himself down on the coverless bed and thought of the sudden desire that had swept over him when he'd held Elizabeth Martin in his arms. For a moment, he dreamed of holding her naked body against him until his loins began to ache.

"Shit," he said and jumped up from the bed as he pushed angrily at his growing erection. "I'm acting stupid."

Then he began to pull off his clothing and almost at a run, headed for the shower where he turned the cold water on full blast. Gradually, his desire waned, and as he began to dress in preparation for the drive to Washington, he realized that it would be necessary to watch himself around Elizabeth. Perhaps it was good that Brandy had told him of her feelings, for Elizabeth Martin had proved, beyond any doubt, that she was an extremely desirable young woman.

In his whole lifetime, Jericho had never been as lavishly entertained as by the Martins.

Kate, because of Jericho's impending visit, had seized the opportunity to accompany Emily Martin, Schuyler's mother, to Kansas City where she would assist the elderly woman in the opening of her summer residence. The thought of having to spend days with the young man she now knew was her son was mind boggling at best, and she still had to learn how to deal with the situation, without being too obvious to Schuyler and the family, of course.

Elizabeth was in her glory and took her mother's place at the dining room table. It was apparent that she was in total command of the household staff, and of her father and brothers as well, who bowed to almost her every wish.

Jericho watched with amusement at how easily she managed to have her way, but he also had to admire her, for when she requested a special favor it was in a sweet and compelling manner and he never once heard her complain if she were refused.

Her attitude toward Jericho proved much the same as on the previous occasions when they'd been together, but this time he discovered that she was not only beautiful, sexually desirable and charming, but that she was bright and talented as well.

The week of his holiday passed much too quickly and when it was time for him to head back to Kansas he left Georgetown with a degree of reluctance. He'd come to realize in that short a period of time that his own home life now appeared unimaginative and dull in comparison with the complex and interesting lives of the Martins.

Elizabeth Martin, with tears of regret in her eyes, had taken him aside for a private goodbye. "I do wish that you'd stay the whole summer," she'd whispered softly.

Jericho felt somewhat embarrassed by her obvious show of emotion, and although he'd found himself almost coming under her spell like her father and her brothers, he'd held back. He knew that Elizabeth was far too young for a man of twenty-five.

"We'll see each other from time to time," he'd offered in reply.

"But you'll be so far away," she'd protested. "And when you pass the Bar, you'll be practicing with Paul Moran," and a look of envy crept into her eyes.

"That's true, Elizabeth, but I'll undoubtedly be called upon to come to Washington on occasion for business, and you can be certain that I'll see all of you," he'd responded, failing to single her out.

"All of us?" she'd replied sharply.

"Why, of course."

"Goodbye, Jerry," she'd said abruptly and turned away and walked into the house, her head held proudly, and not once did she look back.

Brandy came plunging out of the house with the balance of his luggage and after he'd placed it in the trunk of the convertible, he turned to Jericho. "Did you say something to upset Elizabeth?"

Jericho shook his head.

"Then why the hell was she crying when I passed her in the hall?"

"Crying?"

"Yes. Crying," and Brandy took Jericho's arm in a vise-like grip.

"Brandy, I said nothing. I merely mentioned that if and when I returned to Washington I'd enjoy seeing all of you. Perhaps she took exception to the *all*," and he looked at his friend with a certain coolness. "Now, if you'd please take your hand off me, I need to get on my way."

"I'm sorry, Jerry, but she's crazy about you. Please accept my apology."

The two young men shook hands, and then, without saying another word, Jericho got into the white convertible, started the

motor, and with a smart salute and a smile, sped down the long
drive.

In her bedroom on the second floor Elizabeth Martin had
watched the man that she loved go out of her life once again.

"Damn," she said aloud. Then her face brightened. "I'll have
Daddy fix it," knowing full well that in time he would.

15

Upon his return to Wichita, Jericho discovered that Paul Moran had made arrangements for him to sit for the Bar examination within a week's time in Topeka, the State capitol.

When he'd asked Paul about the rush, his mentor had laughed. "Damn it, Jerry, we've waited a long time for you to be with us on a permanent basis," and he sighed. "To be honest with you, I've got more work then I can possibly handle. I hate to admit it, but I'm not getting any younger, and besides that, I'm the Democratic Party Chairman for Kansas."

With this explanation, Jericho accepted the arrangements he'd made and although he felt rather ill prepared, he went to Topeka with confidence that he would pass. The all day test was given in three sections of four hours each, and he was extremely grateful for the additional knowledge he'd gained by working in a law office. Late that night he returned home to await the results.

Within a week the letter arrived from Topeka announcing that he'd passed the Bar, and with exceedingly high marks. He'd shown the results to his parents who seemed pleased, but it was Paul and Dolly who were rightfully overjoyed. Jericho had also called Brandy to inform him, and when they'd finished speaking, Schuyler Martin had taken the phone.

"Congratulations, Jerry. We're all mighty proud of you."

"Thanks, Mr. Martin. I've waited impatiently for this day to come."

"We all have," Schuyler replied, and then paused. "Elizabeth would like to speak with you."

"Jerry," Elizabeth ventured, and it seemed almost shyly for her, "I'm very happy for you."

"Thanks, Elizabeth," he'd replied. "Knowing that you're interested means a lot," and then he suddenly became at a loss for words.

"Please come see us," she said, with an almost pleading tone in her voice.

"In due time. I'll say goodbye for now, and please thank your father and Brandy for their good wishes. I'll be in touch."

As he replaced the phone he could visualize Elizabeth Martin's plaintive look and then her brave smile. He shrugged slightly and placed her image in the recesses of his mind.

During the first few months of practicing law, Jericho played 'catch-up' for Paul Moran. He'd noticed that the older man seemed to tire more easily these days and in a private moment he mentioned it to Dolly.

"I was certain that you'd notice it in time, Jerry," she'd admitted. "Paul didn't want you to know, but he had a slight heart attack awhile back."

"But for God's sake why didn't he tell me?"

"It happened while you were in your last year at Harvard, and he didn't want to cause you any worry."

"He never even mentioned it when you came to graduation."

"I know," and she paused. "Paul's a very proud man, Jerry. He even swore his doctors to secrecy."

"How can I help, Dolly?"

"Paul's going to ask you to work with Stonewall Barton," and she gave an audible sigh. "Mr. Barton can be very difficult, and frankly, Paul doesn't need the stress."

"You mean that I'm going to take over Pride Oil?"

Dolly nodded. "When you have your feet set firmly on the ground."

For a moment Jericho was too surprised to comment. Finally he asked, "Has this change been mentioned to Mr. Barton?"

"Yes, Paul discussed it with him, and he seemed to be agreeable. But be prepared to have phone calls at all hours of the day and night. He's very demanding."

"Tell me, Dolly. Do you personally think that I'm ready for Stonewall Barton?"

Dolly looked at the bright young man with affection. "Yes, Jerry, you're ready. You know the law, and you are just as smart as he thinks he is. He's also taken a liking to you, and that's a help already."

"Is this to be kept a secret?"

"For the time being. Paul wants to tell you himself, but I felt I had to warn you. I don't like telling tales out of school, but sometimes it's necessary."

"I know, Dolly, and I appreciate your confiding in me. This gives me a lot to think about."

"Then I'll leave you alone," and without further comment she returned to her office.

When Paul Moran had informed him, and to Jericho it had seemed almost piously, that he'd be handling Pride Oil and the great Mr. Barton on his own, he'd soon discovered that Dolly Moran had spoken the unvarnished truth where the man was concerned.

He'd also been a guest in his home. There he'd met Julia Barton and their rather plain daughter Adele who, like her mother, weighed well over two-hundred pounds and resembled her father not in the least.

It had also been obvious that there had been little pride in Stonewall's voice when he'd introduced his family to him, and then he'd almost dismissed their presence at the dinner table, speaking to them only in a commanding fashion to get more of this or of that. Jericho had found his degrading performance repugnant, and he had waited impatiently for the day that he could return to Kansas.

When he did return, he went straight from the airport to the office.

As he entered the reception room, Dolly had taken one look at the dark scowl clouding Jericho's face, and for a moment she felt alarmed. Then, completely out of character, he slammed his heavy briefcase, which was filled with the files of Pride Oil, down on a chair and threw himself on the divan.

"Whatever's wrong?" Dolly asked as she moved from her desk to take a place beside him.

"That damn Stonewall Barton. That's what!"

Secretly, Dolly Moran had been more then a little afraid that the 'outlaw oilman,' as she and Paul had on occasion referred to him, would ask this fresh new lawyer to do something that in his mind would be viewed as completely unethical.

"Would you care to tell me?" Dolly asked, the sound of her voice soothing.

Jericho looked at her and smiled, and then reached over to take her hand. "Thank God you're here. I've even considered asking Paul to take me off of Pride," and he paused before continuing, "I'm sure that Barton's at least some part of the reason for Paul's heart attack." Then he whispered, "He's not here, is he?"

"No, Paul's attending a Party function, and he'll go straight home from there."

"Good. Then I'll tell you what this character wants."

"Go ahead," and the older woman settled back to listen.

"Have you ever met his family?" Jericho asked.

"No."

"Well, I did, and Dolly, he treats them like dirt. He's rude, degrading, overbearing . . . a real jerk," and he laughed wryly. "You know, even with all their money, I feel sorry for them."

"That's a shame, but perhaps there's a reason," she replied.

"Maybe so, but he should be grateful, for many of the oil wells that he now owns once belonged to Joe Walowski, his wife's father."

Dolly nodded in agreement, a thoughtful look on her face. "You know, Paul did tell me some time back that Stonewall had confided in him when he was on one of his rare drinking bouts. It seems he insinuated that there was a secret in his past, but Paul never told me what it was, and I didn't ask."

"Well, whatever it is, it's eating his guts out," Jericho replied caustically.

"Would you care to tell me what he's asked you to do?"

"He wants to be introduced to Schuyler Martin," Jericho replied, obviously disgusted.

"What's wrong with that?"

"Stonewall insisted that it's because of Martin's prominence in Washington, but he also insinuated that he'd be willing to pay a large sum of money in return for a favor."

Dolly laughed and Jericho looked at her in surprise.

"Sounds just like him," she said, and patted the confused young lawyer's hand.

"Stonewall's testing you, Jerry. He's probably sitting in his office waiting to see which shoe will drop. He dearly loves cat and mouse games."

"But why would he want to test me?"

"To be sure that you're honest. You see, he wants nothing to do with a shyster lawyer."

"Well, I'll be damned," Jericho muttered. "Do you think that he really wants to meet Schuyler Martin, or is that just another one of his games?"

"No, that's undoubtedly true. And if he happened to mention money, he's probably interested in helping provide the Party with funds for the coming election."

"I wish that Paul had told me some of this before I went out there," Jericho complained.

"Paul wanted you to make up your own mind about Stonewall. By the way, how do you feel about his business ability?"

"There's little doubt that he's smart as a whip; that's very obvious. It's the way he acts personally that concerns me the most, but then that's really not my business."

"Truer words were never spoken, Jerry," and Dolly glanced at her watch. "It's nearly six. Care to drive me home?"

"That I'd like to do," Jericho replied, got up from the divan, stretched, then picked up his briefcase and deposited it in his own office before rejoining Dolly.

"Taxi, lady?" he asked, and then gallantly opened the door.

"Thank you, sir," Dolly replied demurely her eyes sparkling. "Glad that you're home, Jerry," and she reached up and kissed him, and with that they left the business of law behind.

16

A few weeks after his return from Montana, Jericho had received a call from Washington. That morning he'd substituted for Paul Moran in court, and when he got back to the office he'd found the telephone message from Dolly with the word URGENT written on it in red. The number was familiar and he knew that it had to be Brandy.

Without hesitation he picked up the phone and dialed, hoping that there was nothing seriously wrong. However, the telephone rang only once, and when Brandy Martin answered it his words were obviously slurred.

"Brandy, this is Jerry. I just got your message, What's up, old friend?"

"Thank God you called, Jerry," Brandy mumbled, and then there was a long pause on the line as he made an attempt to clear his head.

"You still there, Brandy?" Jericho asked.

"Yeah, still here. I'm trying to get my wits together. Guess I've had too much to drink," he replied.

Jericho was now becoming concerned, as Brandy Martin had to his knowledge never used alcohol to excess.

"Okay. What's bothering you?"

"Jerry," he said almost plaintively, "You won't hate me, will you?"

"Why would I hate you? Just what have you done?"

"Well, it's this way," and he paused to cough loudly. Then Jericho could hear him taking a drink, and hoped that it was only water.

"What's this way?" he pursued.

"It's this girl."

"What girl?"

"The one that I've been dating. She's secretary to one of the Senators."

"So? What's wrong with that?"

"I got her knocked up. That's what's wrong!"

Jericho made no response while he let the words sink in.

"What do you expect me to do about it?" Jericho replied curtly, each word cutting like a knife.

"I need to get out of this mess, and you're a lawyer. I don't love her or want to marry her, and she's threatening to tell the POST if I don't."

Blackmail Jericho thought, but in a way he felt that his friend just might deserve it.

"Were you her first?" he asked.

Brandy laughed. "Hell, no! She's far from being virgin territory, if that's what you're refering to."

Jericho gave a sigh of relief, but he knew that the tactics he might be forced to use would be extremely distasteful as far as his own moral standards were concerned.

"Before I promise you anything, I'll have to talk with Paul Moran; then, hopefully I can get away and come to Washington. In the meantime just hold on, and for God's sake try to keep her from talking." Then in disgust he added, "Your family certainly doesn't deserve this."

"I know, but I hoped that you'd help."

"Don't count on it yet, Brandy. It may take some doing and since I've never had to face this type of situation before, there's no telling what it could cost.

"I've got plenty of money, if you need it."

"That might prove to be a factor, but there's also other information that we'll need on the girl's background. Give me her name."

"Janet Harrison," Brandy responded promptly. "She's a cute little trick but she's in the market for a husband, and I don't intend to be either that or a father, not at this stage of the game."

"I'll talk with you soon, and try to stay out of her pants in the meantime."

At this admonishment Brandy Martin laughed, as he'd never heard Jericho speak in this manner.

When Jericho hung up he went to Paul Moran's office where he also found Dolly.

"Excuse me for butting in, but I need to talk with you, Paul. It's rather urgent."

"Does this have anything to do with the call from Washington?" Dolly asked.

" 'Fraid so," Jericho replied and sank into a chair.

"What's the problem, Jerry?" Paul asked kindly, and then added, "is this private, or can Dolly stay?"

"She's welcome. In fact, she might be of help."

"Okay, shoot," and the older man and woman gave Jericho their full attention.

When he'd explained Brandy's predicament, Paul and Dolly had exchanged glances. It was obvious to them that Jerry was now facing a problem that he'd never learned to handle, yet he wanted to help.

"Janet Harrison," Paul mused. "Name sounds vaguely familiar. That all you know?"

"Yes. I didn't even ask which Senator she works for."

"We'll find out. I have plenty of people that I trust who can be of help. Give me an hour, Jerry; then I'll get back to you."

"Thanks, Paul. I really didn't mean to burden you with this."

"You're not. But there's little doubt you'll have to go to Washington."

Jericho returned to his office and made an effort to work on some of Pride Oil's legal matters, but his mind refused to function properly. As he mulled over the manner in which Brandy had said *knocked up* he gave a slight shudder. It was amazing to him how anyone could speak so lightly about someone that he'd been intimate with. His friend was obviously out of his depth with this girl, or else he was running with the wrong crowd.

A very sober and white faced Brandy Martin welcomed Jericho on his arrival at Washington's National Airport. They shook hands rather formally, and without the usual exuberance that both usually displayed at seeing each other after a long period of time.

Jericho had packed the few things that he found necessary for the trip in a carry-on bag, so they weren't delayed at the baggage claim area and moved directly toward the entrance of the busy terminal. As they went out into the hot and very humid summer night, Jericho saw that the Martin limousine waited at the curb with James, the chauffeur, engaged in an animated conversation with a cab driver. Brandy gave a sharp whistle and the old black man turned. With a broad grin, he hurried to meet them.

"Good to see you again, James," Jericho said pleasantly as he relinquished his bag.

"Mighty nice to have you here, Mr. Smith," he replied, and his eyes held a trace of amusement. Then he turned to Brandy.

"Mr. Brandy, where would you two gentlemen like to go?" and waited expectantly.

"The Mayflower," and then as an aside to Jericho he said quietly, "that good enough?"

"Fine with me," Jericho replied and then the two young men entered the limousine.

While James drove them to their destination, few words were said other than to mention the hot weather. On occasion the old chauffeur had glanced in the rear view mirror, puzzled by the rather cool attitude that Jerry Smith had displayed.

Once in the suite that Brandy had reserved at the Mayflower, they settled comfortably into wing-backed chairs directly facing each other and with only the small coffee table separating them. Brandy had poured two cold beers, and for a few minutes they sat in complete silence.

Then Jericho got up to move restlessly about the room, nervously running his hands through his thick, dark hair. When he finally turned to look at Brandy, his face was twisted with anger.

"Why the hell did you get yourself involved in this thing?" he stormed. Not waiting for an answer, he went on. "You, of all people, should know the reputation of the women you date! I'm shocked by what we've uncovered about Janet Harrison," and his eyes blazed as he looked at his friend. "You're just another one of her suckers, and I thought you were smart. What was it? A free tumble in the hay?''

Brandy Martin had never seen Jericho this angry in their years of friendship, and his behavior was completely out of character.

"If you'd let me explain," Brandy protested, his face now flushed with angry red spots.

"There's no explanation for something stupid," Jericho lashed back.

"So I made one mistake."

"One mistake like this is one too many!"

"In your opinion," Brandy snarled. Then, "How come you're so Goddamned perfect, Jerry?"

Suddenly the room became very still and Jericho turned to look at the red haired young man whose ire he'd aroused.

"I never said I was perfect. Ever," he replied quite deliberately.

"Well, I hope to hell you find out someday what life's all about."

Jericho threw himself back in his chair and took a long swallow from the still cold beer. He proceeded to stare out the window at the brilliantly lit skyline.

Brandy returned to his chair and sat down gingerly, waiting for the next explosion. However, nothing further happened, and it was Jericho who finally broke the silence. "I'm sorry, Brandy. I don't know what's got into me. I've been working so damned hard, and with Stonewall Barton of all people. He's enough to drive anyone off the deep end. In fact, I sound just like him," and he smiled apologetically. "Still friends?"

"God, yes, Jerry."

"Get my briefcase and I'll give you the information that we've pulled together about Janet Harrison."

Brandy got up and retrieved the leather case, handed it to Jericho, and waited apprehensively as his friend leafed through a sheaf of papers. Then, putting the case to one side, Jericho looked at the nervous young man who faced him.

"You really don't care about this girl?" he asked soberly.

"Oh, she was fun to go out with; you know, a good party girl. And she seemed to know all the right people. I know that I've been drinking too much, and that's when it first began. Then it just continued on and on. I never dreamed that this would happen. But care about her?''

"That's what I asked."

"Not really. Not the way I should."

"All right, then this is what we'll do."

Jericho began to speak slowly and deliberately in an effort to explain the plan that Paul Moran and he had devised. Brandy's eyes never once left his face.

Through Paul Moran's network of friends on Capitol Hill, they'd learned that Janet Harrison, the girl in question, had been a known 'hot' number for the past several years, and that on one specific occasion in the not too distant past she'd used the pregnancy ploy on a young, new, junior senator from the South. Being a newcomer to the Washington community and a Southern gentlemen besides, he'd almost been taken in, and would have been had it not been for the action of one of the senior senators in whom he'd felt inclined to confide his plight. The sordid affair had quickly and quietly been hushed up. However, the mystery still remained as to just how Janet Harrison was allowed to stay on in her trusted position, and this fact had rightfully confused many.

"Does your father know?" Jericho asked.

At this question, Brandy turned away from his friend's direct gaze and slowly nodded.

"Did he suggest that you call me?"

Once again Brandy nodded his head.

"Is Schuyler providing the money for the clinic and the 'bonus'?" Jericho continued, and waited. Then, with patience worn almost thin, he said curtly, "Brandy, answer me."

"Yes, Dad's paying for everything," and the youngest Martin son hung his head in obvious shame.

"Do you have the money?" Jericho pursued, "and have you made arrangements for me to meet with this girl?"

"Yes, to both," and then Brandy got up to move around the room, glancing frequently at his watch.

"By any chance is she coming here tonight?" Jericho asked, hoping that he would receive a negative reply.

"Janet thinks that we're meeting here tonight to discuss our wedding plans."

"Oh, my God," Jericho groaned and threw up his hands in despair.

"Well, you told me to stay out of her pants, and this was about the only way that I could handle it."

A soft knock sounded at the door and both young men hastily gathered the legal papers that were strewn on the table and shoved them unceremoniously into Jericho's briefcase. He had but a few brief moments to straighten his tie before Brandy opened the door.

"What took so long?" the girl asked accusingly. Then she saw Jericho.

"You have a guest?" and her look became even more puzzled.

Brandy smiled, then took her firmly by the arm and escorted her into the living room which gave Jericho the opportunity to study the girl with whom his friend had become involved.

"Janet, this is my friend, Jerry Smith," Brandy remarked pleasantly. "We were roommates at Notre Dame."

At this announcement, Janet Harrison gave Jericho a dazzling smile and fluttered her long and obviously artificial eyelashes coyly, every ounce the flirt, even though she was pregnant with another man's child.

"Nice to meet you, Jerry," she said sweetly, and then turned to Brandy. "I thought we had other plans."

"That's why Jerry's here."

The look on the girl's face turned to one of bewilderment as she looked from one to the other.

"What do you mean?" she almost whispered, the tone of her voice rising as though she sensed that something was wrong.

Jericho had looked Janet Harrison over from head to toe, and he could well understand now how Brandy had become infatuated with her. There was no doubt that she was cute, as his friend had stated, with flashing dark eyes, luminous pale skin, and a figure that most women would envy.

She took hold of Brandy's arm possessively and drew him to the divan where she sat so close beside him that she was for all practical purposes glued to him. Brandy glanced at Jericho with obvious embarrassment.

Jericho moved to the chair he'd recently vacated, sat down, and then directed his attention to the young woman who now seemed to be growing apprehensive.

"Janet," he began, and paused to smile pleasantly. "May I call you Janet?"

"Of course. Any friend of Brandy's is certainly a friend of mine," and she gave him a slight smile, which faded quickly.

"It seems that you and Brandy have a problem, and I've been asked to help resolve it."

"Problem?" she replied, her look questioning. Then she turned to Brandy. "Just who is this man?"

"Jerry's my attorney," Brandy replied tonelessly, without so much as looking at her.

"Attorney? Why do we need an attorney?" and she almost spat out the word.

Jericho knew that now was the time for him to interrupt.

"We want to make this as easy as possible for you, Janet. There's really no need to be alarmed."

"Make what easy?"

"From what Brandy has told me, you're holding him accountable for the fact that you're pregnant," Jericho replied flatly.

Janet Harrison turned pale, but then her courage returned. "That's between Brandy and me," she snarled, an ugly look creeping over her face.

"I'm afraid not," Jericho replied kindly.

Janet started to rise from the divan, but Brandy pulled her back.

"Let me alone," she whimpered.

"I'm sorry, Janet, but we have to settle this tonight," Jericho said with firmness in his voice.

Suddenly all the strength seemed to go out of the young woman and she slumped in a heap in the corner of the divan. For a brief moment Jericho felt almost sorry for her.

"Will you listen?" Jericho asked.

Janet Harrison nodded and remained silent, her eyes glued on Jericho.

"We've made arrangements with the Hyde Clinic to take care of you. They're exceptional people, and you'll be given the best of care. There'll be no publicity, and we've already advised the Senator that you'll be away for a few days."

"You've taken care of everything, haven't you? Just like that!" and she snapped her fingers. "Don't you care about your baby?" she whispered, a sob catching in her throat.

Brandy winced and then replied calmly, "I'm sorry, Janet. You see, Jerry learned that you tried the same thing on someone else, and not too long ago. My baby? Who knows?'' and he threw up his hands as though in dismissal.

"You know damned well that it's yours, you bastard," she screamed.

Before Brandy could form a reply, Jericho interrupted. "Janet, I'm sure that you believe the child is Brandy's. However, there's serious doubt on our part," and at this point he withdrew the legal documents from his briefcase. "You see," and he looked at the frightened young woman, "an investigation was made of your past reputation," and he gave an audible sigh, "and what we've uncovered left a lot to be desired."

The girl listened intently, her face a frozen mask while a lone tear trickled slowly down her cheek. Then she covered her face with her hands and began to cry, at first softly and then in hard sobs that racked her body. It was obvious that she was on the verge of near hysteria.

At her sorrow Brandy started to put his arms around her in an effort to comfort her, but Jericho shook his head, and with obvious reluctance Brandy got up from the divan and moved to the window where he turned his back. After what seemed an interminable time, Janet started to regain some semblance of control and made an effort to repair her makeup. When she appeared satisfied, she looked at Jericho, a hint of hardness in her eyes.

"All right, Mr. Smith," she said coolly, without so much as a trace of emotion, "what's the deal?"

This dramatic change from a young woman in the throes of complete despair to one prepared to 'make a deal' shocked Jericho to the core, and he was almost at a loss for words. At this point Brandy turned and stared at Janet in disbelief. He'd been considering asking Jerry to drop the whole thing, but with this mercurial change in attitude his Irish temper got the better of him.

"Pay her off, Jerry," he directed coolly and then headed straight for the door.

"Where the hell do you think you're going?" Jericho demanded.

"To get some fresh air. This place stinks," and without another word Brandy opened the door and slammed it behind him, leaving Jericho behind to pick up the marbles.

After his friend had deserted him, Jericho informed Janet of what she would be required to do and she agreed readily. However, Jericho wouldn't allow her to leave until she'd signed the papers which absolved one Brandon Martin of all responsibility where she was concerned. Jericho provided her with the clinic's address and the name of the doctor to whom she was to report, and then finally produced a sealed envelope which contained, to the best of his knowledge, ten-thousand dollars in unmarked bills supplied by Schuyler Martin.

Janet grabbed the envelope, pushed it into her purse, and then prepared to leave. But then she changed her mind and turned back to face Jericho, an ironic smile on her lips.

"You know, Jerry Smith," she said evenly, "although I don't like you very much right this minute," and she laughed huskily, "you have an excellent knowledge of legal matters. Perhaps someday you'll do something worthwhile with your ability." Then she paused. "Tell Brandy goodbye for me," and it was only then that her voice broke. "It's been nice meeting you," she managed.

Then, with shoulders thrown back and with a smile fixed on her lips, she strode to the door. Once there, she gave Jericho a slight wave and disappeared into the dim hall of the Mayflower Hotel.

Jericho saw or heard nothing more from Brandy Martin that evening.

The following morning, after he'd spent an almost sleepless night, Schuyler Martin called.

"Heard you were in town, Jerry," and his voice held his usual contagious enthusiasm. "How about meeting me for lunch today, or do you have an early flight?"

"It would be my pleasure, sir," Jericho replied and for the first time since he'd arrived in the nation's capitol he'd experienced a feeling of eagerness. Following the settlement of the sordid affair of Schuyler Martin's youngest son, he felt the need for something and someone positive in his life.

"Good; then I'll come by your hotel. Say, one o'clock?"

"Fine, I'll be glad to see you."

After he hung up, the phone rang again. It was Paul Moran.

"Good morning, Jerry. How did things go?"

"As we expected. Brandy got off snow white."

Paul detected a faint tone of disgust in his young friend's voice.

"I'm sure that it wasn't pleasant, but sometimes we have to do things we don't really approve of," Paul said.

"That's for sure. By the way, I'm meeting Schuyler for lunch, and wondered if this might be a good time to approach him about Stonewall Barton. What do you think?"

Paul Moran smiled to himself as he'd also talked with his friend Martin that morning.

"Couldn't think of a better time. Go ahead. Set up whatever you think advisable. You know that Stonewall will expect you to be with him."

"Is that necessary?" Jericho replied, a feeling of disappointment coursing through him.

"That's part of the job, son," Paul answered. Then, "When will you be back?"

"Late tonight. I'll see you first thing in the morning."

"Good. Dolly and I'll be expecting you."

Just before one o'clock Jericho went to the lobby floor to await the arrival of Schuyler Martin. On the stroke of the hour the Martin limousine pulled to a stop in front of the Mayflower. Without waiting for the chauffeur to open the car door, Schuyler Martin emerged and strode purposefully into the hotel. He spotted Jericho immediately and moved forward with hand outstretched, a broad smile creasing his face.

"Mighty nice to have you in Washington, Jerry," Schuyler said. "Ready for lunch? We've got a lot to catch up on."

Jericho looked at him questioningly, but assumed that it had mainly to do with the purpose that had brought him here.

As soon as they were seated and their luncheon orders had been taken, Schuyler leaned across the table, his look serious.

"Thanks for helping Brandy. You don't know how much it means to me and to the family."

"Did Kate know?" Jericho asked.

Schuyler nodded. "Yes. Nothing escapes her. She knows me like the back of her hand," and his smile was one of affection. Then he frowned. "But Elizabeth? No. She'd have been completely crushed."

"I know," Jericho agreed. "How is she these days?"

At his question, Schuyler laughed. "Funny that you should ask. She's already given me instructions to tell her everything about you when I return home," and a twinkle came into his eyes. "You know, Jerry, someday when Elizabeth is older, you two just might become close friends.'' Then he saw that Jericho seemed embarrassed. ''Nothing intended. She's just a kid.'' And with that Jericho nodded in agreement.

When their coffee had been served Jericho brought up the subject of Stonewall Barton and the contribution that he wanted to make to the Party.

''I'd be glad to meet with him, Jerry, but you seem a bit hesitant. Any particular reason?''

''He's a rather strange individual. A westerner from Montana,'' and then Jericho laughed slightly. ''He dresses like a cowboy a good share of the time.''

''I understand that he's in oil.''

''Up to his navel!'' Jericho replied, sounding almost derogatory.

''I take it you don't care for him,'' Schuyler noted as he'd heard the inflection in his friend's voice.

''Oh, he's all right. Just demanding, that's all.''

''Set up a time that's convenient for him and I'll see that he gets the royal treatment.''

''Thanks, Schuyler. I do appreciate your help.''

''Think nothing of it. Now I've a favor to ask of you.''

''Shoot,'' Jericho replied.

''I'm certain that you're aware of Paul's health problem?'' Jericho nodded.

''Well, he'd like to be relieved of the Chairmanship of the Party.''

Jericho frowned slightly. ''But what can I do?''

''Paul wants you to step in and take on the job,'' and before Jericho had a chance to refuse he hurried on. ''He'll be right beside you, Jerry, and frankly Kansas needs some new young blood, and you're the best.''

Then he sat back and waited for the onslaught that he felt surely would come.

''You're pulling my leg,'' Jericho said, but he had the feeling that his host meant every word.

Schuyler smiled pleasantly. ''Jerry, we don't kid about things as serious as being Chairman of the Democratic Party from Kansas.'' Then he continued. ''Would you be willing to give it a try?''

Jericho looked at the handsome, grey-haired man sitting across from him and knew that he usually managed to have his way, yet it was always handled with a definite degree of finesse.

"What about my law practice?"

"We're aware that that will have to take a back seat, at least for the time being, but this will provide you with the opportunity to get your feet wet," and Schuyler chuckled. "You'll be getting in just in time to work on the Kennedy campaign, and who knows where that might lead?"

Jericho had known that he couldn't refuse, since he felt indebted to both Schuyler Martin and Paul Moran.

"I'll accept on one condition," he replied seriously.

"What's that?"

"That Paul stays on as my consultant."

"Agreed!" '

Schuyler Martin held out his hand and Jericho grasped it, not realizing that this was the sealing of a trust that would mark the road for Jericho's ultimate success.

17

When Jericho returned to the office, Paul and Dolly Moran greeted him effusively. Then, following a debriefing concerning the resolution of Brandy Martin's case and his meeting with Schuyler Martin, Paul informed his protege that Stonewall Barton had been bombarding the office with calls.

"What's his problem?" Jericho asked almost sullenly.

"He wants to have that meeting with Schuyler, and he says the sooner the better." The white haired man paused, "Jerry, I know he can be a pain in the ass, and I'm sorry you've been pressed into representing him, but we need his support. In fact, we need all the support we can get. Please give him a call and do something to calm him down."

Jericho laughed wryly. "Sure I will. The news I have should make him happy."

"What news?"

"Oh, Schuyler said to set up a time convenient for Barton and he'd show him the royal treatment."

"Wonderful!" Paul exclaimed, obviously relieved, although he'd noticed the rather disdainful look on his friend's face. "Some catch to it?"

Jericho nodded, and for a few minutes he drummed his pen on

Paul's desk. "You see, Paul, I'll have to go to D.C. with him."

"I told you that was part of the deal."

"Yeah, and frankly, I'm not looking forward to it a helluva lot."

"Tell you what, we'll just let Schuyler handle it. He'll do as he said, and you'll merely have to stand on the sidelines."

"God, I hope so. Stonewall gets on my nerves." He paused, "It's funny, but I really can't seem to put my finger on why."

"We all react to people in different ways. Now give him a call."

Dutifully, Jericho returned to his private office where he placed the call to Pride Oil's headquarters in Salmon, Montana. In a matter of minutes, Stonewall Barton's gruff voice answered.

"Mr. Barton, Jerry Smith here. I understand that you've called several times. What can I do for you?"

Without so much as a salutation, the westerner launched into an almost accusatory barrage. "Understand that you were in Washington this week."

"That's correct. We had some urgent business come up."

"Did you happen to get in touch with Martin while you were there?"

"Matter of fact, I did, and he's anxious to meet you."

"He is?" There was a trace of astonishment in his voice.

"Absolutely, and if you'll set a time that's convenient for you, I'll contact Mr. Martin and he'll work out all the details."

There was a long pause while Stonewall Barton leafed unhurriedly through his desk calendar. Now his attitude had changed dramatically. "I'll be available in a couple of weeks. How about you?"

"My time is your time," Jerry replied.

"Good. I'll come to Wichita and we'll go together."

"Will Mrs. Barton be with you?"

The answer Jericho received was cutting and cold. "Of course not. This is business," and with that Stonewall hung up, leaving Jericho with a buzzing instrument in his hand.

Slowly he replaced the phone, and with almost measured words said, "Go to hell Stonewall Barton. Just go to hell!"

Schuyler Martin had taken great pains with plans for Stonewall Barton's entrance into the political scene of Washington. He'd invited his most influential friends on Capitol Hill and had extended an invitation to Sam Rayburn, Speaker of the House. It was only natural that he'd also included the Kennedys. Barton's contribution, Jericho had informed him, could run well into millions, and he'd expect royal treatment in return.

Schuyler had informed Kate that they'd be entertaining an important client of Paul's and Jerry's, but had failed to mention his name, indicating only that he was contributing heavily to the coffers of the Party. Kate had never been one to mix with the politicians, nor was she that interested in the political arena. However, she was always more then willing to take her place by her husband and serve as the gracious hostess.

The reception and dinner were to be held at the Martin's George-town mansion, giving a personal touch to the gathering, and the decorators, florists and caterers descended in hordes on Kate's home. Young Elizabeth Martin reveled in the excitement, but Kate seemed almost reclusive and willingly left the planning in the hands of her husband and his very capable assistants.

Upon their arrival, Jericho and his companion were met at Washington National Airport by the Martin limousine. James, the chauffeur, had greeted Jericho warmly, but had turned a jaundiced eye on Stonewall Barton. True to form, the man from Montana had clothed himself in a trimly tailored cowboy suit, with intricate embroidery depicting oil rigs and mountains on the jacket, and complemented by the finest black leather boots that Frye offered. The Stetson hat which crowned his thick grey hair was of stark white felt with a wide black band where his initials were worked in with golden thread, and the belt that adorned his still trim waist sported a gold buckle that was studded with diamonds and emeralds. Most assuredly, he was a sight that most native Washingtonians could never have imagined existed.

Schuyler had instructed James to take his guests to the Mayflower where he'd reserved two separate suites, and they were delivered to the hotel in record time.

Jericho settled Stonewall into his suite and then went to his own. As he inserted the key in the lock, the telephone began to ring and he rushed to answer it. "Hello," he managed, short of breath.

"Jerry? That you?" Schuyler Martin asked.

"Yes, it's me. Sorry it took me so long to answer but I had to run for it," and he lowered his lanky frame into an easy chair and put his long legs up on the coffee table in front of him.

"Is your companion happy?"

"Seems to be," and then Jericho laughed. "I wish you could have seen James' face when he met us."

"What do you mean?" Schuyler replied, a trace of annoyance in his voice.

"Well, anyone who's a native here would have had the same reaction that James did at seeing Stonewall," and he chuckled. "Don't blame James."

"What the hell does he look like?"

"As I told you before he's a strange man. This time, he's a true Hollywood cowboy. You'll get to see him in all his regalia."

"You mean that he won't be wearing a dinner jacket?"

"Hell, no. But at least he'll be a stand out." He paused, "Are you sure the Party needs his money? You know, this is no pleasure trip for me."

"Sorry, Jerry. Of course we need Barton's support," and an audible sigh escaped him. "We'll simply have to accept him for what he is.

"What time do you want us to make our appearance?"

"I'm sending James for you at 7:30. We'll have dinner at nine."

"Fine. See you then," and Jericho hung up.

He pulled himself up from the chair and threw himself fully clothed on the bed. His mind began to wander, and he wondered if Elizabeth would be present. He knew that Kate, as always, would be the gracious hostess, and that Emily Martin, Schuyler's mother, would also be in attendance holding court among her old friends. But Elizabeth? Only time would tell. He glanced at his watch, noting that it was only four, closed his eyes and drifted off to sleep.

Promptly at 7:30, the limousine pulled into the drive under the canopy of the Mayflower Hotel. James stepped out, touching his cap with respect.

"Good evening, James," Jericho said pleasantly, but Stonewall completely ignored the black man and lunged inside. Before Jericho entered he paused, placed his hand on James' shoulder and whispered softly, "It's only for tonight." The chauffeur nodded and a slight smile creased the wrinkled ebony face.

Because of the social events that Jericho had attended as a guest
of the Morans, he'd been required to invest in the proper formal
wear, and tonight he looked every inch like someone who had
participated in many such functions. Only Stonewall Barton looked
out of place. However, he'd had the foresight to change from the
black suit he'd first worn into a white western outfit, but he still
sported the jewel encrusted belt and the white hat.

Little conversation of any consequence transpired between the
two men on the ride to Georgetown. Jericho did make some
attempt to direct his companion's attention to various historical
landmarks, but the older man seemed uninterested and
unimpressed. Had the truth been known, Stonewall Barton felt
completely out of his class, and his apparent indifference was
merely a form of camouflage.

As James drove slowly up the long drive which approached
Magnolia Hill, Jericho became acutely aware of the large number of
limousines (some official), complete with chauffeurs, which
crowded the parking area. Stonewall had moved to the edge of the
seat and his eyes literally devoured the magnificent estate that
Schuyler Martin called home.

Then he turned to Jericho. "Jesus Christ, this guy must be in oil,
too," he said in awe.

Jericho laughed. "No, Stonewall, Schuyler Martin has nothing
to do with oil. His family has been wealthy for many years. This is
only the end product of successful early settlers. Then he turned to
look at the man beside him. "You haven't done so badly yourself."

"Guess you could say that," and the older man almost preened
at the unexpected compliment. "But this place looks like something
out of the movies."

"I know, but the people who live here are very nice and they
deserve everything they have, believe me."

"I take it that you like them."

"Of course. Their son and I were roommates at Notre Dame and
I feel as though they're my second family."

Stonewall's look became speculative. "Understand they have a
daughter. Got your eye set on her? And their money?"

At this question Jericho felt a surge of rage beginning to build,
but he made a concerted effort and controlled himself. "I'm afraid
not, Mr. Barton," he replied sharply. "Money doesn't interest me

as it does some others that I've met."

His remark silenced his companion, since he was well aware that Jerry Smith knew how he'd started his fortune.

By now they were at the entrance leading to the house. Jericho moved up the steps slightly ahead of Stonewall, and when the butler opened the door they heard the sound of loud voices and laughter.

"Sounds to me like there's a damned good party going on in there," Stonewall remarked, laughing nervously, and then nudged Jericho in the ribs, almost conspiratorially. Schuyler Martin, who'd been on the lookout for them, excused himself from a group of friends and hurried to join them.

"Good evening, Jerry," he said with obvious affection.

Then he turned to Stonewall Barton, quickly assessing the man from Montana. He saw immediately that he was everything Jerry had said he was, yet the stranger who seemed hard as nails on the surface had the look of someone almost afraid.

"And you're Stonewall Barton," Schuyler said enthusiastically, thrusting his hand out, only to have it gripped in a tight, vise-like hold. "I'm delighted that you could find the time in your busy schedule to come to Washington," he said, all the while nursing his hand which felt as though it had been crushed by a heavy stone.

"Nice to meet you, Martin," Stonewall replied abruptly.

"Shall we go in so you can meet some of the guests. You know that you're the guest of honor this evening."

Stonewall glanced at Jericho and saw that he was engrossed in scanning the room.

"You coming, Jerry?" he asked, searching for support.

"No, you go ahead. I want to see the family," and he moved down the steps into the midst of the milling crowd.

"Nice kid," Stonewall remarked, which brought a smile to Schuyler's face.

"He's a mighty fine young man. He has great potential."

"Think so?"

"Yes, I do. We've known Jerry for quite sometime. I simply wish that my own children had the determination and discipline that he has," and he turned to his companion. "He'll be an important man some day. Mark my words. Now, shall we go in?"

"Sure," his guest replied and with Schuyler leading the way they moved into the room.

Jericho finally found Elizabeth who was seated with her mother. Kate Martin was sheathed in a white evening gown and looked awesomely beautiful, but it was Elizabeth with the blush of youth that Jericho had trouble keeping his eyes from, and he stared at her until she blushed from embarrassment. When he noticed her discomfort he was amused as she had always been the forward one.

"Wonderful seeing you again, Mrs. Martin. You, too, Elizabeth," and his look was filled with admiration. "You ladies are lovely."

Elizabeth glanced at her mother who seemed pleased by the compliment, and then she gave Jericho a radiant smile.

"Thank you, kind sir," she said and curtseyed. When she looked up her eyes held the mischieviousness that he'd grown used to.

Then Kate commanded his attention. "Jerry, I understand that you accompanied this great benefactor," and she grimaced slightly. "I haven't met him as yet, and Schuyler seems to have disappeared."

"He's taking our guest through the hoops. Has to meet all the wheels," he replied. Then, "Would you mind if I spirited Elizabeth away?"

Kate noticed the sudden flush of eagerness that had appeared on her daughter's face and for a moment she hesitated. Then she decided that it would be too obvious if she refused such an innocent request.

"Go ahead," she said, "and should you run into Schuyler, tell him not to become too involved. I'll go check with the chef about dinner." She got up from her chair and disappeared into the throng.

At Kate moved down the hallway which led to the kitchen wing, Stonewall Barton caught a glimpse of her and stopped in the midst of the conversation he was having with one of the senators. He suddenly turned pale.

"Something wrong, Mr. Barton?" his companion asked with concern.

Stonewall Barton shook his head. "Just thought I saw someone I used to know, that's all," he managed. "Now, where were we?"

As the dinner guests drifted into the dining hall to be seated at the exquisitely set tables, Kate, almost at a run, came from the kitchen in search of her husband only to find him in conversation with Jericho and Elizabeth.

"Where have you been?" she demanded heatedly, her dark eyes flashing. "The chef has been holding dinner for the past half hour and he's beside himself."

Schuyler drew Kate aside and made an effort to take her in his arms, but she pushed him away.

"You know how I dislike these affairs. The least that you could do is to be with me."

"Where's mother?"

"With her old friends. What else would you expect?"

"I'm sorry, darling, but the top echelon and I have been having a meeting," he explained, knowing that it mattered little to her.

"Well, let's go in. And the guest of honor? Where is he? I haven't even met him!"

"One of the Kennedys is with him."

Kate heaved a sigh and with a forced smile on her lovely face, took her husband's proffered arm while he escorted her into the large room to her place at the foot of the main table.

The man sitting on Kate's left proved to be a senator that she'd met at a previous function, and she greeted him pleasantly; the man on her right introduced himself as a senior member of a Wall Street law firm, and she smiled and murmured a pleasantry.

Then Schuyler, who now stood at the head of the table, touched the crystal champagne glass before him with a knife to gain attention, and the ringing sound carried throughout the room and brought sudden quiet.

"Good evening, friends," he began. "It's a pleasure to have you as guests in our home. Mrs. Martin," and he nodded toward Kate who smiled briefly, "and I welcome you." There was a light round of applause.

"This evening, we've gathered to honor a man from the State of Montana, who has proved to be one of the staunchest supporters of the Democratic Party," and again polite applause resounded. "My friend, and I do call him friend, has offered the Party a large and most welcome contribution toward the next Presidential campaign," and he paused dramatically. "May I introduce to you, and especially to those who as yet haven't had the privilege of meeting him . . . Mr. Stonewall Barton.''

When Schuyler said Stonewall Barton, the tall, still handsome grey haired man rose to his feet and the guests rose in unison to applaud him. For a moment, Kate Martin stared at him as though transfixed, then suddenly felt as though she were going to be ill.

"It can't be," she murmured. "Oh, God, not Stoney, not here, not in my home . . , and Jericho." Her hand which held the glass of champagne started to tremble and she carefully set the glass down.

Stonewall Barton smiled warmly at the reception and then he turned slightly and looked directly into Kate Martin's eyes. He held his glass high and said, "To my host and hostess, Schuyler Martin and his lovely wife, Kate." A cold shudder swept over her, but she smiled stiffly and sat down.

To Kate, the dinner dragged on interminably and she barely touched the delicacies that the chef and caterer had spent long hours preparing. She consumed glass after glass of champagne and began to feel giddy. She laughed loudly at some of the almost urbane remarks that her dinner partners offered.

Schuyler Martin was astonished by his wife's behavior. She's probably paying me back for leaving her alone, he decided, but he still felt concern.

After coffee was served, he watched as Kate pushed herself from the table and tipsily maneuvered out of the room. He glanced first at Jericho who was seated next to Elizabeth and then saw the look of utter shame on his daughter's face.

"Excuse me, Schuyler," Stonewall interrupted, "but I left my cigar case in the library." Before his host could offer to send one of the maids to retrieve it, Barton was gone.

Although Kate had a head start on her long ago lover, the wine she had consumed caused her to move rather slowly and as she started up the stairs a voice from out of the past said, "Kathleen, wait for me." She froze in her tracks.

Stonewall moved to her and placed his hand gently on her arm, but she pulled away.

"Can we talk?" he asked quietly.

Kate turned to look into the piercing blue eyes of the man who had scorned her years before. "We have nothing to talk about," she whispered harshly.

When Stonewall replied, his voice was ragged with anger. "Oh yes, we do. Do you prefer a scene?"

"Of course not."

"Then where's a place we won't be disturbed?"

"The garden," Kate replied coldly, and moved ahead of him to the front door. They went out into the warmth of the summer evening. Silently, they walked down the path until they reached a wrought iron bench. Kate sank onto it and Stonewall joined her.

"Why are you here?" she asked.

"You know why. I'm contributing to the Democratic Presidential campaign."

"Are you sure that's all?"

"Kathleen," he said, and he noticed that she shivered when he used her given name. "I'm not here to hurt you. God, I didn't even know you were Martins' wife."

"This is merely a coincidence?"

"Of course."

"Then what is it you want to talk about. I have nothing to say to you."

"I'm afraid that you do," and he turned to look into her lovely eyes which reflected her fright.

After a few moments of silence, Kate said, "What is it you want to know?"

"I'd appreciate it if you'd tell me what happened to the child that you claimed was mine."

By now Kate was stone-cold sober, but her Irish temperament was obvious in her reply. "You disclaimed any right to that child," she snapped, and her eyes clouded. "I remember only too well how you treated me," and the look she gave him was filled with loathing, "but if you must know, the child was stillborn."

"Dead?"

"Yes, dead."

"Was it a boy or a girl?" he asked softly, taking her hand.

"A boy," and she sighed deeply, but did not pull away.

"God, I'm sorry, Kathleen. If only I'd been older."

"It's all in the past now and there's nothing more to be said. Only one thing."

"What's that?"

"Please don't call me Kathleen."

"But why?"

"Everyone here knows me as Kate Martin, and that's the way it has to be."

For a period of time they sat silently remembering the past. Then Stonewall Barton looked into the face of his first and only love. "You know, Kate. I loved you then," and he turned away to look into the darkness, "and I love you now."

Suddenly, footsteps could be heard coming toward them, and Schuyler Martin stepped out of the dark. "So here you are," he said, glancing from one to the other.

Stonewall got up from the bench very much at ease. "Schuyler, your missus wasn't feeling too good, so I brought her outside to get some fresh air." He turned to look at Kate and saw the gratefulness in her eyes. "Mrs. Martin, now that your husband's here, I'll go back to the party," and he turned on his heel and hurried off up the path.

Schuyler took the seat that Stonewall had vacated and placed his arm around Kate. "Now that you've had the chance to spend some time with the man from Montana, what's your opinion of him?" Schuyler asked.

"You really want to know?"

"I value your opinion, my dear."

Kate looked down at her hands and then into the eyes of the man she loved. "He's a very decent sort. I'm sure that he'll prove to be a great benefit to the Party."

"That's good to hear, coming from my strongest political opponent," and he laughed.

"Sometimes we have to change our minds," Kate replied. "Shall we go back now?"

"Feel up to it?"

"Have I ever failed you?"

"Never!" and he pulled her into his arms and kissed her passionately. Then, hand in hand, they returned to the brilliantly lit house.

18

Later that evening, after the festitives at the Martin estate had come to an end, Jericho and Stonewall were driven back to the Mayflower. Within the limousine an almost uneasy quiet reigned. Jericho had glanced at his companion several times but had found the older man's expression inscrutable. Once he'd made an attempt at some light conversation, but received only a grunt in reply.

When he accompanied his friend to his suite, Barton finally broke his self-imposed silence. "Care to join me for a night cap?" he'd asked, pleasantly enough.

Jericho glanced at his watch. It was now well after two o'clock in the morning, but shaking off his tiredness he smiled. "I'd like that," and the two men entered the suite.

"What'll you have?" his host asked.

"Brandy, if you have it available."

Stonewall nodded assent and poured the drink. Then, taking a larger one for himself, he moved to where Jericho had taken a seat. He sank into a chair opposite him, all the while studying him.

"Something on your mind?" Jericho asked.

For a moment, Stonewall remained silent and proceeded to swish the thick amber liquor around his glass. Then he looked up. "Jerry," he said, "What do you know about Kate Martin?"

The question took Jericho completely by surprise.

"Know about her? Just what do you mean?"

"Wondered if you knew anything about her background, that's all."

Jericho shook his head. "Can't really say that I do. She and Schuyler have been married for a long time, and very happily I might add.

"How can you be so sure?"

"Really, Stonewall, aren't you being a little presumptious? I know that Kate drank too much tonight. That was obvious, and it isn't like her at all, but she was pissed with Schuyler for neglecting her," and he smiled. "You see, Kate's not interested in the political scene, and prefers to stay in the background. She adores her husband, his sons and their daughter, and frankly I thought she was very congenial. Was she unpleasant to you?"

"No. Not really. We had a chance to talk briefly and she was nice enough. She's certainly a very beautiful woman," he added softly, and a rather sorrowful look crossed his face.

"Anything else you'd like to discuss?" Jericho asked rather abruptly, changing the subject.

"No, and I'm sorry to have kept you up so long." Stonewall rose to his feet and accompanied Jericho to the door. "See you later."

While Stonewall Barton was drinking himself into a stupor, Jericho slept peacefully, while miles away Schuyler and Kate were passionately making love.

The sharp, staccato sound of the telephone awakened Jericho, and for a brief moment he almost forgot where he was. He picked up the shrilling instrument and cradled it against his ear. A bright and cheerful, "Good morning, Jerry," greeted him and he smiled. It was Elizabeth.

"Good morning, yourself," he replied sleepily.

"Did I wake you?"

"Yep. What time is it, anyway?"

"Almost noon."

"Oh, my God," he exclaimed and sat straight up in bed.

"Something wrong?"

"Mr. Barton and I have a luncheon engagement with your father."

"You do?" she said plaintively, her disappointment obvious.

" 'Fraid so, Elizabeth. May I call you later?"

Pleased that he'd asked, she replied softly, "Of course."

After a rather hasty goodbye, Jericho asked the hotel operator to ring Stonewall's suite. The phone rang and rang but there was no answer. Puzzled, he hurried through a shower, dressed quickly, and then ran down the stairs to Barton's suite and knocked loudly. When he received no response, he continued to knock and finally he heard a movement inside, then a low moan.

I wonder if he's sick? Jericho thought. Then, "Stonewall," he said loudly. "Are you okay?"

Following an interminable period of time, the door finally opened a crack. Stonewall Barton clung to the door jam with all his strength, and it was now obvious that he was dead drunk. Jericho took him by the arm and assisted him back to a chair.

"What the hell's the matter with you?" Jericho stormed. "We have a luncheon scheduled with Schuyler and the Party heads. You're supposed to present them with a check! How could you do this when I've worked so damned hard to make it all possible?"

"Sorry, kid," Stonewall muttered. Then his head fell back against the chair and lolled to one side.

Jericho looked down at him with disgust written on his face. He placed a call to the Martin residence and was fortunate to catch Schuyler as he was about to leave.

"Yes, Jerry; I was on my way out to meet you."

"Schuyler, I hate like hell to tell you this, but we've got one big problem."

"Did Barton change his mind and leave?" he asked, a trace of alarm in his voice.

"I wish to hell he had," Jericho replied sarcastically. "He's drunk and just passed out. I found him only a little while ago."

"Did he give you the check?" Schuyler asked.

"Hell no, and I doubt if I could get him sober enough to write one."

"Perhaps he already has," and Schuyler paused. "I dislike asking you to do this, but could you take a look around? You might just be lucky and find it."

For a moment Jericho hesitated. His childhood upbringing was such that you never touched anyone's personal belongings, but he knew this was vastly different. "Hold on, Schuyler, I'll take a look in his brief case."

While Schuyler waited for Jericho to return to the phone, Kate entered the library. "I thought you'd gone," she said with surprise.

Her husband nodded. "I was on my way out when Jerry phoned."

"Something wrong?"

"Yes. Barton's drunk, and he's passed out. Jerry's looking for the check."

Kate turned away so her husband couldn't see the concern which came into her eyes, for she knew the reason behind Stonewall Barton's actions.

"Okay, Jerry. Thanks. Be there shortly," he said into the phone, and then replaced it in the cradle.

"Jerry found the check, thank God. Now I'll get on my way." But before he left he gathered his wife into his arms. "You okay, darling?"

Kate smiled gently. "Why shouldn't I be?"

"I'm not sure why I asked," Schuyler said, and looked deep into her eyes. "But you did act a bit strained when I mentioned Barton. He didn't offend you last evening, did he?"

"Certainly not. Why should he? After all," and she laughed huskily, "I was a little tipsy myself last night, and he did help me get some air."

"I know. See you this evening, darling," and he kissed her deeply, then strode out the door.

As soon as Kate heard the car leave, she moved slowly up the stairs and entered their suite where she slumped on one of the lounges as tears of sadness trickled slowly down her cheeks.

Jericho waited impatiently in the lobby of the Mayflower for Schuyler. When he saw the long black limousine approaching, he moved outside. Without waiting for James to open the back door, he stepped inside. Then, once again, they moved swiftly down the drive.

"I presume you've had a bad morning," Schuyler remarked and glanced at his companion appraisingly.

"I guess you could say that."

"Well, these things happen at times, and I'm sorry as hell that you had to be the one to handle it. By the way, do you know if he drinks like this all of the time?''

It was then that Jericho remembered what Paul Moran had told him about Stonewall Barton occasionally hitting the bottle.

''Matter of fact, I do,'' and he paused. ''It seems, according to Paul, that on occasion he indulges himself in this manner. Frankly, ever since I first met the man I've had the feeling that he's extremely unhappy.''

''Can you think of any plausible reason?'' Schuyler pursued.

''Yes,'' Jericho responded. Then very carefully he chose his words. ''You know, I visited Stonewall in Montana some months back and he was always in the best of spirits and humor until we went to his home.'' He shook his head sadly. ''It was soon obvious to me that his marriage to Julia Walowski is nothing but a charade, and he treats her and their only child, Adele, like slaves.'' He turned to look at his friend, then continued, ''You know, Schuyler, there must be something that he'd hiding, and I can't for the life of me figure out what it could possibly be. He has money, prestige, almost everything.''

For a moment it was very quiet, and then Schuyler said softly, ''He has everything, but love.''

The words ''everything but love'' caused Jericho to stop and think. That could very well be the reason, as he'd personally witnessed the hell that Paul and Dolly Moran had gone through, and there was a good chance that Stonewall's life was much the same.

''You're undoubtedly right, Schuyler. Now, let's forget about our friend,'' and he raised his brows cynically, ''and enjoy this lunch.'' Then he patted his jacket pocket. ''Inside, I have a check for one-million dollars,'' he smiled almost ruefully, ''and I'm the one who'll have the pleasure of presenting it!''

Schuyler, secretly, was well satisfied. With Stonewall Barton now removed from the picture as the benevolent contributor, Jerry Smith would be placed in the limelight, and presenting a million dollars toward the campaign, even though it came from the funds of another, could easily make him the golden boy of the year where the Party members were concerned. He'd not soon be forgotten.

It was Schuyler who chaired the meeting, and many of those in attendance had also been present at his home the previous evening.

After the luncheon dishes had been cleared away, Schuyler rose to his feet and the conversation ceased.

"I know that you'll be disappointed to learn that our good friend, Mr. Stonewall Barton, was unable to make it today."

Several of the guests snickered aloud and others whispered to each other and then laughed.

Schuyler simply ignored them and continued, "In his stead, Jerry Smith, our new Democratic Party Chairman from the great midwestern State of Kansas, has the honor of presenting Mr. Barton's contribution. I hope that you've all had the pleasure of meeting Jerry, but if not, it's with great pride, and I might add a great privilege, that I present Jerry Smith."

Schuyler stood aside as Jericho got to his feet. He was still a bit overwhelmed by the sudden turn of events. He knew that his host could have insisted on doing the honors, and he was doubly pleased that Schuyler had voiced no objection when he'd remarked, "I'll get to present the check." Jericho smiled openly and held up his hand to quiet the applause.

"Thank you all for being here today. I know that you miss Mr. Barton's presence, however, I'll try to do my best to take his place." As an afterthought, he added, "That's really difficult to do," and his words were followed by a ripple of laughter which gathered momentum as it careened around the table. Jericho frowned, and for a moment he thought they were laughing at him. He looked at Schuyler, who smiled and nodded his support.

As the room gradually quieted, Jericho's glance swept around the audience who made up the top hierarchy of the Democratic Party. Although at first he'd felt apprehensive that he might botch this special moment, from deep within confidence in himself and his God-given capabilities emerged. He removed the cashiers' check from his coat pocket and with a slight smile, touched it to his lips. Then he looked up to discover that everyone's eyes were focused on him.

He smiled warmly and then began his presentation. "Mr. Chairman," and he turned first to acknowledge Schuyler Martin, "and honored members of the Democratic Party. As mentioned by Mr. Martin, our good friend Mr. Barton is unable to be with us today and I've been given the honor of taking his place. I'd like to acknowledge the deep and abiding dedication and pride Stonewall

Barton has not only for his country, but also for the Party. He is a true product of America, and a self-made man. Since I have been afforded the opportunity to work with him closely the past few years, I've grown to respect him, not only for his obvious business ability, but also for the generosity he's shown to others in less fortunate circumstances. I'll admit there were times that it wasn't always easy to agree with him, but I've discovered that he was right more often than wrong, and coming from a lawyer . . ." This brought a ripple of laughter. "That's admitting a lot.

"Most of you probably are not aware that as a young man Stonewall Barton left his native Kansas, in the depths of the depression, and journeyed west to the State of Montana. It was in Montana that he met and became friends with a Polish immigrant who'd left his war torn homeland to come to a free world that offered opportunity. That man was Joseph Walowski, the founder of Pride Oil. Perhaps some of you may have heard of him, and perhaps not. However, Joe Walowski was the man who recognized the talents of Stonewall Barton, and following his long illness and then death, he wisely left the company that he'd founded in the hands of his capable protege. Under Mr. Barton's guidance, Pride has grown into one of our largest oil suppliers and is an intregral part of our economy."

A slight round of applause followed, and Jericho paused. Then very carefully he picked up the check which had been placed on the table face down so that no one could possibly see the amount of the contribution, with the exception, of course, Schuyler Martin.

"Now comes the best part," he said and Jericho laughed slightly. "In my hand I hold what to me is a fortune, and one which Stonewall Barton hopes will further the aims of the Democratic Party and ultimately the course of our government. It is with pleasure that I present to you," and he paused to look into the expectant faces, "a check for the sum of one-million dollars," and he turned and gravely handed the check to Schuyler Martin.

At first the silence in the private room was almost tangible. The shocked expressions on the faces of those present were indescribable. Then pandemonium broke loose.

When the noise finally abated, Schuyler Martin joined Jericho and patted him on the shoulder. "Good speech, Jerry." Then he directed his attention to his compatriots.

"On behalf of the Party, and with our deepest appreciation to Stonewall Barton, I accept this contribution."

Then he turned to look at the young man who stood beside him. "As you know, Jerry Smith has just accepted the Chairmanship for the state of Kansas. We'll be seeing a lot of him here in Washington, and some of you will undoubtedly run into him on the campaign trail. It's been my personal privilege to have known Jerry since his fledgling days at Notre Dame, where my son Brandy was fortunate enough to become his roommate," and he paused. "I believe with all my being that Jerry Smith will some day become one of the great leaders of our country."

Enthusiastic applause exploded, and then the party began to break up. As Jericho started to leave he felt the pressure of a hand on his shoulder. When he turned he found himself looking into the eyes of Robert Kennedy. "Nice speech, Jerry," Kennedy said. "I trust we'll be seeing a lot of you in the days ahead."

Almost speechless, Jericho smiled. "Thanks, Mr. Kennedy. I'll do my share. You can rest assured of that."

Then Schuyler joined them. "I'm glad that you could make it, Bob," he said. "What do you think of this young man?"

Robert Kennedy's look became serious. "He'll go far, Schuyler," and a twinkle came into his eyes. "But who wouldn't, under your wing?"

At Jericho's request, Schuyler accompanied him back to the hotel. Although there wasn't the slightest doubt in his mind that he could handle Stonewall Barton by himself, he hoped that Schuyler might be able to talk some sense into him.

When they reached the Mayflower they obtained a key from the desk clerk and went immediately to the suite. It was obvious that the rooms hadn't been cleaned for they were in the same state as when Jericho had left. The silence which permeated the room seemed almost eerie.

Jericho hurried across the living room to the bedroom door and knocked. When he received no answer, he opened the door and stepped inside. A cry of alarm escaped him for lying on the floor was Stonewall Barton. The moment Schuyler heard Jericho's outcry he ran into the room and then stopped dead in his tracks. Sensing the emergency, he quickly moved to Stonewall's side and felt for a pulse . . . but found none.

"Call the medics, Jerry," he directed and then knelt beside Stonewall and began artificial respiration, knowing that in all probability his efforts would prove to be in vain.

Within minutes an ambulance crew arrived accompanied by a young doctor who very efficiently took over. Schuyler and Jericho were instructed to remain in the living room and they waited together in silence. After what seemed a interminable period of time, the doctor joined them.

"I'm sorry," he said quietly, "but he didn't make it. He's been dead well over an hour. We'll need to have the coroner come," and he glanced at the two men who both seemed in a state of shock. "Are either of you a relative?" he asked. Numbly, both shook their heads.

"Who found him?"

"I did," Jericho managed.

Then Schuyler spoke up. "I was here with him. He wasn't alone," and murmured to himself, "thank God."

"Where's the telephone" the young man asked, and Jericho pointed to it. While the doctor spoke briefly into the instrument to someone named "Sam," Schuyler took Jericho aside. "I don't mean to pry, Jerry, but how was Stonewall when you left him?"

"Just as I told you. He'd passed out, and before I left I poured the balance of the liquor down the drain. Then I came to meet you. Why?"

"Oh, there'll be lots of questions. There always are when tragedies such as this happen," and then he noticed the look that came over his young friend's face. "I'm not blaming you, Jerry. He was alive when you last saw him, and they'll undoubtedly reach the conclusion that he suffered a heart attack. But being a lawyer, you know all that."

"Sometimes I wish to hell that Paul had kept him as his own client. This man has caused me nothing but trouble, and now this. Jericho threw up his hands in despair.

In a short time the coroner arrived accompanied by several plain-clothesmen. Schuyler identified himself and fielded the majority of the questions which provided Jericho an opportunity to gather his wits. Then it was his turn to be questioned.

"Your name?"

"Jerry Smith."

"Any relation?"

"No, sir. I'm his lawyer."

"You're his lawyer?" the man replied with astonishment, as he'd noticed his youth.

"Yes, sir. Mr. Barton had been a client of mine for several years."

The detective looked at Schuyler as though seeking confirmation.

"Yes, Mr. Smith is his lawyer, and he's also Chairman of the Democratic Party from the State of Kansas. At my request, he accompanied Mr. Barton to Washington."

"Why was he here?"

"Mr. Barton was honored at a dinner at my home last evening. It's undoubtedly in all the newspapers by now, if you'd care to check."

The policeman shook his head. "We'll make our own investigation, thank you," he replied coolly.

At this moment in the interrogation, the coroner returned from the bedroom with the doctor in tow. "Seems to have been a heart attack brought on by alcoholic shock. I really don't feel there's any need to detain these people. We'll take the body down to the morgue for an autopsy."

As the coroner's men removed the body of Stonewall Barton, Jericho and Schuyler both turned away. Deep within, Jericho knew that the man who was now dead had exhibited a facade of someone who cared for no one, and had held deep in his heart a secret that had finally brought him to his death. For a moment a lump formed in his throat and tears misted his eyes.

"You okay, Jerry?" Schuyler asked softly.

"Of course," he replied firmly, "Shall we go?"

"I think that's best," Schuyler said, and the two men made their way out of the suite.

19

Funeral services for Stonewall Barton were held in Salmon, Montana. Paul, Dolly and Jericho attended together. Schuyler Martin, accompanied by a large and impressive contingent from Washington, arrived by chartered flight. Julia Walowski Barton and Adele, throughout the ordeal, had clung to Jericho as though he were their last refuge. Although he'd found their seeming helplessness cumbersome, he knew that he'd cared for Stonewall in a manner that he didn't readily comprehend, and therefore he accepted their dependence gracefully.

Jericho, Paul and Dolly stayed on after the others had left. Paul had brought Stonewall's Will and Trusts, and after a few days they had met at the family home with Julia, Adele and Belle for the reading of the documents.

Stonewall had wisely seen fit to hire some of the most learned men in the oil industry to assist him with the operation of Pride. Although the company automatically reverted to Julia and Adele upon his death, he'd given explicit instructions as to just how the business was to be conducted. He'd also included instructions that Moran and Smith, his attorneys, were to be allowed access to the company's financial records at any time that they might deem it necessary. When the proposed arrangements had first been discussed, Jericho had objected strenuously.

"Why the hell do we have to be responsible for the company and his family if something ever happens to him?" he'd demanded.

"Jerry, Jerry," the older man had said kindly in an effort to placate him. "You kow that Barton has the company holdings tied up tighter than a drum. There'll probably be little need for our services," and he sighed, "unless his widow makes it impossible."

"Then I won't be a party to it, Paul," he'd replied heatedly.

But even though he'd objected strongly at the time, he now found himself involved not only in Barton's company, but with his family as well.

The reading of the Will was handled by Paul Moran, and since Jericho had read it over very carefully before Barton had signed it, he soon found himself not listening to the legal mumbo-jumbo.

Then suddenly Belle, the Walowski's housekeeper, burst into a torrent of tears that brought him back to reality. He looked over at the white haired woman whose head was bowed in grief, while Julia Barton comforted her. He'd personally handled the trust that Stonewall had insisted be set up for Belle, and in private both Paul and he had chalked up his generosity to one of his many eccentricities. Now the woman wept openly. Poor soul, Jericho thought, and then dismissed any concern.

The monotonous hum of Paul's voice continued on and Jericho began to feel drowsy. Then Paul cleared his throat loudly.

"The following clause which I'm about to read is an addendum to the original Will and Trusts, and was initiated just prior to Stonewall's trip to Washington."

Jericho straightened in his chair and looked at Paul questioningly, as he'd known nothing about any addendum.

Then Paul began, "I, Stonewall Barton, herewith bequeath to Jerry Smith, the sum of one-million dollars as a token of my appreciation for his outstanding help, guidance and friendship."

Paul paused to look at Jericho who'd turned pale. Then he continued. "As God has not seen fit to bless me with a son of my own, and since I have been inspired by the brilliance and caring manner of Jerry Smith, I trust that he will, in his wisdom, accept this bequest with my wholehearted affection. Signed, Stonewall Barton."

The silence which followed was almost tangible while Paul

Moran solemnly folded the legal documents and slipped them into his briefcase.

Julia was the first to approach Jericho. "Jerry, I do hope that you'll accept my husband's gift," and she paused to gather courage. "Stonewall spoke of you so much," and then her voice caught with emotion. "It seemed at times almost as though you were his son. I'm only sorry I couldn't give him one." Then taking Adele by the arm, she quickly left the room, leaving only Belle, Dolly Paul and himself.

Belle moved to him and spoke hesitantly. "Mr. Smith, Stoney had a real affection for you," and she stared at him long and hard. "You know, if I didn't know better, you just could be his son. There's a striking resemblance, especially along the jaw line." Then she, too, hurried away.

Jericho appeared stunned and at a total loss for words following the remarks made by both Julia Barton and Belle. The look that he gave Paul and Dolly was one of complete bewilderment. "God," he whispered hoarsely, "Why me?"

Paul shook his head and Dolly merely shrugged her shoulders.

"Jerry," Paul said, "let me explain," and he paused until he'd gained his young friend's attention. "When Stonewall first came to me about this bequest I'll have to admit that I made a concerted effort to dissuade him. I had the gut feeling that you'd be uncomfortable with it, and I also knew that you didn't want to be forced into a commitment with the Barton family."

He shook his head and smiled, although there seemed to be a trace of sadness. "But you know Stonewall. He always got his way and, it *was* his money." Then he laughed ruefully. "That man even went so far as to threaten that if I didn't do it, he'd find someone who would. So, I did it, and of course was sworn to secrecy."

Then a faraway look crept into his eyes. "I've wondered of late, since all of this happened, if he didn't have some kind of a premonition. Some people do, you know."

Then he looked almost sternly at his wife and Jericho. "Don't you both think that it's about time we all got back to our own lives? We've buried Stonewall and, God willing," and he crossed himself, "this will be the final page of his story."

As they left the Barton residence, it was Belle, the housekeeper who watched from an upstairs window. She murmured to herself,

"I wonder if Stoney ever saw the same thing that I did?"

Then the black limousine swept out of sight, leaving behind an unexplained mystery.

Upon their return from Montana, Jericho buried himself in matters that had been pushed aside. He also found himself deeply involved with the upcoming election in the capacity of Chairman of the Party and had made numerous trips to Washington to confer with the incumbent senators and representatives who were running for re-election that Fall.

Then, the Democratic National Convention was held in early July and after taking part in that weeklong wild and chaotic affair, he discovered he was becoming even more serious about politics.

Schuyler Martin constantly appeared at his elbow to introduce him to other State delegates and also to many top ranking officials. There were times when he felt as though he were being put on display, and if the truth had been known . . . he was, for Schuyler had extensive plans for his future.

After the nomination of John Kennedy to run for the Presidency, and the selection of Lyndon Johnson as his running mate, Jericho began to spend more and more time in the nation's capitol. Following one such stay he returned home to Wichita, feeling literally pulled in both directions. He liked the practice of law, but he had discovered that politics was much more exciting. Still, there was Paul and Dolly to consider.

One evening, after a long and hectic day, the three had shared a late dinner, and Jericho brought up the subject.

"Paul, you know how much I've been away of late and with the campaign ahead, it's apparent to me, at least, that I'm not going to be able to do my share with the firm. I'm sure you both know how much this concerns me. I owe my allegiance to you and Dolly, and I feel as though I'm shirking my responsibilities."

Paul and Dolly both smiled.

"Jerry, we've managed so far without you," Paul said kindly, "although at times it hasn't been all that easy. However, you have a long road ahead of you and we won't stand in your way."

Jericho knew that his friend meant every word.

"I do have a plan which I wanted to discuss with both of you," and he toyed with his coffee spoon for a moment, deep in thought.

"I've considered leasing an apartment in Virginia until the election's over and will undoubtedly be spending most of my time there. How do you two feel about it?"

Paul and Dolly looked into each other eyes and then nodded in agreement. "It's a good idea, Jerry," Paul replied.

"You're absolutely certain you wouldn't mind?"

"We'll mind not seeing you every day, but if we should need you, there's always the telephone," Dolly interjected.

"Then, I'll go ahead. Brandy Martin has offered to help me find a suitable place, and it'll sure save on the hotel bills." His voice held the excitement of a small boy. Then in a rush of emotion he said, "What would I ever do without the two of you?" and he reached across the table to take Dolly's hand.

"What would *we* do without you, is really the question here," Dolly replied softly. "Go for it, Jerry. Whatever it is that you feel you have to do, go after it," and she paused. "With our blessings."

Jericho arrived in Alexandria at the beginning of September. Brandy Martin, true to his word, and feeling somewhat indebted to his friend, had found a nicely furnished one-bedroom apartment within an easy drive of both the Democratic Headquarters and the Martin home in Georgetown. It had been Brandy's suggestion, after Jericho had put away his belongings, that they join the Martin family for dinner. Although their relationship at the moment seemed to be a bit strained, Jericho accepted.

When they arrived at the Martin residence they found Elizabeth waiting on the veranda, her smile radiating excitement. "My two favorite men," she bubbled and placed her arms through theirs as they entered the house.

"Mother, Father, they're here," she called out by way of announcing their arrival.

Schuyler came into the foyer where he greeted Jericho warmly. Then, with Elizabeth chattering a mile a minute, they returned to the drawing room where they found Kate and Emily Martin enjoying a glass of wine.

First, Jericho went to Schuyler's mother to pay his respects, and she expressed pleasure at his being in Washington again. Then he turned to Kate whose smile appeared warm though her eyes remained cool.

"How nice to see you, Jerry. I understand that you've taken an apartment," she remarked politely.

"Yes, Brandy found one for me, and I'm here for the duration," he laughed. "Of course I'll be returning to Wichita whenever Paul gets in a bind."

"How nice," she responded, and glanced at her daughter who was obviously in seventh heaven.

During the course of the evening meal the conversation drifted almost automatically to the upcoming election. Although Jericho had made his own plans and itinerary in order to work closely with the incumbents from his home state, Schuyler was insistent that he share his large suite of offices. Jericho listened attentively to his reasoning, saving money, and so on, and it seemed logical, but he sensed that there was much more to Schuyler's offer than saving a few dollars.

Elizabeth had found the conversation to be boring and when they had finished dinner and adjourned once again to the library, she managed to pull Jericho aside. "When can we talk?" she'd asked, an almost pleading tone in her voice.

Jericho's glance swept around the room. Schuyler had been called away to take an important telephone call, Brandy had disappeared upstairs to change his clothes in order to take a dip in the pool, and Emily and Kate were engrossed in conversation.

"What about now?" he whispered, smiling conspiratorially.

Elizabeth took his hand and they slipped out a seldom used side door into the garden. Still holding hands, they walked down the path in silence, while the rays from the moon made it seem almost like it was daylight. When they came to a bench, they sat down. Jericho slipped his arm around Elizabeth and she moved close to him and laid her head on his chest. The fragrance from the delicate perfume she wore and her proximity aroused Jericho. When she looked up into his eyes, he not only saw her longing, but felt his own.

"Kiss me, Jerry, Please kiss me," she whispered, and without any further invitation he pulled her into his arms and kissed her with all the pent-up emotion that he'd so successfully hidden.

As they caressed each other in their newly discovered desire, they failed to hear footsteps coming down the path, Schuyler, at the insistence of his wife, had gone in search of Elizabeth and Jericho.

When he stumbled upon the romantic scene, he discreetly stepped into the shadows . . . but still he listened.

"Jerry," Elizabeth said breathlessly, "you know that I've loved you since the first day I saw you." She laughed huskily. "I made up my mind then that someday you'd discover me."

Jericho pulled her even closer and whispered softly, "I love you, Elizabeth. God, how I love you," and for a moment he was overcome by emotion. It was obvious that he wanted her physically as well as emotionally, but he was also aware that because of their religious upbringings, he would not take her.

"Do you want me?" Elizabeth asked.

"Want you? Can't you tell?" and he took her small hand and placed it against his erection. For a moment a look of fright came into her eyes, but then she saw the love in Jericho's face and she stroked him gently.

Suddenly he jerked away and got to his feet.

Alarmed, Elizabeth rose from the bench and stood before him.

"Did I do something wrong?" she asked.

Jericho shook his head and then crushed her in his arms. "It's just that I want you so much, Elizabeth," he said gently, "and I'm older than you."

"I'm almost nineteen," she replied indignantly, "and I'm a woman now, not some child." Her dark eyes sparkled. "If you want me, I'm yours."

Jericho moved away and looked up into the stillness of the star filled night.

"No, Elizabeth," he finally said, "we'll not do that. We need to get to know one another far better and spend more time together." Then he paused and turned to look at her. "God only knows when that will ever happen. There's so much to do," and a deep sigh filled with frustration escaped him.

"Jerry," she said as she placed a hand on his arm, "I understand that probably better then anyone," and she laughed slightly. "My mother is a classic example of the woman who waits," and then she frowned. "You know, if I were her, I'd become more active both politically and socially." Then she shrugged. "Oh well, we're all different."

Jericho nodded in agreement, then took her arm as they returned to the bench.

He put his arms around her. "Elizabeth," he said softly, "I love you," and looked into the depths of her eyes, "but we'll simply have to wait until the right time. The next few months are going to be hell."

"How well I know, darling. But please understand one thing. I'll also be working on the campaign for John Kennedy as a volunteer."

Her statement came as a complete surprise since she'd always appeared somewhat detached and indifferent whenever politics became the issue.

"Who got you involved?" Then he saw the look of amusement in her eyes.

"Who else but my father," and she let out a giggle.

"That figures," Jericho replied and then joined in her laughter.

Schuyler Martin had eavesdropped quite enough on their conversation and felt well pleased. With extreme caution, he left his hiding place and headed back up the path toward the house. Kate would simply have to be satisfied that he knew what was best for their daughter, and as he walked along the smile on his face was one of quiet satisfaction.

20

The weeks of autumn rushed by and more often than not, Jericho found himself working alongside Elizabeth. One of the many tasks that he'd been assigned was the recruitment of volunteers to man Democratic Headquarters and he'd discovered very quickly that Elizabeth possessed an almost seductive knack at securing them.

Some nights it had been well past midnight when the two of them finally left headquarters, and on one such occasion Jericho had suggested that Elizabeth stay over at his apartment.

When he'd first mentioned it, she'd looked at him in a puzzled manner since he'd been the one who'd refused to become intimate. For a moment, she thought that he might have had a change of heart. But she was to be disappointed for Jericho had taken a pillow off the bed and with a blanket had curled up on the davenport, while she had the bedroom to herself.

Kate Martin had objected strongly to Elizabeth's sudden change in behavior but Schuyler had turned an almost mute ear to her complaints.

"Kate, my dear," he'd said pleasantly. "Have you forgotten how young you were when we fell in love?" But even his teasing manner couldn't shake her dark mood.

"Life is different now," she'd replied hotly. "All we read and hear about these days is the sexual revolution,'' and she glared at him. ''Do you want our daughter to have the reputation of being a whore?''

For a moment Schuyler remained immobile and when he turned to look at Kate his face was flushed with anger. ''Don't ever say that about Elizabeth again, or even imply it!'' he snarled. ''I happen to know a lot more about their relationship than you do!''

''He's not the man for her,'' Kate protested vehemently. ''He's too old for Elizabeth . ... she's still a child.'' Kate rose from her chair and paced around the room. ''I wish to God that Jerry Smith had never come into our lives.''

Schuyler's look was speculative. ''I don't understand why you dislike him. He's a wonderful young man.''

Kate's eyes clouded. ''Forget it,'' she said abruptly.

Schuyler stared at her for a moment, then said, ''Well, my dear, like it or not, you might as well prepare yourself for the inevitable.''

''What do you mean?''

''They will be married.''

''Over my dead body!''

Schuyler frowned. Kate had never reacted so violently to any of Elizabeth's other suitors, but then she had never shown any serious interest in them until Jerry.

''Well, just what do you intend to do about it? Banish her to some Godforsaken school?''

''That's not such a bad idea,'' Kate replied, her eyes flashing.

''Well, my dear, that will never happen,'' Schuyler replied. ''I'm the head of this household . . . don't ever forget it, Kate!'' and he strode masterfully from the room.

''What will I do?'' Kate moaned. ''They can't marry!''

Yet deep within she knew that even though she continued to voice her objection and would make whatever efforts she could to keep them apart, Schuyler would ultimately win.

''Oh, God,'' she said, ''Why?''

A few weeks prior to the election, Jerry had returned to Wichita as he felt that it was a necessity to be with the congressional candidates.

Paul Moran, with Dolly by his side, had attended many party

functions on his behalf in his absence, and they'd also traveled from one end of the State to the other. Paul was a well known and well loved figure on the campaign trail, and although Jerry was now rightfully the Chairman, he was grateful that his friend had been willing to do his 'dirty work,' as he called it, while he was performing what he deemed to be more important tasks in the nation's capitol.

Even though the final weeks and days were filled with total involvement in the campaign process, Jerry placed a call to Elizabeth every night. Often it was very late, but she was always waiting. He remembered how she'd stated that her mother Kate was the classic example of the woman who waited, and he knew that Elizabeth would be the same.

After one long and hectic day, when nothing had seemed to go right, Jerry forgot how tired and wretched he was when Elizabeth answered the phone.

"God, but it's good to hear your voice," he said with obvious relief.

Elizabeth sensed immediately that he was experiencing difficulties. "Darling," she said gently, "is something wrong?"

In a rush of desire and emotion, Jerry blurted into the phone, "When will you marry me?"

Elizabeth Martin wasn't the least bit surprised at his spontaneous outburst. Since the final nights they'd spent together at his apartment, they both were having difficulty in being apart.

Very gently, she replied, "Whenever you like, Jerry."

"Thank God," he murmured. "Tomorrow I'm going to the jewelers, no matter who or what falls apart. Would you be willing to be engaged for now at least?"

"Yes, my love," Elizabeth replied softly, feeling her physical need for him beginning to mount within her.

Dolly Moran didn't appear to be the least bit surprised when Jericho approached her about accompanying him to the best jewelry store that Wichita offered, and secretly she'd been pleased that he'd taken her into his confidence.

"Are you going public with your engagement to Elizabeth?" she'd asked.

"Not yet," he replied. "There's so much happening now with

the election that the announcement of our engagement would undoubtedly be back page news." He smiled ruefully. "Not that I care personally, but you know the Martins. They'll want it plastered all over the *Post*."

Dolly nodded in agreement. She'd become quite fond of Schuyler Martin over the years and when she and Paul had been guests in their home, she'd found that Kate Martin, although a gracious and charming hostess, had seemed to be almost distant and her actions had mystified her.

As they approached the entrance to the jewelry store, Dolly suddenly placed her hand on Jerry's arm. "Jerry," Dolly said, "will you tell Elizabeth that I accompanied you?"

He laughed slightly at her obvious concern. "God, Dolly, since I've never done anything like this before, I haven't given a thought to what her reaction might be." Then a twinkle came into his eyes. "Shall we keep this as our secret?"

"I think that would be wise," and she laughed pleasantly. "Every woman wants to believe that her 'knight in shining armor' chose her engagement ring by himself." She paused, then went on, "I'll help you select several that I think would be suitable, but the final choice is up to you, or you can choose something different. Fair enough?"

"Fair enough." Then, taking her by the arm, they entered the jewelry store.

When Dolly and Jericho entered the store, the owner rushed forward to meet them, rudely brushing aside a sales clerk.

"Good morning, Mrs. Moran," he almost gushed, and Dolly smiled slightly and murmured a reply. Then he turned to Jericho. "And how's our up and coming Chairman these days?"

Without waiting for Jericho's reply he rushed on. "Now then, what can I do for you today?" and he glanced from one to the other.

Dolly looked at Jericho who seemed to be almost in a daze, so she answered. "Mr. Smith would like to see some of your best diamonds," and she nudged Jericho who nodded in agreement.

A gleam came into the proprietor's eyes. "Is this to be an engagement ring?"

At this remark Dolly silenced him with a look.

"Please try to be a little discreet," she said between clenched teeth.

"Oh, yes, ma'am," he replied, mollified. "Would you care to come into my private office."

"That would be nice," Dolly said, and taking Jericho by the arm she guided him down the hallway to the man's office.

While they waited for the jeweler to return they remained silent, and within a short time he reappeared bearing several velvet lined trays.

"Well, here we are," he remarked, smiling pleasantly, and placed one of the trays on the table in front of his guests.

Dolly's well trained eye saw immediately that these rings were far too flamboyant and gaudy for someone like Elizabeth.

"These won't do," she said emphatically.

Quickly the tray was removed and another replaced it.

This time Dolly scrutinized the rings carefully and saw several that would be appropriate for Elizabeth. Jericho remained quiet and watched her closely. He had been rather surprised when she'd dismissed the first tray so quickly. Carefully she selected several rings from the second tray and placed them to one side. When her selection was complete she turned to Jericho.

"You might like to take a look at those I've selected. They are all quite lovely, and I believe you'll find something that Elizabeth will like."

Then she settled back in her chair while Jericho looked at one ring and then another. The last ring that Dolly had selected from the tray had caught his eye, for the cut of the stone was quite different. The setting was also delicate and he could almost visualize Elizabeth accepting it from him.

"I like this one," he said and indicated the ring.

"Good choice, Jerry," and Dolly smiled. "It would have been mine, too."

The jeweler beamed as the ring that Jericho had selected was one of the finest and most expensive that he carried.

Jericho picked up the ring and handed it to him. "I'll have this one."

"You and Mrs. Moran have made an excellent choice, Mr. Smith. I presume you'll want to take it with you?"

"Certainly," Jericho replied, then paused. "By the way, what's the price? I haven't asked."

"This ring is fifteen-hundred, and a bargain at that price I might add."

"Fine. Please see that it's placed in a suitable ring box."

"Of course. I'll personally see to it," and the man left Dolly and Jericho alone.

"Dolly, this will be the only engagement ring that I'll ever buy, so the hell with cost!" and he reached over and gave her a hug.

Late that evening he placed his usual call to Elizabeth. After exchanging small talk concerning the election, Jericho asked, "Is there a chance that you could fly out here for the weekend?"

"Does it have something to do with the campaign?"

"No, Elizabeth. I simply want you here with me."

"I don't know how mother would feel," she replied, sounding a bit hesitant.

"Ask your father," Jericho answered. "I'm sure that he'd be willing to let you. In fact, Dolly and Paul Moran would enjoy having you as their house guest, if that will help."

"Oh, how I'd love to. It's been so long since we've been together," and she sighed. "I'll go find Daddy. Hang on."

Jericho waited patiently for Elizabeth to return, but when the phone was picked up, instead of her voice he heard Schuyler Martin.

"What's this about Elizabeth coming to Wichita?" he asked.

"Schuyler, you know that it's impossible for me to get away now, and frankly we miss each other. That should surely come as no surprise to you. The Morans have offered to be chaperones."

For a moment Schuyler hesitated, as he knew that Kate would give him hell. Then he quickly made up his mind.

"She'll be on a flight Friday, Jerry. Take good care of her."

"Thanks, Schuyler, I will. Now, may I speak to Elizabeth?"

"Certainly, and I'll see you after the elections."

"Yes sir," he replied.

Elizabeth returned to the phone and her voice soared with excitement. "I'll count the days," she whispered softly.

"You can bet that I will, too," Jericho responded. Then, "Do you mind staying with Dolly and Paul?"

"Certainly not, but I do hope that we'll have time alone."

"That's the first order of business, believe me," he replied.

"Will you meet my plane?" she asked.

"Of course. Have your father call the Morans with your schedule. I'll be in and out so much that I could possibly miss his call."

"Only four more days," Elizabeth murmured and Jericho could almost visualize the longing in her eyes.

"I know. Now I must go, darling. I'll call again tomorrow. Sweet dreams, my love."

"Good night, Jerry, I love you."

"Good night, Elizabeth."

After he'd replaced the telephone, he leaned back in his chair and then carefully removed the velvet box from his jacket pocket and slowly lifted the lid. Almost entranced, he gazed at the sparkling diamond and his thoughts drifted back to Mother Jean Marie. He smiled in remembrance. "How pleased she'd be," he murmured to himself, then pushed himself out of the chair to head back for another round of meetings.

21

As Jericho waited impatiently for Elizabeth's plane to arrive, he thought of the meeting he'd bypassed in order to meet her. He'd found it necessary to ask Paul Moran to take his place. For once, he was pushing politics aside to welcome the woman who'd soon become his wife.

When Elizabeth entered the terminal from the jetway her startling beauty caused heads to turn, but she had eyes only for Jericho. In welcome, he held out his arms and she walked into them. For a time they said nothing, completely ignoring the amused looks of the other passengers. Then their lips met and they became totally oblivious to the titterings of several older women who passed by.

After retrieving Elizabeth's luggage, they entered Jericho's convertible and headed for the Moran house.

Elizabeth slipped close to Jericho and placed her hand lightly on his knee. At her touch, his desire mounted and he wondered if he'd be able to control himself.

When they pulled into the driveway at Dolly's home, Elizabeth said reluctantly, "I promised mother that I'd call."

The slight smile that Jericho gave her was sardonic, still he knew that it was imperative he please Kate Martin. He nodded, then took the key that Dolly had given him and unlocked the door. After the door closed behind them, Jericho pulled Elizabeth into his arms; his mouth covered her willing one and they were lost in desire.

The sharp staccato ring of the telephone shattered the romantic moment.

"Damn," Jericho muttered and moved to the telephone.

"Smith here," he said, his voice sounding almost belligerent.

"This is Kate Martin," was the cool reply.

"Oh, Mrs. Martin," he said and quickly made an effort to sound pleased. "Elizabeth and I have just arrived from the airport and she was preparing to call you. Just a moment and I'll put her on."

He beckoned to Elizabeth to take the phone. It was obvious from the dark look on his face that she was angry.

"Yes, mother," she said sharply, then listened.

"We just got here. The plane was late. No, Mrs. Moran isn't here right now. Yes, I will," and then she banged down the phone.

Elizabeth turned to Jericho. "Hold me, please hold me," she said and almost threw herself into his arms.

"What's wrong?" he asked gently.

Elizabeth remained silent, but when she finally drew away he could see a trace of tears in her eyes.

"Oh, it's mother. Who else?" she replied dogmatically, then nervously ran her fingers through her long dark hair. "She's been a bitch ever since Daddy said I could come visit you. I don't know what her problem is, but it seems to get worse by the day."

"Come, little one," Jericho said softly, and guided Elizabeth to the loveseat. "Want an opinion from someone who's never been a parent?" he asked jokingly.

At his remark, Elizabeth half-smiled. "I'd welcome any kind of reasoning if it would explain why she's so awful! You'd think that I was twelve, instead of nineteen!"

Jericho picked up her hand and caressed it gently. He'd known from the beginning that Kate Martin really didn't like him and in fact, didn't like anyone who courted her daughter.

Elizabeth's look was expectant. "Well, what is it you have to say?"

Then he began. "You see, my sweet, you're Kate's only child."

Like a flash, she interrupted him. "No, Jerry, she has Sky and Brandy too, and she never gives them a hard time."

Jericho laughed gently. "Sky and Brandy happen to be her stepsons, and you are her own flesh and blood. That does make a difference."

"I suppose so, but she'll never keep me from you. Never!" she cried vehemently.

"I hope not," and he paused momentarily. "I have something for you," and he reached into his jacket pocket and brought out the ring box. With a flourish, he handed it to her.

Elizabeth looked at the box for a moment and like an eager child, opened it. Her face was flushed with excitement and her eyes sparkled when she saw the beauty of the ring. She turned to Jericho.

"Oh, darling, it's simply beautiful. Please put it on, oh, please," and she held out her left hand, arching her fingers gracefully. Very carefully, Jericho removed the ring from its resting place and placed it on the third finger of her hand. Together they admired the symbolism, both acutely aware that the ring meant total commitment.

"Any doubts?" Jericho asked as Elizabeth seemed unusually quiet.

When she turned to look at him her smile was radiant.

"Oh, no, Jerry, no doubts at all." Then she was in his arms.

The few days that Elizabeth and Jericho shared passed much too quickly.

Dolly Moran saw to it that the young lovers spent every possible moment together, and she'd even gone so far as to fend off the calls that religiously came each day from Kate Martin. Her usual reply to Kate's continual barrage of questions was polite but noncommital. "Elizabeth and Jerry were attending party functions and the hour was late when they returned." At times she could almost feel Kate's rage from afar when she continued to receive the same stock replies. Although Dolly respected her concern for her only daughter, if the truth were known she thought she was making a royal ass of herself.

On the night prior to Elizabeth's return to the East coast, she and Jericho had had a private supper with Monsignor O'Connell. Peter O'Connell, when he'd met Elizabeth, had given his hearty approval of Jericho's choice for a bride, for he'd found her to be not only enchanting, but also of the same strict Catholic upbringing as his young friend.

"When do you plan on announcing your engagement?" he asked point blank, his shrewd old eyes sweeping first to Elizabeth and then to Jericho.

"We've not really discussed it," Elizabeth replied and looked at Jericho. "When do you think it would be appropriate?"

For a moment Jericho remained silent. "Are you in any rush?" he asked.

Elizabeth frowned slightly, not quite fully understanding his hesitation.

"Don't you want people to know?" she replied almost rudely.

Jericho reached across the table and took her hand, as Peter O'Connell put his napkin to his mouth in order to hide the smile which touched his lips.

"Of course I do, Elizabeth," Jericho replied quickly and pressed her fingers.

"Then what's the problem?"

Suddenly she realized that they were having a tiff in front of the Monsignor, and she turned to him. "I'm sorry, Father O'Connell. Please excuse our behavior."

Peter O'Connell's smile was almost paternal. "You have no need to apologize, dear girl. I probably shouldn't have butted in."

"You had every right," Elizabeth responded, giving Jericho a dark look.

Embarrassed, Jericho hastened to explain. "I want to announce our engagement when it's right. I'm sure that you're aware your father and mother will want it in the *Post* and if we do it now, just before the election, it won't receive the attention they'd expect. It's that simple."

"Oh, pooh on my family," Elizabeth retorted. "Is that the only reason?"

"Of course. I'd be happy to tell the world," and the smile that he gave her melted her anger.

Monsignor O'Connell interrupted them. "May I give you some advice?"

"Certainly, Father," Elizabeth replied directing her attention to the old priest.

"I'd advise that you do as Jerry has suggested and wait until all the hullabaloo's over with the election and the inauguration. Then, if Schuyler and Kate want to make a big splash, the papers will be ready." He glanced from one to the other. "Of course, your family should know, Elizabeth; and yours too, Jerry," he continued matter-of-factly.

"I agree," Jericho replied and Elizabeth nodded.

"I do so wish that you'd be with me when I tell mother and daddy," Elizabeth said plaintively.

"Would you like me to be?"

"Could you?"

Monsignor O'Connell chuckled at their obvious need to be alone and he realized that he'd taken up most of their final evening. Pushing himself back from the table he rose to his feet, straightened his cassock and addressed his guests.

"Elizabeth, Jerry, I think this is the time for me to turn in. Stay here in the garden as long as you like." He turned to Jericho, "You know the way out," and he winked solemnly.

By now both young people had risen to their feet. Jericho shook the priest's hand, and Elizabeth, acting on impulse, kissed him on his wrinkled cheek.

"Well, now, that's what I like," he said smiling rakishly, "having a lovely young woman kiss me." Then he turned and went into the darkness of the rectory.

On the drive back to the Moran house both remained silent. Morning would find Elizabeth on her way back to Washington and neither looked forward to saying goodbye again.

When they entered the house a single lamp had been left burning. Jericho moved to it and swiftly turned it off, leaving as the only light the rays from the moon which filtered through the draperies.

Taking Elizabeth into his arms he pressed her body close to his almost devouring her with his kisses. As the minutes went by they failed to hear the soft footsteps on the staircase. Then, suddenly, the room was ablaze with light and Kate Martin stood before them, fury written on her face.

Elizabeth was the first to recover from the shock of seeing her mother, and she quickly moved away from Jericho, smoothing her dress almost automatically. Still, they all remained silent. The only sound was the slight tapping noise of Kate's long fingernails on the stair bannister.

Finally, Elizabeth turned and moved toward her. "Mother," she said, each word measured, "just what are you doing here?"

As she'd been speaking, Jericho had moved across the room to take his place beside her, while Kate, from her vantage point on the stairs, looked down on them almost as though she were judge and jury.

"This is the reason," she replied coldly, indicating the disheveled look of both young people, and her lips curled slightly in distaste.

"Jerry and I have done nothing wrong. When will you ever learn to trust me?" Elizabeth asked.

Kate looked first at her daughter and then at the flushed face of her companion. For a moment she remembered how passionately she'd loved Stoney.

"I believe that I have every right to be here," she replied, sounding almost contemptuous. "You've never bothered to return my telephone calls, and your father . . ." and her look became ominous, "doesn't seem to have much common sense these days. What do you think our friends will think when they hear about you sneaking off here?"

"Oh, mother. I didn't sneak off. I asked and received permission. You know that!" Her composure was now growing thin. "After all, I am nineteen." It was then that she held out her hand, "And if we must satisfy you, Jerry and I are engaged!"

Kate turned pale when she saw the ring sparkling on her daughter's hand. As she looked into Elizabeth's eyes she saw a gleam of triumph.

For a moment, Kate Martin was at a loss for words. Then she murmured, almost as though she were talking to herself, "Engaged?" However, she quickly regained her composure, moved down the steps and settled herself on the davenport, motioning to the two young people to join her.

Elizabeth and Jericho returned once again to the loveseat and seated themselves, with Jericho holding Elizabeth's hand. Kate noticed his gesture and the smile on her face as sardonic.

"So you're engaged, and without your beau asking either your father or Me? May I ask who gave you that privilege?"

Elizabeth glanced at Jericho whose look remained impassive. then she replied, "Mother, this isn't the Dark Ages. My God, you

were engaged to daddy and lived in the same house long before you
were ever married!''

"That was an entirely different situation," she hissed, "and your
father had great respect for me."

Those words caused Jericho's anger to rise and his lips trembled
with emotion as he replied to her obvious attack. "Mrs. Martin,"
he said slowly and distinctly, "I respect and love Elizabeth far more
then you could possibly imagine. When she spent time at my
apartment, I slept on the davenport and she was alone. We've done
nothing wrong." He paused. "If you don't want to believe us, then
I'd say that it's you who have the problem."

Completely ignoring Jericho, she turned to Elizabeth. "Does
your father know?"

"No. We were going to tell both of you when the election's over.
We thought it might be advisable to keep it quiet until that's
settled. However, if you wish to announce our engagement, please
feel free to do so," Elizabeth replied indignantly.

"That will be quite enough, young lady," Kate replied sharply.
"Now," and she quickly switched her attention to Jericho, "if you
don't mind, our plane leaves very early and I do need to have some
rest. This trip has been far from pleasurable."

When Kate remained seated and made no noticeable effort to
leave, Elizabeth got up from the loveseat and indicated that Jericho
should follow her. Without so much as saying good-night, the two
young people left the house and ran to the car. As the motor started
and the headlights flashed on, Kate rushed out the door, arriving
just in time to see her only child disappear into the darkness of the
night.

Kate turned to re-enter the house but found Dolly Moran
blocking her way.

"Excuse me," Kate said coolly and brushed passed Dolly
heading toward the stairs, but Dolly grasped her arm.

"I think that you and I need to have a talk," Dolly said quietly.

Kate shrugged but did not move. "What have we to talk about?
You've been involved from the beginning in this clandestine love
affair between my daughter and your fair-haired boy," she
snapped.

"I resent your inference, Mrs. Martin," Dolly replied, trying desperately to control her anger. "You've known both Paul and me for a long time, and Jerry, too." Then she shook her head in bewilderment. "For the life of me I don't understand why you can't accept the fact that Elizabeth and Jerry love each other and want to marry."

"She's much too young," Kate replied.

"How old were you when you and Mr. Martin were married?" Dolly countered.

"That was a long time ago and has nothing to do with Elizabeth."

"Oh, but I think it does. If I'm correct, from the stories I've heard, you lived in Mr. Martin's household for months prior to your marriage," and the look she gave Kate Martin was slightly contemptuous.

Kate Martin had never really been a fighter. She knew that she had little ground to stand on, and when she looked up at Dolly tears had formed in her eyes and she moved to the davenport. Dolly joined her and for a time the two women sat quietly, one making an effort to stem the flow of tears, and the other calming the anger that had claimed her.

It was Dolly who broke the uneasy silence. "Kate, I'm sorry if you feel that I've overstepped my bounds, but you should trust Jerry. He's a wonderful young man."

Kate dried her eyes and smiled wanly, knowing that no matter how much she wanted to, she could never reveal the terrible knowledge that she was Jericho's mother. There was simply too much at stake.

"I'm sorry for my behavior, Mrs. Moran. You see, when I was a young woman, my life was not all that it should have been," and she sighed. "I want only what's best for my daughter."

"I understand, Kate, but you also have to learn to trust. After all, Schuyler Martin took you as his wife when you were very young and look how fortunate your life has been."

"That's true." She sighed, "Schuyler insists that Jerry is the perfect husband for Elizabeth; I don't know if he'll ever forgive me for coming out here."

Dolly looked at Kate compassionately. She touched her shoulder gently which produced a torrent of tears.

"Oh, Kate," Dolly said softly and pulled her into her arms. "Everything will be fine."

Dolly remained silent as the ticking of the old grandfather's clock was the only sound as Kate Martin released all the pent-up emotion that had almost consumed her.

22

The presidential election came and went with John Fitzgerald Kennedy being elevated to the highest office in the land.

And in the late Spring of 1961 Kate and Schuyler Martin hosted a lavish party at Magnolia Hill, attended by the elite of the nation's capitol, to formally announce the engagement and forthcoming marriage of their daughter, Elizabeth Marie to Jerry Smith.

The wedding was planned for mid-June and because Jericho had insisted, his old friend, Monsignor Peter O'Connell, had been invited to officiate at the ceremony. Kate wisely refrained from making any comment because she knew that if she voiced any objection there would be hell to pay, not only from her husband and Emily Martin, but from her daughter as well.

Unfortunately, Jericho's parents, due to ailing health were unable to be present; however, both Jericho and Dolly Moran, who had now become a close friend of the elderly couple, kept them abreast of all of the exciting happenings.

Next on Jericho's agenda was to find a suitable home for his bride-to-be. As had become his custom over the years, he turned to Dolly Moran for assistance.

When they'd discussed the situation, Dolly knew that Elizabeth, although a very rich and pampered young woman, would have been satisfied to live in a tent simply to be with the man she loved, but she was also very much aware that the Martins would expect a suitable residence in the 'right' part of town for their daughter.

When Jericho had approached her, Dolly saw that he was literally worn to the bone, and she quickly agreed.

"Let me do the searching, Jerry," she'd said kindly.

"But you shouldn't have to do it alone," he'd protested, although his protest was rather feebly made.

Dolly laughed. "From the look of you, my dear boy, you need to go fishing." Then she paused, a look of contemplation in her expression. "Why don't you and Paul have a long weekend at the lake?" she asked.

A look of relief came into Jericho's eyes. "You really mean it?"

"Of course, silly. Paul needs to get away, too. He's been covering for you the past few weeks and I think he needs to get away from this heavy pace. How about it?"

"Should I ask him?"

"Go on in. If he starts to say 'no' just give me a nod. I'll straighten him out," and Jericho knew that every word she spoke was the truth.

He went to Paul's door and knocked softly.

"Come in," said the familiar voice, and at the sound Jericho felt a tug at his heart for he dearly loved the old lawyer.

When Paul Moran saw his young protege he rose from his desk and crossed the room where he placed an arm around Jericho with obvious affection.

"Well, look who's back," he boomed, in his deep and resonant voice.

"It's good to be back, Paul," Jericho replied, then immediately headed for the leather couch and sank on it, while the older man returned to his desk.

Paul scrutinized his young friend and saw the dark circles that ringed his eyes. "Washington too much for you?" he asked and laughed slightly.

"God, Paul, all they do is party," Jericho replied. "It beats me how they can do it and then perform on the hill."

"Practice, my boy, practice," Paul replied. He paused. "You're absolutely sure you want to try politics?"

At his question, Jericho smiled slightly. He knew that Paul

wanted more than anything to have him remain in his law office to become a full partner.

"Perhaps, someday. But right now I think that both you and I need to get away."

"Oh, but that's impossible," Paul said without hesitation.

"Excuse me," Jericho said and went to the door.

When Dolly saw him give a slight nod she quickly joined the two men.

"What do you mean you can't get away" she demanded, speaking directly to her husband.

"Too much work. You ought to know better than anyone else how it's been."

"Well, my love, you and Jerry are both completely worn out and I'm ordering you two to leave on Friday night and not show up until Monday."

For a moment her husband was taken by surprise.

"But how about you?" Paul asked. "What will you do?"

Dolly's smile was almost like that of a Cheshire cat. "I'm going house hunting!"

"But we have a house!" Paul remonstrated, staring at her in bewilderment.

"Jerry doesn't," she replied, "and I'm in charge."

"Is that right?" and the older man directed his attention to Jericho.

"She volunteered, Paul, and you know Dolly," he replied, an almost sheepish grin on his face.

"Well, I'll be damned," Paul Moran said and suddenly burst into laughter. "You game, Jerry? I snore."

"Hell, I wouldn't hear a freight train go through my room," he replied.

"Then it's all settled," Dolly broke in very matter-of-factly. "Now if you two will excuse me, I have a million things to do," and she turned on her heel and marched from the room.

When Paul and Jericho returned from the few days holiday, they were refreshed and rested. And Dolly, who'd done her research very carefully while they'd been away, produced a list of the most desirable properties that Wichita had to offer. Several of the homes were located in the immediate vicinity of Foxboro Estates where she and Paul resided, and one in particular had captured her imagination.

Jericho carefully read over the list and was surprised at the modest price of most of the homes. He also noted that Dolly had indicated the ones that she felt would be most suitable. That afternoon he met with her.

"Thanks for all you've done," he said.

Dolly waved her hand as though in dismissal.

"I loved every minute of it, Jerry. In fact, I'm almost sorry that it's over."

"But I need you to accompany me. I don't have the vaguest idea what to look for."

Dolly's smile was pleased. "I'd hoped you'd say that. Let me tell Paul that we're going house shopping," and she went to inform her husband that they would be away.

The balance of the afternoon they spent driving up one street and then down another. At a few houses they stopped and were shown through but Jericho hadn't seemed overly impressed. Finally, Dolly stopped in front of the one that had taken her fancy. She felt strongly that Elizabeth would like it, and hoped that Jerry could see it's possibilities. Best of all, it was within a block of the Moran residence.

Fortunately, the house had just recently been vacated and Dolly had had the wisdom to keep the keys over the protest of the real estate broker who hadn't seemed at all pleased. Skillfully, Dolly opened the front door, and with Jericho tagging along behind her, she guided him through the house, pausing occasionally to give him an opportunity to see the possibilities.

The decor of the house was cheerful and bright, for it had been freshly painted inside and out. The small yard was carefully groomed and it was obviously ready for new occupants.

When they entered the master bedroom suite Dolly stood to one side while Jericho appraised it carefully, with a slight smile touching his lips. He could almost visualize Elizabeth waking to the brilliant sunshine which flooded the room, and a thrill of anticipation went through him. When he turned to join Dolly he looked slightly embarrassed and a flush swept over his face.

"Very nice," he said formally to hide his feelings.

"I thought you might like it," Dolly said, her attitude almost off-handed.

"What's the procedure to purchase it?" Jericho asked point blank.

Dolly's face lit up. "You're serious?"

Jericho nodded. "It's exactly my idea of a home. I'm sure that Elizabeth will like it, too."

Now in a hurry, Dolly almost pushed him out of the house in her eagerness to get to the real estate office.

Once in the car she took the wheel and drove recklessly through the streets. When they reached the realtor's office he was just preparing to lock up and go home, but then Dolly and Jericho burst in.

"I've a buyer for the house on Glen Drive," Dolly announced as she swept dramatically through the door, and turned to indicate Jericho who'd followed behind more slowly.

The man's first annoyance at being interrupted quickly vanished and a broad smile creased his face.

"You're Jerry Smith," he said, as he recognized the young lawyer and then extended his hand.

"Jerry wants to buy the house," Dolly said, and added, "he's being married next month."

"How nice. Won't you please be seated." Then apologetically, he continued. "My secretary's gone for the day so I'll have to make up the papers myself."

Dolly interrupted. "I'll be glad to help. You see, I work with my husband and Jerry, and I'm very used to a typewriter."

The man heaved an audible sigh of relief, as it was now well past five o'clock and he knew the paperwork would have taken several hours with his hunt and peck system.

"Thanks, Mrs. Moran, I'll be glad to let you take over." Then as an afterthought he added, "You've undoubtedly had a part in home purchases in the past."

When she'd finished she handed the paper to Jericho who examined it carefully. He removed his pen and check book from his jacket pocket and signed the offer, and without hesitation wrote the necessary deposit check, then gave both back to Dolly. Once again she looked at the paper and Jerry's check, then handed them to the realtor.

"Easiest sale I've made in a long time," he said, eyes twinkling.

"Thanks to you, Mrs. Moran."

Dolly acknowledged his appreciation with a smile and then glanced at her watch.

"My God, Jerry, it's past six and Paul will be wondering whatever's happened to us."

As they rushed from the real estate office, the man called after them, "I'll be in touch." Then Dolly's Cadillac went roaring down the street.

Within a few days Jericho received news that he was now the proud owner of a house. He'd refrained from telling Elizabeth until he was certain, although at times when they'd talked she'd specifically questioned him as to where they'd live. On the day the news arrived, he called her.

"Great news, darling," he'd said when she answered.

Rather puzzled, she inquired. "News? About what?"

"Our new home."

"What home?"

"The one that I've just purchased for us," Jericho replied proudly.

By now Elizabeth could hardly contain her excitement. "Oh, Jerry, when can I see it?"

"Just as soon as you can catch the next flight out here," and he paused. "That is, if Kate wouldn't mind."

"You know I don't care what my mother minds, Jerry. I *have* to see our house. After all, there's shopping to be done. We'll need to have furniture, you know."

"Then by all means come ahead," Jericho replied, and paused. "I'm so anxious to see you. It's been too long."

"I know," Elizabeth responded softly, her voice a bit tremulous. "I'll be so glad when we're married."

"Me, too. Now pack a bag and I'll be waiting at the airport."

"Wonderful. See you soon," and Elizabeth hung up.

Before mentioning the trip to her mother, she packed an overnighter, called the airport, secured a reservation, and informed James to stand by for a quick trip to National.

When she went to look for Kate she was informed by a member of the household staff that Mrs. Martin had complained of a headache and that she was now taking a nap and wasn't to be disturbed.

"I'll leave a note," Elizabeth decided and sat down and dashed off a brief message.

Then she hurried from the house, got into the limousine and was on her way.

The reunion between Elizabeth and Jericho was as to be expected. They had eyes only for each other and they seemed to be in their own private world.

Dolly Moran escorted them to the house on Glen Drive, and when she saw the expression on Elizabeth's face she knew that she'd made the right choice. The young woman's enthusiasm as she wandered through the house that would be her home as Mrs. Jerry Smith almost ran rampant.

"Oh, Jerry," she said enthusiastically, "can't you just picture how perfect it will be? I love the brightness. It makes me feel," and she paused for a moment, her look contemplative, "as though I've just come through a dark tunnel to the light at the end."

Both Jericho and Dolly glanced at her sharply, neither quite understanding.

"Whatever do you mean, darling?" Jericho asked, as he slipped his arm about her trim waist.

"Oh, you know. Magnolia Hill is so big and there's so little natural light." she shrugged. "At times it seems almost artificial." Then her look became radiant. "This house is simply wonderful . . . how did you ever find it?"

Dolly had moved away but Jericho went to her and took her by the hand. "This lovely lady found it, so we have her to thank."

Elizabeth rushed to Dolly and with utter abandon threw her arms around her.

"Oh, Mrs. Moran," she whispered, "How can we ever thank you?"

Dolly slowly extricated herself from Elizabeth and then stood back. "I had a dual purpose," she stated smartly, her eyes twinkling.

Elizabeth and Jericho looked at each other, both puzzled.

"Dual purpose?" Jericho asked.

"Yes. I'm certain at this point that you don't remember but Paul and I live just around the corner. You'll be our neighbors."

For a moment the young couple seemed stunned. Then Elizabeth burst out. "How absolutely wonderful," and Jericho echoed her pleasure.

On their return to the Moran house the telephone began to ring.

Dolly picked it up immediately and then frowned slightly without saying a word. Finally, she managed, "Elizabeth, it's for you. It's Kate."

"I don't wish to speak with her."

"But why not?" Jericho asked. "You haven't had another fight, have you?"

"No, but she'll give me hell as usual," Elizabeth replied with defiance.

"Then I'll talk to her," and he crossed the room and picked up the telephone.

"Hello, Mrs. Martin," he said waxing cheerful.

"Where's my daughter, Jerry?"

"She's right here. Is something wrong?"

"Something wrong?" Kate almost shrieked. "Elizabeth sneaked out of here knowing that there's a shower being given in her honor this evening. That's what's wrong." The sound of her voice was chilling.

"I had no idea," Jericho replied and felt a trace of anger toward his fiancee.

"Well, now you know. By the way, would you mind telling me why she's there?"

"Of course not. Elizabeth came at my invitation, Mrs. Martin, so she could see our new home. It's that simple."

"I see," Kate replied coolly. "I'll make the necessary excuses for her," and she hung up.

When Jericho turned away from the telephone he saw that Dolly had disappeared, leaving him alone with Elizabeth.

Elizabeth had taken a seat on the divan and was studiously scrutinizing her ring, a soft smile playing about her lips. Jericho felt a tug at his heart because he loved her so desperately, yet he knew that it was imperative that she become more responsible if she were to be the wife of a future politician.

Taking a seat beside her he took her hand in his and when she look up into his eyes his anger quickly dissipated.

"Elizabeth, why didn't you tell me that you were committed?"

"Because I'm tired of mother's friends, grandmother's friends, and all the damned hullabaloo. You'd think that our marriage was a three ring circus. I wish that we could just run away, honestly," and the look she gave him was serious.

Jericho frowned. His desire for her was so demanding that her mere presence had become almost more then he could bear. Suddenly an idea flashed into his mind. They could have a private civil ceremony without anyone suspecting and then have the church wedding in June to please the Martins.

"Do you mean that?" he asked as he looked deep into her eyes. Elizabeth nodded.

Suddenly Jericho jumped to his feet. "I have to find Dolly," and rushed from the room to the kitchen where he found their hostess enjoying a glass of iced tea.

"Some tea?" she said sociably and indicated the pitcher and glasses on the table.

"Not now. We need your help."

By the seriousness in his voice she knew that whatever was needed was important.

"Sit down, Jerry."

After sinking into a chair opposite her, for a moment he didn't quite know what to say or how to begin. Then he blurted it out.

"Elizabeth and I want to be married in a civil ceremony tonight," and he placed his head in his hands. "We can't stand being apart any longer."

Dolly Moran, being the woman she was, could well understand for she'd known for weeks how passionately they loved one another.

"But what about the wedding plans that Kate's made?" she asked.

"Oh, that," Jericho replied ruefully. "We'll go through with it just as though we weren't married. You know the church won't consider that we're married anyway."

"That's true. Now what can I do to help? It's getting late."

"We'll need to have a license and a judge that won't talk, and we'll want you and Paul to be our witnesses."

By now Dolly was already on her way to the telephone to call the Court House and arrange for the license; and then her husband, who would certainly know a trustworthy judge.

Jericho returned to Elizabeth who looked up expectantly as he entered the room.

Kneeling before her he looked up into her eyes. "Darling," he said gently, "We're going to be married in a civil ceremony tonight."

Elizabeth's eyes sparkled. "Oh, Jerry, how I want you," and within herself she felt the stirring of desire for the man that she loved.

"No more than I want you," he replied with emotion. "Dolly's taking care of the arrangements."

Without warning he saw a look of concern cross her face. "But what about the wedding?" she asked, knowing that both Kate and Schuyler would be embarrassed if it were cancelled.

Jericho laughed. "We'll keep this wedding as our secret, my love, and give them a performance that they'll never forget," then he pulled her into his arms and kissed her.

In the dusk of the warm Kansas evening, on the flower decked patio of the Moran residence, Jerry Smith and Elizabeth Martin became husband and wife. Dolly had pressed the one dress that Elizabeth had with her, and Jericho had returned to his apartment and changed into a dark suit. Paul Moran had stopped by the florist shop on the way home and had selected an orchid corsage for the bride-to-be and a boutiniere for the groom. And, for something borrowed, they'd used Dolly's wedding ring.

Following the brief ceremony, Dolly announced that she and Paul were going to the lake for the night, and that the house was theirs.

Later that evening the Morans took their leave, while Jericho and Elizabeth toasted each other with a bottle of Paul's finest champagne. Then they made their way to their bridal chamber.

23

The following month Jericho and Elizabeth were married at The Washington Shrine of the Immaculate Conception with all the fanfare and publicity afforded such a prestigious event.

As Elizabeth came down the aisle on her father's arm, Jericho's thoughts turned to their first wedding and more especially to their wedding night which had proved to be a night that he would never forget. A tender smile brushed his lips and his eyes were bright with love for this beautiful young woman who had first claimed his heart years before. Then he glanced at Kate Martin whose smile was fixed and rather sorrowful; however, Schuyler's face was flushed with pleasure, in marked contrast to that of his wife as he gave his daughter willingly to the man that he had hoped she would marry.

Monsignor Peter O'Connell performed the nuptial Mass, and although this had not been Kate's plan, his participation was not disputed since both Jericho and Elizabeth had been insistent that he be the officiant.

Following the hour long ceremony, a reception was held at Magnolia Hill. While the guests were enjoying themselves, and after Elizabeth and Jericho had performed the ceremony of cutting the wedding cake, they slipped into the Martin limousine with James' assistance and were whisked to Washington National where a private jet awaited them.

The Bahamas proved to be their destination and they spent ten love filled days and nights completely hidden away from the public eye. Because of their previous marriage in May, they now lacked the usual frustrations of newlyweds, and their sexual fulfillment had now reached the point of near perfection. Jericho had never dreamed it was possible to love someone as deeply and passionately as he did his bride, and Elizabeth, who'd also been a novice, had become a willing and seductive sexual partner. They were perfectly mated, much the same as Kate and Schuyler.

With reluctance, Elizabeth and Jericho left their island paradise to return home, flying directly to Wichita where Paul and Dolly Moran awaited them.

During their absence, and following Elizabeth's instructions, Dolly had supervised the moving in of the new furniture that the young couple had selected when Elizabeth had visited in May. Dolly had also seen fit to have her own maid clean the house from top to bottom, but chose to make up their bed herself. The day of their arrival she'd picked bouquets of flowers from her own garden and had placed them in special places, and as she moved slowly through the house she decided that it was indeed perfect.

Paul had watched the obvious enthusiasm that his wife had shown at being so much a part of Jericho's and Elizabeth's lives, and he regretted deeply that they'd never had a child. But, even 'second-best' was better than nothing.

The Smiths settled comfortably into the routine of being married and Jericho returned to his law practice. Elizabeth, with Dolly's assistance, met the 'right' people in Wichita. The young couple were feted at many parties and their social calendar was always full. At times Jericho felt as though they were living on a merry-go-round, but Elizabeth appeared to enjoy every moment. He accepted their lifestyle, although he would have enjoyed, on occasion, having a few days when nothing was scheduled.

The role he'd acquired from Paul Moran as Party Chairman also took up a good share of his time, and it was a welcome turn of events when he found it necessary to go to Salmon, Montana, for the distribution of Stonewall Barton's estate. Paul had given him full authority and had more or less washed his hands of Pride Oil and the Barton family. It was now up to Jericho to keep everyone happy.

That September, Jericho made the trip to Salmon alone. Elizabeth, in the few months that she'd been living in Wichita, had become involved in volunteer work, and had joined the Women's club, with both activities keeping her occupied. When her husband had suggested that she accompany him on the trip to Montana, she'd refused with reluctance. Jericho knew, however, that in all probability her decision was the correct one, since Julia Barton would undoubtedly expect him to devote the majority of his time to her.

When Jericho arrived at his destination, Julia insisted that he stay at the Barton residence, and though he'd protested, he'd finally acquiesced to her demand. Since the time of Stonewall Barton's death, Julia had proved to be a surprisingly astute business woman, and Jericho had to admit that in those few months she'd become extremely knowledgeable of the inner workings of Pride Oil. Once again he was dealing with a determined, strong willed person who headed one of the largest oil conglomerates in the country.

Late one evening, following a long and tiring day spent with Julia and the other officials of Pride, Jericho ventured out on the large veranda and had settled into the comfortable old fashioned wooden swing. Alone, he stared up at the sky which was now dark as pitch with only the stars, which sparkled like diamonds, to light it. Deep in his own thoughts, he failed to hear the screen door open.

Belle, the Barton's housekeeper, had found it difficult to fall asleep and she'd put on her old flannel robe and slippers and had quietly slipped down the stairs and then out the front door. When she saw Jericho in the swing she paused to study him intently. Even though it was in the dark of night his profile was outlined by the brilliance of the stars and in that light he looked much like Stonewall Barton. Belle had experienced a rather strange feeling when she'd first set eyes on this young lawyer from Kansas, and she felt fortunate indeed that she now had the opportunity to speak with him alone.

"Mind some company?" she said, and the sound of her voice in the stillness of the night startled Jericho. He turned quickly to see who was there, and when he realized that it was Belle, he relaxed.

"Belle!" he said, "of course not," and moved over on the

swing. "Please join me," and indicated the space beside him.

He watched as the older woman moved slowly across the porch and then smiled pleasantly as she seated herself.

"Guess you couldn't sleep, either," he said, his manner friendly.

Belle nodded her head in agreement and for the first few minutes they sat quietly enjoying the motion of the old swing as it swung to and fro.

Then she turned to Jericho. "I'd like to talk with you," her look appraising.

"Of course, Belle. Some way that I can be of help?"

The smile she gave him was contrite. "No, Jerry. I don't need any help. Just some answers, that's all," and once again she looked out into the dark night. By now Jericho's curiosity was aroused.

"Answers about the trust Stonewall set up for you?"

Belle shook her head.

"Well, then, tell me what it is."

With a show of deliberation Belle turned to face him. "What do you know about Stonewall's past?" she asked, her eyes piercing into his.

Her question took Jericho completely by surprise and he stared at the elderly woman for a long moment before forming a reply. "I didn't know that Stonewall had a 'past,' other than that he was born in Kansas and came out to Montana when he was a young man. The rest is history," still his look remained puzzled.

When Belle looked at Jericho her eyes searched his face. From his expression, it was clear that he really knew very little about Stonewall Barton. She sighed deeply and wondered if she should tell him the story that Stonewall had made her promise never to reveal. Once again, deep in thought, she turned away and looked into the distance.

Jericho's gentle touch brought her back to reality.

"Belle," he said softly. "Is there something I should know?" and when she failed to respond to his question, he went on. "You know, I've had the feeling many times that something was eating at Stonewall, say intuition," and he laughed slightly. "I'll have to admit that I did like him, although he exasperated the hell out of me a good share of the time."

His statement produced a smile from his companion and then it quickly faded, leaving the wrinkled face without expression.

As they sat silently in the still of the night only the sound of the barn owls and an occasional cry from a lone coyote could be heard. The fireflies flickered brightly and as Jericho watched them he became almost mesmerized. Then he yawned, stretched, and started to get out of the swing, but Belle stopped him with a touch.

"You have to listen to me," she whispered hoarsely, and then glanced around the porch to see if they were still alone.

By now Jericho was once again alert and he seated himself, then directed his full attention to Belle.

"What is it, Belle? I've never seen you this troubled," he said kindly.

A trace of a tear formed in the corner of her eyes and at this unexpected show of emotion, Jericho took her gnarled hand in his and gently stroked it. Then, her voice breaking at times, Belle began the tale of Stonewall Barton's beginning. "My young friend," she began, her wise old eyes crinkling at the corners as she smiled almost dolefully, "I knew Stonewall Barton from the day of his birth," and she looked at Jericho to see his reaction, but his look was stoic.

"Stoney," she said, the tone of her voice almost caressing his name, "was the only child of Bess, the Madam of the house I worked in down in Kansas." Once again she glanced at Jericho, but his face remained impassive.

"We all took turns taking care of him," and her face took on a look of gentleness. "You see, we all loved Stoney just as though he were our own."

By now Jericho's interest had been aroused. "Please go on, Belle," he urged.

"Stoney was such a darling little boy," and she laughed huskily, her voice fraught with emotion, "but when he got to be in his teens he ran away." She sighed deeply, then shrugged her shoulders. "Can't say that I blame him much. The kids at school teased him unmercifully."

"But how did you ever come to work for him after so many years?" Jericho asked.

Belle smiled. "That's another story. It can keep."

Jericho nodded and waited for her to continue.

"When Stonewall ran away," Belle said, "we heard that he hired on as a ranch hand out in Western Kansas, and that's where it all began.''

"I don't understand," Jericho replied, his manner puzzled.

"You will."

Once again Jericho waited, noticing that the first flush of a new day was breaking over the far horizon.

"While Stoney was in Kansas," Belle continued, "he fell in love with a young girl."

"What's so unusual about that?"

"Well, being an inexperienced kid of eighteen, he didn't quite know how to handle the problem when it came up."

By this time Jericho was completely mystified and chose to remain silent.

"You see, the girl became pregnant with his child, and like a young fool he ran away from her," Belle said sadly.

"But why?"

"He was scared. So he hot-footed it out here to Montana where he had the good fortune to meet up with Joe Walowski," Belle replied.

"So that's what was bothering him."

Belle nodded slowly.

"His life might have been different had he accepted his responsibility," Jericho said almost cruelly.

"I suppose so. But he paid for it dearly every day of his life, and now he's dead," and then Belle began to cry.

Jericho put his arms around her and held her gently as the light of first dawn streaked across the sky. This was the scene that Julia came upon when she looked out at the fresh new day.

Before Jericho's return to Wichita, Julia Barton requested a private meeting and he arranged his schedule accordingly. On the afternoon before his departure they met over cocktails at the newly built country club, the pride of Salmon.

Once comfortably situated in a secluded corner of the bar, and after their refreshments had been served, they chatted casually about Pride Oil and the future. Jericho knew, however, that this couldn't possibly be the reason that Julia had insisted they meet, for they'd spent many hours going over Pride's affairs with the other officers of the company. So he was not surprised when Julia rather abruptly changed the subject.

"Were you aware that I saw you and Belle the other morning?" she asked, her manner direct.

Jericho smiled. "Matter of fact, I wasn't."

"The two of you seemed to be very chummy."

"Really?" Jericho replied and he looked straight into her accusing eyes.

"Yes, really," her response short.

"I suppose you're curious why we were together," Jericho said.

"Naturally. I didn't realize that you were that close to my housekeeper."

Jericho toyed with his glass, then slowly took a sip from it before he answered. "Please don't insinate that there's anything between Belle and me," he said rather caustically. "I couldn't sleep and neither could Belle, so we both ended up in the porch swing, if you must know. Besides, she's like a grandmother to me."

"But you had your arms around her," Julia pursued.

Jericho smiled slightly. "That's true."

"Why?"

"Have you ever taken the time to talk with Belle?" Jericho asked.

"Well, not really. She and Stonewall spent a lot of time together and I could never for the life of me understand why. Then he had the audacity to set up that trust fund for her. Honestly!," and it was obvious that this had angered her.

"He had a very good reason, Julia."

"My God, what could it have been. She was only a maid."

"That's not true," and he paused. "You see, Julia, Belle knew your husband when he was a small boy."

The look in Julia Barton's face was one of complete astonishment.

"But how could she have known him?"

"She happened to be a close friend of his mother back in Kansas. They go a long ways back."

"But why didn't he tell me?"

"Probably because you wouldn't have been interested," Jericho replied truthfully.

At this point Julia gulped down the balance of her drink and signalled the bartender for another.

After Julia's drink had been served she continued on with her questioning.

"What did she tell you about Stonewall?"

"Not very much, really," Jericho said, knowing that he had to give much thought to his choice of words.

"Go on, go on," Julia said impatiently.

"I'll tell you what I know," and he paused. "It seems that Belle once worked for Stonewall's mother many years ago. She was there when he was born and saw him grow up. They shared a special bond, Julia, for a long time. Then he left to work on a ranch, but when the dust storms hit the Kansas plains he decided to move on to greener pastures. That's when he came to Salmon. You know the rest."

"I thought I heard Belle crying."

"Well, she was. Belle has few friends and no family. Stonewall came the closest. She's devastated by his death, but chose to hide her real feelings."

"But why did she tell you?"

"Beats me. I guess she thought that I'd be a good listener."

For the first time since they'd met Julia smiled slightly. "You know something, Jerry Smith," she said and paused, then looked directly into his eyes, "you're one hell of a man."

Jericho felt embarrassed but managed, "Thanks Julia, I try."

"I'm going to be nicer to Belle," Julia announced, then shrugged her shoulders. "After all, Adele and I haven't much family either, and what we do have is scattered all over the country."

Then an almost forlorn look crept over her face. "I just wish that Stonewall had told me. Perhaps he'd have been happier."

"We'll never know, Julia. Now we'd better be getting back. I have an early flight tomorrow and a new bride waiting."

Julia reached across the table and squeezed his hand with affection and understanding. Together they left the club.

24

Jericho and Elizabeth were now well settled into the role of domesticity, but within a few months Elizabeth became restless and bored with the rather mundane and lackluster lifestyle afforded her by a farming community such as Wichita. She was also deeply concerned by the fact that she hadn't, as yet, become pregnant, and as a result was dispirited and depressed.

Almost mechanically she lived through the weeks, then months, and in the Spring of 1962 she came to the decision that, even though she loved Jerry deeply and respected his profession as a lawyer, they should consider returning to Washington, not only for her own well being, but to further his career.

Because of Jericho's sensitive nature, it was impossible for him not to notice Elizabeth's growing discontent, but he naturally assumed that it was primarily because she hadn't become pregnant. He continued on with his law practice, completely oblivious of the real meaning behind her moods.

On a bleak, dark day in April, as the howling winds of early Spring swept across the Kansas plains, Elizabeth placed a call to her father. Schuyler Martin listened closely to the desperation in his daughter's voice as she told him of her unhappiness with the life that she led, and her almost frantic need to return home to the nation's capitol. When she finally gained the courage to ask him to intercede on Jerry's behalf for a position in the Kennedy administration, he agreed without the slightest hesitation. However, before he proceeded with her request, he'd questioned her.

"Does Jerry know that you're this unhappy?"

"Oh, I think he knows that something's bothering me, but I'm sure he attributes it to the fact that I'm not pregnant."

"How would he feel about leaving Paul Moran?" Schuyler asked. "You know he loves him like a father."

"God, Daddy, I have no idea, and frankly I don't give a damn! I need to come back home. I'm definitely not a small town person."

"This won't be easy, Elizabeth," Schuyler warned her. "You know that Jerry's deeply loyal to Paul and Dolly, and I frankly don't know how far we can stretch that loyalty."

"I love Paul and Dolly, too. In fact, they're the only ones who've made my life here bearable and I really do care about them. Jerry's parents are nice to me, but they're so old and we have absolutely nothing in common." She paused. "Frankly, I miss you, mother, the boys, grandmother and my friends. I feel like some stranger in an alien world."

By this time Schuyler Martin had been well sold on his daughter's plight.

"I'll give Bob Kennedy a call and see what he can do," and then he laughed slightly. "He owes me one."

"Oh, thank you, Daddy. But Jerry should never know that I instigated this."

Schuyler smiled to himself. She was definitely his daughter, so much like himself. Get what you want, no matter how you do it.

A few days after Elizabeth had talked to her father Jericho arrived home from his office unusually early. When he entered the house he found Elizabeth curled up on the davenport engrossed in a magazine and he dropped down beside her and gave her a light kiss.

"What are you doing home?" she asked and glanced at the clock on the mantle. "It's only 2:30. Don't you feel well?"

"I'm fine. I needed to talk with you."

"Something wrong?" and a frown creased her brow. "It's not Paul," she said sharply with dread in her voice.

Jericho shook his head and smiled. "No, Paul's fine. I got a rather strange telephone call a little while ago."

"Really? What about?"

"Came from Bob Kennedy's office in D.C."

"You must be teasing me. Why would they call you?" this in an almost deprecating tone.

Jericho laughed aloud. "So you don't think that I was noticed during Jack's campaign?"

"I didn't mean it that way. It just surprised me. What did they want?"

"They've got a spot they're certain that I can handle. Has to do with the new Civil Rights legislation that Jack's pushing."

"Oh, that!" Elizabeth replied, almost as though she were dismissing it as unimportant.

"They need me to come to Washington indefinitely. However, if you're happier living here then I'll tell them to forget it. I haven't given them an answer yet."

"But what about your law practice with Paul?"

"Well, that would have to be put aside for the time being. We do have a new law intern who can assist Paul, so he wouldn't be left completely in the lurch. However, you really don't seem to be very enthusiastic," and he looked at Elizabeth appraisingly.

"I want only what's best for you," she replied, and then her voice took on a serious tone. "If you want to be in the Kennedy administration, then that's what you should do. There is one thing, though."

"What's that?"

"If we decide that this it the best move for your career, I insist that we keep Kansas as our official residence," and then a sly look crept into her eyes. "Just in case you might want to run for office someday."

Jericho looked at his wife with some surprise, as he hadn't realized until that moment how politically astute she was.

"I had no idea you knew about residency," he managed at last.

"I know a lot more than anyone gives me credit for. After all, I am Schuyler Martin's daughter," this with a definite degree of pride.

"Then you think we should accept?"

"Have you discussed this with my father?"

"No. I think this is one decision that's between you and me. No one else needs to be involved. It *is* our life.''

"I agree, darling. So what will it be?''

"Washington?'' Jericho asked tentatively and then looked into her eyes.

Elizabeth smiled and leaned over to touch his cheek.

"Washington it will be, my love,'' as she pulled him into her arms and kissed him passionately, and without further conversation they headed for the stairs.

The return of Jericho and Elizabeth to Washington was celebrated by the Martins with a private family gathering. Brandy was pleased that Jericho had chosen to return to the nation's capitol, even though he, himself, spent the majority of his time in Kansas City overseeing the financial interests of the family. He was, however, a frequent visitor.

Kate and Schuyler Martin were openly overjoyed to have their daughter back, and Kate had, at Schuyler's direction found a suitable house for them in Old Alexandria within a short drive of Magnolia Hill.

After dinner was over, Schuyler cornered Jericho and indicated that he wanted a private conversation. The two men left the house and walked down the same path that Jericho and Elizabeth had taken a few years before, and then settled on the same wrought iron bench. While Schuyler meticulously lit his expensive cigar, Jericho breathed in the fresh spring air and waited for his father-in-law to speak.

"So you're going to try working with our government?'' Schuyler remarked pleasantly as he opened the conversation.

"I guess you could say that,'' Jericho responded.

"Well, you're in the right place with the right people, believe me,'' and he paused. "By the way, how did this all come about?''

"It was rather strange. I received a telephone call from one of Bobby Kennedy's aides asking if I'd be interested in helping them on the Civil Rights legislation and it was just too good a chance to miss.''

Schuyler nodded. "I have to agree with you,'' he said, smiling smugly to himself.

"Elizabeth and I have decided to keep our legal residence in Kansas,'' Jericho said, abruptly changing the subject.

"Really? And why?" The older man's interest was apparent.

"Elizabeth was the one who suggested it. She insisted on it because at some future time I might run for an elective office."

Schuyler smiled slightly.

"I'd have to agree that's a wise decision and any time that I can be of help just let me know," and he patted Jericho on the leg with fatherly affection. "Now we'd better get back to our ladies or they'll begin to wonder what's happened to us."

But before they started up the path, Schuyler turned to Jericho. "I'm mighty happy that you've come back. This is where you belong."

It was with some degree of trepidation that Jericho entered the hallowed halls of the nation's capitol. The Attorney General's office had provided security with a temporary indentification pass for him, and after he'd found his way to Robert Kennedy's office he found himself playing the waiting game. The minutes ticked by; first a half-hour, then a full hour, and still he waited. People hurried in and out of the reception area and most seemed to know each other well and on a first name basis.

Finally the very proper and stoney-faced secretary looked up and announced, "The Attorney General will see you now."

Then, without warning, one of the highly polished oak doors swung open and Robert Kennedy appeared, shirt sleeves rolled up and hair a tousled mop.

"Jerry Smith," he said pleasantly, his eyes crinkling at the corners. "Nice to see you. I have a few minutes. Please come in."

Jericho stood aside to let him go first and then followed him into the cavernous office and took the chair he indicated. Once face to face with Bob Kennedy he began to feel more at ease.

"I understand that you're joining the staff," and before Jericho could respond, he went on, "I'm glad to have you with us." Then he paused. "I believe that you're interested in the Civil Rights legislation that Jack's working on. Right?" his eyes boring into Jericho's.

For a moment Jericho was speechless as he had confided his interest in only two people, one being Schuyler Martin, and the other his wife. Then he stammered, "Yes, sir."

"We have a place for you in the group that's involved on this project. I'm sure you already know that my brother is vitally interested in it and was long before he was elected. We both highly respect Martin Luther King."

"I share your feelings, sir."

"Good, and call me Bob." Then a look of recognition crossed his face.

"I remember some time back when you gave a speech and presented the contribution in Stonewall Barton's name. You did one helluva job. Now you'll have to excuse me."

With those few words Jericho was summarily dismissed. Silently he opened the door and then confronted the woman at the reception desk.

"Mr. Smith," she said, "someone will be here shortly to show you to your office."

In a matter of minutes a young man, who appeared to be about the same age as Jericho, came rushing into the reception room.

"Jerry Smith?" he asked, and when Jericho nodded, he put out his hand.

"Greg McElroy."

"Nice to meet you," Jericho replied.

"Understand you saw the boss."

"Matter of fact, I did," then added, "we've met before."

"Really?" and Greg's attitude changed dramatically.

"I haven't seen you at Hyannis," he said, his curiosity aroused.

Jericho smiled. "That's because I've never been there. You've undoubtedly seen my father-in-law though."

"Who's that?"

"Schuyler Martin."

"So you're Martin's fair haired boy," and then the young man stopped. "Sorry, I shouldn't have said that."

"Wherever did you hear me called that?" Jericho asked.

It was with reluctance that Greg McElroy provided the answer. "Common knowledge," and he paused briefly. "Or better still, the grapevine."

"Does everyone on the team know that I'm Martin's son-in-law?"

" 'Fraid so."

By now Jericho's anger had become apparent.

"So he's the one that recommended me for this job," and he

looked directly at Greg McElroy who knew that he'd really blown it.

"That's the word we received. And you're to be shown preferential treatment. Not many get to see the boss."

"Well, I'll be damned."

"Sorry I mentioned it," the young man said, obviously displeased by his own performance.

"I'm glad that you did. At least now I know what I'm up against."

"You said it. I didn't."

"Interesting," Jericho mused out loud.

By now they had reached the area which had been assigned to the legal staff that worked on the Civil Rights legislation. As they entered the room and moved past various offices several turned to look at Jericho with knowing smiles.

Undaunted, Jericho followed his escort, head held high, until they came to a small office in the farthermost area of the room. He saw that an old desk, a sadly worn chair, and a beat up filing cabinet made up its total complement. He smiled ruefully. It was certainly a far cry from his comfortable, spacious office in Wichita.

Jericho moved slowly into the small room scrutinizing his surroundings as Greg stood in the doorway and watched.

"Suit you?" he asked.

"It's fine. Now, when do I start to work?"

"Beats me. That answer I don't have," and as Greg prepared to leave he stopped. "By the way, Jerry, I'd like for us to be friends."

"No reason why we can't be," Jericho replied and the two men shook hands warmly.

"Now I need a telephone where I can speak privately," Jericho said.

"You're welcome to use mine, and I'll get lost."

They retraced their steps and entered a similar cubicle, but one which had obviously seen much use. After Jericho seated himself at the paper strewn desk, Greg gave him a smart salute and closed the door.

It was now time that Schuyler Martin heard from him.

When Jericho's call was announced by his secretary it came as little surprise to Schuyler Martin.

"Jerry, my boy," he said, "how nice that you managed to find time to call.''

For a moment Jericho's anger subsided somewhat, although he was still upset by Martin's interference and wondered if he'd ever be able to do something for himself without the elder statesman becoming involved.

"Schuyler,'' Jericho said, his tone of voice almost rude, ''Why have you been up to your old tricks again?''

"Tricks?'' Schuyler replied, feigning surprise.

"You know damned well what I'm talking about. The job that I looked forward to just became one of your missions. There's no use skirting the issue by telling me that you had nothing to do with it. Everybody around here knows, and frankly I feel like an ass!''

"That's what I like about you, Jerry. You're smart as hell,'' and he laughed. "Can't get away with a damned thing where you're concerned.''

"I want you to know that even with all these preconceived ideas about me, I'll give it my best, although truthfully I now wish that we'd stayed in Kansas.''

"Don't say that, Jerry. You needed a stepping stone, and your life in Wichita would have become stifling sooner or later; after all, politics is what you've always shown an interest in.'' Then he paused, his words muffled, "Sorry if my actions offended you.''

"Did you speak directly with Bobby Kennedy?''

"Matter of fact, I did. Kate and I were guests at Hyannis one weekend and during one of our conversations he asked me what you were doing. I told him, but when I mentioned that you were interested in Civil Rights he picked right up on it. Your appointment to his staff came directly from him.''

So Kennedy had remembered him, after all, he thought. Perhaps this would prove to be a worthwhile opportunity even though he still harbored a trace of resentment toward Schuyler.

"Thanks for giving me the lowdown. Now I may be able to handle the rest of this gang that I'm working with. The word's out that I'm to have special treatment, and you know how that makes me feel.''

"I know, Jerry, and I'm sorry. I'll try to stay out of your way from now on, although I do hope that you and Elizabeth will join us on special occasions.''

"We'll consider it. Now I have to go as I've been using someone else's office."

"Thanks for calling, Jerry. We'll see you soon?"

Jericho laughed slightly, realizing that the man would never give up.

"If Elizabeth has anything to do with it, I'm sure we will," he replied stiffly, letting Schuyler know that he still objected to his methods.

Following the end of their conversation, he wandered back to his small office and once again surveyed it. It sure as hell wasn't much, he thought, but he'd do everything within his power to prove himself.

25

Jericho's first year on the Kennedy staff proved to be frustrating at best. With the utmost enthusiasm he had arrived prepared to wade into important legislative issues, but it wasn't long before he discovered that the role he played didn't seem to be all that important. However, for his own self-satisfaction he kept his hand in the Civil Rights legislation, although there had been times when he'd experienced an almost hostile attitude from some of his young compatriots. A few came from out of the deep South and they looked at him with an almost jaundiced eye. On one such occasion he had overheard his name mentioned and then a voice stating in a derogatory manner, "He's a nigger lover." For a moment the ethnic remark had made his blood run hot; however their attitude failed to dissuade him and he continued to follow the legal process and the actions being taken by the president on the negro's behalf.

Martin Luther King was the negro's champion and during the 1960s he made enormous strides in their fight for equality, while Jericho watched with growing interest and concern.

King's march on the nation's capitol proved to Jericho to be the crowning achievement and he had literally demanded that Schuyler Martin accompany him to hear King speak.

Kate was horrified when her husband announced his intentions.

"Whatever are you thinking of, Schuyler?" she protested.

Before giving Kate a reply he carefully considered just how he should answer. "Kate, my dear," he said patiently, "I think that now is the time you should understand the reasoning behind my actions."

"Go ahead," she replied, "I'm willing to listen, but don't expect me to be overwhelmed by your oratory."

Schuyler smiled. "First, you have probably suspected, and rightfully so, that I have great plans for Jerry." He paused, noting the frown that momentarily crossed Kate's face.

"You've been aware that Jerry and Elizabeth have been actively involved in politics, and even though Jerry's not aware of it himself, I've had excellent reports about his ability. Jerry's a bundle of energy; inquisitive, extremely bright and a young man who will go far . . . with the right people backing him."

Once again Kate frowned. "I presume that you mean by 'right people' yourself, the Speaker of the House, and the rest of your cronies on the Hill."

"You're a smart lady, Kate!"

"Where do you think that all this will lead?" she asked.

Schuyler chuckled. "Who knows? Right now he's being provided an inside view of how complicated the government is, and so far he hasn't seemed too impressed."

"But why is he so interested in this Civil Rights thing?"

Schuyler remained silent and looked off into the distance.

"Well," Kate said, her manner showing impatience.

"It may just help him to the top."

"You can't mean the Presidency?"

"That's exactly what I do mean. This is only the beginning for Jerry. First the Senate, where he'll learn the ropes; then when the time is right he might consider running for the Presidency," his eyes took on a dreamy quality.

It was Kate's voice that brought him back to reality. "You'd like that, wouldn't you?" she said. "You've planned this from the first time you met him! How I wish that Elizabeth had married someone who would have given her a normal life."

Schuyler frowned. It had become more and more evident to him that Kate harbored some ill will toward Jerry, and for what reason he couldn't comprehend. However, he ignored her comments and continued. "You're right, Kate. I saw Jerry's potential a long time ago, and believe me that's what counts. He's honest, fair, sensitive to the needs of others, and more than willing to walk the long mile. He'll make an excellent head of state when he's seasoned."

Kate had remained silent, her mood thoughtful, and when she looked up into her husband's eyes she saw in them the bright fire of challenge. She smiled and said softly, "I don't suppose there's the slightest chance that I could talk you out of this?"

Schuyler shook his head. "Sorry, Kate. I know the burden this places on you, but I can't miss this one last chance." Suddenly an almost forlorn look crossed his face. "Neither Sky nor Brandy were born with the potential of greatness that Jerry possesses, and for that I'm truly sorry."

Kate got up and moved to her husband.

"Darling," she said, "whatever makes you happy I'll go along with." She brushed his lips with a kiss and glided to the door, then disappeared from view.

In the dark of early morning on the day of the Freedom March, Schuyler Martin, with a somewhat reluctant James in tow, met Jericho at Washington's Union Station to greet the contingent arriving from Kansas. There they discovered military police doggedly watching every movement as the march participants from across the land disembarked from special trains to take part in what was to be the largest civil rights demonstration in history.

When Jericho spotted the small band of men from Kansas coming down the brick platform carrying a banner which portrayed their sentiments, he turned to Schuyler, eyes shining.

"See what I mean? This is a moment that none of us should ever forget!"

Because of the noise from the trains and the growing crowd Schuyler merely nodded his assent.

Jericho introduced Schuyler and James and then, with Jericho holding one side of the banner, they headed for the streets. It had been many years since Schuyler Martin had walked for other than his own pleasure, and though the heat and humidity were stifling he still walked on. James, who at first had been reluctant to join them, was now one of the most enthusiastic as they strode masterfully down Pennsylvania Avenue, past the White House, to the

Washington monument, and ended the long trek before the Lincoln Memorial.

When Martin Luther King stepped to the podium the crowd went wild. Then as he began his address an almost eerie silence filled the air, interrupted only by the occasional cry of a child. During King's speech Jericho's eyes never once wavered from the face of the man who, to his own people, had become a Black Messiah, and the man who would ultimately achieve equal opportunity for all of them in the years ahead.

James' face shone with admiration for his brother, and even the unflappable Schuyler Martin's heart beat faster as he listened intently to the words of King demanding freedom and peace for all, and his final words, "Free at last, Great God Amighty, We are free at last," shook Jericho to the core.

As they drove back to Georgetown, both emotionally and physically exhausted, Schuyler voiced his feelings. "I really had my eyes opened today," he said quietly.

Jericho turned to look at the older man and saw how solemn he seemed. "Good or bad?" he questioned.

"Good! I've never considered all the liberties that the blacks have never enjoyed. We've always taken our own for granted," and he paused. "I guess that's a trait that goes way back."

"Do you think it will make a difference?" Jericho asked.

"I'm sure that it will. I know for a fact that Kennedy has personally made calls around the country about the Civil Rights legislation."

"Really?"

Schuyler nodded. "That's not common knowledge, Jerry, so I trust you won't repeat it."

"Of course not. I do hope that he's receiving positive reaction."

"Only time will tell. But after today, who knows? You may even become more personally involved with it."

"I'd like that. I wish that Bobby would do something about it."

In the darkness Schuyler smiled. He'd already come to terms with this and knew that his son-in-law would be recognized for his ability and given the knowledge needed to help with the pressing issue.

When Jericho dropped James and Schuyler off at Magnolia Hill, he turned to the old black man. "James," he said, "how do you feel about all this? You've heard what King had to say, and I'd be interested in your feelings.''

James stared into the darkness, deep in thought. It had been years since he'd given up his own burning desire for 'freedom,' as Martin Luther King had so aptly put it. The years he'd served the Martin family had been comfortable ones, and although he knew that his life would be on the fringe of the Martins, it had also become apparent that they cared about him a great deal. On the other hand, had he been an eager younger man, today would undoubtedly have been a turning point, so Jericho's question was one that he didn't quite know how to answer.

"Mr. Jerry," he said, "I have mixed feelings. You know I'm nigh on to seventy now," and he chuckled. "Had Mr. King been around in my youthful days, it might have made some difference," and he sighed. "Now the real hope is for my grandchildren and their children, not for old codgers like me."

Schuyler and Jericho exchanged glances, both mindful of the words of truth he spoke.

Then as he stepped from the car to the driveway the old man continued. "I want to thank both you gentlemen for taking me with you today."

"We're glad that you came along," Schuyler replied, placing a hand on the old man's shoulder with affection. "You're a good man, James, and I'm mighty proud to have you for a friend."

"Lordy, lordy," James said, his voice betraying his emotion. "Now if you two gentlemen will excuse me, it's been a long day. Goodnight," and he doffed his always present chauffeur's cap and started for the carriage house.

Schuyler and Jericho watched him go. When he had disappeared Jericho got into his car, gave his father-in-law a wave, and started for home where he knew that Elizabeth would be waiting.

26

Once again Schuyler Martin met with Robert Kennedy to help further Jericho's career, and much to his young protege's surprise, in a few weeks he was invited to join the Kennedy staff on a different basis.

It was about this same time, November 1963, that the President embarked on an early campaign swing through the Southwest that included a stop in Dallas.

When the news of the assassination attempt on the life of Jack Kennedy reached the nation's capitol, Jericho was on his way to join Elizabeth for lunch and knew nothing about it until he entered the hotel lobby where he found his wife in tears. He rushed to her side, suspecting that something could have happened to either Kate or Schuyler. Elizabeth was unable to speak and instead pointed to the television set in the lobby which was surrounded by a mass of people. Leaving Elizabeth unattended, he joined the silent group and saw the replay of the film of the assassination.

"My God," he said to no one in particular and almost in a daze rejoined Elizabeth who was making an effort to control herself, but when he reached her she threw herself in his arms.

His first thought was, *I must go back*, but with his wife in such an emotional state he knew that it was imperative he get her to

Magnolia Hill.

"Come on," he said and took her arm to guide her through the crowd. When they reached the street the quiet seemed almost foreboding, but he hailed a cab for the ride to Georgetown.

When they arrived at the Martin residence, Elizabeth opened the door and they entered the house where the only sound heard was that of the television. She ran through the foyer and down the hall with Jericho keeping pace behind her. Kate and Schuyler were huddled together on the sofa with James sitting on a straight back chair.

They all turned, but it was Schuyler who sprang to his feet as Elizabeth rushed toward him. James rose, but Kate remained seated, head bowed.

"Daddy," Elizabeth wailed, her voice echoing her sorrow. "What's happened? How could this be?"

Schuyler held her tenderly as her words continued but in time they were almost inarticulate. Over her shoulder Schuyler nodded to Jericho, a sad smile touching his lips.

Jericho slumped in a chair, eyes glued to the television set, and just in time for the announcement that Lyndon Johnson had taken the oath of office and that he, Mrs. Johnson, and the President's widow Jackie Kennedy, would return to the capitol on Air Force One with the body of the late president.

Kate had taken Elizabeth upstairs and James had gone to his own quarters, leaving the two men alone. After a time Schuyler got up from the sofa and went to the bar where he mixed himself a drink.

"Care for one?" he asked.

"Don't mind if I do," Jericho replied and gratefully accepted the glass Schuyler offered.

As they nursed their drinks the television news continued to hammer out the details of the story and finally, in disgust, Schuyler switched off the television and returned to take a seat near his son-in-law.

"Bobby's going to need all of us," he said, "now more than ever." He glanced at Jericho. "And you especially." This very matter-of-factly.

Jericho glanced at the older man in surprise.

"He hardly knows that I'm around, Schuyler."

"That's not true, Jerry."

"You'd never know it. I've seen him perhaps half a dozen times in the past eighteen months."

"You've not gone unnoticed, believe me."

"What are you suggesting?"

"Well, we all know that Johnson will serve out this term, at least. Whether he's strong enough to win the coming election is, at the present, questionable. He's not like Jack," and for a moment his voice quavered. "Lyndon made it up the hard way, and I have to admit he's been successful. Of course he married rich, so that did help, but his personality leaves a lot to be desired."

"And where did you conjure up this opinion?" Jericho asked.

"I've known Lyndon Johnson since he was a freshman senator from Texas, and his manners leave something to be desired."

"Pray tell," Jericho replied, his manner sarcastic.

Schuyler's look was one of surprise. "Now why would you say that?"

"For God's sake, give the man a chance. After all, he does know a lot about the Civil Rights legislation and he's the one who can pull it off if anyone can," Jericho replied, adding, "manners or not."

"You think so?"

Jericho nodded. "Anyway, I think I'll just hang it all up and go back to Kansas."

"You can't do that!"

"And who says we can't?"

"Where's your loyalty, Jerry? I've already told you that Bobby would need his friends, and I know he'll look to you to help Johnson through the transition period."

Jericho took a long sip of his drink and gazed thoughtfully out the window. "Maybe you're right. This has all happened so fast that perhaps I'm jumping the gun." Jericho got up from his chair and placed the empty glass on the bar. Then he turned to the older man.

"Would you mind if James takes me to the office? I should be there. No telling what's going on."

"Certainly not. We'll tell Elizabeth where you are and we'll expect you to come back and stay the night."

"Thanks, Schuyler," and Jericho walked slowly to the door, then turned to his father-in-law. "I'll round up James and send him right back. Take good care of my wife."

Schuyler smiled. "That we'll do."

As he watched the handsome young man leave, he could almost visualize him in the years to come . . . a stately senator from Kansas, and he smiled softly, then the Presidency; it could all happen, but it would take time.

When Jericho returned to Capitol Hill he was immediately drafted to assist in the plans for the rites of the President. He'd seen Bobby in passing and had pressed his hand in understanding, but then the Attorney General had disappeared.

The day of Kennedy's funeral, Schuyler Martin joined Jericho and together they followed the caisson which held the slain president. The world had literally come to a standstill that day and it hardly seemed possible that from the beginning in Dallas, to the lowering of the casket into the grave in Arlington Cemetery, had taken only four days.

Schuyler and Jericho returned to Georgetown drained both physically and emotionally. Elizabeth smothered Jericho with affection and had stayed close beside him during the evening.

After they retired for the night Elizabeth caressed him gently.

"Darling," she said, "Daddy mentioned that you might consider returning to Kansas," and waited for his response.

"I did give it some thought, but Schuyler pointed out that Bobby will need me to help Johnson. I hope he's right."

"I'm sure he is. You need a few days of rest; then things will look brighter."

Jericho looked at her appraisingly. "You wouldn't like going back to Kansas, I take it?"

She shook her head. "No, I like it here, although I hate what's happened." Sudden tears misted her eyes. "But there's so much more to offer here and that's what's important."

"You could be right," and he yawned and reached over to kiss her.

"Good-night, sweet," he said and snuggled close to her.

"Good-night, darling," she whispered against his chest and smiled to herself as his breathing became even.

Jericho stayed on to help Lyndon Johnson through the transition period. But peace was not to come that easily for Jericho, as in the Spring of 1968 Martin Luther King was murdered in Memphis,

Tennessee.

At that point in time, Jericho resigned from the Johnson administration. He willingly agreed to accompany the Kennedy faction to King's funeral in Atlanta, and from that experience he realized that he couldn't turn back and that his loyalty to Bobby Kennedy was unchanged. He became one of his top aides to assist in his bid for the Presidency.

Following his return from Atlanta, Schuyler approached him about running for the Senate from his home state. However, Jericho refused, believing that he could accomplish far more by staying with the Kennedy organization. Wisely, Schuyler Martin refrained from pushing the matter further.

Jericho embraced his new role with relish, and he and Elizabeth spent long strategy planning weekends at the Kennedy Compound in Hyannisport, as well as at Hickory Hill, the McLean, Virginia home of Bobby and Ethel. Jericho, by now, had learned a great deal about the behind the scenes political schemes and it was fascinating to him.

Schuyler Martin, with growing pride, watched in the wings, pleased with how easily Jericho fitted into this old-line Massachusetts family.

Whenever Kennedy embarked on a campaign tour, Jericho was always included. Elizabeth, although lonely, graciously accepted her role of 'the woman who waits.'

On occasion, she and Kate discussed her barrenness, but her mother provided the excuse that their manner of living hadn't been exactly normal. She reassured her that, once she and Jericho began to lead a more conventional life, she'd undoubtedly become pregnant.

June 1968 was the time scheduled for a tour of the Western states by Kennedy and his staff. On this occasion, the wives, relatives and even a few of the Kennedy children had been invited to accompany them. However, a few days prior to the departure, Elizabeth had sprained her ankle while playing tennis and all her plans for an exciting political trip disappeared.

At every stop Kennedy was surrounded not only by his aides but by local security as well, yet when he moved through a crowd he paused to listen to young or old, and would grasp the hands that were thrust out to him. His obvious lack of concern for his safety was becoming a matter of great concern, but he dismissed his staff's worries almost like a duck shedding water.

The last appearance was to be in Los Angeles, winding up what had been, with the exception of Oregon, a successful tour.

On that final day, Tuesday, June 4, 1968, Robert Kennedy was with his family, staff and key supporters, and at times he seemed almost withdrawn. He was deeply concerned about the results of the California primary. He'd come in second to Eugene McCarthy in Oregon, and that loss had been a mind boggling blow. It was apparent, beyond any doubt, that it was imperative he win in California.

As they waited for the voting reports to come in, a party was going full swing in Kennedy's suite at the Ambassador Hotel.The early returns showed McCarthy ahead, and this caused him to sequester himself in his bedroom with his immediate staff. At that time, Jericho noticed that Bobby had seemed almost dejected, and it was only after two of the nation's television networks had projected him to be the winner that his usual rakish smile and good humor returned.

When midnight approached, and he was assured of victory, Bobby and Ethel left the suite on the fifth floor to appear in the Embassy Room which had been packed with his supporters for hours.

When he'd managed to quiet the chanting of the crowd, Kennedy first introduced members of his family, and then his staff, which included Jericho. Strangely enough, it was only Jericho who found himself dazzled by the contingent of celebrities who had now become a permanent part of the Kennedy team.

Jericho, filled with excitement, watched the man who, only a few short hours before, had been distant and almost uncommunicative. His whole personality had changed to one of optimism, gratitude and caring, and at the end of the speech Jericho joined in the applause as Bobby Kennedy left the podium.

Accompanied by his aides, he started on his way to a room reserved nearby for a scheduled press conference; however, to hurry matters along, he turned to take a short cut through the kitchen. As he moved through the kitchen he stopped to shake hands with the staff. Then, without warning, a short, swarthy man appeared and opened fire. Eight shots rang out and Kennedy fell to the floor mortally wounded.

As Jericho followed Kennedy from the Embassy Room he'd been waylaid by an eager reporter and when he entered the kitchen it had been just in time to see the gunman fire and to witness the result.

Within minutes Kennedy was rushed to the Central Receiving Hospital and later transferred to Good Samaritan where a team of top surgeons performed surgery.

Jericho, along with other staff members, joined in the long wait, hoping against hope that Bobby would survive. Restlessly they waited all through the day and far into the night. Then at two o'clock in the morning of June 6th, Kennedy's press secretary announced that he had succumbed to his wounds.

During those trying hours Jericho had been in touch with both Schuyler and Elizabeth, and although he never openly voiced his feelings, it soon became obvious that he'd had enough of politics to last him a lifetime. Wisely, Schuyler and Elizabeth kept their own counsel, realizing that Jericho had experienced enough tragedy.

After the services for Robert Kennedy had drawn to a close, Jericho and Schuyler Martin left Arlington Cemetery and in a brooding silence returned to Georgetown. It was obvious to the older man that his son-in-law was deeply troubled by the violent and unnecessary deaths of the two Kennedy brothers and Martin Luther King.

It was two subdued women who greeted their husbands and when Elizabeth saw Jericho's face she hurried him up the stairs and to the privacy of their room. Jericho remained silent, and although Elizabeth longed to take him in her arms, she refrained.

Morosely, Jericho paced the room to pause occasionally and stare out the window into the darkness. Then he turned to face Elizabeth.

"I'm through," he stated flatly. "I'm through. There's no possible way that I can go on. Politics has become a monster and I simply can't stay in Washington." Then he paused, noting the look of despair on her face. "We're going home, and the sooner the better."

"But darling," she said in her most persuasive manner,

"tomorrow things will look brighter."

It was then that he cut her short.

"There is no tomorrow for me here, Elizabeth," he said, his voice echoing with emotion. "I need to go home."

Then he paused as a look of reflection crossed his face. "I had such dreams that I could help make the world a better place," and then his eyes became dark and he said savagely, "it's a lost cause." Before Elizabeth could reply he went to the door and said curtly, "I'm going for a walk."

He opened the door, strode down the hall and went out into the stillness of the night, leaving Elizabeth crying softly as she knew that she had lost.

27

When the announcement of Jericho's and Elizabeth's impending return to Kansas reached Schuyler Martin's ears, it came as little surprise. However, it was Kate Martin who was affected the most, as she and Elizabeth had enjoyed a close mother-daughter relationship when they were political widows.

Within a month's time the Virginia house had been closed, all goodbyes had been said, and the young couple were ready for their return to Wichita.

As soon as Jericho had reached his decision he'd immediately phoned Paul Moran.

"So you're coming home?" Paul happily bellowed into the phone, although Jericho thought he heard a trace of concern in his voice.

"Yes, we are," Jericho replied enthusiastically. "Am I still a member in good standing with the firm?"

At that Paul let out a laugh. "Good standing? My God, Jerry, you can't imagine how much we've missed you these past years. Your office is waiting and Dolly will be delighted."

For the first time in many months a surge of happiness swept through the young lawyer.

Elizabeth had fought the move tooth and toenail and had

become despondent when he'd refused to reconsider. It was also the first time in their married life that there had been bitter words between them.

Elizabeth Martin Smith, being a product of Schuyler Martin, was every bit as ambitious for her husband's career as her father, and she'd voiced strong objection to the move.

"Why must you insist on doing this stupid thing?" she'd stormed, tears of anger flowing down her cheeks. "You'll never be anything but a small town lawyer! Why can't you forget what's happened?"

With complete objectivity, Jericho had looked at his wife and her tears had left him cold. He was seeing for the first time the self-centered, self-indulgent rich young woman she'd always been. Before he attempted to respond to her accusation, Jericho calmed the sudden wave of anger that enveloped him.

Then, in a cutting tone, he replied, "You weren't there, Elizabeth. You haven't the vaguest idea what's happening to our country. The Martin family has always been fit to stay on the fringe of things and have appeared as the untouchables. They've simply walked away and continued on as though nothing had happened." Then he paused, "You know, I could handle Jack's death, but then there was King and finally Bobby," and he shook his head as a dark look crossed his face. "It's simply asking too much."

"But you can't do anything about that. It's all behind us," she protested.

"Perhaps. But I do need to go home, to rest and find out who I am, who we are. There's so many questions that I need to find answers for."

When Jericho had said 'who we are' Elizabeth had been startled. She loved her husband deeply and she began to wonder if her actions had caused a change in his feelings where she was concerned.

"Don't you love me?" she asked plaintively.

When he looked at her it was again with objectivity. "Of course I love you. However, for once we're going to do what *I* think is best. If you really wanted to, Elizabeth, you could be happy in Wichita, and that would make me happy," his eyes filled with torment. "God, why can't you understand?"

"I'm trying, Jerry, but you know how I love living here. I'll miss my family and my friends. However, if going back to Wichita is what you really need, there's nothing more for me to say."

Without another word, Elizabeth left the room and in that moment Jericho realized that the day would undoubtedly come again when he'd be faced to accept the ambitions of his wife and her father.

However, today was his.

When they returned to the midwest, the hot, dry July weather left much to be desired. After Jericho and Elizabeth had reopened their house with the help of Dolly Moran, they settled into a routine once again with some degree of normalcy.

It wasn't long before Elizabeth discovered how nice it was to have the man she loved all to herself. Because of her upbringing and her father's frequent absences from home on business or political matters, that had seemed to her to be the norm; now she and Jericho were like newlyweds in their solitude, and they'd shared more time in those first weeks than they had in the past years.

She'd also remembered her mother's words, *When you have a normal type of life, you'll undoubtedly become pregnant.* With this thought prominent in her mind, Elizabeth consulted one of the local doctors and following a rather cursory examination he'd told her there shouldn't be any problem unless, of course, her husband was sterile.

When she informed Jericho he'd immediately made an appointment and had a sperm count taken. The verdict in his case was the same.

With a near frantic zeal, Elizabeth focused all her attention on the required routine of their sexual activity in an all out effort to become pregnant. She'd followed the doctors temperature instructions to the nth degree and Jericho didn't have the slightest inkling just when he might be called home from his office to 'perform' because, according to the thermometer, it was the right time. They followed in this pattern religiously for several months; however, much to their chagrin and disappointment, nothing happened.

Dolly Moran had observed the almost fanatical behavior where Jericho was concerned, and one day when he'd gone flying at a whirlwind pace out of the office while in the midst of dictating a brief to his bewildered secretary, she determined that now was the time for a talk. When Jericho returned late that afternoon looking spent and tired, Dolly had asked that he join her in her office. Once there, he'd literally thrown himself into a chair, an uneasy smile playing about his lips.

"Jerry," she began quietly, "what I'm about to ask you may feel is none of my business. Stop me if it isn't."

But before she could question him, he interrupted. "I know exactly what you're going to ask," his smile sheepish. "My actions of late have been rather strange at best," and he laughed huskily. "I'll have to admit it's strange to me, too, but still necessary."

Taking note that whatever it was seemed to be somewhat of a source of amusement, Dolly relaxed. "Well, for God's sake, kid, do tell me what's going on," she said, her curiosity now fully aroused.

"Well, it's like this. You are aware that we've not been blessed with children so far," he said rather matter-of-factly.

Dolly nodded.

"Now Elizabeth is hell bent on getting pregnant though we've never lacked for effort in the past and it's been a total mystery to the both of us why she hasn't." He blushed slightly.

"I understand," Dolly said, smiling pleasantly. "Having a child of our own is the one thing that Paul and I have missed the most," and for a moment a look of sadness touched her face. Then she brightened. "Any luck so far?" she asked and gave him a wicked wink.

Jericho laughed out loud and shook his head. "Not yet, but we're still trying. I really wish that it would happen, not only to make Elizabeth happy but so I could get back to a normal work routine."

Dolly leaned back in her chair and her look became serious. "Have you ever considered the possibility that you might not be able to have children?"

A dark look crossed the young man's face. "It's been in the back of my mind on occasion, but I hope that's not true. Elizabeth wants a child so much, and frankly, so do I."

"Well, good luck, Jerry," and the older woman rose from her chair and moved around the desk. "You have both Paul's and my blessings, but I'm sure that you already know that," and she put her arms around him.

"Thanks, Dolly." As he started to leave he stopped and turned back. "When we do have a child, would you and the old man be Godparents?"

The smile that creased Dolly Moran's face was one of exultation and her voice when she answered rang with excitement. "You've got a deal, Jerry!" and she blew a kiss in his direction as he left.

After weeks and months had gone by and Elizabeth hadn't become pregnant, she approached Jericho about visiting her grandmother, Emily Martin, in Kansas City. When she'd asked if he'd mind, he'd seemed somewhat surprised.

"Any special reason?"

"No. Not really. Grandmother's close and it's been a long time since we've shared any time alone, that's all."

"Then by all means go. I wish that I could join you but I'm in the middle of that criminal trial."

"I know, but that's all right," Elizabeth had responded quickly, her manner almost pleased that he was busy. "Grandmother and I'll enjoy being by ourselves."

On a warm, October day Elizabeth Smith told her husband an affectionate goodbye and took an early flight to Kansas City. Upon her arrival, the maid directed her to the sunroom where her grandmother waited.

Emily Martin had been somewhat surprised when her only granddaughter had telephoned to ask if she could come for a short visit, but since her own plans called for her not to return to Washington until late November, she'd readily agreed. During Elizabeth's youth they'd been rather close, but since her marriage the time they'd spent together had been almost non-existent, so she was rightly curious as to the reason for her sudden visit.

"Darling" Elizabeth said and rushed into the room where she smothered her grandmother in a warm embrace. "How wonderful to see you. You look simply marvelous."

"What a lovely compliment; do come sit beside me," and Emily Martin moved to make room for Elizabeth.

After taking a seat where the elderly woman had indicated, Elizabeth took her grandmother's small jeweled hand in hers and then pressed it gently.

"Tell me now, what brings you here?" her grandmother asked,

knowing full well that it couldn't have been primarily to see her.

"I did want to see you Gram, but you're right. There is another reason."

"Is there something wrong between Jerry and you?" she asked with a trace of alarm.

Elizabeth shook her head. "No, grandmother. We're very happy," and with that she smiled brightly. "It's something else."

"Well, if I can be of any help at all, please feel free to ask. You know that I'd do anything for you and the boys," and she paused. "Well, almost anything."

"It's rather difficult to talk about," Elizabeth said almost shyly.

"For heaven's sake, child, I'm your grandmother and the mother of your father. I've lived close to eighty years now and I'm sure that there couldn't possibly be anything that would shock me."

"I'm glad. I'd hoped you'd respond that way, and I do need your help."

Emily Martin's wise old eyes noticed the sudden look of sadness which had crept across her granddaughter's face, and she patted her hand gently.

"Elizabeth, please tell me," and then she laughed good naturedly. "The suspense is killing me."

The young woman looked up into her eyes and then saw the concern in them. She sighed deeply, then began, but paused occasionally to control her emotions.

"You see, grandmother, we haven't been able to have a child as yet, and I've about come to the end of my rope."

"Have you seen a doctor?"

"Yes. Both Jerry and I have, and he's assured us that there's nothing really wrong. But I'm not so sure," she replied.

Emily Martin felt a deep compassion for her beautiful grandchild since she, herself, had been able to bear only one son.

"Well, we'll have to see that you get to a specialist. I'm certain my personal physician will know the best gynecologist in the city," and she paused. "I presume that you're in a hurry."

Elizabeth nodded. "I have to know."

"And if you can't have children, then what?"

"Oh, I don't know. We'll both be so disappointed." Suddenly her expression changed. "Let's not talk about it any more. I have to call my husband. Please excuse me,'' and Elizabeth hurried from the room, but it was obvious to her grandmother that she was close to tears.

The following afternoon Emily Martin's limousine deposited Elizabeth at Dr. Melvin Johnson's office building on the Plaza. Melvin Johnson was the most popular OB/GYN man in Kansas City and his reputation was well known throughout the State of Missouri. When he'd received the request from his physician friend and golf partner, Spencer Hathaway, inquiring if he would see Mrs. Martin's granddaughter, he'd almost automatically shifted his appointments to make room in his busy schedule.

With a degree of apprehension, Elizabeth entered an examining room where she disrobed and then covered herself with a green garment. The nurse had taken her history and now she waited for the doctor, wishing with all her heart that Jerry were there with her.

Accompanied by his nurse, Melvin Johnson entered the small compartment. It was quite apparent that the young woman who waited for him was extremely nervous. The medical gown she worn was pulled tightly around her slim body as though she were afraid he might see what lay beneath it. The look in her eyes as their gaze met was a dead giveaway; she was not only frightened but fearful of what he might discover.

Even though his friend had informed him that Elizabeth Smith was the only daughter of scion Schuyler Martin and the grand-daughter of Emily Martin and needed his expertise, he'd simply considered her as a woman that he might be able to help. As he had moved down the hall he'd glanced almost perfunctorily at her chart and noted that she was now twenty-seven and her husband was thirty-five. The information also included that both she and her husband had recently undergone complete physical examinations and both had passed with flying colors.

When Melvin Johnson looked at the young woman he gave her his warmest smile and the calmness in his voice caused Elizabeth to relax.

"How nice to meet you, Mrs. Smith," he said softly, then proceeded to settle himself comfortably on the examining table.

Elizabeth smiled briefly in acknowledgement and murmured, "Thanks for seeing me on such short notice."

"No problem," he replied with a wave of his hand as though in dismissal. "Now, why don't you tell me a little about yourself and the problem you seem to have."

Elizabeth straigthened and with the utmost care chose her words. "Jerry and I have been married almost eight years and so far we've been unable to have a family." Then she paused. "We're Catholics and we do so much want to have children, but so far . . ." and then her voice trailed off as a sob choked her words.

Melvin Johnson patted her shoulder gently as Elizabeth poured out wracking sobs.

"Mrs. Smith," he said kindly, "I know how much this concerns you. I've seen others with the same problem as yours and have been able to help some." Then rather brusquely he announced, "I'll have Miss Fletcher prepare for you the examination and then I'll be back." But before he left he paused. "Just remember one thing. If there's a possibility you can have a child I'll tell you, and if there isn't, I'll be honest." With that he left the room.

After the rather long and drawn out examination was over, Elizabeth dressed and an aide escorted her to the doctor's office where she waited impatiently. When the doctor entered the room she noticed immediately the grim look on his face, but still he gave her a fleeting smile. Once settled in his chair he leaned forward and placed his elbows on the desk in front of him. He looked straight into her eyes.

"Mrs. Smith, I told you that I'd be honest," he said, and Elizabeth inclined her head to acknowledge his statement.

"Well, the prognosis isn't good," and he shook his head almost sadly. "In fact, it's not good at all."

Alarmed, Elizabeth moved to the edge of her chair. "What's wrong?"

"I'll try to explain my findings in layman terms so you'll be able to understand."

"Please do. We have to know."

"From what I've been able to determine, your fallopian tubes which carry the egg have grown together and there's no way for the ova to be conveyed from the ovaries to the cavity of the uterus. It would be my best guess that it might require several surgeries to correct the problem, and I couldn't assure you it would be a sure thing."

"In other words we can't have a child?"

"At this stage of the game, the answer is no, unless you're willing to have surgery."

The thought of undergoing surgery was frightening to Elizabeth and she shook her head 'no.'

"I'm sorry, Mrs. Smith that I didn't bring you better news," and Melvin Johnson rose from his chair eager to be on his way to see another patient. "Have you and your husband ever considered adoption?" he asked.

Elizabeth shook her head. "No, and I wouldn't."

Very carefully Elizabeth got up from her chair. "Thank you, Dr. Johnson for your honesty." She touched his hand briefly and then quickly strode from the room.

When Elizabeth returned to her grandmother's house she discovered that Emily Martin had gone out to play bridge with some of her old cronies, and it was then that she made a snap decision. She hurried up the stairs to the guest room and packed her belongings. She then returned to the lower floor where she sat down at her grandmother's desk and wrote a note.

Dear Gram,"
The news from Dr. Johnson was negative so I've decided that it's best for me to go home to Jerry. Sorry to rush off this way, but I'm sure you'll understand.
Love, Elizabeth

Without calling the airport, she commandeered the Martin limousine and was driven straight to the terminal. When she arrived she found that a flight for Wichita would be ready to depart within a half hour and after purchasing a ticket she hurried to a pay phone.

The telephone in Moran and Smith's law offices rang several times before a breathless Dolly answered.

"Moran and Smith," she said rather formally. "May I help you?"

"Dolly dear, this is Elizabeth."

"My goodness, where are you, home?"

"No, I'm just leaving Kansas City. Is Jerry in?"

"I'm sorry, darling, but he's still in court. What time will your flight be in?"

Elizabeth glanced at her ticket. "Six o'clock. Would you ask Jerry to meet me?"

"If he hasn't come back from court by then I'll come myself."

"Thanks, Dolly, but I do hope that Jerry can make it."

"I'll see what I can do." Then Dolly asked. "Are you okay?"

"I'm fine, Dolly, just fine," she replied as she savagely bit her lips to keep from screaming.

It was Dolly Moran who welcomed Elizabeth on her return to Wichita. She'd quickly observed the stark look of disappointment on her young friend's face, and had said, almost apologetically, "I'm terribly sorry, Elizabeth, but Jerry was in the midst of summation and there simply was no way he could meet you."

"Of course," Elizabeth had snapped, and then had remained silent on the ride home.

When she took her bag from the car she failed to utter even a thank you, which had puzzled Dolly even more. Still, she knew that something had to be drastically wrong and so she accepted, though reluctantly, the obvious rudeness of her younger friend.

As soon as the judge had given final instructions to the jurors, Jericho had rushed from the court room and then raced home. Dolly, during the proceedings, had managed to slip him a note that his wife would be arriving on the six o'clock flight. It had been five o'clock then and the summation hadn't as yet begun.

The house was quiet when he entered and he noticed Elizabeth's unopened bag sitting in the hallway. He moved through the downstairs and when he failed to find her, made his way up the stairs only to discover that their bedroom door was closed. Suddenly a sense of foreboding coursed through him, and he knew that there could be only one reason for her action.

Softly he knocked on the door, but when he received no answer he turned the knob and entered. The drapes had been drawn tight and the room was dark and in the stillness only the muffled sobs of his wife were heard.

Making his way to the side of the bed he reached out and touched her but she pushed him away.

"Darling," he said softly, "Let me help."

"No one can help," she mumbled and pushed her face even farther into the pillow, her body trembling with emotion.

Tenderly and with great care, Jericho drew her across the bed and only then did she throw herself into his waiting arms.

"Darling, please talk to me," he whispered against her cheek as he gently held her.

Even so, Elizabeth failed to answer, but as he continued to hold her while murmuring words of endearment, she gradually quieted.

When she finally pulled away she brushed at her tears and then tried at a smile. "Oh, Jerry," she wailed, "we can't have a baby. Never! Never! Never!" Once again she burst into tears.

"What do you mean, Elizabeth?" he asked almost sternly, hoping that his words would curtail the outburst.

She turned to stare at him, shocked by his curt manner.

"It's just as I said. We can't have children. Would you like me to shout it from the housetop?" she said bitterly.

That was the moment when, through his sadness and anger, he completely lost control and slapped her with all his might across the cheek.

The shock of the sudden violence brought Elizabeth to reality. "Don't you ever hit me again," she spat at him and got up from the bed and moved to the door. "God damn you, Jerry Smith and everybody else," she said between clenched teeth, and then rushed out the door and went flying down the stairs.

Before Jericho came to his senses, he heard the car door slam and at top speed go plummeting out of the drive and down the street.

"What have I done?" he said aloud as he hurried down the stairs. When he reached the front door he heard the loud squeal of tires and then a resounding crash.

Dolly and Paul Moran had been sitting quietly in their den watching the evening news when they heard the crash. They both bolted from their chairs and rushed from the house only to see Jericho go flying down the street.

"My God, Paul," Dolly said, "something must have happened to Elizabeth," and she began to run after Jericho with Paul behind her moving at a slower pace.

When Jericho reached the battered car that had come to rest against a light standard he saw his wife lying unconscious and crumpled on the front seat while blood trickled down her face from a ragged gash in her forehead. With all his strength he pulled at the door until it finally yielded.

As Jericho bent over Elizabeth, Dolly Moran came running up.

"Whatever happened, Jerry?" she asked breathlessly.

"Don't ask. Just help me get her out," and together they very slowly and carefully removed Elizabeth from the car.

Because of the movement her eyelids fluttered and her eyes opened and she looked into the anxious faces of her husband and her friend.

Then she began to whimper. "I'm sorry, Jerry; so sorry."

"Hush. Don't talk. There's nothing to be sorry about."

At that moment a siren was heard and an ambulance came hurtling down the street and came to a halt. The two attendants jumped out and knelt beside Elizabeth who was now lying on the curbside covered with a light blanket.

While the medics checked Elizabeth for broken bones, Jericho hovered close to them. Then one attendant stood and addressed the small crowd that had gathered at the crash scene. "Any relatives here?" he asked.

"I'm her husband," Jericho said, "Is she going to be all right?"

"Your name, sir?"

"Jerry Smith."

"Mr. Smith, it would be advisable to take your wife to the hospital so she can be examined thoroughly. The cut on her forehead will undoubtedly need stitches, but otherwise we've found nothing obvious. However, we don't make diagnoses."

After Elizabeth was placed on a stretcher and put in the ambulance, Jericho got in and sat beside her, but before the ambulance door closed he said to Dolly, "Would you come?"

"Of course, Jerry. I'll go get the car," and as the ambulance pulled way with its red light blinking and its siren blowing, Dolly Moran ran back to the house, grabbed her purse, stopped to pick up her husband, and at break neck speed they went careening down the highway.

Fortunately for Elizabeth the only major injury, if it could be called that, was the jagged three inch gash on her forehead. Jericho held her hand as the emergency room doctor skillfully repaired the damage, and after he'd applied a bandage to the wound he told them that they were free to leave.

"You're sure she shouldn't stay overnight?" Jericho asked, voicing his concern.

The young intern smiled patiently and shook his head. "No,

she's fine. I'll give you a prescription for a few sleeping pills and she should be able to get a good night's rest. However, Mrs. Smith will undoubtedly experience some minor aches and pains because of the accident, but those will disappear within a few days. I might suggest that good hot showers will do wonders.''

At that point the young doctor was paged and he excused himself, but not before giving Jericho the prescription. Then he was gone.

When they were quite alone, Elizabeth turned her face to the wall to avoid looking at her husband.

"Elizabeth," Jericho said gently, "we have to leave now. Dolly and Paul are here and will take us home."

"I don't want to face them, Jerry," she implored. "I've made such a fool of myself."

"That's utter nonsense," he replied emphatically, "and I'd suggest that you forget tonight for now. Tomorrow's soon enough. As for Dolly and Paul, they're our friends and won't ask questions."

With care, Elizabeth managed to sit up and swing her legs around the side of the examining table. She winced slightly as Jericho helped her down and he placed his arm around her to give her support.

When Dolly saw them, she rushed over. "Honey," she said, "I'm so glad you're okay," and embraced Elizabeth who began to cry. Dolly drew back. "Hey, young lady there's nothing to cry about. You're fine and that's what's really important. Now let's get out of this place," and she laughed slightly, "it gives me the willies."

On the drive home they stopped at a drug store where Jericho had Elizabeth's prescription filled and as they approached the corner where the accident had occurred, the car had disappeared and the neighborhood was quiet.

"Where's the car?" Elizabeth asked, suddenly alarmed.

"It's been towed away," Paul replied softly.

"Can it be fixed?" she asked.

"Certainly. There's really only some minor damage and I've made arrangements for a loaner until it's repaired," he replied.

"Oh, Paul," Elizabeth said, "thanks so much. I'm so ashamed."

Both Dolly and Paul laughed. "Just remember that there are lots
of others who've had accidents and much more serious ones.
You're a very lucky young woman," Paul added, almost
paternally.

"I know," Elizabeth said, sounding remorseful.

Jericho had listened to the conversation between his wife and
their friends and was glad that they were accompanying them
home. Not one word had been mentioned about the reason for the
accident and he knew that until he volunteered the information
neither would question him.

After the Morans dropped them off with Elizabeth refusing
Dolly's offer to stay and help, they entered the silent house
together. Elizabeth settled on the divan and pulled an afghan over
her, but Jericho immediately headed for the bar where he poured
himself a double scotch. She watched with growing alarm as he
downed the drink and then with extreme care put the glass on the
bar counter and pulled up a chair alongside her. When he looked at
her his eyes were cold and the smell of liquor on his breath
permeated the air.

"Would you like to go to bed?" he asked point blank.

Elizabeth shook her head.

"Shall we talk?" he asked.

For a moment she was in a quandary as to what tack to take, but
then she nodded her head.

"Good. Now I have something I'd like to say," Jericho said.
"First, I'm glad that you're okay and I'm sorry as hell that I
slapped you." Then a dark look crossed his face and his anger was
apparent. "Secondly, why did you run away? Don't you think that
I have any feelings?"

Once again Elizabeth inclined her head in agreement.

"It's high time that you grew up, Elizabeth, You're a woman
now, not some spoiled brat, although at times I've wondered. Sure,
we're both disappointed that we can't have children, but that
doesn't mean that life comes to an end. It goes on and we accept
what is, not what could have been."

Abruptly he rose from his chair and moved restlessly around the
room, then returned to sit beside her.

"Now I'd suggest that you go upstairs, have a hot shower as the
doctor said, and then take your sleeping pill."

"But what about you?" Elizabeth ventured.

When Jericho laughed it was filled with irony. "Don't be concerned about me. I'll be fine. Now let me help you up the stairs."

After Elizabeth was situated for the night, Jericho brushed her cheek with a kiss, turned out the light, closed the bedroom door and returned to the downstairs where he poured himself another drink. With glass in hand he went out on the patio, and though the October night air held a trace of Fall in it, he dropped onto the lounge and stared out into the blackness of the night.

"What do we do now?" he mused aloud. "God, what do we do now?" he asked almost beseechingly.

As the warmth of the scotch relaxed him he started to drowse and then fell into a deep sleep. It was only the chill of early morning that awakened him. He glanced at his watch and saw that it was almost six o'clock. He jumped up from the lounge that had served as his bed for the night and entered the house. His mind was clear as a bell and he knew full well what he had to do.

28

Because of her youth, Elizabeth's recovery was rapid and within a few days the stitches were removed from the cut on her forehead leaving only a hairline scratch. The strain between herself and her husband was still there, and although he'd returned to their bed he'd made no attempt to make love to her. She knew that he was miserable and rightly so, and watched with growing apprehension as he literally threw himself into his work, taking on far more clients then he could comfortably handle.

As Jericho's actions continued unabated for weeks on end, Elizabeth reached the conclusion that it was now time to talk with her father.

When his daughter's call came, Schuyler Martin wasn't the least bit surprised, as Elizabeth had written a long and depressing letter to Kate and himself about her inability to have children. He knew then that it would only be a matter of time before she became restless and unhappy.

"Darling," Schuyler exclaimed, "I'm so happy that you called. How's everything?"

"Terrible. In fact, just awful," Elizabeth replied dejectedly.

"I'm so sorry. What can we do to help?"

"You can get me out of this God forsaken place, that's what."

she replied vehemently. "Jerry's acting as though I don't exist and I'm bored stiff! He spends a good share of his free time with Monsignor Pignelli," and then added caustically, "but at least it's not another woman!"

Schuyler laughed, although he really wasn't amused. The laughter was only for his daughter's benefit.

"Do you have any suggestions?" he asked.

"Well, I know one thing. He won't come to Washington to work for the administration since Nixon's in. There has to be something and I'm certain that you could come up with one of your brilliant plans."

"How about my flying out on the pretext that I want to see you?" her father asked.

"Oh, Daddy, that would be wonderful. Could you make it soon?"

"Let me check my calendar. Hold on." Quickly he leafed through the desk calendar and saw that there were a few days available in the following week. "How about next week? I can fly in Wednesday but will need to be back no later than Friday. Kate and I are invited to a State dinner at the White House on Saturday evening."

"That would be super," Elizabeth exclaimed. "It's the first good news I've had in ages." Then almost forlornly added, "Promise me that you'll speak to Jerry, Daddy."

"You can rest assured that I will, little one," Schuyler Martin replied, already aware of the role that he'd selected for his son-in-law.

When Elizabeth told Jericho at breakfast the following morning that her father would be spending a few days with them, he seemed pleased.

"Any special reason?" he'd asked.

"No. He had to take care of some family business in Kansas City and make the arrangements for grandmother to return to Washington. I presume as they say, 'He's killing two birds with one stone' by taking the time to see us, too" and she laughed lightly.

"You certainly seem excited," Jericho remarked.

"Well, why wouldn't I be? It's been nearly six months since we left Washington and I'm dying to hear the latest gossip," she replied, a mischievous twinkle to her eyes.

"Schuyler gossip?" Jericho said with obvious surprise.

"Well, not exactly, but he does share some things with me that he'd not discuss openly." Then she bridled a bit. "After all, I'm his only daughter and we've been extremely close. You should know that," and the last was almost like a reprimand.

"I do, I do. Now I must run," and Jericho got up from the table and started for the hall closet to get his coat.

Elizabeth tagged along after him.

"Will you be home for dinner on time?" she asked, and it seemed almost plaintively.

For a moment Jericho stalled. He realized that his indifference toward her the past few weeks had caused her concern so instead of providing some inane excuse, he said, "I'll be here no later than six. I promise."

"Oh, good. It's been so long since we've had a decent meal together," and she moved close to him.

For a moment he felt as though he were trapped but when she put her arms around his neck and pulled his face to hers and kissed him with all the pent up passion she'd withheld for weeks, his arms tightened around her and they were locked in an embrace. When she drew away she looked up into his eyes and whispered, "Do you have to leave so early?" her desire echoing in every word.

Without any hesitation, Jericho picked her up bodily and moved up the stairs. In moments they'd shed their clothes and began the lovemaking that they'd both sorely lacked.

The ringing of the telephone was the catalyst that broke the spell, and Jericho grabbed for it. "Smith here," he growled.

"It's Dolly, Jerry. Just wondered if you were okay. Your nine o'clock appointment is waiting."

"Oh hell, Dolly, I completely forgot. I'll be there shortly. Please make my excuses," and he tossed the phone back into its cradle and then lay back on the bed stroking the lovely body of his wife who was on the verge of starting to make love to him again.

Gently pushing her hands away, he said, "Elizabeth, I'm sorry, but I do have to go."

"Damn it, Jerry, why can't you let someone else wait?" she said bitterly.

"Please don't act this way. I've already told you that I'm sorry, and I'll be home for dinner on time. We do have the whole night," and he smiled at her suggestively.

Realizing that if she wanted to have her way she'd have to let him go she smiled, although a bit wistfully.

"I'll be waiting, dear husband," she said as she gently stroked his back.

When Jericho had finished dressing he bent and kissed her longingly, then pushed at his erection. Elizabeth saw and laughed aloud. She had her husband and her lover back. To hell with Monsignor Pignelli and his backgammon games, and she mockingly crossed herself.

Schuyler Martin's visit was one of utmost diplomacy. He sympathized openly with both Elizabeth and Jericho about their inability to have children and with that problem faced, as soon as he deemed it appropriate, he began to explore Jericho's reaction to the possibility of running for public office. The subject came up late one afternoon in Jericho's office and just before they were to meet Elizabeth, Dolly and Paul Moran at the country club.

"Getting tired of being a small town lawyer?" he asked in a joking fashion.

Jericho had looked at him sharply. "Whatever gave you that idea?"

Schuyler paused, his look thoughtful. "Well, you have to remember that I've seen you in action in Washington."

Jericho nodded, knowing full well that his father-in-law had some plan to try and pique his interest.

"What is it you want, Schuyler?" he said almost resignedly.

"You don't appear overly enthused, Jerry," the older man remarked as he tugged at his mustache, a habit of long standing.

"Just speak your piece. Elizabeth and the Morans are waiting."

"All right, Jerry. Let's go back a few years," he began and Jericho looked up at him in surprise.

"I'm sure you'll remember our many conversations about politics when you were attending Notre Dame and then Harvard Law. Right?" and he raised one eyebrow, his look now almost cynical.

"Of course I do. But that was a decade ago and as I indicated, I did my part, first with Jack and then with Bobby. What more is there?"

Schuyler let out a laugh. "What more? I can't believe that you'd ask me that!" and he got up from his chair and paced restlessly around the room. He came to a stop before the window where he stared down at the quiet street below, and almost shuddered with revulsion.

"Come here, Jerry," he said, and Jericho moved to the window where the two men looked down at the scene below. It was now well past five o'clock and the streets were nearly empty with the exception of a lone car filled with teenagers racing down the street toward the main highway.

"See what I mean?" Schuyler said.

To Jericho it appeared as it always had, but Schuyler's connotation caused him to think. Deep in thought Jericho returned to his desk, placed some files in his briefcase and then turned to his guest.

"Shall we go? We're already late."

"Certainly. Sorry to have detained you," Then added, "Aren't you the least bit curious about what I have in mind?"

Jericho's smile was knowing. "We'll discuss that later. Tonight's party night in Wichita."

Schuyler Martin's laugh seemed almost hysterical. "Party time? That's a good one!" Then together they left the law offices and headed for the country club.

The evening with the Morans proved to be a pleasant one, but at one point Schuyler had asked Paul to take him on a tour of the club's facilities, leaving Jericho to entertain the two women. When they were well out of hearing range, Schuyler suggested that they share a brandy in the bar and Paul agreed. Having been a close friend of Schuyler Martin's for well over thirty years he was always aware when he wanted to ask a favor, and being old comrades most of his requests had been granted without reservation.

When they were settled in a booth that had seen better days and was far removed from the crowded, noisy bar, Schuyler had proposed a toast. "Here's to our years of friendship," and then ceremoniously he raised his glass.

Paul's look was shrewd, still he smiled and touched Schuyler's glass. Then he slowly took a sip of the brandy, his eagle like eyes never once leaving his friend's face. Before Schuyler had a chance to speak, Paul Moran asked, "What is it you want?"

"I'm that transparent?" Schuyler replied and laughed softly.

" 'Fraid so. We go back a long way."

"That's true, Paul, and I do value your friendship and trust."

"Then get on with it. We're keeping Jerry and the girls waiting."

Schuyler Martin looked into the depths of his brandy glass and then leisurely took a sip.

"I'm sure that you and Dolly are aware that Elizabeth and Jerry can't have children."

Paul nodded.

"Well, since that's become an established fact, Elizabeth has been depressed."

"I'm sure that she has. Jerry hasn't been himself of late, either," Paul remarked, a frown touching his brow. "But what has that got to do with your favor? I'm sure that you want one."

"You're right. I do." Schuyler paused. "There's no reason to beat around the bush," and he took a deep breath. "I'd like Jerry to run for the Senate."

Paul Moran's expression didn't change the slightest but he leaned back against the booth, his mind racing, for he knew that if Jerry chose to run for public office it could well mean the end of Moran and Smith.

Schuyler had watched his old friend and although he knew that he was asking almost too much, he continued on. "After the Senate . . . well, there's always the possibility of the Presidency."

"My God, Schuyler," Paul exploded, "have you discussed this with Jerry? He does have a right to refuse, you know."

"I don't think that he will."

"How can you be so sure?"

"He loved Washington, and he knows how much Elizabeth misses it. It was only after the Kennedy boys and King were assassinated that he became so disillusioned. He's young, it's time, and he's a brilliant young man whose talents shouldn't be wasted. I could go on and on, but you know all that already."

"Have you mentioned this to our friends in the capitol?" Paul asked.

Schuyler nodded. "Matter of fact I have, and they're in accord. The time to act is *now*, not later. We've got a year-and-a-half ahead of us to help plan his campaign strategy for the next congressional election," and Schuyler paused. "I need your help to convince him, after I've given him my best shot.''

"Than you haven't approached Jerry as yet?"

"I've hinted that I want to discuss something with him, and figured that after Elizabeth had retired, tonight would be a good time.''

"She wouldn't mind?"

Schuyler shook his head. "No, she'd be happy. Washington's her home,'' and then he paused. "Did you know that it was Elizabeth's idea that Jerry retain Kansas as his legal residence?"

"You're kidding!"

The grey-haired man's smile was filled with pride. "She's a lot like me, Paul. A chip off the old block.''

At that Paul Moran had to smile, for he'd observed some of the same characteristics in Elizabeth as he had in her father.

"Will you support me in this, Paul?"

The old lawyer slowly nodded in agreement. "Just keep me informed of your progress. That's all that I ask.''

"Thanks, old friend,'' and Schuyler patted him affecionately on the back. "Now, shall we rejoin our companions?''

"Wouldn't be a bad idea,'' Paul replied, then stopped. "You know how I'll hate losing Jerry. He's my right arm.''

"I'll find someone to replace him.''

Paul Moran sighed. "It wouldn't be the same. It'll be like losing a son.''

"I know. But we have to think of the future. We've done our part.''

Silently the two old friends left the bar, a momentous decision behind them.

When Elizabeth found a moment to speak with her father privately she'd asked if he'd had an opportunity to talk with Jerry.

"Not really,'' Schuyler had replied seriously. "However, Paul and I came to terms about Jerry running for the senate, and he took it much better than I thought he would.'' He paused. "He considers Jerry his son, but I'm sure that you're already aware of that.''

"I know, daddy, and I'm really sorry about Paul and Dolly, but I simply can't stand much more of this small town existence. Had we been able to have a family, perhaps things might have been different,'' and for a moment her eyes were washed with tears.

"Don't worry, sweet," Schuyler said with fatherly affection. "We'll have you home before you know it. It will take some time, since the next election is nearly two years down the road; however, there'll be the campaign to organize and you're a true genius at that," and he smiled with paternal pride. "I remember well how you worked for Kennedy, but this time it will be for your husband, and that's far more important."

"Oh, daddy. Thank you, thank you," and Elizabeth threw herself into his arms much as she'd done when a little girl.

When they returned home, Elizabeth went right upstairs, leaving the two men alone.

Jericho had made a fire in the fireplace since the fall air now had a definite nip to it. Then he went to the bar and prepared two night caps, a brandy for his father-in-law and a scotch for himself.

They both settled before the blazing flames, each in the privacy of his own thoughts.

Jericho had watched with interest as Schuyler had manuevered Paul away from the table when they'd been at the country club, and he knew that whatever was coming had already been discussed with his senior partner.

"Nice evening," Schuyler remarked, breaking the silence.

"Yes, Paul and Dolly are great company. Elizabeth and I see a lot of them."

"That must make life pleasant."

"For me it does. But Elizabeth seems distracted these days.".

"Really? I hadn't noticed." Schuyler replied and looked to Jericho for an explanation.

"Ever since we learned that we couldn't have children she's been so different and she's acted as though it were my fault. Finally, I began to spend my evenings with Monsignor Pignelli."

"I had no idea, Jerry. Please accept my apologies for her behavior."

"Thanks, Schuyler. But she appears, on the surface at least, to be somewhat better now. I'm also sure that your visit has helped."

"That's good to hear."

Jericho got up from his chair and moved to the fireplace where he poked at the burning logs and then turned to face Schuyler. "Okay, my friend, let's hear it. Having Paul take you on a tour of the *facilities* wasn't the greatest excuse.''

Schuyler threw back his head and laughed. "That's what I like about you, Jerry. You never miss a thing!''

Then his look became serious. "I did speak with Paul, that's true,'' the older man admitted. "However, he plays an imporant role in our plan and I felt it advisable to have his reaction. And you're right. It does have to do with you.''

"Well?'' Jericho asked, showing growing impatience.

Schuyler took a sip from his brandy and then set his glass on the table. When he looked up into the eyes of his handsome son-in-law a sudden eagerness swept over him.

"Jerry,'' he began, "You've been the subject of many discussions throughout the Democratic Party and you can rest assured that I'm not the only one who's acutely aware of your abilities. The performance that you gave with the Kennedys and, of course with Johnson, didn't pass unnoticed. It's now time that you consider what you really want for the future,'' and he paused. "I'm sure that you thought my joke about being a small town lawyer was a jibe at your profession, and in all honesty perhaps it was, but you have so much more to offer that I can't stand idly by and see you turn into a recluse.''

"Recluse?'' Jericho replied. "That's a good one,'' his tone filled with sarcasm.

"I know that you help people here in Wichita with divorces, adoptions, and a criminal case now and then; and of course, there's still Pride Oil. But that's nothing compared to what you could do for all the people of the state of Kansas if you were their Senator in Washington.''

Jericho had now guessed what was ahead since Schuyler Martin would never have mentioned his running for Congress unless he was dead serious.

"I gather that you want me back in Washington. Right?''

"The whole family would like for you and Elizabeth to be there, but what's even more important is what you can do for your country,'' and a look of remembrance clouded his eyes.

"Remember Jack Kennedy saying 'Ask not what your country can do for you; ask what you can do for your country.'?''

Jericho nodded. He'd long admired both Jack and Bobby Kennedy with the passion of youth, and now he was being asked to take the same step that they'd both taken by becoming a Senator. The mere thought of it was almost more than he could handle and he shivered slightly although the room was warm.

"But why me? The Kennedys were a far different breed than I am. I'm a midwesterner, and that's where my roots are."

"Truman was from Missouri and didn't even have a college education, yet he became president. Jerry, it makes no difference where you're from, it's what you *do*." Now Schuyler knew that he almost had him. "Would you consider running for junior Senator in the coming election?"

"But what about Elizabeth, and Moran and Smith? They both have to be considered."

Schuyler Martin smiled. "They have been. Elizabeth and Paul are both waiting for your answer."

Jericho frowned slightly as the thought crossed his mind that perhaps his wife might have been the instigator of this latest ploy to get him to return to the Nation's capitol.

"Something troubling you, Jerry?" Schuyler asked, smiling amiably.

"A thought just occurred to me and I'd appreciate an honest answer before I make any commitment to run for anything."

"Okay, shoot," Schuyler replied, and for the first time that evening he had the sinking feeling that perhaps his plan would fail.

Jericho poured himself another scotch and offered his guest more brandy, but Schuyler refused. He knew now that he'd need to have his wits about him.

"May I ask if our darling Elizabeth might have had anything to do with this?" Jericho asked, sounding almost accusing.

"What do you mean? You've always known how she loves Washington, and I think that she's done a terrific job out here away from her family and friends."

"I really don't appreciate your comments, my friend. All I want from you now is an honest answer."

Schuyler Martin got up from his chair, poured himself a snifter of brandy, and then looked into the amber liquid. Finally he took a long sip and then faced Jericho. "For the life of me I can't understand why you should bring this up, Jerry," and he paused to take another sip from the glass. "Elizabeth is devoted to you, and like all of us wants only the best for you."

Then his expression saddened. "As you're well aware, neither Sky nor Brandy have ever expressed any interest in politics. Finally, your record as far as the Party is concerned is impeccable; and frankly, we need young men like you. We lost two of the best in the sixties and now for some reason you want to blame my daughter for the fact that you could become a Senator? That's ridiculous! Naturally she'd be proud to be a Senator's wife, and she'd also be a hell of an attribute, but Elizabeth had nothing to do with this, Jerry. I did mention it to her, but she'll abide by any decision you make."

Jericho couldn't help but smile at Schuyler's soap box speech and realized that there was every possibility that if he were elected, he could turn things around if he had the authority and the right people to back him. It seemed obvious that he already was assured of the latter, at least.

"What part would Elizabeth play if I should decide to take this on?"

"You saw her ability when she worked for Kennedy, and I'm certain that she'd accompany you wherever you go. She'd do a great job at organizing the women of Kansas on your behalf, and besides that, both Dolly and Paul would be right beside both of you all the way," and he stopped. "Would you like to give it a whirl?"

"You make it sound almost flippant," Jericho rebuked.

"I didn't mean to, as I know what a serious step it is," the older man replied.

"Can I have a few days to consider it, or do you have to have an answer immediately."

"Take your time, but remember one thing. The sooner we get started, the better off you'll be. You know, you do have one thing in your favor already."

"And just what might that be?"

"You served as State Party Chairman, and people will recognize your name."

Jericho laughed. "How could anyone possibly forget the name Smith?"

Schuyler finished his drink and then moved toward the guest room. "I'll say good-night for now. See you in the morning."

After the door had closed behind his guest, Jericho sat on the edge of the divan and stared into the smoldering coals. For a long time he remained silent, then finally picked up his coat and tie and headed for the stairs, knowing that he really had little choice and that the decision was already made.

29

The weeks and months which followed that fateful evening seemed to evaporate before Jericho's eyes, and he soon found himself completely divorced from his law practice and involved in the campaign. Both Schuyler and Elizabeth, and even Paul and Dolly Moran to some degree, had been exuberant when he'd announced that he'd decided to run for the Senate. But in all reality, he knew that it wasn't entirely his decision. He realized that as long as Schuyler Martin lived he'd find himself embroiled in politics.

At times he'd wondered why Schuyler himself hadn't sought political office since he had obviously acquired all the necessary attributes. Jericho finally reached the conclusion that Schuyler would much rather sit on the sidelines and play God. And, had the full truth been told, Schuyler Martin was deathly afraid of failure and consequently, he was more than willing to let someone else bear the brunt of the emotional crisis that losing entailed. He was, to Jericho, becoming more mysterious and secretive as time went on and Jericho firmly believed that, if it had been another time in history, Schuyler could easily have charmed Cleopatra's asp.

Brandy Martin, his long time friend and brother-in-law, happily accepted the job of financial advisor and campaign manager and worked diligently to raise funds to further Jericho's election.

Elizabeth had been drafted to manage the campaign headquarters in Wichita and in addition, regularly accompanied him on the campaign trail. On other occasions Paul Moran took her place, and because of his prominence his personal endorsement of Jericho would garner votes that he otherwise might not have received.

Jericho's opponent was a respected Republican—and the incumbent—and he knew from past experience that it could prove to be much more difficult to unseat someone who had already successfully served two terms. However, wherever Jericho appeared, the young people, now in the midst of social revolution, flocked to his rallies and he slowly became aware that in him they saw a new hope for the future. Also, his former close association with the Kennedys had proved beneficial, and when Ted had shared the platform with him at a Jaycee's meeting, his presence alone had made his ratings go higher in the polls.

From a rather slow beginning, Jericho's popularity gradually gained momentum and it wasn't long before the *Kansas City Star* assigned one of their political reporters to travel with him. As election day approached, the days never seemed to come to an end, and occasionally he'd awaken after just a few hours of sleep and actually wonder where he was. However, when Elizabeth accompanied him, the time that they spent alone proved to be the balm he needed to heal his jangled nerves.

Schuyler Martin never left him alone during those final and crucial weeks and was on the telephone several times daily waving his banner of encouragement. Then, a few days prior to the election, he and Kate flew in from Washington to await the results. On the day of the election, Jericho's headquarters were crowded with his most loyal supporters. Even as the polls were preparing to close, the telephone crew was still manning the phones urging people to get out and vote for their candidate.

When the first returns came in his opponent was well ahead and Jericho had remarked to Schuyler, "Do you really think I've got a chance?"

His father-in-law had replied, "My God, Jerry, that's only a sprinkling of the precincts and from what Paul's told me, they've always gone Republican. Just wait for the suburbs and the young people's vote. You'll see," he said, smiling smugly.

Even though his words were encouraging, Jericho was already

psyching himself up to accept a loss, should it come. He knew that if that should happen, the whole Martin family would come face to face with their first real defeat.

As the evening progressed the vote tally started to change, slowly at first, and then Jericho drew even with his opponent. But when the final votes were counted it was Jerry Smith, the bright young lawyer, who had unseated the veteran Republican, and the Smith headquarters went wild. In the chaos which followed Jericho lost sight of Elizabeth, but Schuyler Martin, as always, was right at his elbow to share in his glory as the crowd pushed Jericho toward the front of the room.

"JERRY, JERRY, JERRY," they shouted over and over.

In quite desperation he held up his hand, but the chanting, clapping and stomping of feet continued unabated and he finally relaxed and enjoyed the excitement. Elizabeth had somehow managed to reach him and she hugged him enthusiastically. Then the crowd began to chant again. "Jerry & Liz, Jerry & Liz."

Jericho glanced at his wife and saw the flush of happiness reflected on her face as she smiled and waved to his supporters. Finally, it was Schuyler Martin who quieted them.

"Friends," he said smiling benevolently. "We appreciate your enthusiasm and support of Jerry. It's been a long, hard road for my son-in-law," he said proudly and turned to smile at Jericho, "and I know that you want to hear from him personally," and he relinquished the microphone to Jericho.

"Thanks, Schuyler," he said and then nervously ran his hands through his dark tousled hair, his eyes serious.

"First, I couldn't have done this without all of you," and once again the crowd burst into applause, but stopped as he held up his hand.

"These past months have seemed like an eternity at times, but it's all been worth it and I intend to represent both the young and the aged to the best of my ability when Elizabeth and I get to Washington," and he turned to draw Elizabeth close to him. "This lady has been my staunchest critic and supporter, and without her constant strength and help I don't know if I could have gone through this. I knew when I married her that she was a winner, and today not only my dream has come true, but hers as well. We thank you for the long hours you've spent on my behalf, and you'll not be forgotten. Good-night and God Bless You."

Jericho withdrew to his tiny office that had served him well to collect his composure while the others saw to the departing constituents. His musing was interrupted by the sound of footsteps and he saw Schuyler Martin in the doorway. Schuyler moved purposely to where he was sitting and pulled up a chair.

"Good feeling?" he asked, eyes twinkling.

Jericho nodded. "I'm numb, Schuyler, simply numb. To be honest with you, I didn't think I had a chance in hell," and then he smiled broadly. "Just goes to show that you were right all along, and you deserve most of the credit."

"Not on your life, Jerry," Schuyler replied, although it was obvious that he was pleased. "You and Elizabeth are the ones that took on the Republican Party. Don't ever sell yourself short."

"Did someone call my parents?" he asked.

Schuyler nodded. "Dolly took care of that, and they're happy for you."

"You know, my friend," Jericho said solemnly, "I wonder just what they think now. They did so want me to become a priest."

Just as he finished speaking, Monsignor Pignelli wandered through the open door. Jericho jumped to his feet and the two men embraced warmly, then Schuyler shook the priest's hand, though rather formally.

"Nice seeing you, Father," Schuyler said. "I presume that you've heard our boy won," and he touched Jericho's arm possessively.

"I heard it on the evening news, and hoped that he might still be around." Then he glanced around the paper littered room. "So this is what it's like," he mused and bent to pick up a discarded placard which had Jericho's picture on it.

"Yep, this is the winner's circle," Jericho replied laughing. "When you win, you're in, and I haven't the vaguest idea whose going to clean this mess up."

"Don't worry," Schuyler interrupted quickly. "I've made the necessary arrangements." Then he turned to Monsignor Pignelli. "If you'll excuse us, Father, Jerry's tired and needs to go home." Almost rudely, he began to steer his son-in-law toward the front door, but Jericho stopped in his tracks.

"Schuyler, if you don't mind I'd like to have a moment with my friend."

"Whatever," the grey-haired man replied and the look he gave Monsignor Pignelli was one of distrust. "I'll send the others on home and wait for you in my car."

"Thanks. I'll be along shortly."

With Schuyler gone, Jericho turned to his long time friend. "You'll have to excuse my father-in-law. Sometimes he acts as though he owns me."

"Does he?" the priest asked point blank.

His question came as a surprise and Jericho hesitated briefly before he answered. "Perhaps he does in some ways. He's been my mentor since I attended Notre Dame, and I'll be the first to admit that he does know how to make things happen. However," and he stopped, "I'm quite sure that he was short with you because Elizabeth undoubtedly has told him that we've become rather close."

"Is he jealous?" Pignelli asked matter-of-factly.

"That well could be, Michael, but he'll not come between our friendship, I can assure you of that." He paused. "I suppose I really should go. We'll get together when things are more settled."

"I understand, Jerry. Just be your own man," the priest said, his look serious.

Jericho laughed slightly. "I remember many years ago when you told me not to let anyone push me into something I didn't really want," and he sighed. "I do like politics, that I can't deny, but there are days when I wonder if I really made the right choice."

The older man looked at him sharply. "You're right where you belong. We all have our roles to play in life."

"I'm sure you're right. Now I'd better go."

As they went to the door, both men turned to look back at the disorderly room. Jericho switched off the lights and pulled the door shut.

"Come by soon, Jerry."

"I will, Michael," and then his look became serious. "According to Schuyler, this is only the beginning," and he frowned. "Wherever will it lead?"

"Only God knows, Jerry, but I'll be here for you."

Once again the two men embraced and Jericho watched his friend drive into the night.

When Jericho joined Schuyler in the car he slumped in the front seat as his father-in-law headed for home. Both men had remained silent and neither referred to the visit of Monsignor Pignelli. However, he was quite sure that Elizabeth had discussed his friendship with the priest with her father, and he'd been right.

In any event, Jerry and Elizabeth would be leaving for Washington and Monsignor Pignelli would be staying behind.

Elizabeth and Jericho returned to Washington and within a short time were settled once again in their home in Old Alexandria.

After Congress convened, and following months of intensive indoctrination into the intricacies of the body which governed the United States, Jericho became acutely aware of the secret manueverings behind closed doors. On several occasions he had been approached by lobbyists who were actively interested in promoting legislation that would prove beneficial to the special interests they represented. However, very quickly these individuals discovered that the newly elected junior Senator was a man to be reckoned with as he was blunt and hard as nails to their proposals.

The first few years passed quickly and when Richard Nixon and Spiro Agnew became the victors in the 1972 election, Jericho wasn't too surprised. However, a few months after the inauguration, rumors began to surface that all had not been right within the Republican campaign and these accusations were attributed to two young reporters on the *Washington Post*.

At first, like most everyone else, Jericho had chalked the stories up to idle gossip but when the Watergate story became a known fact, he watched in horror not wanting to believe that the President of the United States would take part in such a heinous crime.

One evening, following a family dinner at Magnolia Hill, Jericho and Schuyler took refuge in Schuyler's office to discuss the political situation. Jericho immediately broached the subject of the Watergate issue and his host listened attentively as the younger man vented his anger and frustrations.

"God, Schuyler," he said, "why are people so damned dishonest and stupid? I'll have to admit that I've admired the man's foreign policies, but his present actions are totally beyond my comprehension."

Schuyler had listened attentively and continued to puff on his expensive cigar. When Jericho had finally exhausted his anger and slumped into a chair, he knew that now was the opportune time. Very carefully the older man stubbed out his cigar in the heavy crystal ashtray and then leaned back in his chair, eyes riveted on his son-in-law.

"Well, Jerry, you've got to understand one thing up front. The political game is riddled with bad apples," and he laughed slightly. "The majority of those who commit the crimes get away with their underhanded operations and only a few are dumb enough to get caught." For a moment he paused. "I'll cite one example that has concerned not only me, but the entire Democratic party, and that's Ted Kennedy's fiasco at Chapaquiddik." Once again he paused, then continued.

"Money, as you are undoubtedly aware, plays an important part, and please don't take offense at what I'm about to say. Have you ever considered the fact that if you hadn't met Brandy at Notre Dame, you would probably be in Kansas and would have given up the idea of becoming a lawyer? Who knows? But fate stepped in, in your case, and your life has changed dramatically because of circumstances."

"Are you insinuating that you bought my election?" Jericho interjected.

"No, but my influence goes a long way, and the Martins happen to be one of the more fortunate families who have accumulated vast wealth. It happened to be my connections that first brought you to Washington where you worked on Jack Kennedy's campaign, and then you volunteered to help Bobby. You've proven yourself . . . there's little doubt of that."

"Thanks," Jericho replied tersely.

"Now about Nixon. The scenario from all indications will go like this. He'll undoubtedly resign, if they don't impeach him first, and I have to admit that's a good possibility. However, that would make the country look like a big asshole to our allies, and in all probability he'll have to vacate the Oval office on his own accord. Then Jerry Ford will step in. And his first act will be to grant Nixon a pardon to keep up appearance. There'll undoubtedly be loud cries that justice isn't being served but what good would impeaching Nixon do? He merely got his hand caught in the cookie jar and was an idiot to surround himself with imcompetents and con artists.

"Now, all you have to do," Schuyler continued, "is keep your nose clean."

When Jericho started to protest, he tempered his words. "I don't mean to imply you've done anything wrong."

"Schuyler," Jericho almost shouted, "can't you give me credit for having my own good judgment?"

"Don't get excited, Jerry," the older man cautioned, "I merely want you to be extra cautious," and a far away look crossed his face. "You have a great future ahead, mark my words."

Then he suddenly stopped speaking and got up from his chair, almost as though he were dismissing him.

"Shall we join the ladies?" Schuyler asked, smiling pleasantly.

It was obvious to Jericho that their conversation had ended and he followed his father-in-law from his office to join Elizabeth and Kate on the terrace.

Schuyler Martin's prophecy about Richard Nixon proved to be correct and in a matter of weeks the whole Washington scene had changed.

After listening to President Ford's announcement that Richard Nixon had been given a full pardon, it was Schuyler who voiced his anger. "The damned fool should end up in jail like the rest of those bastards," he stormed. When Jericho failed to react, he went on, "I suppose you think that pardoning him is all right?"

"There's no reason to be so upset, Schuyler. It's finished."

"You feel sorry for him, don't you?" he said accusingly.

"Matter of fact, I do. If you'll recall, you were the one who made the statement that he got his hand caught in the cookie jar, and then you pointed out Ted Kennedy's problem! I'm thinking about the future. There's every chance that we'll have a Democrat back in the White House the next election. The Republican Party has lost it's morality."

Schuyler seated himself at his desk and when he looked at Jericho it was with obvious pride. "Now you're thinking, and you're right! It's over. Ford will never be elected," then his look became serious. "Besides, your own election comes in 1976," and his eyes held a wicked gleam. "You've got plenty of ammunition."

"Schuyler," Jericho said solemnly, "I wouldn't lower myself to rub salt into someone else's wounds," and he sighed deeply. "I'm rather surprised at your attitude."

When Schuyler looked at his protege it was with new respect for it was apparent that Jerry Smith was showing the true depth of his character.

"I'm sorry," he apologized. "I simply got carried away."

"Apology accepted," Then Jericho leaned forward. "I'll serve another term," he stated positively.

"You're certainly sure of yourself," Schuyler replied softly.

"Why shouldn't I be? I've performed well in the Senate and people like me, Schuyler." He paused. "You helped me get here, and I do appreciate that, but I'm the one who has done the job . . . no one else." His eyes shone with enthusiasm. "We have a rough road ahead of us; legislation has gone to hell since Watergate, and we've got to get back on the right track."

"You're going to make it big, son," Schuyler said with pride. "I knew that you would."

Schuyler knew in his heart that this was the man who would eventually become a candidate for the highest office in the nation.

30

When it came time for Jericho to hit the campaign trail again, Elizabeth accompanied him only sporadically. Because of her reluctance, he once more turned to his former law partner, Paul Moran. The two men, even though they had been apart for a number of years, still enjoyed a close relationship and Jericho knew that whatever he confided in his friend would never reach Schuyler Martin's ears.

After a long day of campaigning, they had sought refuge in Jericho's hotel room. Rather abruptly, Jericho had dismissed Brandy Martin and the other staff members so that he and Paul could enjoy an evening alone.

When he had left Washington it was with some apprehension and an intuitive feeling that his father-in-law was up to his old tricks.

"What's bugging you, Jerry?" Paul asked.

"Am I that transparent?" he replied, laughing slightly as he untied his shoes, kicked them off, and stretched out his legs.

" 'Fraid so, son." The word 'son' rolled off his tongue automatically.

Jericho took a long sip from his scotch and then placed the glass on a table. He got up to move restlessly around the room, an expression of concern on his face. Then he faced the white haired lawyer. "Schuyler's up to something," he said.

"Any clues?" Paul asked.

Jericho shook his head. "For the life of me I can't seem to put my finger on it. Before I left on this trip, Elizabeth and I were paraded to a bunch of parties," he made a face, "and you know how much I like that," he said sardonically.

The older man laughed. "Want an honest opinion?"

"Hell, yes. Elizabeth even started to complain, and that's unusual. You know how she dearly loves the limelight."

Paul Moran smiled and indicated that Jericho should take a seat.

"Jerry," he began, "as you know, I've been friends with Schuyler since college days, and as much as we've been together over the years, at times he's a complete enigma. However, I'd be willing to bet my last dollar that he's priming you for the presidency."

When Jericho started to interrupt, he held up his hand. "Not this time. Carter and Mondale will be the ticket," and his look became secretive. "Just you wait."

"You can't mean it!" Jericho replied in astonishment.

Paul nodded. "I've seen Schuyler operate time and time again, and I'll tell you something in strict confidence. If Nixon hadn't screwed up, Carter wouldn't have a chance. But it doesn't make any difference. We're merely biding our time."

Jericho got up, poured himself another Scotch and freshened Paul's brandy, a frown on his face. "You've given me a lot to think about, Paul."

"I know, my friend, but I wanted you to have fair warning of what Schuyler will expect of you."

"I'd never win," Jericho said, almost sadly.

"Now why would you say that? Your term in the Senate has been outstanding, and you must remember that you've been a confidant of the Kennedy clan and, I might add, you possess that All American Boy image!"

"Oh, shit," Jericho growled. "Sounds like some Wheaties advertisement."

Paul Moran howled. "Now, what do you think your constituents would think of your attitude, let alone Schuyler Martin?" and he cocked his head to one side, eyes twinkling.

"That's a helluva lot to ask a man, and I don't know if I'd even consider it."

"Only time will tell," Paul replied softly and got slowly up from his chair. "I think I'll turn in now," and he yawned, "it's been a long day. Don't worry about it, Jerry. Your senate race is what's important now. Just keep what I've told you in the back of your mind."

Jericho escorted the older man to the door and as they paused, he placed his hand on his shoulder and looked deep into his eyes. "Thanks for being my friend, Paul," and his voice softened. "I love you and Dolly."

"We know, Jerry," Paul replied, a trace of tears in his eyes. Then he ambled down the hallway, but turned at the door to his room to give Jericho a smart salute.

Jericho successfully retained his seat in the Senate and had been well satisfied with the turn out which had given him an overwhelming victory. He was appointed to the Foreign Relations Committee, and he openly applauded Carter's Camp David Treaty between Israel and Egypt. His respect for Carter had grown somewhat.

It was well into the second year of his term that Schuyler Martin called and invited him to join him for lunch. On most days, Jericho simply forgot to eat so his father-in-law's invitation was a welcome diversion. He'd blocked out the time almost gratefully.

At the hour scheduled to meet Schuyler, Jericho left his office, but instead of finding his host waiting for him, the Martin limousine stood curbside, with James beside it.

"Good-afternoon, James," Jericho said pleasantly. "Where's the boss?"

"He's been delayed by an overseas call, Senator, and sent me to pick you up."

"But what about our engagement?" Jericho asked and glanced at his watch with obvious impatience.

"I believe the cook's preparing lunch. The ladies of the house, including your Miss Elizabeth, are attending a luncheon today," James replied politely.

"I see," Jericho said. "Well, we'd better hurry. I've got to be back by three for an important meeting."

James held the door open while Jericho got in and slumped down on the soft leather upholstery. With skill, the old chauffeur took the wheel and manuevered the sleek, black limousine through the heavy noon hour traffic. When they arrived at Magnolia Hill, Schuyler was just winding up his call and motioned to Jericho to take a seat.

After a few minutes of additional conversation, with Schuyler doing most of the listening, he finally replaced the phone in its cradle and then rubbed his ear which had turned a brilliant red from the pressure of the instrument.

"Some people are sure long winded," he complained.

"That's true," Jericho replied, "and thanks for sending James."

Schuyler nodded. "I thought that was the best solution under the circumstances. Now, shall we have lunch? I know that you're pressed for time." As they entered the pleasant breakfast room he saw a table had been set for two and a bottle of wine was cooling in a silver container.

"This is certainly out of my class," Jericho remarked, laughing slightly. "If I do get to eat, the food usually comes out of the vending machines and is brought in by my secretary. Come to think of it, she goes out for lunch every day," and he smiled, "some people are just lucky, I guess."

"That will undoubtedly change," Schuyler remarked as he poured two glasses of chilled Chablis and handed one to his guest.

"Really?" Jericho replied. "That would certainly be a welcome surprise to me."

After the maid had served their entre of poached salmon, the two men ate hungrily and almost in silence.

When he'd finished, Jericho said, "That was delicious, my compliments to the cook."

Schuyler smiled. "Jessie's been with us almost forever, it seems, and she always knows exactly when to add the right touch."

"Couldn't agree more." Jericho paused. "Is there a reason for this luncheon? Something you need to talk with me about?"

His host nodded. "Why don't we have our coffee in the drawing room. We'll be more comfortable there."

He gave the order to the servant and they adjourned to the palatial room. Jericho had long admired the magnificent decor and knew that the old masters on the walls had belonged to the Martin family for many years. He took a seat near the bay window which afforded him a view of the picturesque grounds; it was Spring and the Magnolia buds looked as though they were ready to burst into bloom.

Then he turned his attention to his father-in-law, who was obviously deep in thought. "Is there something wrong?" he asked.

"Perhaps," and Schuyler looked out the window and then back to his guest. "I have something of importance that needs to be discussed."

By now he'd peaked Jericho's curiosity.

"Is Kate or your mother ill?" he asked, with a trace of alarm in his voice.

The older man shook his head. "No, thank God. Everybody's fine, Sky and Brandy included."

"Then what is it?"

"To begin with, I'd like to have an honest opinion of Carter's performance."

"You mean my opinion?" and he shook his head almost sadly. "What difference would it make?"

"To me and some others it means a great deal," Schuyler replied.

For a moment Jericho studied the man who confronted him and the conversation that he'd had months before with Paul Moran crossed his mind.

"So, you're asking that I hold nothing back?"

Schuyler nodded.

Jericho gave a deep sigh and then began.

"Jimmy Carter is a nice person; a good Christian and a family man; however," and when he said *however* he could almost see Schuyler's ears prick up.

"Please go on," his friend encouraged.

"Well, with the exception of the Camp David treaty, Carter's done almost nothing for the country. However, I do respect him because he's the President. Does that satisfy you?"

Schuyler smiled and nodded. "Yes. Would you support him if he chose to run for re-election?"

Jericho shook his head, got up from his chair and roamed around the room. He was certain of what he was going to be asked and a chill went through him. Then he turned. "Just what is it you want from me?''

"A lot.''

"That figures. Go ahead and spill it,'' Jericho replied almost rudely.

"I've been having some discussions with some of the other party members and we'd hoped that you'd consider running for the presidency in the next election,'' he stated flatly.

"Me?''

"Yes, Jerry. You possess all the necessary attributes. You've been in the political scene for a long time. First, with the Kennedys, then Johnson, and now you're serving your second term in the Senate. Everyone who's important likes you, and respects your judgment. It's also become obvious that you're nobody's man, and your image is—''

Jericho interrupted him. "The All American Boy type,'' he said so softly that it was almost impossible to hear him.

Schuyler's look was one of surprise. "That's not all bad.''

"I don't know, Schuyler. I'll have to give it a lot of thought,'' and he paused, "And I do mean a lot!''

"That's one of the main reasons we wanted to have your reaction before too many others toss their hats in the ring. We're almost certain the Republicans won't nominate Ford, but they'll come up with someone. No matter who it is, should Carter and Mondale run we'll lose, and we don't want that to happen.''

Jericho glanced at his watch and saw that it was approaching two thirty.

"I have to go. I've a meeting at three,'' and he moved to the door. "I'll let myself out and send James back.'' Then he paused. "How long do I have?''

"We'd like your answer as soon as possible.''

"I understand. Thanks for lunch,'' and with a nod he hurried out.

Schuyler went to the window and watched as Jericho got into the limousine and was driven away. He'd made his pitch and with the help of Elizabeth he hoped that the answer would be 'yes.'

31

Just before leaving his office that afternoon he placed a call to his long time friend, Monsignor Pignelli, and had asked a favor.

"Of course, Jerry," the priest replied without any sign of hesitation. "Ask and it's yours."

"It's imperative that I come out there for a few days," he said, and then added, "I need a cover."

"Would you care to be a little more explicit?" his friend had asked, sounding rather puzzled.

"I've just received an important proposition."

"What kind of proposition?"

"I'm sorry, Michael, but it's hush-hush at the present. Even the Morans can't know that I'll be in the area."

"What about your family?"

"Frankly, I never gave them a thought," and Jericho paused. "Would it be asking too much if I told Elizabeth you'd called and said that my folks aren't doing too well?"

"Whatever it is, it sounds urgent," the priest replied solemnly.

"It is, and it's going to require some research on my part."

"Research?"

"I'll explain that later."

"Then, of course. If anyone should ask, and I doubt if they

will," and he laughed wryly, knowing how the Martin family viewed him, "I'll tell them that your family needed you. I'd be glad to meet your plane."

"There's no need for that, I'll have a rental car available."

"Will I see you?"

Jericho laughed. "Of course. You know that this is completely against my nature," and he gave an audible sigh.

"I know, Jerry. But sometimes we have to do things that we normally wouldn't even consider. I'll be looking forward to your visit."

"Thanks, Michael," and their conversation had ended.

When Jericho arrived home he found an expectant Elizabeth waiting and he knew that she had talked with her father.

After Jericho had prepared Elizabeth's Martini and a Scotch for himself, he sprawled in his favorite chair and swung his feet up on the hassock.

"Something wrong?" Elizabeth asked sounding almost too solicitous.

"Just before I left the office I received a telephone call from Monsignor Pignelli." When he glanced at his wife he saw that her pleasant look had changed to a frown.

"What did he want?" she snapped.

"My folks aren't very well; he'd just been to see them."

"Oh, I'm sorry. Anything serious?" but there was only the slightest trace of concern in her voice.

"They're simply up in years and they do miss seeing me."

"I'm sure that's true."

"You know, Elizabeth, as I was driving home I came to a decision."

"What?" she asked eagerly.

"I'm going to take a few days off and fly out to see Mother and Dad." When he looked at her he saw her disappointment though she made a concerted effort to hide it.

"Perhaps you should. Would you like for me to go along?"

Jericho laughed. "No, darling. I appreciate the offer, but I know how you dislike going out there. This one I'll do alone."

"If you insist," she replied. Then, "Is there anything else you'd like to talk about? Your day?"

"Oh, yes, I had lunch with your father."

"How nice. What did Daddy have to say?"

"Oh, the usual. Politics. What else?" his laugh was ironic.

"Is that *all*?"

"What did you expect?"

"My dear husband, Daddy called and told me about your conversation and I'd hoped for once that you'd tell me about it without my having to literally pry it out of you," she replied with obvious disgust, her eyes flashing.

"There's nothing to get excited about, Elizabeth. Not yet, anyway."

"Than you haven't given it any consideration?"

Jericho shrugged his shoulders. "Of course I have. Who wouldn't? But it's a giant step, and I don't know that I'm ready."

"But you are," she said, almost agonizingly. "You are, Jerry. You have everything to offer. My father wouldn't consider approaching you or anyone if he didn't believe that you'd be a winner. Honestly! Men!" and she got up and refilled her glass, every gesture filled with anger.

"While I'm visiting the folks I'll have lots of time to think about it, and when I come back I'll undoubtedly have my answer."

Elizabeth sank to her knees beside his chair and then looked up into his eyes. "Oh, Jerry, I do so hope you'll agree."

Like a loving father he patted her hair and then bent down to kiss her.

"You'd make a beautiful First Lady, my love," and he paused to stare at her intently. "In fact, you have the same class as Jackie Onassis," and he cocked his head to one side and then smiled rakishly. "Perhaps even more."

For a moment Elizabeth hugged his knees and then got up and crawled into his lap where she began making love to him.

A few days later Jericho flew to Wichita. He secured a rental car and headed directly out of town to the farm, skirting the business district just in case one of the Morans might spot him.

Since their conversation, Monsignor Pignelli had seen fit to pay Jacob and Martha Smith a visit and had told them that Jerry was coming home. The elderly couple were overjoyed at the prospect of seeing their son for since his election to the senate, his visits had been few and far between.

Even though they were both well into their eighties, Martha Smith insisted on doing her own cooking, though not as she'd done in the past; however, with the priest's announcement, she immediately started to prepare Jericho's favorite dishes.

The meeting between parents and son proved to be an emotional one for even when Jericho had resided in Wichita it was apparent that Elizabeth hadn't enjoyed their company and his visits were made alone.

After they'd devoured Martha's farm style dinner, the hired girl shooed them from the dining room and they'd gone into the old-fashioned parlor of the farmhouse. Once Martha and Jacob were settled in their favorite chairs, Jericho pulled up another.

"Mother, Dad," he said, "I need your help."

Martha and Jacob looked at each other in surprise.

"Of course, son," Jacob replied without hesitation. "What is it?"

"I know that what I'm about to ask of you will undoubtedly stir up old and perhaps sad memories," and he paused. "But you see, I want to know about my past."

"Whatever for, Jerry?" Martha asked.

Jericho looked at the questioning faces knowing that he couldn't possibly tell them why.

"I presume that it's basic curiosity. You see, I remember Mother Jean Marie and the life that I led before you adopted me. But I've never known who my real mother and father were, and I have to know."

"We really don't know that much," Martha had replied and it seemed to Jericho almost reluctantly.

"But why? Surely the adoption papers would show my parents' names."

Sadly, Martha shook her head. "I'm afraid not, son."

"But who signed them?" he asked.

"Mother Jean Marie."

"How could she? I'm a lawyer and that's most unusual."

"Not in those days," Jacob suddenly interrupted. "Mother Jean Marie produced a Power of Attorney giving her the right, and naturally we accepted it without question. The papers had apparently been drawn by an attorney and seemed proper to us."

"My God," Jericho said and got up from his chair to move restlessly around the room. Then, "Did she happen to mention any names?"

For a moment Jacob seemed puzzled, but then his eyes brightened.

"By golly, she did."

"Tell me."

"She did tell us that your mother's name was Kathleen."

"Thank God," Jericho said. "Do you remember anything more?"

Jacob shook his head. "That's all we know, son. I'm sorry."

"How about the Convent in Staley? Is it still there?" Jericho continued, almost as though he were interrogating a witness.

"As far as we know it still is. You were the last one to visit Mother Jean Marie just before she died. And there really wasn't any need for us to go back after that."

Jericho smiled sadly. "Did I ever tell you when I was there that last time that Mother Jean Marie referred to herself as 'Kathleen' and believed that I was her son?"

"You never mentioned it to us."

"Why didn't I think of the Convent before?" Jericho murmured almost as though he were talking to himself.

"Are you sure that you really want to do this?" his mother asked.

"It's a necessity. The day has come for me to know my own heritage."

Jacob shook his head an a sadness seemed to envelope the elderly people. "Then you'd better go to Staley. Perhaps they can give you the answers you need."

By now it had grown quite late and Jericho kissed his parents good-night and watched them move slowly to their downstairs quarters. After they'd disappeared he went out into the cool Kansas night and stared up into the dark sky, a sudden surge of excitement creeping over him. Tomorrow he'd know who he really was.

As the dawn of a new day erupted over the stark plains of Kansas, Jericho slipped out of bed, shaved and dressed, and then left a note for his parents informing them that he was on his way to Staley. After he'd driven for an hour he'd pulled into a small roadside cafe where he enjoyed a hearty, home-style breakfast. As he ate, his thoughts drifted back to his early days.

What a truly wonderful experience that had been for a very small boy, he thought, and as he remembered the happy times he was overcome by emotion and tears welled in his eyes. He remembered vividly the day he'd discovered Jean Marie alone in the Chapel sobbing her heart out before the Virgin Mary because she had to give him up and once again he was overwhelmed by his emotions.

"Perhaps I should never have left her," he murmured to himself; yet, he knew that her sacrifice had proved to be right, even though it had been one that was filled with much anguish and much pain.

Refreshed from breakfast, he returned to the car and proceeded on his way down the old familiar highway. As he drew near the small rural community where the Convent was located, excitement pulsed through him. It had been almost forty years since he'd left the Convent to live with Martha and Jacob, and when he pulled in front of the weatherbeaten building that had once served as his home, tears formed in his eyes. Here was his beginning. For a moment, he quietly sat in the car and stared at the brick structure, then he got out and flew up the long flight of stairs. When he reached the door he saw that a new bell system had been installed and he pushed the button.

The door opened, and he came face to face with a young novice whose angelic look took him aback.

"Yes, sir?" the young woman asked, smiling pleasantly.

"I'm Senator Smith," he said, "and I'd like very much to meet with the Mother Superior."

"Have you an appointment?" she asked.

Jericho shook his head. "I'm afraid not. But it's imperative that I see her," and he pulled his congressional card from his wallet and handed it to her.

The Sister glanced at it briefly and then back at Jericho.

"I'll see if the Mother Superior can see you. Please come in," and she pushed the heavy door open to allow him to pass in front of her into the familiar musty foyer.

The nun indicated that he should follow her and she led him to the small small sitting room where years before he had first met his adoptive parents.

"Please have a seat. I'll return shortly," and she hurried away, the skirt of her habit rustling crisply about her legs.

Time passed slowly and Jericho glanced at his watch several times, his impatience growing. Then he looked up to see an older woman staring at him from the doorway. He jumped to his feet, embarrassed that he'd been caught off guard.

"I'm Sister Noel, the Mother Superior," she announced as she moved into the room. She extended her hand to Jericho, who took it in his own.

"Allow me to introduce myself. I'm Senator Jerry Smith."

"I know, Senator. Sister Mary informed me that you have an urgent need. How may I serve you?" she asked as she took a chair with Jericho following suit.

"It goes a long way back," he began, "and I'm not sure if you'd remember or even know anything about it."

"Please continue. I'll do what I can."

"Forty-five years ago I was born here in the convent," and with this statement the Mother Superior turned almost pale.

"Born here?" she whispered incredulously, her brows furrowing.

Jericho nodded. "Jean Marie was the Mother Superior at the time."

"Oh, yes," the nun replied and smiled. "I've heard many stories about her."

"I lived here at the Convent for almost five years and then was placed for adoption." He looked down at his hands and then up into understanding eyes. "Mother Jean Marie and I had a wonderful relationship, even after I went to live with my adoptive parents, and when she died it was almost more then I could bear."

The Mother Superior reached over and touched his hand with understanding.

"My quest is this," Jericho continued, making an effort to sound more businesslike. "I'd like to know if, by chance, there's a record of my birth that might provide some clue to my parentage."

For a moment the sister frowned. "Even if there were, I don't know if we could release the information."

"Would you be kind enough to look? There might be a folder, or an envelope, with my name written on it."

Sister Noel got to her feet and Jericho rose.

"If you'll come to my office I'll see what I can find," and then she turned back and looked him directly in the eyes. "I can't promise you anything, but I'll try."

"Thank you, Sister," Jericho replied.

He followed her down the hall where they stopped at the room that had once served as Mother Jean Marie's office. With a feeling of trepedition he entered and then saw that the room had been changed. He let out an audible sigh.

The nun looked at him questioningly. "Something amiss?"

"It's changed, that's all," and he took a chair beside her desk.

The Mother Superior began rummaging through a drawer and found a small key. Quickly, she went to a small closet like room where it was apparent the old files had been locked away. There she hastily went through them, and she returned with a yellowed folder in her hands on which the name JERICHO was printed boldly in black.

"You were right, Senator. There was a record. If you'd care to look at the information alone, I have other things to attend to. Please excuse me," and suddenly she was gone.

When he was quite alone, Jericho held the folder for a few moments. Then taking a deep breath, he started to open the file that would reveal his past.

As Jericho opened the yellowed container he noticed Mother Jean Marie's orderly filing system and a smile touched his lips. He remembered with fondness how she'd drilled him day after day on promptness, orderliness and cleanliness, which, in her opinion were some of the most valuable traits a person could possess.

The first paper he touched was of the thinnest parchment and a few pieces crumbled as he picked it up. Even so, he could still read Jean Marie's fine script; noting the date of his birth, his given name, the name of his mother—Kathleen Muldoon—and her age. But there was nothing mentioned about his father.

"Sixteen," he murmured. "She was so young," and a touch of sadness swept over him for her lost youth. "Why did she have to die?"

After he'd carefully laid aside his birth record he saw that there were copies of letters that Jean Marie had written to his mother. The ink had faded somewhat and only a few words were still legible, but it was apparent that she'd harbored a deep obligation to keep his mother informed on his progress. The letters appeared to have been written in great detail and he knew that she'd sat at her desk long into the morning hours laboring over them.

A few faded postcards from his mother had also been filed away but the dates were blurred and it was apparent that in time they'd gradually ceased. It had been only Mother Superior who'd kept on with the one-sided correspondence. "I wonder why," he mused. "Perhaps that was when my mother was taken ill," and he sighed, satisfied with his reasoning.

At that moment the Mother Superior returned. "Is everything in order?" she asked, obviously curious.

"So far. Mother Jean Marie was a wonderful woman," and he smiled. "She was way ahead of her time," and he laughed lightly.

"I don't want to rush you, Senator, but will you be staying much longer?" Sister Noel asked, a certain sharpness to her voice.

"No. I'll hurry," It was apparent that she wanted to have the use of her office.

As he continued to sort through the papers he found that Jean Marie had kept his first efforts at writing and then he uncovered the letters that he'd written to her long after he'd gone to live on the farm with Martha and Jacob. These she'd tied with a frayed yellow ribbon, almost as though they'd been love letters.

"She treated me as though I were her son," he mused.

The last item was an envelope made from a heavy linen material that had been sealed shut.

"I wonder why," he thought. "Perhaps it has to do with my adoption," and with great care he slit open the envelope with the help of Sister Noel's letter opener.

With care he removed the smaller envelope that was enclosed and he saw Mother Superior Jean Marie name was written in bold letters across it. This one wasn't sealed and slowly he removed the card that was enclosed.

Then he began to read:

IT IS WITH PLEASURE I ANNOUNCE
THE MARRIAGE OF
KATHLEEN MULDOON
TO MY SON
SCHUYLER CARTER MARTIN
SEPTEMBER 1, 1937
ST. JOSEPHS CATHOLIC CHURCH
KANSAS CITY, MISSOURI

EMILY CARTER MARTIN

For a moment Jericho was so shocked that he couldn't move and he finally shook his head as though to remove a bad dream. Then rage surged through him, his face turned scarlet, and his heart began to beat like a trip hammer.

"Why?" he screamed to the empty room. "WHY?" In anger and frustration he threw the contents of the folder to the floor.

The young Sister who had greeted the Senator upon his arrival had heard the mournful sound and rushed to tell the Mother Superior.

As the two women entered the room she took in the scene, then whispered for the younger sister to leave.

"Whatever's wrong?" she asked him with concern.

When Jericho turned to look at her she saw the devastation written in every line of his face. She quickly poured a tumbler of water and went to him. Almost rudely, he pushed the glass away, spilling the water on the floor. Then he fell into a chair, buried his face in his hands and began to sob as though his heart were breaking.

"My son," Sister Noel said kindly. "Can I help?"

Through muffled sobs he mumbled, "No, no, there's no one that can help."

Sister Noel withdrew and took a chair in the farthest corner of the room. With compassion, she watched the complete despair of a broken man.

When Jericho quieted he got up and slowly began to retrieve the papers and return them to the folder.

"May I help?" the woman volunteered.

Jericho tried to smile. "No. I have to go;" and he held the folder to his chest.

"I'm not sure that you should take the papers with you," the Mother Superior protested, although rather half-heartedly.

"I must have them. They're no good to anyone else."

Realizing that she was dealing with a man who'd obviously experienced a view of hell, she nodded. "May I show you out?"

He shook his head, opened the door and then almost at a run went down the hall and out the convent door. Quickly she moved to the window and watched as he threw himself into the car. Like a mad man, he went roaring down the dirt road, a cloud of dust billowing behind him.

32

Monsignor Pignelli was enjoying a glass of fine wine, a product of the vineyards of France and a gift from one of his parishoners, before his evening meal in the small garden that adjoined his office. It was the most peaceful and quiet part of the day and he was in deep contemplation when the wrought iron gates burst open and Jericho rushed in. For a moment he was shocked at the appearance of his friend as his expression was that of a wild man.

Automatically, he rose to his feet, As he did so, Jericho crashed into his arms with sobs tearing from his throat.

The rectory housekeeper, who had just made a trip from the kitchen to call the Monsignor to supper, appeared and a frown of disgust crossed her face. The priest indicated with a nod that he shouldn't be disturbed, and with obvious reluctance she returned to the kitchen muttering that supper once again would be late. She had immediately recognized the Senator and briefly wondered if something could have happened to his family. Then she shrugged her shoulders in dismissal and proceeded to prepare her own supper.

With gentleness, Michael Pignelli extricated himself from Jericho's arms and guided him into his office.

"Jerry, my friend," he said, "whatever's happened?"

Jericho shook his head.

The priest noticed the manila file that Jericho held and asked softly, "May I see the folder?"

Once again his friend shook his head.

"Then how about sharing a glass of wine?"

Jericho nodded and the priest poured a glass of wine, handed it to him, and retrieved his own glass from the table in the garden. When he returned he found Jericho in what appeared to be a more rational state.

"I was just going to have supper. Would you care to join me?"

"No, thanks. I'm not hungry. You go ahead."

"I won't do that, Jerry. It can wait. Excuse me while I tell the housekeeper," and he hurried from the room.

While the priest was away Jericho gulped down the wine and then poured another glass. The warmth of the wine relaxed him and his reasoning now began to return.

When Monsignor Pignelli returned he slipped into an easy chair and took a sip of his wine as he searched his friend's face. "Jerry," he said kindly, "we've been friends since you were a boy, and I hoped that if you ever had a problem you'd feel free to confide in me. You know that it would go no farther than these four walls."

Jericho nodded. "I know."

"This quest that you mentioned. What was it? Perhaps you found your answer and it wasn't quite what you expected."

"You're right, Michael. It wasn't what I had hoped to find." Then he lightly tapped the folder which he had now placed on the divan beside him. "In here is the answer."

"But you still haven't answered my question," the priest persisted.

Jericho took a deep breath. "I'd better start at the beginning."

"Please do."

"Sometime back, Schuyler Martin approached me with the prospect of becoming a candidate for the presidency in the upcoming election."

"How wonderful," the priest replied, his eyes brightening. "Did you accept?"

"No."

"And pray, why not?"

"You've been aware of the fact that I was adopted when I was five, but you've never known about my beginning."

"That's true. But what has all that got to do with politics?"

Jericho smiled wryly. "A helluva lot."

The priest frowned. "Your reputation is impeccable; whatever would cause you to worry about the past?"

"Ever heard of Woodward and Bernstein?"

"Of course. They're the young reporters who uncovered Watergate."

"Need I say more?"

"Then you've been afraid of what someone might discover about your past?"

"Correct. I had to find out for myself before I could possibly give consideration to Schuyler's proposal."

The priest got up, went to the wine cooler and brought back the bottle of wine to refill their glasses.

"So that was your quest," he murmured thoughtfully. "And just what did you find out about those first years?"

"As I said, it's all there in the folder."

"May I take a look?"

"Go ahead. You might as well know the truth, too," and he handed the folder to the priest.

With care, Monsignor Pignelli opened the manila container and, as Jericho had done only a few hours before, he meticulously read the papers acknowledging that Kathleen Muldoon was his mother. When he came to the elaborate ivory envelope he opened it carefully, pulled the card out and then started to read. When he finished the silence that filled the study was almost tangible.

Slowly he got up from his chair and moved to the window where he stared unseeingly into the night, not really knowing what to say or how to say it. Then he turned to find his friend smiling sadly.

"Oh, Jerry," he said, every word filled with anguish. "Why didn't Mother Jean Marie tell you?"

"She never had any reason to believe that someday I might meet and fall in love with a woman who would just happen to be my half-sister. I can forgive her for that."

The priest frowned. "But what about Kate? It's obvious that she has no knowledge that you're her son."

"I'm sure she doesn't. Can you imagine any woman letting her only daughter marry her half-brother?"

Monsignor Pignelli shook his head. "There's no mention of your father."

"That's true. I suppose that Kate, for whatever reason, simply didn't want to tell her."

"What a shame. Perhaps he would have come forward and claimed you for himself."

"Who knows? At this point, it's all just speculation."

"What do you plan to do?" the priest asked quietly.

When the senator looked up he displayed his normal somewhat lopsided smile, but the pain was evident in his eyes.

"I wish I knew," he said softly. "On the way back from Staley, I was asking God Almighty the same thing, but I can't say that I received any good answers." He paused as though expecting a response, but the priest remained silent.

Finally, Jericho continued. "At one point, it occurred to me that I could destroy those," waving his hand toward the folder, "and no one would be the wiser . . . except me." Then he slowly shook his head. "But I wasn't sure that I had it in me to carry that knowledge alone."

Father Pignelli frowned slightly before he replied. "Could it be that your coming here *was* His answer? Stranger things have happened, you know. You're really not alone in this. Kate Martin couldn't have known either. If she had, she would never have allowed your marriage to her daughter."

Jericho slowly nodded his assent.

"You realize, of course," the Monsignor continued, "that Mrs. Martin—at least—will have to be told, since that's really where this all started."

The younger man rose to pace the room in apparent agitation.

"I thought of that, too, but even though she's never really cared that much for me, I'm not sure I could hurt her that much." Then defiantly, "Burning those damned papers would be a lot easier for everyone."

Playing for time to organize his own thoughts, the priest interjected quietly, "And just what, Jerry, are you going to tell Elizabeth?"

"To be honest, I don't really know," and he looked up at the priest. "I'm sure it will come as no surprise to you that we've shared a wonderful intimacy over the years, and indeed still do." He sighed deeply. "Michael, I really don't know what to do. Hearing from me that I'm her half brother and that Kate is also *my* mother could destroy her completely."

"Are you really so sure of that?" Pignelli interrupted.

"Damn it, no!" Jericho barked, "but I care enough that I don't want to risk it. Besides," and his voice saddened, "there's the church. In Rome's eyes we've been living an incestuous life."

Almost automatically the priest nodded slowly, his mind racing to absorb and evaluate all that he'd learned in the short time since Jericho's return. In the lengthening silence, Monsignor Pignelli absently gathered the papers together into a neat pile in the center of his desk. He was yanked back to reality by the sound of his friend's voice.

"Shall we light a fire, Michael?"

"A fire?" The priest frowned as the enormity of the question struck home. Then, as he looked at his companion, he placed his hand firmly on the pitiful stack of papers and when he replied his tone carried an edge of harshness for the first time. "Not yet, at least, my friend. You're moving much too quickly to expect my immediate endorsement."

Jericho's protest of "But, Michael," was cut off by a peremptory wave of the priest's free hand.

"Jericho, you know that my being a priest was not entirely voluntary at the outset," he continued in a more kindly tone, "but I did take certain vows and accept definite responsibilities," he now smiled slightly, "and I cannot set them aside lightly."

"Then you *won't* help me?"

'I did not say that at all," came the quiet response. "I merely have to consider the alternatives and be aware of the consequences."

There was a long pause, and then Jericho wearily asked, "Michael, when will you *know*? I'm sure you realize that I haven't much time."

"In eternity, one day is nothing," came the measured reply. "Come back tomorrow; by then I should be able to decide what I can reasonably do."

Jericho nodded in numb agreement as the priest escorted him out of his study and back to his car. The Senator was half way back to the Smith farm before he remembered that he'd left his precious papers behind, but by then he was too emotionally exhausted to care.

While Jericho spent a restless night at the farm, in the rectory Monsignor Pignelli wrestled manfully with himself, his conscience, his church and his God while his now stale dinner was totally forgotten.

After Jericho's car had disappeared from view, like a man in a daze, the priest had moved slowly through the garden and into the study where he slumped into the chair that he had so recently vacated. For several minutes he sat with head bowed and in total silence while his mind raced in an attempt to assess the possible consequences of what Jericho had related. Finally, with a sigh, he raised his head and as he did so a lone unnoticed tear trickled down his cheek.

"Oh, my God," he cried out to the empty room. "Why?" Then he breathed deeply to regain some semblance of control.

The truth of the matter was that Michael Pignelli looked upon the younger man as a friend, possibly even as a younger brother, rather than as parishoner. Over the years he had watched the progress of Jericho's career with pride and satisfaction, and now this! He vaguely felt that it might have helped to have someone to blame, but even that small comfort was missing. Jericho and Elizabeth were unknowing victims of fate, and poor Kate! He shook his head sadly. To him it was obvious that she'd had absolutely no inkling of the truth or she would never have permitted the marriage in the first place.

Finally, weary and sick at heart, he crossed the hall to the small chapel that had been the legacy of Father O'Connell. There he knelt and, in the simpler way of his youth, prayed first for his own guidance and then for God's compassion for Jericho, Elizabeth and Kate.

Later, when he returned to the study, he felt curiously refreshed and found himself now able to view his friend's predicament with a certain degree of objectivity. When his eyes fell on the open folder lying on the desk he shook his head.

"Poor misguided woman," he muttered in obvious reference to

the Mother Superior. "If she hadn't let him see those papers, none of this would have happened." A frown of annoyance shadowed his face briefly, then "And to make matters even worse, she let him keep them."

There was little doubt in his mind that Jericho was probably entitled to a copy of his own birth certificate, but he was also quite sure that the Mother Superior's release of the entire file would be viewed as a serious breach of trust if it should ever reach the ears of the hierarchy. Since he himself had now managed to become involved, he knew intuitively that such an eventuality had to be, and would be, avoided. Father Pignelli was by no means a fool, although he was still in somewhat of a quandary.

There was still the matter of Jericho's marriage to his half-sister. To fulfill his obligations as a priest he was certain that he should counsel his younger friend to confess his sin, however unwitting it had been, and seek the foregiveness of the church and of his wife. In the back of his mind, however, the thought rose almost unbidden. *The quieter the handling, the better the result for everyone concerned.*

Like most men, Michalel Pignelli harbored at least some degree of personal ambition. Now, with the knowledge that his friend was being seriously considered as a possible Presidential nominee, he began to consider the personal implications. As the possibilities began to tick off in his mind, he shook his head irritably. "Michael," he muttered, "you shouldn't be thinking like this. Damn it, think of your vows," but the lure was almost irresistible. There was the definite possibility of getting out of Wichita and to the Nation's capitol since he was reasonably certain that a grateful Jericho could exert at least some influence on his behalf. And now, of course, there was the added possibility of becoming a confidant and advisor to the President, not to mention that of becoming his personal priest and confessor.

It was past midnight when the weary priest filled a snifter with fine old brandy and contemplated his vision of the future. There were still many things to consider, but the basic decisions were made.

As he finished the brandy, his eyes fell on the papers still lying in the center of the desk. Very slowly, he rose to gather them up and lock them away before going to bed. As he reached the study door he paused and looked back for a brief moment, then crossed himself and turned out the light.

When Jericho opened his eyes the following morning he was puzzled as to where he was, but as he looked around the room he soon recognized the familiar setting and realized that he was home. From below he could hear the voices of his parents as he got out of bed, noting by the clock that it was now well past ten.

Jericho slipped into his robe and went down the hall to the bathroom. When he looked into the mirror over the porcelain sink, the face that stared back at him reflected a new hardness. Inside he felt numb, and almost automatically he stepped into the shower. After he had toweled dry, he shaved and then returned to his bedroom where he put on fresh clothing. He decided that he would tell his parents nothing about the trip to the convent.

When Jericho entered the kitchen, Martha and Jacob greeted him with smiles of pleasure. To the elderly couple having their son at home seemed almost like old times, and it was apparent that his visit had made them happy.

Martha got up and hustled to the stove to prepare his breakfast. "How about pancakes?" she asked.

Although he really wasn't hungry, Jericho knew that he couldn't refuse, so with a smile he replied, "Only a short stack, mother. I don't eat as much as I used to."

Meanwhile, Jacob had squeezed a glass of fresh orange juice, brought it to the table and had pulled out a chair.

"How did things go yesterday?" he asked, his eyes filled with curiosity.

Jericho toyed with his glass. "It was a trip into nostalgia," he said and shrugged.

"What do you mean by that?"

"Oh, you know. The old days, all the memories," and he took a sip from the juice.

"Were you able to find out anything about your mother?" Martha interjected as she skillfully flipped the pancakes.

"There was nothing. It was merely a wild goose chase."

Martha and Jacob exchanged glances and it was obvious that they were both relieved.

"Well, son," Martha said as she placed the plate of hot cakes before him, "it's probably just as well. Now it's off your mind once and for all."

He nodded. "You're right. I'll never go back," and he laughed wryly. "I believe that it was Thomas Wolfe who said, 'You can never go home again,' and he was right. Nothing's every really the same."

After he had finished breakfast, Jericho drank a second cup of Martha's fresh home ground coffee and then pushed himself away from the table.

"I'll have to go back to Washington today."

Their faces fell. "You can't stay for Mass tomorrow?"

Jericho shook his head. "I'm sorry, but we're still in session. I really shouldn't even have been away these past few days."

Martha sighed as she had hoped the three of them could attend Mass at St. Peters together, like old times.

"If you have to go we'll understand," Jacob said, more resigned than Martha to the fact that his son was a busy man.

"Will you see the Morans?" Martha asked.

"I can't take the time this trip and I would appreciate it if you wouldn't menton my visit. I don't want to hurt their feelings."

"Of course," Jacob readily agreed.

When Jericho had packed his belongings, he came back downstairs where Martha and Jacob followed him to the car. There he kissed Martha and shook Jacob's hand.

"Don't stay away so long," Martha said softly.

"I'll try not to," and he looked out over the fertile fields that surrounded the farmhouse. "There are some days when I wish that I had stayed here and worked the farm. Oh well, that's the way it goes," he said, and got into the car.

As he drove down the dirt lane that led to the highway he turned and looked back, waved, and then headed for his meeting with Monsignor Pignelli at St. Peters.

It was almost one when Jericho arrived at the rectory. He had awakened that morning to a gray day and light rain, an atmosphere that seemed to fit perfectly with the sense of foreboding which permeated his thoughts. What if his old friend couldn't, or wouldn't, help him in the course that he had planned? Tormented, he sighed audibly. From his own perspective, all the conceivable alternatives to the actions he had proposed could lead only to disaster, and he had conceded to the priest's right to at least try for a solution that would be more acceptable.

When the Monsignor admitted him to the study there was a noticeable air of restraint between the two men. The papers were nowhere to be seen, but a small fire burned cheerfully in the fireplace and Jericho noted that a decanter of wine flanked by two filled glasses rested on the coffee table.

Noticing the direction of his glance, Monsignor Pignelli said softly, "I thought we would have a glass of wine, for old times sake," as he retrieved the glasses and offered one to Jericho. "To the future," he proposed with a smile.

After Jericho had raised his glass and drank to the toast, he looked straight at the priest. "Well, Michael, have you reached a decision or discovered some alternative?"

The priest shifted uncomfortably and frowned. Finally he replied. "Obviously, there are several different ways that this could be handled. Of course, each choice carries its own risks but there are alternatives available."

"Name one," the senator said angrily.

"Under the circumstances, I'm certain that your marriage could be annulled. After all, there was never any intentional sin."

"But then Elizabeth would have to be told," Jericho said tersely.

Monsignor Pignelli nodded. "Yes, and the church, and probably the family." He paused, then continued. "Quite frankly, with your political prominence and that of the Martins, there is little chance that it could be handled quietly, though I'm sure the church would bend every effort to discretion."

"You're saying there would be high risk of extensive and negative publicity?"

Soberly the priest nodded.

"That's totally unacceptable!" Jericho exploded; then more quietly, "that leaves my original plan."

"That, too," Pignelli replied in a steely voice, "is totally unacceptable."

When Jericho pivoted to face Michael Pignelli, his face had paled. "My God, Michael," he said almost savagely, "what are you saying? I thought you were a friend I could trust!"

"I *am* your friend," came the quiet reply, "and you *can* trust me. I will not, however, become your accomplice, nor will I sanction your destruction of those records just because they happen to displease you.''

"But they're mine now," Jericho started to protest.

"Not really," Pignelli countered. "They belong to the Church. You have merely removed them from the convent and brought them here so that we can more conveniently discuss the matter.''

There was a long pause as Jericho considered the priest's response. Finally, "What are you trying to tell me?" he questioned.

"Aside from the fact that I can't possibly condone it, it would be foolish for you to destroy those papers.''

"Convince me of that.''

"What about Kate Martin?" his friend seemingly digressed. "Are you going to discuss what you've found with her?''

"I feel that I should, but I'm still not sure.''

"You realize, of course, that she won't want to believe you, that you'll undoubtedly need every possible bit of proof.''

Jericho nodded slowly, "I'm sure you're right.''

"Jerry, don't you see it?" the priest questioned softly. "Even if I agree, all that you would destroy are the momentos of a dead woman. The very things that you should *keep*.''

As the silence lengthened he glanced at his watch, then rose and moved to the study door.

"I'll tell the housekeeper you'll be staying for dinner," he announced. "We can discuss this further after you have had time to consider it more carefully." Then the door closed softly behind him.

As the two men sat quietly sipping wine following dinner that evening Monsignor Pignelli finally broke the silence. "Well, my friend, what have you decided to do?''

Jericho shrugged, then sadly replied, "When the time is right, I suppose I'll have to go to Kate and tell her.''

"I don't envy you that," he said softly. Then he rose and moved to the desk where he retrieved the folder. "You'll be needing these.''

Jericho accepted the papers wordlessly and finally looked up. "You trust me that much?" he questioned.

"As their custodian, yes. I know they'll be used with

compassion." Then he continued, "And what about Elizabeth?"

The younger man shook his head. "One decision at a time, Father. That one will have to wait," and he sighed. "I'm not quite reconciled to giving up my wife."

The priest frowned slightly but said nothing. Then his face cleared and he smiled almost impishly. "Tell me, now. What have you decided about running for the presidency?"

Jericho paused, carefully considering his response. When his reply came it was in measured tones. "Not this time, Michael," failing to note the brief look of shock registered in the priest's eyes. "I've about decided not to run as long as Kate is alive."

When he finally noticed the expression on his friend's face, he chuckled. "Surprised? Michael, you've told me to be my own person; this is at least a good beginning."

Father Pignelli slowly nodded his agreement although his reluctance was evident. "I'm sure you're right, Jerry. There's certainly nothing wrong with a few added years of senatorial experience," turning away in an effort to hide his disappointment.

Then the Monsignor refilled their wine glasses.

"Shall we drink to bygone days?" he asked, his look now filled with understanding.

"To the past," Jericho echoed solemnly as they touched the crystal glasses and then drank.

33

When Jericho arrived at Washington National Airport, he found Elizabeth waiting, and in greeting he brushed her cheek with a kiss.

"Hey," she objected. "This is your wife," and then proceeded to bestow a moist kiss on his lips.

"Sorry. I've a million things on my mind."

"How are your parents?" Elizabeth asked as they moved through the terminal.

"Could be better," and he sighed. "However, both mother and dad seemed to perk up a bit while I was there."

"That's good," she replied as they went out the door. There he saw the Martin limousine waiting with James beside it.

"Why your father's limo?" he asked.

"He asked that I deliver you directly to the house."

"Really, Elizabeth, I don't want to go."

"And why not? Daddy's anxious to talk with you."

"I know, but I want to get organized before I see him," and he went to James. "We'll take a cab home. Sorry you made the trip."

At that point Elizabeth exploded. "Well, I'm going whether you go or not," she said heatedly, and got into the waiting limousine.

"Suit yourself," Jericho said and almost nonchalantly hailed a passing cab.

When he arrived home he took his bag upstairs, unpacked and then placed it in the storage closet in the hall, the papers safely inside.

Returning to the lower floor he entered his office where he found a stack of messages waiting. Slowly and carefully he read each one, and then the telephone started to ring. For a moment he let it ring, then on the sixth ring he answered. As he'd anticipated it was Schuyler Martin.

"Jerry! What the hell's wrong?" Schuyler demanded. "Elizabeth's crying her eyes out."

"Nothing, Schuyler. Absolutely nothing. I merely wanted to come home to my own house. Is that a good reason for hysterics?"

After his question the silence that followed was lengthy, then Schuyler said solemnly, "Elizabeth gets carried away. I'm sorry, Jerry, but we do need to talk."

"We will, Schuyler. I have some important matters to clear up before Monday so perhaps tomorrow would be a better time for a chat."

"Whatever you say." Then almost tonelessly, "I'll have James bring Elizabeth home."

Following the conversation with his father-in-law, Jericho realized that Elizabeth would return home much like a child who'd disobeyed her elders and he knew that it was necessary that he start to treat her in a different manner. As he'd told his friend, their sex life was wonderful. Now he was faced with the problem of making changes.

Monsignor Pignelli had also advised him, much to his surprise, that he keep his parentage a secret for now. He'd agreed. But he also realized that it was easy for the priest to say, since he didn't possess a beautiful and sensuous wife.

"God, whatever will I do?" he said, feeling almost as though the weight of the world were on his shoulders. Then he heard a car door slam.

When Elizabeth entered the room her manner was subdued and he knew that her father had properly chastised her. In some ways he felt a touch of compassion for her, as she'd never quite matured and still felt that no matter what, she should have her own way.

Silently she crept across the room. "Are you speaking to me?" she asked in her best little girl voice.

Jericho smiled. "Of course. What a silly question."

"I'm sorry for pushing you, Jerry."

"You're forgiven." Then almost off handedly, he added. "Would you mind if I continued with my work? I have lots to catch up with."

Even though he'd rebuked her, she smiled sweetly and hurried from the room, closing the door behind her softly.

After Elizabeth had gone, he got up from his desk and moved aimlessly around the room, realizing that only with the help of God would he manage to get through the catastrophe facing him. First, he'd have to deal with both Schuyler and Elizabeth and tell them that he'd reached the conclusion, after careful deliberation, not to accept the invitation to run as a presidential candidate. He knew that this decision would cause a horrendous uproar on both their parts; hysterics by Elizabeth and ranting and raving by Schuyler Martin. Yet, it was a necessity.

Around eight o'clock that evening, Elizabeth had brought in a light supper on a tray and then had left him to himself. He'd been grateful for the mountains of work that had faced him, and he hoped that when he retired that she'd have fallen asleep.

It was well after two o'clock when he straightened up his desk, turned out the light, and went upstairs. The bedroom lights had been extinguished and one dim light came from the adjoining bath. Elizabeth was sound asleep, and a book that she'd evidently been reading lay beside the bed on the floor.

Jericho undressed in the dark, slipped into his pajamas and crawled into bed. More than anything he needed to hold his wife in his arms and make love to her, and his loins ached from desire. Still he knew that until he'd talked with Kate Martin, a decision about their future had to be held in abeyance.

The next morning, before Elizabeth awakened, Jericho slipped out of bed, gathered fresh clothing and went down the hall to the guest bathroom where he showered and shaved. Once dressed he continued on downstairs and into the pleasant kitchen. Elizabeth had prepared the coffee the night before, as was her usual custom, and he simply had to plug in the pot.

As he waited for the coffee to finish perking he went to the front door and picked up the Sunday *Washington Post*. When he glanced at the front page, an article caught his eye that concerned a secret presidential candidate, and the man that had given the interview was none other than Schuyler Martin. In disgust he threw the paper aside and went charging back into the kitchen where he poured a mug of coffee and headed for his office.

He picked up the phone and dialed Magnolia Hill. Jessie, James' wife, and the Martin's housekeeper, answered, "Martin residence."

"Jessie, this is Jerry Smith. Is Schuyler up?"

"Yes, Senator. I'll tell him you're calling," and she hurried to the breakfast room. When she entered Schuyler looked up.

"Mr. Martin, Senator Smith is calling."

"Thanks, Jessie," he said and picked up the extension phone beside him.

"Good morning, Jerry."

"Don't you good morning me," was his terse reply. "Have you seen the *Post*?"

"Not yet. Why?"

"That damned interview you gave about a *secret* candidate. For Christ's sake, Schuyler, when are you going to learn to stay out of my business! I've never given you an answer, yet you had to blow it."

"Now, Jerry, calm down," the older man replied almost placatingly.

"Calm down, hell! You might as well know my answer. I'm not going to be your candidate!"

Silence echoed across the distance, and finally Schuyler said, "You can't be serious."

"The hell I'm not," Jericho replied and slammed down the telephone.

When he looked up he saw Elizabeth in the doorway, a look of dismay on her face. Then she burst into tears.

Without speaking he brushed past her and went out the front door, jumped into his car and roared away.

Making an effort to control her tears, Elizabeth rushed to the telephone and called her father. When he answered she started to cry.

Exasperated, and now almost at the end of his rope, Schuyler screamed into the phone, "Shut up, Elizabeth!" His tone of voice and manner chilled her, and within moments she'd regained some degree of control.

"Don't you tell me to shut up!" she snarled, as she dabbed at her eyes. "You're the one that screwed things up. You always think that you're so damned smart. Whenever are you going to listen to *me*? After all, I know my husband far better than you do!"

This was the first time that father and daugher had shown any signs of anger towards each other, and it was Schuyler Martin who apologized. "I'm sorry, baby. I hadn't any idea that the *Post* would print the interview in today's paper. In fact, I'd asked them to hold it up until Jerry had given us the go ahead, then they were to have the first chance. Damned reporters!" he said. Then quietly, "Is Jerry there?"

"No. He left the house and drove off in the car."

"Perhaps he's on his way over here."

"Don't count on it, father dear. You're the last person he wants to see!"

Deciding that he should try another tack, Schuyler asked. "How's he been since he came back from Kansas?"

Elizabeth released an audible sigh. "Aloof. He's barely spoken to me and I don't understand why. For a time I thought that he was concerned about his parents, but he said that they were all right." Then her voice took on a venomous quality. "It could well be that damned Pignelli!"

"Now Elizabeth, you know that they're merely friends."

"Then why would he treat me so coldly? He merely kissed me on the cheek when I met him at the airport."

"Is that so unusual?"

"Yes, father, it is."

"I'm sorry. I presume that he's got a lot on his mind."

"That's obvious. Now what's the plan, Mr. Mastermind?" she asked with sarcasm.

"Acting smart with me doesn't help the situation if you want to be in the White House someday."

She laughed. "That's a helluva long ways off, father dear, and you're the one who'd better realize that you just lost the best man the Democratic Party had."

In anger, Schuyler Martin slammed down the telephone,

realizing this his daughter had spoken the truth.

For a moment Elizabeth stared at the buzzing instrument in her hand, and then screamed into it, "Go to hell, you son-of-a-bitch!"

34

As the weeks went by, the rift between Jericho and Elizabeth grew and at times they barely communicated. After a period of time Jericho had seen fit to move his belongings into the guest quarters and Elizabeth had voiced no objection. She felt not only wronged by her father but her husband as well, and had withdrawn into a protective shell performing her duties as the wife of a Senator in an almost derisive manner.

Schuyler Martin repeatedly left messages with Jericho's staff and in desperation, Jericho had directed his personal aide to refrain from telling him when his father-in-law called. In reality, he was making a concerted effort to divorce himself from any involvement with Schuyler. Still he knew that the time was yet to come when he would find it necessary to meet with Kate Martin; and that opportunity appeared much sooner than he'd anticipated.

Emily Martin, Schuyler's mother, was suddenly stricken by a mild stroke while still in residence in Kansas City and being a dutiful son, Schuyler had rushed to her side. Shortly thereafter, Elizabeth announced one morning that she was going to New York where she could buy some 'decent' clothes. Jericho made no objection since this would leave him a wide open field for with both Schuyler and Elizabeth out of the way, he could see Kate Martin.

When Jessie informed her mistress that Senator Smith was calling, a frown had crossed Kate's face.

"Good morning, Jerry." she said.

"Good morning, Kate," he replied his tone pleasant.

"Is there something you need?" she asked.

"Yes. I'd like to see you."

Once again Kate frowned. Finally she replied. "Of course."

"When would be a convenient time?" Jericho asked politely.

"How is your schedule?" Kate countered.

"I'm free tomorrow afternoon from three on."

"That would be fine, Jerry. We'll share a cup of tea," and she laughed softly.

Jericho smiled, then replied. "Thanks, Kate. I'll look forward to seeing you," and before she could form a reply he had hung up.

Following a sleepless night, Jericho placed an early call to his chief aide and rather bluntly informed him that he'd not be in.

"But Senator, you have several appointments scheduled," the younger man protested, although with a definite show of restraint.

"Tell them that I'm not feeling well," was his terse reply and he had hung up knowing that his action wasn't the norm and could create a flap.

"Who the hell cares?" he said aloud. "I'm getting damned tired of having to answer to everybody else." His whole attitude had changed since his return from Kansas, and it had become obvious to his staff and colleagues that at times he seemed almost indifferent.

After he was finished with his preparations for the day Jericho went to the hall closet, retrieved his bag and removed the papers he had secreted away. However, before he returned the luggage to the closet, he sat down on the bed and carefully examined the documents. Then he placed the envelope in his jacket pocket and hurried downstairs to his office. Once at his desk, he picked up the phone and dialed St. Peters.

When the rectory housekeeper had first interrupted Monsignor Pignelli's breakfast, he had seemed annoyed, but when she informed him that the call was from Senator Smith, his whole manner changed.

"I'll take it in my office," he said and after a final sip of coffee he hurried from the room.

When he picked up the phone he waited until he heard the click of the extension, then said brightly, "Good morning, Jerry."

"Today's the day, Michael," was the solemn response.

For a moment the priest frowned, then the realization of what his friend had said swept over him.

"I gather that you will be seeing Kate Martin," he replied.

"Yes. This afternoon. Both Schuyler and Elizabeth are out of the city and it gave me the opportunity."

"Did she present any objections to seeing you?" Pignelli asked.

"Not really. She seemed puzzled," and he paused. "But she's also aware that Schuyler and I are on the outs and is undoubtedly concerned about what's happened between Elizabeth and me."

"How's that situation? I mean, you and Elizabeth."

Jericho sighed. "Fortunately, on my return she pulled one of her domineering acts and it gave me an excuse. I'm sleeping in the guest room."

"But what about Schuyler?"

"As usual he took the bull by the horns and gave the *Post* an interview concerning a secret candidate," and he laughed wryly. "In a way he helped me, although he doesn't know it. I gave him holy hell for jumping the gun and told him that he'd just lost his candidate. So far I've been able to avoid him."

Michael Pignelli smiled. "God does work in mysterious ways, Jerry."

"That's true, but to be honest I'm not looking forward to this afternoon, although I know that it has to be done."

"I can't say that I blame you," the priest replied. "Let me know how it goes."

"That I'll do, and thanks Michael."

It was raining heavily when Jericho started the drive to Magnolia Hill and his meeting with Kate Martin. The skies over Washington were overcast and the wind thrashed unmercifully at the grey Potomac. The traffic on the beltway was not exceedingly heavy and he arrived at his destination much sooner than he expected. After he parked the car, he pulled his raincoat around him and made a dash for the house.

Jessie had watched the car turn into the drive and before Jericho had a chance to ring the bell, she opened the door, a broad smile greeting him. "Good afternoon, Senator. Mighty sorry day," she said and helped him off with his wet coat. "I'll hang this to dry."

"Thanks, Jessie. Is Mrs. Martin available?"

"She'll be down shortly. You're early."

"I know," Jericho replied.

"James has a fire going in the parlor and I'll be serving tea there," she said, and then walked ahead of him down the hall and into the small, cozy sitting room.

Before the old black woman left, she paused. "How's Miss Elizabeth?"

Jericho smiled as Jessie had served as Elizabeth's nanny for many years.

"She's in New York . . . buying out the stores," he replied.

Jessie's face brightened. "I'm so glad. She hasn't been herself lately."

Jericho looked away. He knew that Jessie was no fool and had noticed Elizabeth's unexplained withdrawal from her usual sunny disposition.

As he waited for Kate Martin to appear he stared into the flickering flames and just for a moment wondered if he was really doing the right thing. Before he had the chance to reconsider his decision, he heard footsteps and then Kate's melodic voice. "Good afternoon, Jerry," she said pleasantly as she glided into the room.

He saw that she was impeccably groomed, as usual, but her dark violet eyes held a trace of concern; however, her smile was warm and she touched his hand in welcome.

"Shall we sit?" Kate said as she moved gracefully to a large wing backed chair.

"Thanks," Jericho replied and took the chair facing her.

"The weather has certainly changed," Kate remarked.

Jericho nodded in agreement.

"Have you heard from Elizabeth?" she pursued.

"No. But she should be back the end of the week. I imagine that she's enjoying shopping and seeing her old friends."

Before the conversation could continue, Jessie appeared bearing a heavily laden silver tray and placed it carefully on the table before her mistress.

"Shall I pour, ma'am?" she asked politely.

"No, Jessie. I'll do the honors," and she paused. "On your way out, would you please close the door."

The aged black woman looked puzzled at Kate's request since she had never asked this before.

"Of course, ma'am, she said softly and withdrew.

Kate busied herself with the tea service, pouring a cup which she handed to her son-in-law and then served himself. When she had completed the task, she settled back comfortably in her chair and looked at Jericho expectantly.

"Your conversation on the telephone indicated that you needed to speak with me," and she took a deep breath. "I do hope that you and Elizabeth aren't have difficulties. You've been so devoted to each other."

"That's true, Kate," Jericho said, "however, in this case it's something you should know about me."

The look she gave him was one of surprise. "What is there to know? We've known you for many years and you're a member of the family."

"I know, but this goes back to my beginnings."

"I don't understand," and she shook her head.

"You will," and Jericho got up from his chair and stood before the fireplace.

"Do go on," Kate urged, "if you think that telling me will help."

"That's what I intend to do."

Suddenly Kate felt a sense of foreboding. "Are you sure that you want to tell me, Jerry?"

"Yes, Kate."

For a long moment Jericho gazed out the window at the rain which continued to pour down, and then turned to his hostess.

"To begin with, I was adopted by the Smiths many years ago."

"Adopted?" Kate questioned, almost inaudibly.

"Yes, adopted. I was nearly five at the time," and he paused. "You see, Martha and Jacob never had children of their own. They found me through Father O'Connell at St. Peter's."

"They're lovely people, Jerry," Kate replied quietly, but with a growing sense of anxiety.

He smiled. "Yes, they gave me a love that I'd never experienced before. However, there was someone who loved me just as much, or perhaps even more.''

"Your mother?'' she questioned, eyebrows raised.

"No, not my mother.''

"Did you know your biological parents?'' she asked apprehensively.

"Not really.''

"How sad. How truly sad,'' and she sighed as her eyes avoided his.

Jericho hesitated and it was obvious that he was experiencing some difficulty. Once again he took the chair that faced Kate and when he looked at her his eyes were filled with compassion. "Perhaps what I'm about to say will help you to understand the differences between Elizabeth and me . . . and Schuyler, too.''

Kate said nothing, and her look remained impassive.

"As I'm sure you are aware, Schuyler asked me to consider becoming a candidate for the presidency.''

Kate nodded.

Jericho continued. "Since this is a giant step for any man, I felt it only reasonable and proper that I make an attempt to find out about my past . . . before some smart reporter did.''

"Did you really believe that was necessary?'' Kate said, her eyes growing dark with fear.

"Yes, I did. I used the excuse that it was necessary for me to visit Jacob and Martha in order to go back to Kansas, and that's where I hoped I'd find the answer.''

"Did you?''

"Yes, Kate, I did,'' he said solemnly.

Kate's face turned pale under her perfect makeup but still she remained silent.

"I really don't find any enjoyment in telling you what I discovered,'' Jericho said, his eyes glistening with tears.

"Proceed,'' Kate said, her tone lacking inflection.

At this point Jericho removed the envelope from his jacket pocket and for a moment held it before offering it to Kate.

"I believe that you have every right to see what this envelope contains.''

Very slowly Kate removed the papers from the envelope. The first ragged slip that caught her eye was the record of her son's birth, signed by Mother Superior Jean Marie. The other was the formal announcement of her marriage to Schuyler Martin. She shuddered and for a moment thought she might faint, as Jericho sat with head in his hands obviously weeping.

With care, Kate returned the fragile documents to the envelope and then placed it on the table.

When Jericho looked up expecting to see Kate fraught with despair, he was stunned to look into the cold eyes of his mother.

"You don't believe me," he said.

"Of course I do," Kate replied.

"But you aren't the least bit upset. Why?"

"It's a long story," Kate replied tonelessly.

"What do you mean?" Jericho said, his anger growing.

"Oh, Jerry," Kate said, "I've had suspicions for a long time."

"But how could you? You never came back to see me or claim me. I don't believe you." He rose from the chair and paced about the room, then stopped in front of Kate. "Why would you even be suspicious? And, for God's sake, if you were, please tell me why you let me become involved with Elizabeth? You have a lot to answer for!" His tone of voice was menacing.

Kate had the feeling that she was locked in a cage with a wild animal, but she knew that it was of the utmost importance that she be truthful. "If you'll stop pacing, I'll explain," she said.

"You're damned well right you will!" Jericho replied, then threw himself into a chair, his look fixed on the woman who had borne him.

"First," Kate began, "I want you to know that when I left the convent I had every intention of returning for you."

"But the fact remains that you didn't," Jericho interrupted. "Schuyler Martin, his family and his wealth, were far more important to you than the small boy who waited at the convent," and a sob choked him.

"Perhaps you're right."

"I know I am, and because of your selfish and self-centered ways, you've ruined your daughter's life and mine, too!"

Ignoring Jericho's outburst, Kate continued. "Do you want to know when I first suspected that you were my son?"

"Of course. How long have you known and how did you find out?"

"I'm sure that you'll remember we met your family on only one occasion and that was when you and Brandy graduated from Notre Dame.''

"So?"

"Martha and I spent some time together, and it was she who created the first suspicion and opened Pandora's box.''

"But how?"

"We took a long walk around the campus and during that time we talked about you. That was when she told me how you came into their lives." She shrugged. "She left little to the imagination."

"But why didn't you say something . . . to someone?"

"I was afraid, and at the time I had no idea that you and Elizabeth would eventually fall in love. Believe me, Jerry, Schuyler and I had many disagreements about Elizabeth marrying you. But when it came right down to the bottom line, I knew the life of the whole family would fall to pieces if the information ever came to light." She looked away and then into the eyes of her son. "I tried, oh how I tried. But you know Schuyler. When he has his head set, no one can change him."

"I'll never understand," Jericho murmured.

"Perhaps you would if you heard the whole story."

"As long as I'm here, I might as well listen."

Kate began at the beginning, telling of her family's move from Boston to Kansas in search of the 'pot of gold' and the ultimate results of her father's decision. Jericho listened intently, his eyes never once leaving her face.

"I met your father when I was fifteen," and she smiled slightly. "He was much in the same boat as me, we had a lot in common." Then her eyes misted and her voice quavered. "We fell madly in love as young people do, and in time became intimate. The result was that I soon discovered I was carrying his child," and she paused as all the memories came flooding back.

"I was so happy about our baby, but when I told him he turned on me and accused me of being a whore." She looked up into her son's face hoping for sympathy, but his look remained impassive.

"In desperation," she continued, "I denounced him as the father and when the time of your birth became imminent, I went to the convent where I was given shelter. There I was loved and cared for by Mother Jean Marie and the other Sisters," and she smiled in memory, "but most of all you were the most important person there."

At this point Jericho interrupted. "And who was my father?"

Kate Martin looked down at her meticulously manicured hands and then up into the eyes of her son. "Your father was Stonewall Barton."

For a moment Jericho was speechless, and then he began to laugh, but when he finally stopped sobs racked his body. In anger, he slammed his fist against the mantle causing a crystal candlestick to crash to the floor. When footsteps approached he became silent.

It was Jessie who knocked.

"You all right, Mrs. Martin?" she asked, an edge of concern in her voice.

"We're fine, Jessie," Kate managed. "Please leave." The old black woman hesitated, undecided as to what to do, then went back down the hall to the kitchen where her husband waited.

When Jessie entered the room James noticed the expression on her face and rose to greet her.

"Everything all right?" he asked.

Jessie sank into one of the chairs that surrounded the kitchen table.

"Something terrible must have happened," she said and shook her head. "It's between Mrs. Martin and the Senator."

James patted her shoulder. "Jessie, might as well leave it be. We can't butt into their affairs."

"I know."

In the parlor silence reigned. Dusk had crept upon them and almost automatically Kate got up from her chair and turned on the lamps.

Jericho had slumped in one of the chairs and sat with head bowed, hands covering his face. His thoughts drifted back to the days that he'd spent with Stonewall Barton, and he remembered the fragile cord that had seemed to bind them together, even though on several occasions he had professed a total dislike of the man. Now he was beginning to understand the secret that had driven him to kill himself.

As he looked at his mother she outwardly appeared composed, but it was obvious that she was filled with turmoil within.

"Kate, oh, Kate," Jericho moaned. "How could you do this to me?"

"There was little alternative, Jericho," she said, and he glanced at her sharply for she'd never before used his given name.

"Stonewall recognized you on the night of the party, didn't he?" Kate nodded. "Yes. We were both shocked to see each other after so many years."

"I hope you realize that you killed him," he said brutally.

"I had no control over your father's actions."

"What did you tell him about me?"

"Under the circumstances, and being aware of the power that he possessed, I told him that the child had died at birth."

"But why couldn't you have let him find me?"

Kate's laugh was laced with irony. "And risk everything that I have? I'm no fool, Jericho." Then her dark eyes blazed. "You have to remember that Stonewall Barton deserted me when I needed him the most. He didn't care then, so why should I have been honest? Answer me that?"

"You're a selfish self-centered bitch, Kate Martin," Jericho snarled. "Just because Stonewall was young and didn't know any better, you denied him the right to his own son. I can never forgive you for that. Never!" He paused, his loathing obvious. "And then you saw fit to abandon me because of wealth and power. You'll rot in hell."

Kate Martin turned pale under his onslaught.

Composing herself, she asked. "What do you plan to do with this information?"

"What do *I* intend to do?" and he laughed wryly. "You're already worried about your life; have you given any consideration at all to *my* life and that of your daughters?"

A frown crossed Kate's face.

"When I learned that you were my mother and that I was married to my half-sister, I was certain that you had no idea and felt only concern for you. However, I went to St. Peters and saw Monsignor Pignelli."

At the mention of the priest's name Kate's eyes filled with fright. "You told him?"

"Yes. Michael knows the whole story. I had no one else to turn to and we've been friends since I was a boy."

"Did he have any suggestions?"

"Yes, but that's our business . . . not yours. This is between Monsignor Pignelli . . . me . . . and God."

"Thank God," Kate whispered.

"Yes, you'd better thank your God, whomever He might be, for the day will surely come when you'll pay dearly for the lies and hurt you've inflicted on me, my father, your husband and your daughter. Mark my words," and with his words echoing in her ears, Jericho picked up the envelope and headed for the door.

Then he turned back.

"I don't ever want to see you again, *Mother.*"

He ran down the hall where he grabbed his raincoat from the hall tree and rushed out into the stormy night.

The sound of the opening and closing of the door brought Jessie on a run and she found her mistress emerging from the parlor.

"Would you like your dinner served, Mrs. Martin?" she asked.

"No, Jessie. I'm going up to bed. I'm not feeling well. Goodnight."

Then Kate Martin, nee Kathleen Muldoon, moved slowly up the curving staircase, knowing that from that day on her life would be one filled with hell.

35

Through the still steady downpour Jericho pointed his car toward home and upon his arrival he found the house blazing with lights. It was obvious that Elizabeth had returned sooner than planned. After he entered the drive, he cut the motor and sat silently for several minutes before getting out. Then he made a dash for the house.

As he placed his key in the lock, the door was pulled open and Elizabeth stood before him. The look she gave him was one filled with disgust. "And where have you been?" she said accusingly.

"A late meeting," he replied and moved past her. He quickly removed his wet coat and placed it on a hanger to dry, then turned to her.

"Have you had dinner?" she asked and it was almost as though she'd asked him out of courtesy.

Jericho shook his head. "No, and I'm not feeling well. It's probably the flu, so if you don't mind I'm going straight up to bed."

"Do as you please," Elizabeth replied cooly and stalked past him, her head averted so he couldn't see the distress in her eyes.

"Good night, Elizabeth," Jericho said and slowly climbed the stairs to the guest room.

After he'd undressed and showered he literally fell into bed, both emotionally and physically exhausted. When he was settled, he picked up the bedside phone and dialed St. Peters. The telephone rang only once and it was Monsignor Pignelli himself who answered.

"I've been waiting for your call," the priest said.

"I just got home and found Elizabeth had returned," Jericho announced.

"Can she hear you?"

"No," and Jericho paused. "Michael, is there a chance that you could come to Washington?"

Without the slightest hesitation the priest responded, "Of course. I'm in need of a holiday and I'd be delighted to be your guest," and he chuckled slightly. "Would you like to tell me about your visit with Kate?"

"Not over the telephone," Jericho replied.

"Fine. We can talk later. I'll let you know my flight."

"I do appreciate your coming on such short notice."

In Wichita, Monsignor Pignelli smiled complacently and said, "Think nothing of it, my friend." In the recesses of his mind he was planning that while he was the guest of the Senator, he would ask him to assist him in his desire to be assigned to the Virginia diocese.

Jericho had just finished his call when a knock sounded at the door. He slipped down in the bed, then said, "Come in."

When the door swung open Elizabeth entered carefully, balancing a small tray. She went straight to the night table and set it down.

"I thought you might like some chocolate and toast," she said, smiling ever so slightly.

"How thoughtful," Jericho murmured, and pushed himself into a sitting position.

While Elizabeth watched, Jericho consumed the toast and chocolate.

"That hit the spot," Jericho said after he'd finished, "and thank you. I'll undoubtedly sleep much better."

"Would you like anything else?" she asked.

"No, thanks. Just rest."

Without further comment, Elizabeth picked up the tray and

started for the door. There she turned. "When are we going to talk, Jerry?" she asked. "We can't continue on this way."

"I know, Elizabeth," and he sighed. "However, Monsignor Pignelli is arriving in a few days and he'll be staying with us."

A curtain seemed to fall across Elizabeth's face and the look she gave him was filled with loathing.

"How nice," she replied coolly, then opened the door and slammed it behind her, the sound reverberating throughout the room.

When all was silent, Jericho turned off the light and lay in the darkness listening to the stacatto sound of the rain on the roof, his mind retracing the hours that he'd spent with Kate Martin.

"Oh, God," he said to the stillness of the night. "What am I ever to do?"

During Monsignor Pignelli's visit, Elizabeth made herself as scarce as possible and joined the two men only at dinner. The priest had made an honest effort to be pleasant and include her in their conversations but she chose to remain silent and avoided any close contact with him. Fortunately for Elizabeth, Pignelli spent the majority of his days at the Arlington Diocese.

It was late evening and after Elizabeth had retired for the night that Jericho and Pignelli had the opportunity to share a private conversation. That evening at dinner Elizabeth had informed them that her mother was not well and when Jericho had questioned her as to the cause, she had merely shrugged her shoulders.

Over a night cap Jericho told his friend of his meeting with Kate Martin.

"Serves her right," the priest said emphatically when Jericho had finished. "You can't play with people's lives."

"I've had some serious doubts about my actions," Jericho replied.

"But why? Kate caused a situation that affected not only you, but your wife, her daughter and your late father."

"But it's not my nature to be unkind, Michael," he protested. "However, you're undoubtedly right. She left me little alternative."

"Then why be concerned? Your concern should be directed to Elizabeth. She is also an innocent victim, just as you are," and he paused to stare into his brandy. "Just what are you planning to do about your marriage?"

A frown crossed the younger man's face and he got up from his chair to move restlessly around the room, then stopped.

"I love Elizabeth, Michael. We've been married for a long time and I doubt if that will ever change." He paused. "The other night Elizabeth said that we couldn't continue on this way, and she's right. However, I can't possibly tell her of my relationship with Kate. The only solution I have is to become a husband again," and when the priest started to protest, Jericho held up his hand. "Don't say it, Michael. It's burnt into my brain like a brand into a cow."

For a time they both remained silent. Then Monsignor Pignelli got up to refill his glass and came to stand by Jericho whose head was bowed.

"I can't condone that, my friend," and he sighed deeply. "I see little reason to destroy others because of the actions of one person, but in view of the facts you should really think again before considering such a step."

By now Jericho was sobbing openly and the priest placed a conciliatory hand on his shoulder.

"How can I ever thank you for being my friend," Jericho managed.

"You have already," Pignelli said with a smile. "Today I learned that I will be transfered to Arlington."

"Congratulations," Jericho said through his tears. "You'll be near."

Michael Pignelli nodded. "Yes, Jerry, I'll be near," and he smiled almost smugly, hoping that the day would come when he would stand at the pinnacle with his friend.

In the interim, Schuyler Martin had wisely refrained from contacting either Jericho or Elizabeth and upon his return to the capitol from Kansas City, he discovered that his wife was ill. When he had asked Kate what was wrong, she had merely said "nothing."

"But you're so listless, and your eyes lack their usual luster," he said gently.

"It will pass," was the reply he received, which left him totally confused.

In near desperation he had phoned Elizabeth and although she was still distant, when he mentioned Kate taking to her bed, his daughter had voiced concern.

"It's strange, Daddy, but ever since Jerry came back from Kansas he seems to be angry with you, me, mother, everyone except Monsignor Pignelli. Have you heard that the priest is being assigned to Arlington?"

"Heavens, no. When did this come about?"

"He paid us a visit while you were away and it happened while he was here."

"How interesting," Schuyler said. "Are you and Jerry on good terms?"

"Not really, and this mystifies me."

Schuyler laughed."Probably middle-age menopause."

"How can you say that?" Elizabeth said indignantly.

"It happens to be true, just as it is with women."

"Thanks a lot!"

"Oh, Elizabeth, don't take things so seriously. Do you suppose there's a chance that Jerry would talk with me?"

"No! And stay away! He'd told me that he hasn't any desire to see you, so leave us alone!"

"Are you serious?"

"Of course. Take care of mother and grandmother. That should give you enough to do. Just stay out of our lives!"

Before he could reply the phone went dead.

"Well, I'll be damned," he said aloud and put the instrument back in the cradle. "One little mistake and I'm off their list." He shrugged. "I'll give it time. It's never too late."

The following months passed rapidly and many changes came about.

Monsignor Pignelli took up his priestly duties at the Virginia Diocese in Arlington much to Elizabeth's chagrin, but a welcome blessing to Jericho.

Emily Martin had died suddenly, the result of a massive stroke, and only this tragedy had brought Kate Martin out of her sick bed to rally behind her husband. Even Jericho had exhibited some degree of his former gentleness at the passing of Schuyler Martin's mother, and with Elizabeth accompanying him they had attended the Wake at Magnolia Hill.

It was Schuyler who greeted them at the door where Elizabeth flew into her father's arms and together they released their long pent-up emotions, not only because of the death of Emily Martin, but also for the reasons that had torn them apart. Jericho stood to one side as Schuyler and Elizabeth become reconciled.

Then the older man, wiping tears from his eyes, approached him. "Jerry, my boy," he said softly, forcing a smile to his lips, "I do appreciate your coming today with Elizabeth."

"I admired your mother, Schuyler," he replied. "We had many conversations over the years and she was always a lady. I'm sorry that you lost her."

Then, as Kate Martin came within hearing, he added, "It must be a terrible blow to lose one's mother."

That afternoon people from all walks of life flocked to Magnolia Hill to pay their final homage to Emily Martin. When Jericho had grown tired of the condolences extended to him as a family member, he sought refuge in the kitchen.

Jessie saw him and scowled, but James greeted him warmly. "Sure have missed you and Miss Elizabeth, Senator," he said.

"We've missed both of you," he replied in all sincerity.

Suddenly the old black woman turned. "Then why haven't you been here?" she asked sullenly, and the look which came over her husband's face was one of total shock.

"You have no right to speak in that manner, wife," James snapped. "Apologize to the Senator."

Jericho was aware that Jessie was suffering since she obviously held the opinion that he was responsible for her mistress's mysterious and sudden illness.

"Sorry," she mumbled, and turned her back to busy herself with food preparations for the horde of guests.

Jericho went to the door and James followed. "Please excuse my wife. She's been very upset because of Mrs. Martin's illness and Grandmother Martin's passing."

"Think nothing of it, James. I understand," Jericho said kindly and went in search of his wife.

After he'd looked through the house, he finally found Elizabeth out on the sun porch with Sky and Brandy.

"Where have you two been keeping yourselves?" Brandy asked.

"Busy. I have another campaign coming up and you know how

that goes."

"Need some help?" Brandy volunteered.

"Help is always welcome, but I don't want to impose on your good nature."

Brandy smiled. "Just let me know when and I'll be there," and he paused. "Will Elizabeth be working on organization?"

Before Jericho could reply, she said sharply, "I haven't been asked."

"Now, Elizabeth," Jericho said placatingly, "You know that you've always been an important part of my campaigns. Why should I have to ask?"

Elizabeth shrugged almost as though his reply were insignificant, which caused Brandy and Sky to exchange looks.

"I think we should leave, Elizabeth," Jericho said.

"Leave? Now?"

"If you'd like to stay please fell free to do so. I'm sure that your father and Kate would enjoy having the three of you to themselves."

"But why must you go?" she protested.

"I have work to do," and he sighed, "Elizabeth seems to think that the government runs itself."

"Then go on," Elizabeth said haughtily. "James will bring me later."

"Fine, and good night, you two," Jericho said, shaking hands with both men.

"Don't forget to tell mother and daddy good-bye," Elizabeth directed.

Jericho glanced around the room and neither Kate nor Schuyler were anywhere to be seen.

"They seem to have disappeared. Give them my regrets," and he turned and walked into the crowd of guests, not once looking back.

36

As the time approached for his campaign, Jericho returned to Kansas to open his headquarters and it wasn't long before Brandy Martin joined him. Jericho had phoned ahead and asked Dolly Moran to see that the house was opened. When they arrived, he found the house neat as a pin and with a well stocked larder.

"Just like Dolly," he'd said to Brandy. "She's one woman willing to go the extra mile."

"The Morans are nice people," Brandy had agreed. Then he looked at Jericho questioningly. "Would you mind if I asked you something personal?"

"Go ahead," Jericho had replied, knowing that it would undoubtedly concern Elizabeth.

"I couldn't help but notice that Elizabeth seems out of sorts these days. She wasn't at all nice to you at Grandmother Martin's Wake."

Jericho smiled slightly. "Well, we've been married a long time now, and there are occasions when we don't exactly see eye to eye."

"She's always been bossy," Brandy admitted, smiling rather sheepishly. "We all spoiled her."

"That's for sure, and I don't. Perhaps that's the reason she seems at odds with me on occasion." He paused. "You see, she'd like to have me devote all of my time to her and that's an impossibility."

Brandy shook his head. "The Martin family, including me, have always been demanding, and especially Elizabeth and father."

The expression on Jericho's face changed at the mention of Schuyler Martin. "I have to agree. Now, shall we get to work?"

"Certainly, but there's one more thing."

"Yes?"

"When will Elizabeth be here?"

"I don't know for sure if she's coming."

"But why?"

"It seems that she'd rather spend her time at Magnolia Hill, and if that's what she wants to do, then she has my blessing."

"Will Paul Moran campaign with you?"

At the mention of his old friend, Jericho's face brightened.

"In all probability. I can always depend on him."

"You can depend on me, too," Brandy interjected.

"I know Brandy, and I do appreciate your help."

For the third time Jericho hit the campaign trail and Paul Moran, who was now getting well up in years, seemed to find the energy to accompany him. However, Dolly had insisted that she join them.

When Dolly had told her husband that she was going, he'd bellowed like an enraged bull. "But why? I'm perfectly fine. The doctor said so!"

"I know, darling," she replied calmly, "but on occasion you do seem to forget to take your medicine."

"Medicine!" he'd roared, but in the end both men had welcomed her presence, for Elizabeth hadn't so much as called or bothered to put in an appearance.

Monsignor Pignelli did join the party on a swing through Kansas, and his presence alone would bring in a goodly number of the Catholic vote.

On election day Jericho, accompanied by the Morans and Brandy Martin, had stayed at his main headquarters in the hotel. The ballroom had been engaged for the victory celebration that evening, and they were correct in their assumption for Jericho had won hands down.

It was a proud and happy moment when Senator Jerry Smith stood alone before his constitutents and thanked them for their loyal support. Elizabeth's absence hadn't seemed to make much difference, and over the previous weeks he'd heard rumors to the effect that the workers were glad that she hadn't been along.

The victory celebration continued on well into the early hours of the morning, and the Senator had joined in with enthusiasm. One lovely young woman had caught his eye earlier in the evening, and when he'd asked her to dance she'd seemed hesitant at first, then accepted him graciously. As they moved smoothly around the dance floor, Jericho found himself enjoying the fragrance of the perfume she wore and the feeling of her fresh, young body next to his. His thoughts drifted back to the long ago days when he'd first held Elizabeth in his arms and had felt the stirring of desire. Now, sadly, he felt nothing.

When the music stopped, the young woman started to excuse herself, but Jericho detained her. "Won't you join me in a victory drink?" he asked, "and please tell me your name."

"I'm Molly Shannon, Senator," she said shyly, "and I'd enjoy sharing a drink with you."

Jericho and his new friend moved through the milling crowd to the bar where he ordered two glasses of punch which was strongly laced with rum, and then sought out a quiet corner. Once settled, Jericho turned to his companion. "Here's to you, Molly Shannon," he said and held his glass to hers.

"And here's to you, senator," she'd replied solemnly.

Their glasses touched and when their eyes met they never wavered. In the Senator's face she saw his longing for her.

"Would you join me later?" he asked abruptly.

Molly knew that to accept was wrong since the Senator was married to Elizabeth Martin. However, she'd also felt drawn to him, and she quickly nodded her assent.

Jericho reached into his jacket pocket and produced a hotel key. "Here's an extra key to my suite. I'll excuse myself shortly."

Then Jericho got up from his chair and told Molly Shannon good-night for the benefit of the others around them and returned their glasses to the bar. He went up the steps to the podium and quieted the crowd.

"My loyal friends and supporters," he said. "They say that the third time is the charm," and he laughed slightly. "However, I wouldn't have been successful in this campaign without all of you," and he opened his arms to include everyone in the room.

The crowd roared their appreciation.

"It's been quite an evening," he continued, "and I've enjoyed every minute of it." He paused, wondering if he should mention Elizabeth, then decided not to. "Now, if you'll excuse me, I'm going to retire. Keep on having fun. You deserve it." With a wave and a smile he walked off the stage.

When he opened the door to his suite he found Brandy Martin waiting.

"What are you doing here?" he asked sharply.

"Thought you might enjoy some company since Elizabeth didn't bother to show."

"I appreciate that Brandy, but I'm beat and all I want to do is go to bed. Do you mind?"

Brandy's look was puzzled, and then he got to his feet and went to the door.

"Congratulations, Jerry. See you in the morning. Good-night," and he let himself out.

As he passed the elevator on his way to his room, the door opened and a beautiful young woman stepped out. He glanced at her and then continued on down the hall.

When Molly Shannon entered the hotel room she found the Senator in his robe, sipping from a drink. Jericho rose to his feet and greeted her warmly. "I'm so glad you came," he said softly, and before she could reply he pulled her into his arms. For several minutes they remained that way, then without further conversation they both disrobed and fell upon the bed.

Jericho made violent love to Molly Shannon as he'd never dreamed possible and she responded fully to his every overture. Their desire for each other was overwhelming and continued unabated until finally they both burst into climax together.

Before Jericho released Molly, he kissed her long and passionately. Then, almost angrily, he pushed himself away tossing a cover across her naked body. He swung his feet over the side of the bed and buried his face in his hands.

Molly slipped from the bed, picked up her clothes and vanished into the bathroom where she slipped into her garments and made an effort to look presentable. When she glanced in the mirror her eyes sparkled and she felt a certain completeness, for her virginity had been taken by the man that she'd admired secretly for many years.

Molly had worked on Jerry Smith's campaigns over the years and her duties had consisted of telephone canvassing, but whenever the young senator had been present and the opportunity presented itself, her eyes had followed him. From the first day, she'd determined that at some future time he would also notice her.

When Molly reentered the room she saw that the Senator had pulled on his robe and was sipping a fresh drink. As she moved into the light, his dark eyes devoured her.

"Come here," he said and placed his glass on the table. He held out his arms and Molly went into them, savoring the touch of his hands as he caressed her. Suddenly he pulled away.

"We have to talk," he said.

"I know," she replied.

"Why didn't you tell me you were a virgin?" he asked solemnly. She shrugged.

"Then why? Why me?"

For a moment Molly seemed at a loss for words, but when she looked into his dark brooding eyes she saw in them his need for love.

"I've loved you from a distance for many years," she said, and then her green eyes blazed. "But I also knew that my prayers would be answered and some day we'd come together."

"But you're aware that I'm married, and this made no difference?"

"Your marriage means nothing to me. Over the past few years there have been rumors that all is not well in your home life," she replied.

"You're right, Molly. Elizabeth and I merely share a house now," and he sighed. "Since we're Catholics, we'll never be divorced. You must realize that."

Molly's eyes danced. "I'm Catholic, too, and what we've just experienced goes completely against all the teachings of our religion." Then she laughed huskily. "However, when people need love why should God frown upon it? I'm free, and you're free. Only your marriage vows bind you. But is that enough?"

Jericho shook his head. "No, it's not, not anymore. Oh, my God, Molly, how I've needed you."

"It's been obvious," and she paused. "I don't know what happened between you and your wife and frankly, I don't want to know. For now, there's just you and me."

"Would you move to Washington?" he asked impatiently.

"Certainly. How soon would you like me to be there?"

"The sooner the better." Then, "Are you acquainted there?" She shook her head no.

"I'll have to find you an apartment."

Molly smiled, her look radiant.

"It will be our apartment, Jerry . . . ours, and I'll be waiting for you whenever you need me."

Once again Jericho pulled her into his arms and began to unbutton her blouse and skirt. He unhooked her brassiere which allowed her full breasts to be released and darted his mouth from nipple to nipple. He tugged gently and slipped her panties down. Once he'd shrugged out of his robe, he took her by the hand and they returned to their love bed.

All the long pentup passion that Jericho had withheld emerged as he made love to Molly with a gentleness and all consuming desire he'd never before experienced. As his fingers caressed her near perfect body he knew that this new love would be a blessing in diguise, and as he mounted her willing body he gazed deep into her eyes and whispered, "I love you, Molly Shannon. Oh, how I love you."

She drew him into her body and said softly, "Jerry, we belong together."

Then, as he thrust deep within her, he realized that a commitment had been made for a lifetime.

It was dawn when Molly left Jericho. They'd spent a sleepless night, talking, planning for the future, and expressing their love for one another. Neither had given the slightest consideration to the possibility that Molly could bear him children, and it was Jericho who'd finally mentioned it.

"You know, my sweet, you could very easily become pregnant," and for a moment the thought overwhelmed him.

"Would you care?" she asked, smiling suggestively. "I do know that you've never had children."

"No, I wouldn't mind," he replied, his voice firm. "However, if that should happen you'll be well cared for and I'll be with you."

"Oh, darling" she whispered against his chest, "I'd love to have your child."

The magic moment was shattered by the telephone's sharp ring.

Jericho picked it up. "Smith here," he growled, then paused to listen.

"Yes, Elizabeth, I was re-elected," he said . . . "I don't know when I'll return. I may stay on for a few days and visit my parents. He listened . . . "You're good at making excuses. Make another," he said, and with that he hung up the phone.

"Sorry," he said to Molly.

"There's no need to be. I have to accept the fact that you do have a responsibility where your wife is concerned."

"You surprise me."

"Why should I. I love you. What's happened between us comes but once in a lifetime. I'll treasure whatever time you can give me." Then, "Will you be leaving immediately?"

Jericho smiled, "And let you get away? Never!" He kissed her soundly and then escorted her to the door.

"We'll meet tonight. I have to rid myself of one brother-in-law."

"I know," Molly said and pulled his lips down to hers. "I'll be waiting."

When Molly had gone, Jericho moved restlessly around the room almost in a daze. Then the phone rang again, but this time it was Brandy. "Did I waken you?" he asked.

"No, Elizabeth did," he replied shortly, knowing that he was now starting to live a lie.

"What did she want?"

"Asked that I come back. There's some social event that she wants me to attend with her."

"Are you going home?"

"No, Brandy. I'm planning on staying over to visit my family. It's been a long time."

"Sounds like a good idea to me. My flight leaves at eleven, so I'll tell you good-bye now."

"Thanks for all your help, my friend, and I'll see you soon."

Jericho hung up the telephone, wishing that Molly was still there as his loins continued to ache from desire.

As he looked out the hotel window across the bleak sky of Wichita, his thoughts turned to Monsignor Pignelli.

"I wonder what the good Father would think now?" he mused aloud.

37

Jericho and Molly miraculously escaped from Wichita and spent three heavenly days together. As they drove along the Kansas highway during a blustering November rainstorm in search of an out of the way motel, they sat close together and acted like teenagers in the discovery of first love. Jericho couldn't begin to remember when he had been so happy. He relaxed and completely dismissed Elizabeth, the Martin family and Washington from his mind. In reality, he was running away from life, and when the three days were drawing to a close he found himself almost desolate.

The last day that he and Molly shared had been one of beauty. It had been unseasonably warm for November. They'd donned light jackets, jeans and walking shoes which had been purchased at a nearby general store and had taken a long walk in the woods that fanned out behind the small motel which had served as their hideaway.

As they walked slowly through the dense forest scuffling their feet in the dried leaves, they were enchanted with the colors of the leaves that still clung to the ancient oaks and cottonwoods. When they came to a fork in the path, they discovered a spot that had been used by campers. An old tree trunk had been pulled close to the dark ashes of a fire that had once burned brightly, and they sat down breathing in the crisp air of late Fall.

"Oh, Jerry," Molly said, taking his hand in hers. "This has been wonderful," and her eyes misted. "I'll never want to let you go," she murmured.

Jericho pulled her into his arms and held her gently. "I'll never leave you," he said, then stopped. "Of course, being a Congressman does require my presence on the hill," and he laughed. "However, knowing that you'll be waiting will make the days go by much faster."

"But what about Elizabeth? You do have to keep up a front."

"I know. But I'll see that things work out."

Hesitantly, Jerry said, "There's something you should know about the future."

Molly looked puzzled. "Please tell me." she said quietly.

"Schuyler Martin asked me many months ago to consider becoming a candidate in the last presidential election, but I refused.

Molly nodded.

Then he continued, "I'll probably be asked to run again," and his look became serious. "To be honest Molly, there's every possibility that I will give it serious consideration." He paused. "Elizabeth wants to become First Lady," and he laughed wryly. "I suppose in a way she does deserve it, should I be elected," and he turned to Molly. "You know what that will mean?"

She nodded, her look disconsolate.

"You'll have to groom me to become your top woman assistant," she said brightly. "After all, selecting a woman from your home State would seem only logical," and she laughed. "I do have a college degree, and my reputation is spotless," but when she said that she bridled a bit.

Then they both burst into laughter and Jericho pulled her to the ground. In the silence of the woods once again they consummated their love for each other.

When Jericho returned to Washington he found no one waiting for him and he smiled smugly. "Good," he thought, "I won't be questioned."

After picking up his luggage he left the terminal, hailed a passing cab and was quickly driven home. As he went up the walk to the house he saw that the drapes were pulled and he frowned. Elizabeth was undoubtedly at Magnolia Hill pouting because he hadn't followed her wishes.

"Who cares?" he said aloud and pushed up the thermostat sending a blast of hot air throughout the house. He went to his office and dialed Molly. She answered on the first ring.

"I'm back," he said.

"I miss you," she replied and at the sound of her voice his body ached for her.

"You'll be here soon. I'll start looking for an apartment today."

"Please do, Jerry."

He smiled, realizing how nice it was to be loved and wanted for no other reason than yourself. Then he heard the front door open and close and knew that Elizabeth had returned.

"I have to go," he whispered into the phone. "I'll call later this evening away from the house," and without saying good-bye he hung up.

Elizabeth had noticed the light in her husband's office and came to the door just as he put down the phone.

"Checking in with Pignelli?" she asked caustically.

Jericho rose from his desk and looked her straight in the eyes. "That's really no concern of yours. Now if you'll excuse me, I have to unpack and get to work." He brushed past, leaving her standing alone in the hall.

After Jericho had made a stop at his office, he returned to his car and headed out the Interstate toward Virginia. A copy of the *Washington Post* lay on the seat beside him with the advertising section turned to rentals. One apartment complex in Fredricksburg had caught his eye and that was his destination. The ad had stressed 'complete privacy,' and that was what he and Molly would need.

When he reached the complex he entered the rental office where an older woman greeted him. "Good afternoon," she said, smiling warmly.

"I saw your advertisement in the *Post* and am looking for a nicely furnished two bedroom apartment."

"For yourself?" she asked.

"No, for a friend."

The look the woman gave him was filled with curiosity and suspicion.

"My friend," Jericho said by way of explanation, "has just recently lost her husband and is in the process of selling her home. Her husband and I were friends for many years, and I volunteered to help out."

"How thoughtful," the woman said and relaxed visibly. "I'm a widow myself and you can't have enough friends these days." Then she took a key from a board behind her desk.

"I just happen to have a unit that's available immediately which you might like. It's off the main thoroughfare, and might meet your friend's needs. Shall we have a look?"

Jericho nodded, the first hurdle past.

Together they walked down a winding path until she stopped in front of a villa type residence. She paused for a moment and then asked, "Shall we go in?"

Once again he nodded.

The grey haired lady opened the door to the apartment and pulled back the drapes to let the late afternoon sunshine brighten the room.

"Please feel free to look around and take your time," she said pleasantly, and then sat down in an easy chair while Jericho wandered through the apartment by himself. As he went through each room he checked very thoroughly, then returned to his companion.

"What's the rent?"

"$750.00 a month including utilities," she replied.

"Is there a garage for a car?"

"Yes, in the back. There's access to it through the kitchen."

For a moment he hesitated, and the woman assumed that he was possibly just another looker.

"I think that Mrs. Shannon would be happy here," he said. "Of course, she'll be bringing her own momentos and belongings."

"Then you'll take it?"

"Yes, and she's authorized me to pay six months' rent in advance."

The woman appeared shocked as some of her guests, as she preferred to call her tenants, had problems paying one month.

When the transaction was completed and Jericho had received a receipt for the rent, the grey haired woman handed him two sets of keys, then looked at him appraisingly. "Your face looks familiar," she said.

Jericho smiled. "My name is Smith. I'm one of the Smith boys." He pocketed the keys, told her good afternoon, and hurried to the car.

When he came to a telephone booth he pulled to a stop and dialed Molly. The telephone rang several times before she answered. "Are you all right?" he asked.

"I was in the bedroom packing."

Jericho gave a sigh of relief. "Good! Catch the next flight to Baltimore.

"You mean it?" she said, and he could almost see the sparkle in her eyes.

"We have a home."

"I can hardly believe it, everything's happened so fast."

"Getting cold feet?" he asked.

"Oh, no. But my boss was furious when I resigned without giving notice."

"Tough. You have a better job waiting for you, and that's with me," he said softly.

"I know, Jerry. I'll be on the early morning flight."

"Good. I'll be waiting at the airport."

The sound of Molly's laughter made him wish that she were there now.

"I'll see you in the morning."

Before he hung up she asked, "What about Elizabeth?"

"She's back. That's the reason I had to hang up when I called this morning. So far I've been able to avoid her. Now I have to go. I'm not looking forward to this evening."

"I love you, Jerry," Molly whispered, and then hung up.

Almost in a daze, Jericho returned to the car and headed for Alexandria. He knew that there was every possibility that Elizabeth would create a scene, yet he also knew that the time was long overdue for a final confrontation.

When Jericho entered the house he found Elizabeth waiting for him in the den. It was obvious that she had been drinking heavily and in her hand she held an unfinished martini.

"I see you're back," she said, her voice thick from the liquor she'd consumed.

"Yes, I'm back. Don't you think you've had about enough?" he asked as he moved to the bar where he saw a half-filled pitcher of martinis remained.

"That's my business," she replied testily, then moved unsteadily to the couch and sat down almost spilling her drink in the process.

"Whatever," he replied and mixed himself a scotch. Then he seated himself so he faced her. "We need to get some things settled, Elizabeth."

"I'll go for that," she replied.

"Our marriage is over," he said, his voice without inflection.

At his statement Elizabeth began to laugh. "You'd better believe it is." Then she took a deep swallow from her drink. "That's the best news I've heard in a helluva' long time."

"I hope you realize that we'll never be divorced," he continued.

Once again she laughed, but this time it was laced with hysteria. "Course not! You're Daddy's fair haired boy," she chortled. "God, if he only knew."

"Knew what?"

"You think that I'm a dumb bell. I've known about you and Pignelli for years," she hissed, her dark eyes filled with loathing.

"Michael's a good friend, but think whatever you want. I couldn't care less. However," and he paused, "we'll continue living in the same house, do the required entertaining, and present a united front."

"What if I don't agree?" she muttered.

"You do want to be First Lady, don't you?" he asked, dangling the carrot before her just as her father had done to him in the past.

"Certainly I do," she replied, her sullenness evaporating.

"Good, that day will undoubtedly present itself, but you'll have to start acting like a politician's wife for a change."

"You're mad because I didn't go campaigning."

"Perhaps. But that's immaterial now," and he got up. "Now that we have the ground rules laid, you can pursue your own interests and I'll pursue mine. Good-night, Elizabeth."

He started for the door but before he got away she jumped from the couch and began to claw at him like a tiger. With one sweeping motion Jericho grabbed her arms and held them tightly, his eyes blazing into hers.

"Don't ever try that again. I'm a different man, Elizabeth, a far different man."

Then he released her and walked away, leaving a tamed Elizabeth Martin Smith standing alone with tears streaming down her cheeks.

Before dawn the following morning, Jericho left the house and as he cruised along the Beltway he considered the scene that had taken place between his wife and himself. He had actually felt a tinge of sorrow for her, yet the insinuations that she had made about him and Michael Pignelli had cut him to the quick.

"God, what a sick mind she has," he said aloud.

After he parked the car at the airport, he put on his dark glasses and made his way through the terminal. He located the gate where Molly's flight would arrive and walked toward it. On the way he stopped to purchase a cup of coffee and sipped from it as he waited for the woman he loved.

He saw the plane entering its landing approach and watched with never failing admiration as the pilot skillfully brought the giant silver streak to the ground. When the plane began to taxi to the jetway, he tossed the cup into a trash container and went to the gate.

The passengers started to enter the terminal. He watched apprehensively until he saw Molly. At the same moment she saw him and gave him a dazzling smile, even though it was only six in the morning.

"I'm glad you're here," he whispered, his eyes caressing her face.

"It seems as though we've been apart forever, Jerry, yet it has been only twenty-four hours," she replied quietly.

"Where's your luggage?"

"I brought this overnighter with me. I'm having the rest shipped," and she smiled. "I didn't think that I'd need a lot of clothes."

"How right you are. Now, let's get out of here."

With Jericho carrying her bag they left the terminal, got into the car, and in that pseudo privacy he pulled her into his arms and kissed her. "Care to make love in the back seat?" he asked.

"In front of God and everybody?" Molly replied huskily, her eyes filled with desire. "Why don't we go home?"

"Gladly," and he started the car and headed for the apartment in Fredricksburg.

38

In his newly found happiness with Molly, Jericho had avoided Schuyler Martin and Elizabeth like the plague, and it was only natural that the patriarch of the Martin family had turned to his daughter. Of late, he'd noticed that Elizabeth had been spending the majority of her time at Magnolia Hill. It had also became apparent that there was a serious problem between his daughter and her husband. He'd also noticed that Elizabeth frequently appeared on the verge of intoxication and there were some nights when she'd stumbled up the stairs to bed that he'd wondered if she'd make it to the top.

But he was also experiencing problems of his own. Since Emily Martin's death, Kate had slipped even further into depression and he'd finally insisted that she seek help. To please her beloved Schuyler, Kate had made an appointment with her internist for a physical examination before seeing a psychiatrist. On the day that she'd scheduled the appointment, Elizabeth and Kate had argued and her daughter had placed the blame on Kate and Schuyler for the problems that now existed between her husband and herself.

"You never liked him," Elizabeth had raved, eyes blazing with fury. "You never thought that he was good enough for me. You and father turned me into a spoiled rotten brat and look where it's gotten me! Jerry doesn't love me now and we're living in a house together to 'keep up a united front,' as he puts it, so father can push him into becoming a candidate for the next election.''

Kate had made an effort to placate her, but Elizabeth refused to listen, stormed from the house, and drove away with tires squealing.

In resignation, Kate had kept her appointment with the doctor and after he had completed the examination and had taken blood samples he joined her in his office. When he entered, his look was glum. "Besides depression, Kate, have you felt well physically?" he asked.

She laughed slightly. "Oh, I have a few aches and pains now and then. Why?"

"I removed a tissue sample from your ovaries for a biopsy," he said. "In all probability it will show nothing, but I thought you should know.''

Suddenly Kate felt alarmed. "Could it be serious?" she asked hesitantly.

"Anything can be serious, Kate, but we'll have to wait for the test results.''

"When will you know?"

"Within a few days. Now, why don't you run along home, have Schuyler take you out on the town and enjoy yourself," and he smiled warmly. "That's my prescription for today.''

"You'll call?"

"Of course.''

Kate left the doctor's office feeling even more depressed than when she had entered. From his attitude, she had an intuitive feeling that what he had discovered was cause for concern, although he had seemingly dismissed it almost lightly.

James drove her back to Magnolia Hill where she found Schuyler waiting. He took one look at her and knew that something was troubling her.

Suddenly she said almost too brightly, "Let's go out tonight. How about the Kennedy Center? Leontyne Price is performing there and we do have season tickets.''

For a moment the fear that he felt was pushed aside and he was pleased with her change in attitude. "Great idea. We'll have dinner at Luigi's in Old Town and then take in the concert." Schuyler paused. "Do you have any idea how wonderful you've made me feel?" and he pulled her into his arms, eyes shining.

"I'm glad," she said and then released herself from his embrace. "I'm going to take a nap," she said and when he indicated that he'd like to join her, Kate held up her hand. "Not now, Schuyler. I need to be alone," and she disappeared up the stairs.

For a moment he felt rejected, then he became angry. He strode from the house and entered the limousine.

"Where to Mr. Martin?" James asked.

"Hell, I don't know," he replied gruffly. "Just drive."

As James drove slowly along the Potomac, Schuyler gazed out the window at the curling water, his thoughts as murky as the river.

Suddenly he let out a cry. "God, oh God!" he wailed, "what are you doing to my life?" Then he began to cry, hard racking sobs. Fortunately the window between Schuyler Martin and James was closed and the despair of this very proud man was kept private.

Molly Shannon was well into her seventh month of pregnancy. When she had first discovered that she was carrying Jericho's child, it hadn't come as a surprise to either of them. Their love for one another had grown stronger with each passing day and Jericho spent every possible moment with her. They kept mainly to themselves and on weekends when he had been able to get away, they'd gone to the hills of West Virginia where they frequented a small Inn.

As the time approached for the delivery of their child, Jericho had asked Monsignor Pignelli to join him for dinner. Up until that time they had seen each other infrequently, but now he wanted his friend to meet the mother of his child.

Shortly after five, on a hot and humid August day, Jericho picked up the priest and instead of heading for Old Town which was one of Pignelli's favorite haunts, they moved into the heavy afternoon traffic and headed toward the Virginia countryside.

"Would you mind telling me where we're going?" Pignelli asked.

Jericho smiled. "I came across a delightful place in Fredricksburg recently. I'm sure that you'll find it enjoyable."

The priest glanced at his friend with the feeling that something was up, and when they turned into the driveway of a large apartment complex he was even more puzzled.

"Are we picking someone up?" he asked.

"No," Jericho replied and pulled into an open garage.

"Are you sure that you're feeling okay, Jerry?"

"Never felt better in my life," and he got out of the car with the priest following.

The door to the kitchen opened and Molly Shannon, very much with child, smiled a warm welcome. Jericho kissed her deeply and then turned to his friend.

"Father," he said, "this is Molly Shannon."

Molly put out her hand to the priest and he touched it briefly, still in a quandary as to why they were there.

"Do come in, Father," Molly said politely and stood aside so he could enter.

As they moved through the small, compact kitchen, delectable odors drifted to Pignelli's nostrils and he sniffed hungrily. Then he realized that this was the 'delightful' place that Jericho had mentioned.

Once they were seated in the living room, Jericho went to the bar and prepared a ginger ale for Molly and two Scotches for his guest and himself. He offered one to the priest, who accepted it gratefully, and immediately took a deep swallow.

"I'm glad that you came, Father," Molly remarked pleasantly.

"I am, too." Then he looked at Jericho whose smile was amused. "But I don't understand."

"We know," Jericho replied and took Molly's hand.

"Michael, you've been my best friend and confidant for many years and both Molly and I want to share our secret with you. We know that whatever we tell you will be safe with you," and he paused. "You see, Molly is carrying my child," and he touched her stomach tenderly. "This new life is a child stemming from our love," and his look turned serious. Then once again he said very solemnly, "A child of love."

At Jericho's announcement the priest almost went into shock and gulped down the balance of his drink before holding out his glass for a refill. Then he managed, "You've got to be kidding! I'd never suspect that you'd take part in a covert act. My God, Jerry, does Elizabeth know?"

"There's certainly no 'covert' act, as you so candidly put it," he said. "Molly and I love each other and she is also aware that because of our religion we'll never be able to marry." He looked at the young woman beside him with open affection and his anger vanished.

"Elizabeth and I," he continued, "have decided to pursue separate lives and I have elected to spend as much of mine as possible with Molly and our child."

"But you and Elizabeth are still living at the house," Pignelli said, looking puzzled.

Jericho nodded. "It's a matter of convenience and necessity. As you're aware, one day Schuyler will seek me out and ask me to consider becoming a candidate again. I told Elizabeth that if she ever wants to become First Lady she'll do exactly as she's told."

"Heavenly Father," the priest murmured and crossed himself.

"Our baby is due before long" Jericho went on, "and I'd like to ask a favor."

"Go ahead," the priest replied, now quite sober.

"Would you be willing to accompany Molly to the hospital? I'm afraid that it would present an awkward situation for me."

Pignelli frowned, yet he knew that by taking part he would ensure his position as religious advisor to a prospective President. Still he hesitated just long enough so that he wouldn't appear to be too eager.

"Well?" Jericho asked.

"All right, Jerry. I'll do it. Just provide me with the necessary information . . . doctor, hospital, whatever, and the story that goes along with it."

Before he realized what was happening, Molly pushed herself up from the divan and knelt at his knees.

"Thank you, Father," she said, eyes brimming with tears. "Oh, thank you."

Michael Pignelli gently patted her head. "Molly Shannon," he said kindly, "I admire you, and I bless you."

Then he helped her up and went to Jericho. "Congratulations, my friend. Now how about a toast to the baby?"

Michael Pignelli's look was solemn as he chose his words, then he said boldly, "To Michael Shannon," and a broad smile crossed his face.

Jericho and Molly looked into each others eyes and laughed.

Then holding their glasses to his, echoed his words. "Michael Shannon, it will be!"

On the day Kate Martin received the call from her physician she was home alone. Elizabeth had returned to her own home that morning and Schuyler was at a committee meeting. When Jessie informed her that the doctor was calling, she'd picked up the extension beside her bed. "This is Kate," she said softly.

"Kate, the results of your tests are back," and there was a slight pause.

"Can you tell me the results?" she asked apprehensively.

"I'd rather that you came into the office," and she knew immediately that there had to be something terribly wrong.

"When should I come in?" she asked.

"I've scheduled a consultation with a specialist for this afternoon," and he paused. "Bring Schuyler with you."

"But he's away for the day," she replied.

"Is there anyone else who could come with you?"

"I'll see if my daughter's available. Then I'll get back to you, and thanks for calling."

As Kate replaced the phone, a cold chill swept over her and she felt like running away, but instead she called Elizabeth.

When her daughter answered her reply was curt. "Yes?" she said.

"Darling, this is Mother. Could you accompany me to the doctor's this afternoon? Your father's not available."

Elizabeth Smith suddenly forgot about her own problems. "Is there something wrong?" she asked. "I didn't even know that you'd been to a doctor!"

"Yes. At the insistence of your father I went earlier this week, and the test results came back. The doctor suggested that someone come with me."

"Of course I'll go. Send James, and I'll see you shortly."

After she had finished speaking with her mother, Elizabeth placed a call to her husband's office.

Jericho's top aide answered and when he recognized the Senator's wife's voice he steeled himself. He had received strict orders from his superior that he wasn't to disturb him for any reason.

"The Senator please. This is his wife," Elizabeth said shortly.

"I'm sorry, Mrs. Smith, but the Senator's not available this morning. If there's something urgent I'll gladly take a message."

"No!" she said crossly and slammed down the phone.

"God damn you, Jerry Smith," she screamed to the empty house. "You're never there when I need you."

When Kate Martin and Elizabeth entered the medical office they were ushered into a small private conference room. The nurse had seemed overly solicitous and her actions caused Kate to become even more apprehensive.

Within a short time the two doctors entered and the oncologist was introduced to the two women. It was the latter who almost impassively, and without any marked inflection to his voice, informed Kate that the pathologist's lab reports had shown that she was a victim of melanoma cancer.

"Oh, my God," Elizabeth had said as Kate turned pale.

"I'm sorry, Kate," the internist said kindly. "My friend will tell you what options there are," and then he excused himself.

"Options?" Kate asked and frowned slightly.

"Yes, you do have several, Mrs. Martin. First, of course, there is always surgery, and if you select that course we would hope to curb the spread of the disease. There's also radiation to consider, and chemotheraphy."

"And what advice would you give?" Kate asked, her voice almost too calm.

Before his meeting with Kate Martin the doctor had carefully examined the tissue culture and had gone over the x-rays with the radiologist. He knew that radiation was all that they could reasonably do as the cancer had already spread through Kate's female organs and was in the progress of destroying her bladder. Yet, she'd told her internist she'd only experienced minor aches and pains and this fact had puzzled him.

"If it were my wife or mother," he said, his voice now taking on a trace of feeling, "I'd recommend radiation treatments, and the sooner the better."

"How long do I have?" Kate asked, every word measured.

At her question Elizabeth let out a sob. "What do you mean 'how long do you have'?" she wailed and began to cry.

Kate ignored Elizabeth's outburst as her attention was directed to the doctor.

"If you're lucky, six, maybe nine months," and he shrugged. "Perhaps even a year. It's very difficult for any of us to make a prognosis since each person reacts differently to the treatment they select."

"Will you take care of me?" Kate asked, liking the distance he kept between himself and his patient.

"I'll be glad to do whatever you decide. Shall we start in the morning?"

"Certainly," Kate replied and then turned to her daughter. "I'd like to go home now, Elizabeth." As they started to leave Kate turned. "Thanks for your honesty." Then she quickly strode from the room.

After they entered the limousine and were on the way back to Magnolia Hill, Kate turned to Elizabeth. "Your father is not to be told," she said calmly, and when her daughter started to object she continued. "So far I've experienced little discomfort, and as long as it continues in this fashion Schuyler will enjoy being with me. I don't want his pity, or yours," and she looked at Elizabeth intently.

"But mother," Elizabeth said.

"Don't fret so," Kate said and patted her hand.

"What about Jerry?" Elizabeth asked.

Kate was silent. She knew that the time would come when he would learn of her illness and perhaps by then it would prove to be too late.

"Tell him if it will help," Kate replied.

"But mother, how will you explain going to the hospital for your treatments?"

Kate's laugh was forced. "Leave that to me," and she sighed. "Remember, Elizabeth, I'm counting on you."

"Oh, Mamma, why did this happen to you of all people? You've always been so loving and kind."

"Sometimes God has his own plans for us," she said quietly. Then, "Elizabeth, I've been far from perfect and there are some things in the past that I wish with all my heart that I'd done differently. Now enough of this," and she touched her daughter's tear-streaked cheek with affection. "Just remember your promise."

Elizabeth nodded, too choked to reply.

39

It was several days after Molly and their son Michael had come
home from the hospital that Jericho returned to Alexandria. When
he entered the front door he found Elizabeth waiting for him.

"Where have you been?" she asked accusingly.

"Out of the city. Why?" and then he saw the expression on her
face. "Is something wrong?"

Without answering, Elizabeth burst into tears and Jericho felt
some degree of sympathy.

"You can't tell me what's troubling you if you continue to cry,"
he said gently and seated himself in a chair near her. "Please tell
me."

"It's mother," Elizabeth mumbled as she made an effort to dry
her tears.

"What's wrong with Kate?"

"Oh, Jerry, she has cancer . . . melanoma. The worst kind."

"Oh, God," he said as a feeling of remorse swept over him.
"Does Schuyler know?"

Elizabeth shook her head. "No, and she doesn't want him
to . . . not until it becomes a necessity."

"Is that fair?"

"What's fair?" and Elizabeth raised her tear stained face to look at the man she called husband.

"I'm truly sorry, Elizabeth."

"Mother asked to see you, but didn't tell me why."

Jericho knew the reason, but for Elizabeth's benefit he forced a smile. "Probably wants to give me some sound advice."

"Will you go see her?" Elizabeth implored. "I know that you've never really cared for her," and she sighed.

"I'll give it consideration," he said as he gazed out the window.

"Please don't wait too long. Mother's a very proud woman and won't want to see you towards the end when she won't be herself."

"I'll let you know in a few days," he said.

"I'm staying at Magnolia Hill, Jerry," Elizabeth said quietly as she wiped her eyes.

"Is that necessary?"

"I need to be with people who love me," she said as she picked up her bag and hurried from the house.

When Jericho returned to Fredricksburg Molly sensed that he was troubled.

"Has something happened?" she asked after they had embraced.

Jericho nodded. "Elizabeth was waiting for me when I got home."

Molly's look was puzzled. "Is that so unusual?"

"Yes. She's been spending the majority of her time with her family and told me that from now on she'd be living at Magnolia Hill."

"But why?"

"Her mother has just learned she has cancer."

"How horrible," Molly said. Then she glanced at Jericho. "You've never cared for your mother-in-law, or am I assuming that?"

"You're right. Kate and I haven't exactly been the best of friends," and he sighed. "Elizabeth told me that she wants to see me."

"Will you go?"

"I really don't know."

"I see."

"Someday I'll tell you the whole story, but now," and he gathered her into his arms and touched her breasts that were heavy with milk, "how I need you," he whispered.

Molly smiled. "I know, darling, but you have to be patient."

At that moment the door bell rang and Jericho released her and got up to answer.

When he opened the door he found Monsignor Pignelli on the doorstep prespring profusely from the hot and humid August evening. As the portly priest entered the air conditioned apartment he gave an audible sigh of relief. "Where's my namesake?" he asked.

"Sleeping, Father," Molly replied, "but if you'll come with me I'll let you have a peek."

The priest followed Molly down the hall to the nursery with Jericho bringing up the rear. As they stood beside the crib and looked at the sleeping infant, an aura of peace seemed to surround them.

"Ah, but he's a beauty," the priest said softly, patting Michael Shannon's soft dark fringe of hair. "Looks just like his father," and he turned to smile at Jericho. Then he looked at Molly whose face was radiant. "And you, my child?" he asked, his arm encircling her waist.

"I'm fine, Father."

Then the priest turned to Jericho. "Now what is this private matter you wanted to discuss with me?"

At his question, Molly excused herself.

When they were alone Jericho went to the bar and prepared their usual Scotches and offered one to his friend, but instead of taking a seat he walked restlessly around the room.

"What's troubling you, Jerry?" he asked.

"It's Kate."

"Kate Martin?" the priest repeated, a frown crossing his brow. "I don't understand."

"You will," Jericho paused. "Elizabeth just told me that her mother has recently learned that she has cancer and has only a few months to live. She asked, through Elizabeth, that I come to see her," and he shook his head. "I don't know what I should do."

"Have you given consideration as to how you would approach her after all that's happened?"

Jericho's laugh was sardonic. "I really have no idea."

"Perhaps she wants to make peace with you, Jerry," the priest volunteered.

"I've given that some thought and I suppose you're right. Elizabeth suggested that I make my visit before it's too late."

"It would be the Christian thing to do," the priest replied.

"I don't know, Michael," and he frowned. "I really have little desire to alleviate Kate's conscience."

Michael Pignelli knew that it would not be wise to force Jericho into an undesirable situation since there was every possibility it could make his own position of less importance.

"The decision is yours, Jerry," he said solemnly, put his glass on the bar and went to the door. "Say good-night to Molly for me." and he went out into the night leaving Jericho faced with a decision he had yet to reach.

A few days following his conversation with the priest, Jericho called Elizabeth and told her that he did not think it advisable that he visit Kate.

"But why?" she cried.

"I have my own personal reasons," he replied.

"I can't believe that you'd treat a dying woman in this manner," Elizabeth said.

For a long time neither said anything, then Jericho spoke. "It's best, believe me."

He hung up the phone leaving a shattered Elizabeth Martin Smith with the task of telling her mother.

It was almost nine months to the day of Jericho's meeting with Kate Martin that her funeral was held. Over the preceding months both Schuyler and Elizabeth had devoted the majority of their days and nights to her.

In the interim, Jericho had told Molly the story of his beginnings and the comfort she had given him had helped ease the pain and to understand the 'why' of the ending of his marriage to Elizabeth. However, even though Jericho and Elizabeth were estranged, it was known only to the immediate family, and his colleagues in the Senate were understanding of his wife's devotion to her mother.

The day of Kate's funeral dawned balmy and warm, a perfect day in early May. As Jericho dressed for the solemn occasion he

knew that had Kate been alive, she would have been happy for the
magnolia trees were now in full bloom and the flowers that dotted
the grounds of Magnolia Hill had shown their bright faces.

Jericho and Elizabeth had reached mutually satisfactory terms and
together they attended the services with Schuyler, Sky, Jr., and
Brandy.

Dolly and Paul Moran had been unable to attend since Paul had
recently suffered a debilitating stroke, but to everyone's surprise
Julia and Adele Barton and Belle had flown in from Montana as a
gesture of respect, not only for Schuyler Martin, but for Jericho as
well.

Washington Cathedral, where Jericho and Elizabeth had taken
their marriage vows, was packed with dignitaries that included
Jericho's colleagues from the Senate. Speaker of the House, and
corporate officials from the United States and foreign countries as
well. Flowers in profusion banked the altar and Monsignor
Pignelli, at Jericho's specific request, had played a small part in the
Mass for Kate.

Both Schuyler and Elizabeth looked haggard and worn from the
long hours spent at Kate's bedside, but they stood hand in hand as
Sky, Brandy and Jericho were almost overshadowed by their
obvious strength.

Following the lengthy service and burial rites, the immediate
friends of the family had been invited to Magnolia Hill for a private
luncheon. It was there that Belle had sought Jericho out.

When the white haired, chubby faced woman came face to face
with Jericho they had embraced and Belle whispered softly,
"Could we have a few minutes alone?"

"Certainly," he replied, and taking her by the arm escorted her
from the crowded room and down the familiar path that he had
traveled on several other occasions. Once they were seated in a
sheltered part of the garden, Belle turned to her companion, her
look searching.

"Jericho," she said quietly, "Stoney was your father." She
waited for his response, expecting denial, but instead Jericho took
her work worn hand in his and when he looked into her eyes his
smile was gentle.

"Yes, Belle, Stonewall Barton was my father," and he paused.
"I've often thought of the night when you and I talked about

Stonewall's death, and believe that even then you suspected, but didn't feel you could overstep your bonds.''

"You resemble him so strongly," she said, and then looked down at her hands. "Was Kate the girl he deserted?''

The seconds ticked off as Jericho considered his reply. Then he reached the conclusion that Belle would never betray his secret.

Slowly he nodded. "Yes, Belle. Kate Martin was my mother.''

"How long have you known?''

"A short time," and he sighed. "You see, Schuyler had asked me to consider entering the presidential campaign, and I knew that somewhere in my background was a secret.'' He sighed audibly. "What I discovered could easily have ruined both the Martin family and my career.''

"Did you tell Kate?'' Belle asked.

"Yes.''

"Did she believe you?''

"She already knew.''

"Then why are you here? And what about your marriage to Elizabeth?'' Belle pursued.

"It's at an impasse. We'll never divorce, if that's what you're asking. However,'' he continued, "I'm only sorry that I didn't know Stonewall Barton was my father before it was too late.''

"Stoney talked to me about the girl he had abandoned on many nights when he couldn't sleep. He never forgot her or stopped loving her. That's the reason he finally killed himself.''

Jericho nodded. "How well I know.'' Then his look turned serious. "I trust that you won't reveal what I've just confirmed.''

Belle smiled. "Jerry, your father saved my life many years ago and now in my golden years I've been blessed with a family of sorts with Julia and Adele. After Stoney died we became quite close; you see, we all loved him, but in different ways,'' and she shook her head sadly, "but he really didn't know how to love anyone but Kate.''

Jericho nodded in agreement, then glanced at his watch. "Now we'd better head back or Schuyler will send out a search party for us!''

When they rose from the garden bench Jericho put his arms around Belle. "You're a lady, Belle, a real lady.''

She pulled back from his embrace, a twinkle in her wise old eyes.

"I remember a long time ago when your father told me the same thing. Thank you, Jericho," and she brushed his cheek with a kiss. Then, hand in hand, they moved back up the path.

Even after Kate had been gone for several weeks, Elizabeth remained at Magnolia Hill, using the excuse that her father needed her. To the world at large that seemed to be a logical explanation, and they assumed when the Senator and his wife refrained from attending important social gatherings that it was because of Elizabeth's mourning.

It was true that Elizabeth and Schuyler mourned together, but as time began to heal the first intense hurt of Kate's passing, they also began to consider Jericho's prospects as a candidate for the next election.

40

Elizabeth returned home but still spent long days in her father's company. However, the handsome Senator from Kansas and his stunning wife, following a period of mourning for Kate Martin, once again returned to the mainstream of political life in Washington and entertained and attended the more important social functions.

Molly and young Michael had remained in the apartment in Fredricksburg. As Michael became more active, and after discussions with Molly, Jericho purchased a charming but modest home in the country of Virginia for his family. And, in time, Jericho had added Molly to his staff. Because she was a native of Kansas his aides thought little about her arrival and within a few weeks discovered that she was not only blessed with a fresh and positive personality, but was also intelligent. She was readily accepted.

On the day that Schuyler had called Jericho's office it had been Molly who had taken his call, and it had been at her urging that Jericho had agreed to speak with his father-in-law, although with a degree of reluctance.

"Jerry," Schuyler said, now once again exhibiting some of his normal enthusiasm which had been sorely lacking since Kate's death, "how about joining me for lunch at the Mayflower? It would be like old times."

Jericho hesitated, realizing that Schuyler was undoubtedly loaded for bear and that he was the hunted.

"I don't know," he finally replied, and then glanced at Molly who nodded her head vigorously as though to say 'go ahead.'

"It's been such a long time," the older man said, his tone almost plaintive.

"That's true. Just what day did you have in mind? I do operate on a tight schedule."

"I'm ever so much aware of that, Jerry. How about this Thursday, at one?"

"Thursday," Jericho repeated as Molly looked through his calendar and then nodded affirmatively.

"It looks as though Thursday might be as good a time as any," he replied. "We will be alone?"

"Of course."

"Good. I'll see you then."

"My pleasure," Schuyler replied. After he replaced the telephone, he rubbed his hands together in obvious glee and turned to his daughter who was sitting beside him.

"He agreed?" Elizabeth asked eyes sparkling in anticipation.

"You bet!"

"Can I go?"

Schuyler shook his head. "Afraid not. He insisted that it just be the two of us."

Elizabeth's look was crestfallen. "I should have expected that," she acknowledged and shrugged, "but I'll be waiting for the results."

"I know," her father replied. Then as an afterthought, added, "How I wish Kate were here."

"But she's not, father," Elizabeth said softly. "You and I must move ahead and our future depends on Jerry and the nomination."

The silver haired man smiled. "I'm really looking forward to this campaign."

"Don't be too sure that Jerry will even consider your offer," Elizabeth cautioned.

"Like to make a bet?" Schuyler said, tipping his head to smile at her rakishly.

"No, no bets. Now we'd better get busy. There's a long, hard road ahead."

Promptly at one o'clock on Thursday, Jericho arrived at the newly refurbished Mayflower and within a short time the Martin limousine deposited its owner at the front door. The two men greeted each other with some degree of restraint and Jericho allowed his father-in-law to provide the conversation.

"Great to see you, Jerry," he said, shaking the younger man's hand.

"Thanks, Schuyler," Jericho had replied, smiling slightly.

As they followed the matire'd into the crowded dining room their presence was noticed by other diners, and it was Schuyler who stopped to exchange pleasantries with some of his old friends while Jericho waited.

Once seated, and after their bar order had been served, Schuyler glanced at his companion who had remained silent and whose look was almost stoic.

"How about a toast?" he suggested, smiling politely.

Jericho's look held a trace of amusement and a slight smile touched his lips. "To what?"

"The future, of course!"

"Whatever," Jericho replied and touched Schuyler's glass.

After lunch was served they both ate hurriedly; Jericho because of an appointment back at his office, and Schuyler because of his need to talk with his son-in-law. It was over coffee that Schuyler finally broached the subject of their meeting.

"Tired of serving in the Senate?" he asked abruptly, eyes scanning Jericho's face.

"I'll have to admit that I've given some thought to not running again, if that's what you mean. Why?" Jericho asked, well aware that they were playing a cat and mouse game.

"Jerry," he said softly as he leaned across the table, "you can have another chance at the nomination."

Jericho drew back, took a sip from his coffee and then countered, "Is that so?"

"You know damned well it is!" the older man replied, sounding on the verge of anger.

"I don't know, Schuyler," Jericho said and paused. "Campaigning gets tougher each time, and traveling all over the country would take up even a considerable amount of my time.''

"But think of the opportunity? How many men ever get the chance?'' Then he rushed on. "You could have had the nomination the last time,'' and he shook his head. "I've never understood why you refused.''

"I had my reasons.''

"Well, whatever they were I hope that they've been resolved.''

"They have been. It just took some time.''

"Then how about it?''

"I presume that Elizabeth still has her head set on being First Lady?'' he replied.

Schuyler's grin was sheepish. "I won't deny that, and besides, you know that she'd make a damned good one.''

"That's true, but I'm sure you know that our marriage has gone sour and there's every possibility that this could come to light.''

"Only the family is aware of that,'' and he scowled. "I don't understand that either. She won't talk about it and I know that you sure as hell won't!''

"Anything else on your mind?'' Jericho asked.

"My God, isn't that enough?''

Jericho pushed back his chair and stood up.

"I'll let you know, Schuyler. Thanks for lunch and I'll see you around.''

Without so much as a goodbye, the Senator hurried from the room leaving behind a mystified Schuyler Martin.

Several dreary winter weeks went by and as the days passed slowly, Schuyler and Elizabeth reached the point where they both believed that the proposition Schuyler had presented to Jerry had somehow turned sour. It was an unexpected surprise when Jessie announced one morning that the Senator was calling.

Schuyler, who was deeply engrossed in the financial pages of the *Post*, had tossed the newspaper aside and went to his desk. Once settled in his leather chair he picked up the telephone.

"Jerry,'' he said, his voice waxing enthusiasm, "it's good to hear from you.''

"Thanks, Schuyler. I've been giving some serious consideration to your proposition,'' Jericho said in his businesslike manner.

This announcement caused Schuyler to become even more alert;

however, he remained cautious and made an effort not to appear overly optimistic. "Glad to hear that," the older man replied.

"I'd like to meet with you, and also Elizabeth," Jericho said.

"I'm sure that that could be arranged," Schuyler had responded, his nerves taut as a violin's strings. "Just when and where did you want this meeting?"

"How about Magnolia Hill?" Jericho replied and laughed ironically. "That's where it all began."

It was impossible for his father-in-law not to hear the sarcasm in his voice.

"Name the day and we'll both be available," Schuyler said, then added, "by the way, have you discussed this with Elizabeth?"

"Frankly no. I felt that it was best that the two of you be present."

"Good. Then name the day."

"I'll arrive this Sunday afternoon around four o'clock, and I do hope that you'll keep this meeting to yourselves. I certainly don't want any publicity."

"Of course, Jerry. We'll expect you Sunday."

"Thanks, Schuyler," and he hung up abruptly.

The silver haired man slowly replaced the telephone and sat back in his chair musing over their brief, but fruitful conversation.

"I wonder," he murmured aloud, then picked up the telephone to call his beloved Elizabeth.

Although Elizabeth and Jericho were both going to Magnolia Hill for the meeting with Schuyler, they left their home in separate cars with Jericho leaving several hours before the appointed hour so he could be with Molly and young Michael. This did not cause Elizabeth any undue concern since she'd accepted their lifestyle with graciousness and at times found herself actually enjoying being able to come and go without any real consideration for her husband's schedule. However, in her heart she harbored a deep hatred and resentment toward Monsignor Pignelli whom, she felt, was somehow the cause of their estrangement. She also believed that there was every possibility that the priest might put in an appearance with her husband at Magnolia Hill.

Elizabeth arrived early to allow plenty of time for a strategy talk with her father on exactly how they should act with this rather strange individual whom at one time they'd both known in a much different manner.

"Darling," he said, "we'll let Jerry do the talking. After all, he's the one who requested the meeting and we do owe him that. We shouldn't force our opinions on him or let him think for a minute that we're pushing him."

His daughter nodded. "You're right, as always. Perhaps this is his way to tell us 'no' nicely. You see," and she sighed, "I've learned not to expect anything from Jerry these days."

"I understand," Schuyler replied with sympathy and touched Elizabeth's hand with affection.

At that moment the door chime rang and Jessie could be heard greeting the Senator and directing him to the library.

When Jericho appeared in the door his eyes held a luster that neither Elizabeth nor Schuyler had seen in months. Schuyler, in particular, seemed taken by this rather startling change in the stoic manner that Jerry had exhibited of late and jumped to his feet to greet him, while Elizabeth gave the newcomer a brief but rather cool smile.

"Come in, come in, Jerry," the older man said, and then proceeded to pull the library doors closed so they were quite alone.

"Thanks," said Jericho as he moved into the spacious room where he settled in a chair that faced both his father-in-law and his wife. "Rather nippy outside," he remarked.

"How about a brandy to take the chill out of your bones?"

"Sounds good to me." Then Jericho turned to Elizabeth. "Would you care for something?" he asked politely.

Elizabeth smiled wanely. "No, thanks. It's a bit early," and she quickly looked away from the man she loved in order to compose herself.

Once the two men were settled, the silence that engulfed the room was almost tangible, each waiting for the other to begin the conversation. Then both started to speak at once and finally broke into laughter with Schuyler Martin deferring to the Senator.

"You first, Jerry," he said and glanced at his daughter, seeing the shadow of pain her eyes.

"It's been some time since we last talked," Jericho said.

"That's true," Schuyler acknowledged.

"At least this time you gave me the opportunity to consider all the ramifications of your proposition."

Inwardly Elizabeth winced as she knew that she'd thrown the monkey wrench into their last effort and that her father had never quite forgiven her for it.

"Would you care to tell us your decision?" Schuyler asked, making an effort to appear calm, although his heart was beating rapidly.

"As you both will remember," Jericho said, and looked from one to the other, "the last time that I campaigned for my senate seat the only support that I had from the family came from Brandy, and from my old law partner, Paul Moran." The tone of his voice evidenced his displeasure.

Elizabeth looked down at her hands, obviously embarrassed, as she knew that there was little reason for her to protest since his statement was true.

However, Schuyler did. "My God, Jerry," the older man literally exploded, "you came back from that trip to Kansas like some stranger to the lot of us, including Elizabeth. What did you expect?" Then he rushed on. "You had that election sewed up anyway."

"I simply want to point out that should I take the bid for the nomination I'll need everyone's support, and that includes money. Campaigns don't run on nickels and dimes," and his laughter held a trace of sarcasm. "Not these days, anyway."

At that point both Schuyler and Elizabeth had renewed hope.

"You know that you'll have everything you need, Jerry—money, campaign strategists, and the backing of the Party—of that I can assure you," Schuyler replied, his enthusiasm soaring.

Jericho took a sip from his brandy, realizing that accepting the challenge for the presidency was at least in part, his way of paying Elizabeth back for all the hurts that he'd caused her. When he looked at her it was with honest affection.

"Elizabeth," he said solemnly, "how would you like to become First Lady?"

For a moment the room was so still that the ticking of the mantle clock was the only sound heard. Elizabeth rose gracefully from her chair and while her father watched she went to Jericho and dropped to her knees beside him.

"Oh, thank you, Jerry. No matter what's come between us, I'll stand beside you every long, hard step of the way," she said huskily, and then burst into tears, her head coming to rest against his knees.

Jericho gently stroked her hair and Schuyler felt tears moisten his eyes. He knew that this moment was one that would remain etched in his memory until his dying day.

After a short pause, Jericho turned to his wife. "Now that *that's* settled, Elizabeth, I really think that you and I need to talk over our own personal strategy."

Elizabeth looked up sharply, her surprise apparent. "Of course, Jerry. When should we plan this little discussion?"

Ignoring the evident sarcasm in her tone, Jericho smiled gently. "How about right now?" was his quiet response. "I have a meeting later today and I'm sure you have plans, too, but I can meet you at the house and we can at least make a start." He rose to his feet and waited expectantly.

Belatedly recognizing a long hoped-for opportunity, Elizabeth nodded her assent. Then, as her husband strode from the room, she turned to her father. "You do understand, don't you? When we're finished, I'll come back for dinner and the two of us can go over our own strategy," her eyes sparkled.

"Of course, dear," Schuyler replied. "Perhaps this will be the turning point for you two that we've both prayed for."

As Elizabeth swung into the driveway of their home, the senator's car was already parked in the side drive. When she entered the house the foor to his study stood open, and she heard him call out, "I'm in here, Elizabeth."

As she entered, Jerry turned to meet her, a glass in each hand. "Martini for you, Scotch for me. Right?" he said almost impishly.

Confused, Elizabeth nodded as she accepted the proffered cocktail.

In an abrupt change of tone and mood, he said solemnly as he touched his glass to hers, "To the White House, and to its next First Lady."

After the toast, Elizabeth seated herself on the sofa, and Jericho sat facing her in his favorite high-backed chair. His manner had now become serious and almost businesslike.

"You realize, of course, that this will mean changes for both of us. If we're to succeed I'll need your total support, at least publicly."

Elizabeth smiled sadly. "Really, there's never been a time when you couldn't have had my 'total support,' or anything else you wanted just for the asking."

Jericho winced noticeably and Elizabeth, sensing a possible advantage, rushed on almost breathlessly, "Damn it, Jerry Smith, I love you!" Then almost pleadingly, "Oh, God, I want my husband back!"

In a flat and almost lifeless tone he replied softly, "I'm afraid that's out of the question . . . not possible."

"But why? In God's name, what have I ever done to lose you?"

"My dear Elizabeth," he replied gently, "in reality it's nothing you have or have not done. It's just," he searched for words, "a matter of circumstances gone wrong."

"That's still not an answer," she snapped stubbornly. "I still don't understand."

There was a long silence. Then Jericho rose slowly to his feet and paced around the room. Abruptly, he turned to her.

Almost instinctively, Elizabeth's heart went out to him, as she asked softly, "Oh, Jerry, what is it?"

As he sank into his chair he glanced at the brown envelope he had removed from his pocket. With torment in every line of his face he finally replied, "Elizabeth, I swore that you would never know, but now," he shook his head slowly as though gathering his thoughts, "I feel that you really *have* to be told."

She started to speak but he raised his hand to silence her words.

"My dear, you really must know that my love for you was very real, for all those years before my world went to hell. That was no sham," and he sighed audibly.

"Then, why—" she began, but again he silenced her.

"The answer is here," he said, extracting a card from the envelope and handing it to her. "I'm sure you've seen this before in one or another of the family albums."

When Elizabeth looked at it, she replied instantly, "Of course, it's my mother and father's wedding announcement. But what—"

"This is the second part," he said, handing her the birth record. "Please be careful; I'm afraid it's not very sturdy."

She took the second document and studied it, then looked from one to the other several times before handing them back.

After a long pause, she looked at him and said, "You're telling me that mother had a son before she married my father, aren't you?" Then defiantly, "What the hell difference does that make now?"

"There's more," he replied patiently, dreading his own words. "You never knew it, but Jacob and Martha adopted me when I was about five. All my life I've been known as Jerry, but" he paused to gather courage. "Oh God, Elizabeth. My given name was Jericho."

As the full import of his words struck home, she turned deathly white.

"Oh, my God," she gasped, "You're—" then her words trailed off in silence.

"I'll say it for you," he said bitterly, "your husband is also your half brother."

When Elizabeth spoke again her voice betrayed her attempt at control. "Oh, Jerry, how long have you known?"

"Since I went to Kansas . . . and came back a stranger."

She nodded her acceptance, then moved across the room to stare blindly out the window. Finally, she turned to face him. "I still love you, you know."

"I believe that," he replied sadly. "In some ways I probably still love you."

"Oh, Jerry," she said, her pain echoing in every word, "I *still* want my husband back!"

Jericho shook his head. "We both know that's not allowed."

Elizabeth moved slowly back to the sofa and sank down before asking quietly. "Who else knows about this?"

Jericho considered his answer carefully, then, "Kate knew."

She interrupted almost savagely, "The dead don't count in this. May God forgive me. Who else?"

"Only Monsignor Pignelli," he replied.

"That son of a bitch!" she snarled. "My God, how could you—"

The voice that silenced her outburst was quiet but firm. "Shut up, Elizabeth." He sighed. "I know you don't like him but I've known him for years, and at the time I found those," nodding at the envelope, "he was the only person I could turn to."

"I not only dislike the man," Elizabeth said bitterly, "I don't trust him."

"But I do," he said. "In all this time he has said nothing, not to the world and not to the church." Then, with a bleak smile. "More to the point, however, he can't possibly hurt us without destroying himself."

As Elizabeth digested his words, she nodded slowly. When she spoke again her voice was quite calm and matter of fact. "Well, what do we do now?"

Jericho shrugged. "I suppose we could confess our sin, seek an annulment, and forget the whole thing," he smiled quizzically, "or . . ." he let his voice trail off.

Without the slightest hesitation, Elizabeth picked up the stale Martini and moved to face her husband. Raising her glass she said firmly, "To the White House and to the next President of the United States."

Jericho rose, retrieved the now watery Scotch, and touched her glass. "To the White House," he replied gravely.

After Jericho had put away the documents and left for his meeting, Elizabeth placed a call to her father.

"Daddy, could I take a rain check? I'm really tired . . ." then paused. "Breakfast would be fine. We could have the whole morning for planning."

She paused again. "Jerry? Everything went just fine. I think we really understand each other now. See you in the morning."

As Elizabeth moved up the stairs carrying a fresh martini, her mind was already busy with the details of the approaching campaign.

After his meeting with Elizabeth ended, Jericho returned to Fredricksburg where Molly and the Monsignor waited. When he entered the door they both sensed the deep turmoil that he'd been through, and without so much as asking, Michael Pignelli went to the small bar and prepared a strong scotch for him. Molly had taken his coat and then returned to sit beside him.

"I guess there's really no need to ask how it went," the priest said.

Jericho's smile was forced as he replied. "I'm sure that you both understand that I still have some deep feelings for Elizabeth." He saw the fright in Molly's eyes and pulled her close. "You have nothing to fear." Reassured, Molly nestled in his arms as he continued.

"Seeking the nomination is the only possible way that I can conceive of to partially repay Elizabeth for all the hurt I've caused her. When I looked at her today it literally tore me apart. She hadn't the vaguest idea why I had to turn away from her."

"I presume then that you accepted Schuyler's proposal?"

Jericho nodded. "You're right. I've agreed to run for the Democratic nomination and the next months will be taken over with meetings, finding support, adding additional staff and securing campaign workers across the country. This time it won't be just the state of Kansas, it will be all forty-nine others, as well."

"What can I do to help?" Molly suddenly interjected into the conversation, almost afraid that she'd be left out of the excitement.

"I've slated you to become my personal assistant. You'll travel with the rest of the staff." Then he frowned. "I dislike having you away from Michael," and he sighed, "but with Mrs. Merrill to care for him, I'm sure he'll be just fine."

Molly's eyes sparkled, then just as suddenly she seemed subdued. "Do you think that Elizabeth will object to the fact that you have a woman on your staff?"

"Elizabeth has nothing to say about who I select or who accompanies me. The one and only obligation that she has is to appear with me at the more important functions and, of course, you'll both have to expect Schuyler Martin to be wherever we go trying to run the show.

He paused as a mischievious look came into his eyes. "You know, I might let the old gentleman be my campaign manager. He's acquainted with almost every Governor and State Party Chairman and can certainly open the right doors."

Monsignor Pignelli interrupted. "Jerry, there's one thing you have to remember and that is that both Schuyler and Elizabeth detest me."

"So? Elizabeth wants more than anything to become First Lady and Schuyler wants to 'clean up the White House.' They really have little choice in the matter as to who becomes my closest advisors."

"If it suits you, then it suits me. Now I have to be on my way. Keep me informed." The priest gave Molly a brief kiss on the cheek, shook Jericho's hand and let himself out.

As he turned back to the city he remembered the long ago day when he'd first met Jerry Smith and a smile touched his lips. Thank God he had taken his words of advice and had not entered the priesthood. Then he laughed aloud, realizing that by entering the clergy, even though it was because of the pressures of his old-line Italian-Catholic family, he would soon have his own days of glory.

41

Following his acceptance of Jericho's invitation to serve as his campaign manager, within a short time Schuyler Martin had acquired the services of the best strategists in the business, a research staff beyond compare, and a cadre of campaign workers from all walks of life. He had also made calls, either personally or by telephone, to the Governors of all fifty states, no matter what their party affiliation, seeking additional support for his candidate-to-be.

Then, on a pleasant late summer weekend, Schuyler and Elizabeth had personally gone to Hyannisport for a meeting with Senator Edward Kennedy. During their conversation, the senator had reminisced at length about Jerry's dedication and devotion to his brothers, Jack and Bobby. Because of his own decision not to run, he indicated that he was more than willing to support his colleague.

This was indeed a feather in the cap of the Smith campaign. When the announcement of Jerry's candidacy and Kennedy's endorsement were made public by the *Washington Post*, the story covered the front pages and included file pictures showing Jerry Smith with former President Jack Kennedy in a rather formal pose, and another with Robert Kennedy in a playful mood at the

Kennedy's McLean, Virginia estate. With its appearance in the *Post*, the story was immediately picked up by the wire services and within hours the announcement of the Smith candidacy had blanketed the nation. The first few days that followed were an education to the core of people that Schuyler had assembled and a source of amazement to the newly declared candidate himself.

For days afterward the grass roots response was unlike anything that Schuyler could remember. The few telephone lines that had already been installed were jammed, telegrams came in boxes, and by the second day mail was being delivered in sacks. When the first surge was over, it was apparent that Jericho's candidacy had touched a chord in many people, young and old, and all across the land. The result had been a spontaneous outpouring of support sprinkled with a sampling of statements of opposition and even a few thinly veiled but anonymous threats.

When the two men met to discuss the initial tabulation of results, it was apparent that both had reached the same general conclusions. The grass roots support was stronger than expected, the opposition about normal, and the few threats too insubstantial at that point to be considered serious.

As the campaign got underway and increasingly heavy demands were placed on Jericho's time, he often found himself going for days at a time without seeing his son. He had added Molly as a member of his staff almost immediately after the *Post*'s announcement had appeared, and as time went on he found himself increasingly dependent on her for news of the boy's progress.

After a long and particularly tiring meeting with Schuyler one evening, Jericho, although worn to the bone, left Magnolia Hill and took the road to Fredricksburg. When he arrived, the house was dark. However, when he entered the kitchen he found Molly waiting, clad only in a wispy nightgown, and immediately swept her into his arms. Then Molly placed her hand in his and together they made their way through the darkened house to her bedroom. There, with total lack of ceremony, Jericho removed his clothes and soon they were locked in each other's arms.

When their needs had been satisfied, Molly raised up on one elbow and tenderly kissed her lover. "Do you have any idea how much I miss you?" she whispered against his cheek.

"I could tell," he replied as his hands explored her naked body, his voice husky with emotion. "It's the same for me. I'm so thankful that you're beside me every day. Otherwise we'd seldom see each other, I'm afraid."

"There's something I have to tell you, darling," Molly then murmured softly.

"What is it? Is something wrong with Michael?"

"No, he's fine," she replied, her voice filled with tenderness. "He'll be celebrating his second birthday soon, you know."

"Then what is it?" he persisted.

"I'm pregnant, Jerry."

For a long moment the silence that suddenly filled the room seemed ominous.

"You're absolutely certain?" Jericho asked, his voice strained.

"Yes."

"When is the baby due?"

"In April, seven months from now."

"That's at the height of the campaign," he said almost resignedly.

"I know and I'm so sorry."

"Don't be. We'll work it out someway," and he pulled her into his arms. "I love you, Molly Shannon."

Then once again in the early hours of the morning, they demonstrated their love for each other.

The months passed quickly and eventually Molly's pregnancy became apparent to the other members of the senator's campaign staff. There was considerable speculation among her co-workers as to how a young widow with one fatherless child and no husband could consider bringing another child into the world. The fact that she remained as the senator's trusted aide seemed to inhibit open comment, and her own quiet dignity allowed her to retain their respect.

When Molly elected to take a leave of absence in late January, Jericho, Schuyler, Elizabeth and the rest of the campaign entourge, were preparing to head for New Hampshire and the first battle-ground on the long road to the nomination. As the Party made its preparations, Schuyler was reviewing the latest reports to come in from his native Kansas City, and felt a glow of pride at the reported results. He himself had been instrumental in securing the convention for his home town, and both the city council and the business community were now responding in a manner that would assure the availability of the necessary facilities and support services. The elderly gentleman's satisfaction was boundless.

However, he was less pleased by the fact that Monsignor Pignelli was accompanying the campaign party to New Hampshire. Being something of a pragmatist, Schuyler had privately conceded that the priest's presence could help bring out the Catholic vote, though both he and Elizabeth would have preferred a different cleric. Only Jericho was aware that Father Pignelli had a second function . . . that of providing an unobstrusive link with Molly Shannon.

As the day approached for their departure, the only dampening to the general feeling of euphoria were the increasing attacks by the right-wing press and an accompanying increase in both the number and severity of the physical threats made against the candidate. Jericho had dismissed the threats almost contemptuously as the outpourings of the lunatic fringe, but his campaign manager reacted more practically and had informed the Secret Service.

When the campaign in New Hampshire was over, Jericho's first victory seemed almost too easy. Later analysis indicated that his support had come from all age groups, but particularly from the young who appeared to regard him as a second Bobby Kennedy, and from senior citizens who viewed him as the potential saviour of their Social Security and Medicare benefits.

It was while Jericho was campaigning in Iowa that he received word from the Monsignor that Molly had given birth to a baby girl.

That evening, in a small wayside motel in a seamy part of Des Moines, Jericho had telephoned her. "Darling," he said, "how are you?"

Molly's eyes opened wide at the sound of his familiar voice and she moved to a more comfortable position in the hospital bed. "I must have fallen asleep," she murmured into the phone.

"You don't sound like yourself," Jericho said. "Are you sure everything's all right?"

"I'm just tired," she replied. "How soon will you be home?"

"Soon, I hope. My main concern right now is you. How did it go?"

"It was far more difficult than I'd anticipated. The baby delivered so fast that they didn't have time to prepare me properly and the doctor has already told me that I shouldn't have any more children."

Jericho could visualize the tears in her eyes from the tone of her voice.

"Please don't worry about that," he replied gently. "Right now we have all we need, a healthy mother and two healthy children." Then his voice took on an intimate note. "You know. As the old song says, *A boy for you and a girl for me.*"

Molly had to smile as she questioned once again, "When will you be coming home? I've asked Father Pignelli but he doesn't seem to know."

"We have to wind things up here and then I'll be back. I'm sure that you should be home by then." Then, very quietly, "Don't forget for a minute that I love you, Molly Shannon."

Tears of happiness streamed down her cheeks and she managed, "I love you, too," as their conversation ended.

When Jericho had replaced the telephone he crossed to the window and looked out into the gathering dusk. From his vantage point he could discern the three young men placed inconspicuously at strategic points along the street, and knew that there were others whom he couldn't see. He shook his head as he turned away to pick up a sheaf of papers.

"Damned security is getting to be a nuisance," he muttered to himself. "A man can hardly have any privacy."

It had been bad enough at the beginning, but since the incident in the Senate Office building, the security around him had become almost oppressive. A man in his middle thirties and armed with a hand gun had somehow eluded the normal checkpoints, and had subsequently been found and taken into custody in the hall outside of Jericho's office. While he had been out of town at the time, the affair had triggered an immediate increase in his Secret Service contingent.

Jericho sighed as he turned to the stack of unfinished work that awaited him. The increased security was just one more problem to be dealt with after his return to Washington.

By the time Jericho arrived back in the nation's capitol, Molly and the new baby had already returned home.

His first stop, of necessity, had been at campaign headquarters for a brief meeting with Schuyler. While there, he also touched base with Monsignor Pignelli. After the priest informed him that Molly, on the insistence of her physician, had been accompanied by a private nurse when she left the hospital, he realized that she must have experienced a difficult time indeed.

As soon as he could, Jericho, accompanied by the priest who had insisted on making the trip with him, had slipped unnoticed out a little used side entrance. With Father Pignelli at the wheel, the two men had taken the road to Fredricksburg in silence.

They were well on their way when Jericho suddenly threw back his head and laughed aloud.

The priest glanced at him curiously. "May I share the joke?"

"Of course," his friend nodded. "It just occurred to me that if anyone misses me I'll undoubtedly catch hell when we get back."

"But why should you?"

"Just think, my friend," the senator chuckled, "No Secret Service!"

For a long moment the priest was silent. Then he himself chuckled softly. "Might I suggest that we go in the same way that we left? That should work, at least this once."

The senator nodded and then lapsed once more into silence, apparently intent on his own private thoughts.

Mrs. Merrill, the housekeeper, opened the door and greeted the two men warmly, but Jericho had noticed the concern in her eyes. "I'm so glad that you're here," she said and stepped aside so the priest and Jericho could enter.

"Where's Molly?" Jericho asked.

"I'll have her come out," giving him a knowing smile.

"Thanks, Mrs. Merrill, you show good judgment."

In a short time, with the assistance of the housekeeper, Molly came slowly down the hall and at the sight of her Jericho was touched to the quick. The smile she gave the two men was forced and it was obvious she was still suffering the after affects of a difficult birth.

Jericho went to her side and placed his arm around her waist to support her as he helped her into a comfortable chair.

"I'm sorry," she murmured as she looked up into his eyes.

"You're sorry!" he said darkly as he turned to the priest. "Michael, why didn't you call me?"

The priest shrugged. "She wouldn't let me."

"But why?"

It was Molly who answered his question. "Jerry, it was far more important that you remain in Iowa. Had you come back because of me, tongues would have started to wag and you know what that could mean."

Jericho considered her answer, knowing that she was right. "You know, there are some days I wish to hell that we weren't living a lie," he said, "and that I didn't feel so damned obligated to Elizabeth."

"But the nomination is what's important," Molly replied, smiling sweetly. "Remember, Jerry, I've listened to all of your dreams. I know you want them to become a reality, and so do I!"

At that moment the nurse came bustling into the room, the baby cradled in her arms. She handed the baby to Molly before hurrying off.

Once assured that they were alone, Molly said softly, "Would you like to see your daughter?" and she gently removed the blanket from the sleeping child's face.

Tenderly, Jericho took his daughter in his arms as a sense of well being swept over him. He turned to Molly and the priest. "Isn't she beautiful?" he said, then knelt beside Molly and kissed her deeply.

The priest hurried to the bar where he noisily prepared their usual scotches to provide the new parents an opportunity to spend a few moments alone.

Later, after Molly had summoned the nurse to take the baby back to the nursery, Jericho asked. "Are you nursing Ashley?"

Molly shook her head. "No, I couldn't this time, and in a way I'm not sorry." The expression on her face became more animated than it had been since their arrival. "You see, when I'm back on my feet I intend to rejoin the campaign. I'll not miss out on the last exciting months simply because I had to take a detour."

"Are you sure that won't be too much for you?"

"Mrs. Merrill is very capable with Michael and I'm sure that she will also be able to care for the baby, especially since I've engaged a cleaning service so she's relieved of that chore," and Molly blushed slightly. "I might add Senator, that you're very generous."

"And why shouldn't I be?" Jericho demanded.

"Every day that passes," Molly said softly, "I'm blessed because you care. Most men in your position would have cast me aside long before now."

"But I'm not 'most men,' Molly." Then softly, "I happen to be in love with you, and I care deeply about our children. Not even the presidency with all its demands could change that."

42

Now the states of Oregon and California loomed ahead, and everyone was aware that the Golden State, with its large number of electoral votes, could equal the strong support the Senator had won in the industrial strongholds of Ohio and Michigan. Even the Southern states which Jericho had visited only sporadically, and which were heavily populated by senior citizens and retirees had gone his way, so it wasn't too surprising that his staff was almost overly confident that their candidate would win the coveted nomination.

On the road, Schuyler and Elizabeth kept mainly to themselves and away from the throngs of people that always seemed to surround Jericho. Elizabeth, however, was always available and by her husband's side at every important function. From all appearances, they seemed to be a happily married couple who enjoyed each other to the fullest.

When Elizabeth appeared on her husband's behalf before the Democratic women's organizations, her concern for his welfare was evident and it became obvious to Jericho that, when she had given him her promise to stand beside him, she'd thrown herself into the campaign with no reservations.

Both her father and Jericho had complimented her but Elizabeth kept her feelings hidden, since it was becoming increasingly difficult for her to ignore the closeness that existed between her husband, the priest, and Molly Shannon.

From the long ago remembered days of 1968 when Jericho had accompanied Robert Kennedy on his ill-fated trip, he had insisted that their headquarters be housed in the Ambassador Hotel. It was with some reluctance that his wishes were acceded to. The security measures surrounding him were even tighter than before. The final days of the campaign were now at hand, and after the long and tiring months of parading up and down the streets and highways of the nation's cities, shaking hands and listening to everyone's needs, Jericho was glad that the time was drawing near when he could see the end.

If it hadn't been for Molly and Michael Pignelli, who had provided him with some degree of normalcy along the way, there were times when he had literally felt like throwing in the towel. Yet, always in the recesses of his mind, was the relentless nagging of his obligation to Elizabeth.

The day prior to the California primary, Jericho, with Elizabeth and Schuyler Martin and his normal retinue of secret service agents and aides, had appeared at several rallys in the rich precincts of Beverly Hills and Orange County as well as the blue collar worker's stronghold. It was almost the identical route that his friend Robert Kennedy had taken. And, like Bobby, he had waded into the crowds to become a part of them much to everyone's dismay. At every stop, Jericho was greeted by both city fathers and crowds that he'd never thought possible, but he was quick to realize that this was fabulous, unpredictable California.

After a long, hot and tiring day, they had finally returned to the Ambassador. After a briefing with his advisors he had excused himself and gone to Monsignor Pignelli's quarters. There he found Molly and the priest watching television.

When he entered the room Molly jumped to her feet and went to him. "I'm assuming that it went well," she said. "Now how about a drink to help you relax?"

"That I'd welcome," he said and slumped into a nearby chair, his eyes glued to the television screen as Michael Pignelli got up to mix his drink.

"Would you care to tell me about it?" Molly asked, "or am I to

believe everything that the media says?'' and she laughed. Then,
"Elizabeth seemed to be enjoying herself," she added without any
trace of bitterness.

"She's done one helluva job. I really can't give the lady enough
credit," and he turned to look into Molly's eyes. "I'm only sorry
that it couldn't have been you."

"Thanks, Jerry, you don't know how much that means to me."

"Now all we have to do is wait," and he sighed, "but I'd sure
like to get away from all this for a few hours. Think there's a
chance?"

Pignelli spoke up. "Let me see what I can do," and he went to
the telephone where he held a long, drawn out conversation. When
he returned his eyes sparkled. "You didn't know it," he said,
addressing Jericho, "but you're going to Mass."

Jericho smiled. "That's not such a bad idea. And where is it?"

"The beach, a very private beach. I do have connections in this
town," and the priest chuckled. "However, we'll both have to go
with you. After all, we're known as The Three Musketeers. What a
group!" and he laughed as Jericho and Molly joined in.

"How soon can we go?"

"Any time. The car will be waiting at the kitchen service
entrance."

For only a moment Jericho felt a trace of apprehension. That
had been the exact spot where his friend had met his death, but
soon shrugged off the feeling. Obviously, lightning would never
strike the same place twice.

"I'll have to change into something more casual," he said and
left the room, tailed as always by a secret service agent.

When they met at the kitchen entrance another agent appeared
and announced that he was to be their driver.

"Can't get away with anything," Jericho said in obvious disgust.

"Sorry, sir, it's regulations."

"I know. Let's go."

The priest joined the driver in front while Jericho and Molly
entered the back of the car where they sat at a respectable distance
from one another. The car's windows were shaded a dark grey
enabling the occupants to look out, but allowing no one to see in.
Once on the freeway Jericho began to feel more at ease, and after a

short drive they left the heavily traveled highway and approached a guarded gate.

When the uniformed attendant approached the driver's window the agent produced his identification, and as the electric gate swung open they passed through. As soon as the car came to a stop the four occupants poured out.

Monsignor Pignelli, knowing that Molly and Jericho needed to be alone, engaged his companion in conversation and they trailed along behind at a distance where the conversation between the Senator and his companion couldn't be heard.

The gentle lapping of the water against the shoreline and the coolness of the evening breeze gave Jericho a sense of well being. He luxuriated in the quiet and took Molly's hand in his as they strolled along the beach. "Have you talked with Mrs. Merrill today?" he asked.

"Of course. The baby's fine and Michael wants us to come home," Molly replied, her eyes brimming with tears. "I do miss them so," and she made an effort to muffle a sob that somehow escaped.

Jericho drew her into his arms, not really caring if anyone should see them. However, the priest was going his part exceedingly well for the two men were engaged in a discussion of religion, and that tool had never before failed the Monsignor. Only once had his companion looked up, but by then Jericho and Molly were moving toward them as darkness was descending on the deserted strip of sand.

"Ready to go?" Pignelli asked.

"If you are," Jericho replied.

"Fine with me. How about you?" and he turned to the agent.

"Whatever the senator says. It is getting rather late."

Once again they entered the privacy of the car, and in the darkness of the California night they returned to the Ambassador for one last night of waiting.

The voter turnout in the California primary election proved to be much heavier than had been expected, and as the day dragged on Jericho's first feelings of confidence began to wane.

Schuyler Martin moved like a whirling dervish in an effort to keep tabs on the various activities taking place and Elizabeth soon became alarmed at her father's almost fanatical pace since he was now well into his seventies. However, when she asked him to slow down, he had actually laughed at her misgivings, his eagle bright eyes reflecting his enthusiasm.

"Slow down?" he had said. "My God, Elizabeth," and it seemed to her almost contemptuously, "I love what's happening. These past months have made me want to live again and if I die with my boots on, then I'll at least die happy!"

When Schuyler had mentioned death Elizabeth had almost collapsed. She couldn't possibly envision life without him and, since she had become a wife in name only, she was aware that she would literally have no one when he was gone.

"Oh yes," she murmured to herself, "Jerry will show me the proper amount of respect and sympathy but once my father is in his grave he'll quickly forget that I exist, even after all Schuyler's done for him."

So, on this momentous day which could eventually lead her to the White House, Elizabeth Martin Smith didn't really give much of a damn whether the Californians voted for her husband or not.

Molly Shannon, Monsignor Pignelli and Jericho remained closeted in his quarters for most of the day while his staff came and went sporadically. The television had been turned on so they wouldn't miss out on a newsbreak, should one occur.

Late that afternoon Molly had ordered room service to bring a light supper to the suite since the lot of them had existed mainly on black coffee all that day, and she knew that it was important that Jericho have solid nourishment to fortify him for the long night ahead. Once the food had been served, Molly, with the insistence of Michael Pignelli, urged Jericho to eat although he vigorously denied that he was the least bit hungry. However, he devoured everything that was placed before him and when he had finished, Molly suggested that he take a nap.

"Sleep?" he said, looking at her as though she had suddenly lost her mind. "Now?"

"Yes, Jerry, now," she'd replied firmly while the priest nodded his approval.

For a moment he hesitated.

"Come on Jerry, a few short winks will do you a world of

good,'' the Monsignor urged.

"Well, if you really think so,'' he replied and headed for the bedroom. "You'll be sure to wake me?'' he asked before he disappeared behind the door.

"I'll personally see to that, Senator,'' Molly said. "It would give me a great deal of pleasure.''

When Molly and the priest were quite alone they remained silent, deep in their own thoughts. Then Molly kicked off her shoes and within minutes she, too, was fast asleep, while the good father, like a faithful shepherd, watched over his flock.

When seven o'clock rolled around, the designated time for the polls to close, Molly, who had awakened earlier, went to the bedroom door, entered and closed the door behind her. As she approached the bed she saw that Jericho was still asleep. She bent down to kiss him gently. At the touch of her lips his eyes flew open and then he smiled and pulled her down beside him.

"What time is it?'' he asked.

"Seven. The polls have just closed. You have plenty of time.''

"Has Schuyler been around?''

"No, but he did call to tell me that he'll be spending the evening with Elizabeth to hear the returns.''

"Good, that gives us some time,'' and they began to make love.

In the outer room, Monsignor Pignelli was fending off Jericho's staff and trying to answer the continual ring of the telephone. For a man now in his mid-sixties he'd been blessed with the energy of a much younger man and because of his experience on the campaign trail he had learned very quickly which calls needed immediate attention and which were from mere curiosity seekers. When a brief respite came, the Monsignor went to the bedroom door and knocked softly. It was Molly who answered.

"You'd both better get out here,'' Pignelli said softly.

"I just got out of the shower and Jerry's gone in. I'll be with you shortly.''

Within minutes Molly appeared, fully dressed, eyes sparkling like jewels.

"Have a good rest?'' the priest asked pointedly.

"Now, Michael,'' Molly remonstrated with good humor. "You know that Jerry needed a little pep talk and frankly, so did I. He'll look and act like a new man when you see him.''

The priest's laughter was spontaneous as he knew exactly what she meant.

And Molly was right, for the Senator returned to the sitting room with every hair in place, dressed in a conservative and freshly pressed Navy suit, sparkling white shirt and a striped tie, with an expression on his face as though he could lick the world.

"Ah, I see Molly's right," the older man said.

"Right about what?" Jericho asked.

"The pep talk you needed!" he said slyly.

"How true," Jericho replied, a slight smile touching his lips, not the least bit offended by his friend's remark. "Now, fill me in on what's been happening," he said as he lowered his tall frame into one of the hard straight-backed chairs. "God, how I wish this hotel would provide some decent furniture," he complained, then directed his attention to Molly and the priest.

Monsignor Pignelli glanced at Molly who was obviously champing at the bit to give Jericho the news, and he nodded for her to proceed.

"Jerry," she said and paused, "the networks are projecting you the winner," and waited expectantly for his reaction.

"Are you sure?" he said, almost afraid to believe her.

"Of course we're sure," she replied emphatically.

At that precise moment Schuyler Martin, accompanied by Elizabeth, came marching into the room much like a grand marshal at a parade.

"Jerry," he bellowed and lunged toward his son-in-law, enveloping him in a bear hug. "We've won!"

Although Elizabeth had a smile on her lips it was apparent that she really felt rather ill at ease at having barged into her husband's headquarters.

"Mrs. Smith," Molly said pleasantly as she moved to her side, "congratulations!"

"Thanks, Mrs. Shannon," Elizabeth replied and the smile she gave Molly seemed almost grudging. "The Senator certainly has to thank you and the Monsignor for all the help you've given him." Then, "I'm certain that you'll both be well rewarded," her last remark was caustic.

Molly merely smiled and returned to take her place beside Jericho.

The Senator smiled his appreciation and then turned his attention to his wife who seemed so very much an outsider. Jericho got up from the chair where he'd been sitting, moved to her side and brushed her cheek with a kiss. "Well, old girl," he said taking her hand, "it looks as though we're on our way to the Convention."

"How nice," Elizabeth replied, a definite coolness to her voice.

"I'll need you with me tonight when the announcement is made," and he paused. "You will be available?"

Schuyler Martin interrupted. "Of course she'll be there," and the look he gave Jericho was one of defiance. "Now, Elizabeth," he continued "let's get back to our suite. I'm sure that Jerry and the staff have plenty to do." Then he asked. "By the way, have you given any thought to a running mate."

"We've tossed a few names around if that's what you mean, and know that it's important we pull in the Southern vote so we may possibly go that route. However, the final decision will come later."

"Good thinking. Now, if you'll excuse me," and taking his daughter firmly by the arm he sailed out of the room, resembling an aged king with his young queen.

By ten o'clock the majority of the returns had been tabulated and it was officially declared that Senator Jerry Smith from Kansas was the winner. The Smith headquarters at the Ambassador was overflowing with excited staff, security personnel, close friends and associates who had supported the Senator. The ballroom at the hotel had been filled for several hours and as the time for Jericho's appearance drew near, he asked Molly and the Monsignor to join him for a private moment.

When they were sequestered in his bedroom, both Molly and the priest noticed a certain uneasiness in his manner.

"What is it Jerry?" Molly asked.

Jericho moved restlessly about the room and then stopped in front of the window to look out at the lights of the City of Angels. When he returned they saw the pain reflected in his eyes.

"Oh, how I wish you were my wife," he whispered against Molly's cheek.

"It's all right, Jerry. Elizabeth needs to be First Lady but I will always remember that she'll be the First Lady of the country," and she smiled securely, "while I'll be the First Lady in your life."

The private moment was shattered by a knock at the door.

Monsignor Pignelli answered. "Yes?"

"They're calling for the Senator," an aide replied. "Is anything wrong?"

The priest gave him his most patronizing smile.

"Wrong? Now why would you say that? Everything's just as we planned. The Senator will be joining you shortly," and he closed the door.

Michael Pignelli turned back to his friends. "The time is now." Then he paused, a contemplative look creeping into his eyes. "I'll be with you every step of the way."

Molly immediately placed a call to Schuyler Martin's suite and advised him that he and Elizabeth should join the Senator and his party in the ante room adjacent to the ballroom. That done, she picked up the speech that Jericho had prepared and slipped it into her briefcase.

"All set?" she asked brightly.

Jericho nodded and left the suite to begin his walk into history.

Secret Service agents surrounded the small group as they entered the elevator which had been reserved for the Senator's use and they were quickly whisked to the ballroom floor. Before they alighted a sweep was made of the path that Jericho would take and when everything proved in order, they moved down the hall and entered the room that Molly had designated. There they found Schuyler and Elizabeth waiting.

Elizabeth Smith had changed from the rather severe suit she'd worn that day into a striking yet understated electric blue gown; her hair had been freshly styled and her makeup was impeccable. The one flaw in her appearance, and noticeable only to Molly, was her bitterness toward Michael Pignelli.

The music from the orchestra filled the room and the excited voices of the crowd were heard, but it was Schuyler Martin's enthusiasm that helped everyone relax.

"This is going to be a great show," he said and slapped Jericho on the shoulder. "You've made me proud, son."

"Thanks, Schuyler," Jericho replied.

Within a matter of minutes, Schuyler was called to give the opening remarks and with a sparkle in his eyes the old war horse strode regally onto the stage, acknowledging with dignity the greetings of the crowd.

Schuyler had made a point of having his speech brief since it was Jerry the crowd was waiting to hear. He held up his hands to stem the flow of applause and when it died down he paused for a moment as a sudden wave of emotion swept over him.

When he began to speak his voice was filled with emotion. "Good friends," he began, and a wave of applause rippled through the ballroom. When the room quieted, he started again, "Tonight we celebrate a momentous victory, not only for our candidate, but for all of you who have followed loyally in his path over the past months."

Once again, clapping, catcalls and whistles erupted.

"This evening," Schuyler continued, "if you'll bear with me, I want to give you a brief," and he chuckled, then said, "I do mean brief," and at this remark good-natured laughter erupted, "background of my long relationship with Senator Smith. Most of you are aware that Jerry is my son-in-law, the husband of my daughter, Elizabeth. However, many years before Jerry became a member of our family, I had the opportunity to get to know our candidate when he was an undergraduate at Notre Dame and the roommate of my son, Brandy. Over these intervening years I've had the distinct privilege of watching Jerry Smith develop, from a novice in the political arena to a true master, and through these decades he's remained not only true to himself but loyal to the people who share his life. Most of all, he's a man who believes with all his heart that he can help our country move ahead and become a better place for all of us."

As an echo of applause sounded, he turned to look into the wings where Jericho waited. Then he faced the crowd and smiled broadly. "It is with the greatest pleasure that I present to you the next Democratic nominee for President of the United States, Senator Jerry Smith."

Sheer bedlam rocked the ballroom and the almost frantic chanting started.

"JERRY, JERRY, JERRY."

In the wings, Jericho nervously straightened his tie and ran a hand through his hair. Then, with a smile on his lips and the same enthusiasm he'd shown throughout the long months of the campaign, he strode to the center of the stage where he shook Schuyler's hand and then moved to take a position at the podium, smiling and waving to his supporters.

Some twenty minutes elapsed before Jericho was able to quiet the crowd and finally he was able to speak.

"First, I want to thank Schuyler Martin for his introduction," and he smiled slightly. "I hope that I can live up to his expectations."

Then his look became serious. "Perhaps it's time for me to acknowledge just how important this nomination is to me. I'm very much aware that we still face the convention in July and that there are other candidates, all of whom have excellent qualifications. However," and his eyes swept over the crowd, "I'm following in the footsteps and beliefs of a great man whom I had the privilege of calling 'friend.' I was also a member of his staff and it seems almost ironic that twenty years later I stand on the same stage and at the same podium where he stood in 1968. Some of you are too young to remember that era, but to others of my vintage I'm sure you will never forget."

Jericho paused while all eyes remained fixed on him. "Now it's late; it's time for celebration and time for me to thank you once again for the long hours you've devoted on my behalf. I won't promise you the moon," and he laughed slightly, "we've already been there. However, I'll give you my best, surround myself with knowledgeable and capable advisors, but most of all," and he paused, his eyes sweeping over the crowd, "I'll be your friend, and you'll be mine."

The rafters of the Ambassador shook with applause as Jericho moved to one side of the podium. At that point, Elizabeth, Brandy, Sky, Monsignor Pignelli, Schuyler, Molly and the other staff members joined him on stage.

With confidence, Elizabeth took her place beside him and together they joined hands and held their arms aloft in a sign of victory.

Then one by one, the members of his staff came forward and he introduced each one to the crowd. Once again he approached the podium and Elizabeth took her place beside him.

"Thank you, enjoy yourselves; you deserve it, and good night."

Amid thunderous applause, Jericho and Elizabeth moved to the front of the stage as the band began to play *Happy Days Are Here Again*.

Overwhelmed by the emotion of the moment, Elizabeth moved to Jericho and embraced him. Then the sound of a single shot rang out and suddenly the shining electric blue gown that Elizabeth Martin Smith had elected to wear in that triumphant moment was covered with blood. Her head fell to one side as horror and shock contorted Jericho's face as for what seemed an eternity he held her limp body in his arms.

43

The following hours were ones fraught with rage, sadness, despair and chaos.

Secret Service agents had literally dragged Jericho from the stage, leaving Monsignor Pignelli, Molly and Jericho's staff to face the steady stream of reporters and television cameras.

Schuyler Martin had forced his way into the ambulance and had accompanied his darling Elizabeth to the hospital, but upon their arrival he had been physically restrained from entering the room where she lay.

"She's my daughter," he had bellowed at the top of his lungs like an enraged bull.

"We know, Mr. Martin," one of the hospital staff replied calmly, having been faced in the past by other angry parents, and then very matter of factly had rolled up Schuyler's shirt sleeve and given him a shot. In a matter of minutes he appeared more subdued, although the sedative hadn't taken its usual quick effect.

"Where's her husband?" he asked, eyes starting to glaze.

"We don't know, sir," was the quiet response.

"Oh, God," he muttered, "why Elizabeth?"

Then suddenly his head fell to one side and mercifully he slept.

* * *

In the same small ante room that they had shared only minutes before, Jericho, surrounded by secret service agents, sat with head bowed.

A knock sounded at the door and one of the agents drew his gun before answering. "Yes?" he said, as he cracked open the door.

"It's Monsignor Pignelli and Mrs. Shannon," the priest stated.

The agent recognized them and opened the door to allow the priest and Molly to rush to Jericho's side.

"Son," the priest said quietly, "what can we do to help?"

Jericho did not reply and Molly moved forward.

"Senator, this is Molly Shannon," and at the sound of her voice Jericho raised his head and it was then that they saw the look of total destruction written on his face. He reached for Molly's hand as she knelt beside him.

"Why?" he managed. "Why?"

Quietly Molly answered. "We have no idea, Senator."

"Is she dead?" he asked, staring from one to the other.

It was Michael Pignelli who answered.

"Yes, Jerry. Elizabeth is gone. She knew nothing."

Shaking his head, the senator lapsed once more into silence.

While the secret service, the Los Angeles SWAT team and hotel security people futilely scoured the building and its grounds, at the hospital the hastily assembled coroner's team had determined the exact cause of Elizabeth's death. A single small calibre high velocity bullet had struck the upper back, penetrated the chest cavity and then had fragmented, rupturing the heart and collapsing the left lung. Death, it appeared, had been almost instantaneous. One of the team, as he looked at the collection of fragments that had been so painstakingly removed, shook his head in disgust. To no one in particular he said, "The lab will have one hell of a time making anything out of this."

As the weary crew left the hospital they were besieged by cameras and reporters. When the noise subsided, their spokesman said firmly, "I'll make a short statement at this time. There will be *no* questions." He paused and glanced at his notes. "Mrs. Smith died as the result of a wound inflicted by a single small calibre bullet that entered the chest cavity from the back. In our opinion, death was instantaneous. We have no further information at this time."

Several reporters started to speak, but were quickly silenced.

"As I said," the man continued patiently, "there will be no questions at this time. Additional information will be released from the Coroner's office after lab tests are completed."

Back at the hotel, security teams were escorting the senator and his party back to their respective quarters. Since the exhaustive search had revealed nothing, security was even tighter and additional agents were assigned to the suits of the senator and his chief aides, while Los Angeles plainclothes police kept a watchful eye on corridors, stairwells and elevators. Even Schuyler Martin, still at the hospital, was under surveillance although he was, for the moment, quite unaware of it. As dawn broke over the City of Angels, the members of the senator's party, with the sole exception of Father Pignelli, who was on his knees beside his bed, were finally experiencing at least some semblance of sleep.

It was well after eleven when Jericho finally awoke from his sleep of exhaustion. For a moment he couldn't place where he was, but then the flood of memory surged over him and a sob of pure rage caught at his throat. Finally, almost out of habit, he moved to the bath and went through his normal ritual.

When Jericho came out of the bathroom he was greeted by a young man whom he did not recognize.

"Dan Jackson, sir. Secret Service," he introduced himself.

"You're new, aren't you?" Jericho asked.

"Yes, sir. I came in with the detachment that arrived from Washington this morning." He paused, then "We were sent out after word came in that we'd be needed. I'm very sorry, Senator."

"We all are," Jericho replied sadly. "Now," he continued in a more businesslike manner. "Please fill me in on what's been happening."

The young man picked up a pad from the table and glanced down the list, obviously selecting the order of the items.

"The President called. He'll be calling again at two o'clock Los Angeles time."

Jericho nodded.

"Mr. Martin called. He's back in his suite and would like to see you at your convenience."

Almost impatiently, Jericho interrupted. "Have someone call

Schuyler and ask him to meet me here as soon as possible. I want him here when the President calls. And have someone order breakfast sent up for two.''

"Yes, sir.'' The young man passed a hastily scribbled message to an associate and then continued. "Monsignor Pignelli asked that you call when it's convenient.''

The Senator scribbled a note, then said, "For now, he'll have to wait. Next?''

"Mrs. Shannon called. She asked me to tell you that she'd like to return to Washington. Unless, of course,'' he added, "you still need her here.''

"Good idea,'' Jericho nodded, "I'll inform security and clear it as soon as we've finished. We'll send most of the staff back, too; anything else?''

"Several calls from the network. I put them off.''

"Good.''

"A number of calls from prominent politicians. I've made a list and told them you'd get back to them.''

The Senator nodded approvingly. "I'd say you've done quite well.''

"Thank you, sir,'' then "nothing else seems that important. I'll give this to one of your aides and you can review it whenever you have time.''

Jericho smiled for the first time.

"Thank you, Mr. Jackson.'' Then he moved to the telephone and picked it up. "Where can I reach your security chief?''

After receiving clearance from the senior agent, Jericho called Molly, his manner almost brusque. "Mrs. Shannon? Senator Smith here. I've checked with the Secret Service and they've approved your suggestion.'' He paused and then smiled gently. "I know that. I do, too.''

He listened and responded quietly. "That will be fine. Get the staff together and make the necessary arrangements. I'll see you back there. We still have some things to finish here so it may be a day or two.''

Schuyler Martin, looking older and tired, was admitted just as Jericho replaced the phone. For a long moment the two men regarded each other in silence and compassion.

Then with evident effort Schuyler spoke. "Oh, Jerry, why now when the dream was so close?'' tears forming in his eyes.

"I can't answer that, my friend,'' Jericho replied past the lump in his throat. "Come on, let's have some breakfast.''

The older man sighed. "Yes, I know that we have to,'' his manner resigned.

As the two men sat over coffee, Schuyler looked up. "I've taken the liberty of contacting the coroner's office. They've released,'' he cleared his throat, "Elizabeth, and I've made the necessary arrangements.''

Tears came to Jericho's eyes. "That was no liberty, Schuyler; that was your right, and I thank you for it.''

Neither had heard the shrilling of the telephone.

When they looked up Dan Jackson was there with the phone in his hand. "It's for you, Senator. The President.''

"Thank you,'' and Jericho took the instrument as the young man moved away.

"Good afternoon, sir.''

He listened for a moment as tears came to his eyes, then, "Thank you, Mr. President; I appreciate that.'' Then, "Yes, he is. Would you like to speak with him?''

Jericho nodded and handed the phone to his father-in-law. "The President,'' he whispered.

Schuyler Martin automatically straightened his shoulders as he accepted. "Yes, Mr. President?''

There was a long silence, then, "Yes, it's been a real shock and we appreciate your call.'' He paused briefly, then replied, "I'm certain of that, and thank you,'' handing the phone back to Jericho.

"Yes, Mr. President? Then, "That's correct, sir. Most of the staff should be on the way back by now.''

As Jericho listened, mixed expressions flickered across his face and he finally replied. "Thank you very much, sir. We'll be ready. Tomorrow morning at six? That will be fine. We'll be there. Goodbye, sir.''

As Jericho hung up the phone he looked at Schuyler and said very quietly, "Well, I'll be damned.''

"What?'' Schuyler said, looking puzzled.

"The President has dispatched a plane.''

The older man's head came up as he stared at his companion.

"You're kidding!"

"No," Jericho replied. "Air Force One will be available for boarding tomorrow morning at six."

"Air Force One?" and Schuyler shook his head. "Well, I'll be damned."

Jericho chuckled gently. "You, too?"

"But not for the same reason," Schuyler responded. "I usually don't agree with him, but I always give the devil his due. That man is a master politician who always knows exactly what he's doing."

"Really, Schuyler," Jericho protested, but the older man merely smiled.

When Jericho finally remembered to call Father Pignelli there was no answer, and when he checked with the desk he was informed that the priest had left with the rest of the staff earlier in the day. He had, however, left a message that he would see the Senator in Washington. It was, therefore, only Jericho and Schuyler who shared a quiet dinner later that evening in the Senator's suite.

44

With the area under heavy security, the Senator's party had boarded the flght in the pre-dawn half-light at Los Angeles International Airport. Jericho and Schuyler had watched together in silence as the plain but elegant solid mahogany casket that would carry their Elizabeth home was loaded, and as the compartment door closed, Schuyler crossed himself and briefly bowed his head.

Then he turned to his son-in-law. "It's better this way, Jerry," he said quietly. "Just the three of us going home together." Then his voice took on a slight tremor. "For this, we really didn't need all those others."

Jericho, for once unable to speak, could only nod in silent agreement as the two men joined hands in quiet understanding. Then the moment had passed and they turned to board the waiting plane.

Once aboard, the flight crew took over with quiet precision. Jericho and Schuyler, with a single secret service agent, were escorted to the spacious center compartment, while the balance of the passengers were seated in the forward cabin. The quarters reserved for the president were not to be used, but the door had been opened briefly and then closed before takeoff.

An hour out of Los Angeles they had been served a light

breakfast, and after the trays had been cleared away Schuyler had gotten up to wander restlessly around the compartment. Jericho had watched in silence as his father-in-law opened the door to the President's compartment to drink in its restrained elegance.

When he returned to his seat he smiled gently and said, "I was thinking of Elizabeth," and paused. "I only wish she could have been seen this."

Jericho nodded. "She certainly deserved that if anyone did," he replied softly and once again the two men lapsed into silence.

It was the older man who finally broke that silence once more. "Honestly, Jerry, I still don't really understand why it had to be Elizabeth?"

He shook his head slowly from side to side and then looked almost apologetically at his son-in-law. "You'll have to excuse an old man, Jerry," his eyes clouding, "it's hard for me to accept that she's really gone."

The Senator had been sitting, elbows on knees, with his head in his hands and as he raised his face the pure anguish that was written there struck Schuyler like a blow.

"My God, Schuyler, it shouldn't have been her," and he paused as though to gather courage. Then, flatly, "That bullet wasn't meant for her. I'm the one who should be dead," and he turned away to stare out the window.

When the older man replied, his voice was strong and very gentle. "Everyone knows that, Jerry, including me, but it doesn't make it any easier. I guess I was just looking for comfort. I certainly don't blame you for what's happened," and he reached out comfortingly to touch his shoulder.

Avoiding the contact almost automatically, Jericho rose to his feet and paced back and forth in the confines of the cabin, using the exertion to restore some measure of control. When he faced Schuyler to respond his face was almost expressionless and his voice was flat. "I appreciate that, Schuyler." Then his voice cracked as he continued with an almost sardonic chuckle, "God willing, I may even be able to find a way to stop blaming myself."

Schuyler started to protest, but as Jericho moved away to take a seat by the window on the far side of the cabin, he decided to let the matter rest. It was, he concluded, probably inevitable for Jerry to be going through some feelings of guilt, even though they were unwarranted. Better to deal with that later, if there was still a need to do so.

He felt a touch on his shoulder and looked up into his eyes of the agent who had been assigned to their cabin.

"Everything okay here?" he asked.

Schuyler nodded. "Yes, as good as can be expected."

The young man nodded in understanding. "Would you like coffee, or perhaps a drink?"

"No, thanks," he smiled slightly, "I think what I really need is a nap," and he leaned back and closed his eyes, leaving the young man to his own devices.

During the balance of the flight into Andrews, there was little conversation. Schuyler, although emotionally exhausted, dozed only fitfully. Somewhere deep inside was a knot of pain that would not dissolve.

As for Jericho, the death of his wife, and particularly its circumstances, had stirred within him a remnant of the love they had once known. Countless memories arose almost unbidden as he relived the good days that they had shared. And from the well where he had locked them away, the guilts arose to haunt him; the blood relationship with the woman he had so unwittingly married, the subsequent relationship with Molly, the children born even as he had been. The total of it all was almost overwhelming.

As the plane banked for its final approach, the thought flashed through his mind that Elizabeth's death might have been punishment for his own transgressions. Then he pushed that thought, too, away and stared numbly out the window as the wheels of Air Force One reached for the runway.

As Jericho followed Schuyler down the ramp, he paused briefly.

Below and a little to the right Sky and Brandy stood waiting. A short distance behind them the Martin limousine waited, obviously flanked by an escort of Secret Service vehicles. Further to the right and moving slowly into place from the rear of the plane came a silver and black Cadillac hearse, its function all too evident. To the left stood another vehicle bearing the now familiar CNN markings. At some distance a line of media vehicles and crews had formed and Jeicho realized with a slight chill that the nation was a witness.

Jericho's absorption in the greeting between Schuyler and his sons was broken by a now familiar voice. "Good afternoon, Senator."

Jericho's eyes shifted abruptly as a half smile that failed to reach his eyes flickered across his lips. "Dan Jackson," he said softly, "it's good to see a familiar face."

"Glad you're pleased," the young man replied gravely. "You see, you're to be my permanent assignment." Then he gestured at the nearby media crew. "They have been allowed here as a courtesy, representing all networks. You don't have to say anything."

The Senator considered his words for a moment and then moved toward the waiting crew. As he approached, cameramen moved into position while CNN's political correspondent, Jay Danforth, moved to greet him.

"Good afternoon, sir," he said crisply. "I'm sure I speak for our audience when I extend our deepest sympathy."

Although Jericho's flinch was discernible, the voice that replied was firm. "Thank you, Jay." Then the pain within flashed briefly across the tired face. "Both the Martin family and I appreciate your support and concern. It's hard to—" and his voice trailed off as he visibly fought for control. Then he turned and faced the cameras as though speaking through them.

"The Martins and I have a lot to do right now, personal things that take precedence at a time like this." There was a brief moment as a sad smile touched his lips. "We need and will appreciate your support and your prayers."

Then he turned back to the visibly shaken reporter. "Thank you, Jay, for just letting them listen," and with that he moved away to join the cavalcade that waited to start the journey to Georgetown.

As they reached the waiting vehicles, Jericho's companion opened the door to the black limousine that stood second in line.

"Senator," he said, "the service sent this along for your use." He paused and then continued. "For the present, my instructions are that it's to be used at all times."

Jericho looked at the massive automobile whose functionality was visible only in its abnormally thick windows. Then, without comment, he got into the back where he found himself wedged between Dan Jackson and one of his colleagues.

As they approached Georgetown he turned to Dan and said, "Dan, please tell me just where we're headed."

"The Martin place, Magnolia Hill," he replied, without taking his eyes from the passing scene.

Jericho frowned. "I'm not sure I approve of the selection," his tone almost harsh.

The agent shook his head in denial. "The choice wasn't mine. You see," his demeanor one of great patience, "it's strictly a matter of security. Mr. Martin's sons arrived here yesterday afternoon, and by this morning all of the details had been cleared with them."

He paused for a moment and then went on. "The Martin estate has many advantages and our people had very little time to prepare."

Jericho nodded slowly. "I understand, but it still bothers me that others share *my* risks."

As his voice trailed off into silence, his shoulders slumped with fatigue and his murmur could barely be heard, "Oh, Elizabeth, I'm so tired."

When Jericho awoke the following morning it took several minutes for the reality of his surroundings to penetrate his sleep fogged brain. Even after his mind had cleared, his memories of their arrival were fragmentary and obviously incomplete. The sensation was akin to looking at widely separated frames from a motion picture.

There had been guards at the gate, for the first time in his memory. Then he'd been hurried into the house. He thought the whole entry drive had been floodlighted, although it had only been dusk at the time. Then he seemed to remember James arguing with someone, something about not driving for Schuyler, and his wife Jessie complaining about being moved into the main house. He thought they had welcomed him back, but he really couldn't be sure.

The picture of Schuyler and Brandy entering the foyer was quite clear. James and Jessie had both quieted, but Jericho had looked in vain for Sky, Jr. When he had asked, there had been an awkward pause before Brandy had replied that his brother had gone with Elizabeth to Cosgroves, and would be coming in later. Then there were sandwiches and coffee in the library, and Jessie telling him how sorry she was while James told her to be quiet. His last clear picture was of Sky entering the library. After that there was nothing.

It was almost seven when Jericho entered the cheery kitchen. He'd bathed and shaved out of long habit, and had followed his nose to the smell of coffee without even noticing the strange faces here and there. He had exchanged small talk with James while Jessie had prepared his bacon and eggs. Then he had eaten in silence, finally leaning back in his chair as he looked at James.

"I was tired last night. Sky came in late, and they told me he had gone to Cosgrove's with Elizabeth." There was a pause while he sipped from his cup. "Just where in the hell is Cosgroves?"

The elderly black man looked first at his wife, then at the floor, totally unable to speak. Then Jessie moved forward to place her hand gently on Jericho's shoulder. "Mr. Jerry," she said softly, "Cosgroves is the funeral home."

There was a brief moment of total recall, total realization, and then Senator Jerry Smith let out a horrible scream, followed by one after the other.

With the help of the Martin household and the augmented security force, Jericho managed to get through the next few days in spite of himself. After the one brief outburst, he had apparently accepted Elizabeth's death but his mood alternated between apathy and deep depression. It was quite apparent that the Senator was engaged in an inner struggle. The few comments that he offered betrayed the fact that he still blamed himself for what had occured.

Schuyler, too, had finally been all but overcome by his grief and had reacted by temporarily secluding himself in his study, effectively leaving the family affairs in the hands of his sons. This, however, proved to be only a continuation of a process the two had instigated themselves when they had first arrived in the capitol, and by the end of the day the results were evident.

When Brandy and Sky met that evening in the sitting room that had been Kate's, the house was quiet and the weariness of each was apparent.

"Have you seen Dad or Jerry?" Sky queried after the two had greeted each other affectionately.

Brandy shook his head. "No, but it's probably just as well, from what James has to say."

"But what have they been doing all day?" Sky persisted.

"Nothing much." Brandy paused to consider his answer. "James says Dad was in his office all day, and Dan tells me that Jerry hasn't left his quarters since he fell apart this morning."

"Have they eaten anything?"

"Oh, yes. Jessie's been carting their food in on trays." Then Brandy moved to the fireplace and turned to look at his brother. "You know, Sky, I almost feel guilty because I can function."

"I don't," Sky responded with a slight chuckle. "Not everyone can be grief stricken or overcome by irrational guilt. Things still have to get done." Tears misted his eyes as he looked up at his brother. "We loved her, too, you know."

Brandy nodded as he brushed at his own eyes before responding. "As for getting things done, just where are we?"

"Everything's arranged," Sky replied, glancing through the notes he had gathered. "We have a private visit at Cosgrove's, family and staff, tomorrow morning at ten. Security is set up."

Sky cleared his throat and continued. "At one tomorrow afternoon, visiting will open to the public for the following day and a half."

He consulted his notes once more. "The following morning, Elizabeth will be moved to the cathedral. Services will be held at eleven, followed by private interment with Grandmother and Kate here in Georgetown."

Sky got up to move slowly around the room. "The details we can go over tomorrow, but that's the gist of it."

"Sounds like everything is under control." Brandy's tone was so businesslike that Sky couldn't repress a slight smile as his brother continued. "Security is complete here at Magnolia Hill; we have a full cadre of Secret Service people, with quarters and communications set up in the carriage house."

Sky actually laughed. "Did you know that Jessie's still bitching?"

Brandy nodded. "She raised hell in a hand basket when they were moved into the back wing." Then he grinned. "Give her time and she might learn to like it. James does already."

"That's one change that should have been made a long time ago," Sky responded, then paused momentarily.

"I know you went to Jerry's headquarters today," he continued.

"How did that go?"

"It should be all right now," Brandy said somewhat shortly. "I just hope that Jerry will approve of what I've done."

"Why wouldn't he?"

"Well, for one thing I sent most of the crew home," was the brusque reply. "When I got there the press was camped outside, the staff was in a daze and almost nothing had been done."

Sky nodded gravely. "That's not too surprising, you know."

"Not surprising maybe, but not acceptable either. Mrs. Shannon and that priest friend of Jerry's, Father Pignelli, were about the only one's who still had their wits, and they were both outranked." Brandy got up to pace around the room, his tension obvious.

"So what was the outcome?" Sky asked almost impatiently.

Brandy stared at him for a moment before he replied. "I assumed a hell of a lot of authority that no one questioned," and he grimaced slightly. "Met with the press first to inform them that I was shutting down the campaign offices until after the services. Then I furloughed most of the people."

He looked at his brother thoughtfully, then went on. "There will be a skeleton staff back the second day after the services with Mrs. Shannon in charge." He sighed. "I told her to contact either of us if anyone gives her a problem."

"Fine," Sky assented, then, "After I left today, Cosgrove's were to contact the press with the schedule for the next few days, so hopefully that at least is covered."

"I hope so. The word I left with the media was that neither the Senator nor Mr. Martin would be available before next Wednesday." Then Brandy lapsed into silence.

After several minutes, Sky Martin looked at his brother and spoke once more. "Let's get some sleep, Brandy. I think that we've more than earned it."

Not surprisingly, media reporting of the events preceding the services for Elizabeth Martin Smith were extensive. However, due in large part to Brandy's early efforts and his conception, the various news agencies made every effort to keep intrusion on the family's grief to a bare minimum.

Under the watchful eyes of the Secret Service the family and staff had made its pilgrimage of love and respect that morning with

Schuyler and Jericho sharing the Senator's limousine. As they entered Cosgrove's together, each seemed to draw strength from the presence of the other and neither appeared aware of the discreetly placed television crew with its security contingent.

Jericho and his father-in-law spent some ten minutes alone in the peaceful room where Elizabeth lay, then seemingly reconciled, they moved to an anteroom to await the rest of the party.

As they waited, Schuyler finally spoke. "Jerry," he said softly, "she looks so beautiful," while the tremor in his voice betrayed his emotion.

"I know," and the Senator swallowed hard, "but we both know that she'd have wanted it that way," and he reached out to place his hand on the older man's shoulder.

Schuyler nodded through the tears that clouded his vision. "For her it was always a matter of pride."

At that moment they were joined by the other party members and soon were on their way back to Magnolia Hill. After they had arrived, Brandy noted that his father and Jerry entered Schuyler's study together and he nodded approvingly . . . the isolation had apparently ended.

Across town in Arlington, Monsignor Pignelli, feeling suddenly older than he cared to admit, rose wearily and turned off the television. Schuyler had looked old and tired, which did not surprise him, but the change in Jerry was almost shocking. He was obviously thinner, his face was lined and drawn and the gray at his temples was certainly more pronounced. What was most disturbing, however, was the fact that he had seen no trace of what he'd sometimes termed 'the look of eagles.' Somehow, the future suddenly seemed much less secure.

Far from living in isolation, Jericho and Schuyler now became almost inseparable. It was as though they drew strength from the presence of the other, and they spent long hours together recalling the good times, the happy times and even the times of contention, as though it were a ritual that had to be completed.

Sky and Brandy almost dreaded the day of the funeral since neither had any inkling of what to expect. To their relief, however, the day came and went without incident. Both their father and thr brother-in-law, though obviously grieved, had carried themselves with quiet dignity during the services and had seemed almost oblivious to the silent throng on the streets outside. Only during the private interment rites did Schuyler allow his grief to surface while Jericho quietly acted as his comforter.

Then it was over. The family returned to Magnolia Hill and the media swiftly turned to other matters with what seemed to be a feeling of relief as the nation continued on with its business.

On Wednesday, true to his word, Brandy had re-opened the Smith campaign headquarters. He had met briefly with Molly Shannon and Monsignor Pignelli to review the old schedule and to suggest some changes. Together they had worked out a timetable for the recalls necessary to bring the staff back to full strength and he had indicated that they could expect to hear from Jerry in a few days. Finally, satisfied with the preparations, he returned to the Martin estate to report his progress to the candidate.

Jericho listened attentively as Brandy outlined the steps he had taken. He'd been encouraged by his brother-in-law's half smile at the mention of Mrs. Shannon and puzzled at the mixed emotions betrayed when he referred to Father Pignelli, but he was totally unprepared for Jericho's response.

"I don't know when I'll be able to get to the campaign office again," he said calmly.

"But why?" Brandy asked in astonishment. "Those people need your direction."

"It's too soon," Jericho replied patiently. "It wouldn't be right. And besides, Schuyler needs me now," and very quietly Senator Jerry Smith got up and left the room, leaving behind a thoroughly puzzled and frustrated Brandy Martin.

The following day Sky returned to Boston, while Brandy elected to delay his own departure until the following week. For the first time in his busy life he now seemed to be marking time as events at Magnolia Hill slipped into a predictable if meaningless routine.

Schuyler and Jerry got up at the same hour. They ate together and took long walks around the grounds under the watchful eyes of secret service agents. When Schuyler took a nap in early afternoon, Jericho sat on one particular bench in the garden staring off into the distance. Sometimes he cried, and sometimes in the middle of the night he could be heard groaning in his sleep. And day by day

Schuyler Martin fought his battle, and little by little he was winning.

Then the break came.

45

As far as Dan Jackson could discern, that day was not remarkable in any way. Brandy had been up early, had eaten a light breakfast with James, and was already back from his run around the estate by the time Jericho and Schuyler appeared. While the two were leaving for their ritual morning walk, Brandy had finished a call to Sky in Boston, and was now in the process of completing a conversation with Molly Shannon.

It was well after ten when, having finished his business calls to Kansas City, he entered the kitchen for a belated cup of coffee. There he found that Dan Jackson had preceded him and was glancing idly through the *Washington Post*. Over coffee, the two exchanged pleasantries, but avoided any mention of Jericho's continuing inaction or of Schuyler's apparent indifference.

"Mind of I join you?" the quiet voice interrupted Brandy's perusal of the notes he had made that morning. With a start of surprise he looked up into the eyes of his father who was obviously very much awake.

Brandy nodded and gestured to a nearby chair, but Schuyler chose instead to take a turn around the room while Brandy waited.

"Has Jerry talked to you at all." Schuyler asked abruptly.

"Only once," Brandy said quietly. "After Mrs. Shannon and I

re-opened the campaign office I went over what we'd done, but he wasn't interested.''

"Just what did he say?" Schuyler demanded.

Brandy frowned in concentration. "As I remember, he said that you needed him, that it was too soon, and that he didn't know when he'd go back.''

"At first I did need him," the old man admitted almost grudgingly. "We needed each other. But I'll be damned if I'll be his excuse.''

"What are you going to do?" Brandy asked curiously.

"Try to remind him that he's still a man," Schuyler barked as he strode from the room.

Then he turned back, his eyes suddenly twinkling. "Anyway, I'm beginning to feel like I'm married to him." With that, he was gone, leaving a startled Brandy behind.

As Jericho returned to the house he found Schuyler and Dan Jackson waiting and looked questioningly from one to the other.

"Come on, son," Schuyler said firmly. "I've asked Mr. Jackson to drive us around for awhile.''

"But, why—" Jericho began when Schuyler cut him off.

"Because I'm getting a little stir crazy. Anyway, it's time we got out of here for a change.''

There was complete silence in the closed rear compartment of the limousine as the agent manuevered the vehicle onto the Beltway and toward the capitol.

They were halfway toward downtown Washington and Jericho was deep in his own thoughts when Schuyler shattered his reverie. "Senator," he said firmly, "You and I need to have a little talk.''

"Just what the hell is this 'Senator' business?" the younger man snapped defensively. "Since when is that necessary?''

Schuyler smiled gently. "Let's just say I needed to get your attention," he replied.

"All right, you have it," Jericho conceded almost grudgingly. "I'm listening.''

After a short pause Schuyler continued. "Jerry, don't you really think it's about time you said something to your campaign staff?" Then, without waiting he went on. "We *have* been waiting.''

"Schuyler, I don't deserve it. You don't know—''

The interruption was almost savage. "Damn it, Jerry, I've

listened to hints and innuendos for days. I've heard it all."

Then he quieted. "You'll have to manage your own guilt, if that's what this is all about, though I have to tell you that sack cloth and ashes are very unbecoming."

A brief smile flitted across the Senator's face but he remained silent.

"Jerry," Schuyler continued, his tone serious, "I'm sure you realize that your nomination by the convention is virtually assured."

"I hadn't really given it much thought," Jericho replied stoically.

"Damn it, you'd better think about it," Schuyler almost exploded. "You've got a staff that needs direction and nothing's happening. It's not fair, to your people or to me."

"I don't know if I can do it," came the defensive reply.

"Who the hell ever does?" Schuyler responded, the tone of disgust unmistakable. "Jerry, you've got a lot of good people. None of us feel that we've backed a loser," Then his tone went flat as he continued. "I hope we haven't backed a quitter."

Jericho flinched visibly but remained silent as his father-in-law continued in a matter of fact tone. "I trust you know that the only way you can avoid being our next president is to give it away through your own damn foolishness."

Jericho stared at the older man with a growing sense of shock.

Schuyler nodded gravely, then turned to stare out the window. When he turned back and spoke again, his voice was softer. "Jerry, I loved my daughter very much, as I loved her mother and my mother before her." He shook his head as tears gathered in his eyes. "I'll mourn her for a long time, and it won't be easy. However," and he crossed himself, "God knows life is for the living and it must go on!"

"Schuyler, how can you sit there and—" Jericho began, but his emotion filled voice trailed off into silence.

"Jerry," came the patient reply, "Elizabeth would have understood because it was her dream, too. Maybe we all owe her that extra mile."

The younger man nodded in slowly dawning comprehension. "I believe I see what you're saying."

As the car swung into the wide street, Schuyler replied strongly,

"Good, because you've got about a week to get it together before the hard work really starts." Then he pointed out the window. "1600 Pennsylvania Avenue. The dream is still possible, Jerry."

As they passed the White House Jericho gazed out the window, every faculty once more alert.

Then Schuyler interrupted once more. "A bit of advice, if you'll accept it."

"Yes?"

"If you can, put some distance between yourself and Monsignor Pignelli."

"Why would you say that?" Jericho asked quietly.

"Because, whether you believe it or not," came the flat reply, "that man is not really your friend; he's been using you for years."

"But why should he?"

"I suspect," Schuyler said softly, "that he has dreams of riding to glory on your coat tails." Then he paused. "At least give it some thought."

Jericho nodded slowly but did not reply. As the limousine made its way back to Magnolia Hill, the two shared the comfortable silence of mutual understanding.

The meeting that took place two days later in Senator Smith's suite in the Senate Office Building was attended only by the key people in his organization. As they filed into the room, Jericho nodded gravely and greeted each one by name. When the room had quieted, he moved around and half seated himself on the front edge of the massive desk as his eyes swept over their faces.

"I'm sorry I've kept you waiting," he began. "The family has had a number of things to take care of; those matters are now complete and it's time that we get this show on the road." Then he paused momentarily. "As far as recent events are concerned, I can only regret that there are those among us who prefer bullets to ballots, and affirm that we are more determined than ever to see this campaign to a successful conclusion."

He raised his hand to still the ripple of sound that started, and then continued, "This dream was as much my late wife's as it was mine, and I have no doubt that she would approve wholeheartedly."